California Boys

A Novel

Axel Schwarz

As always, for Melanie

And for Kurt

1

The curved handle of the revolver rested in the boy's hand, the weight of it pulling down slightly. Six shells sat in their chambers and the gun gleamed in the early afternoon sun. There was no sign of age or tarnish on the metal. It was oiled and polished and clean just as his father had taught him. The boy's clothes and hat were dirty and too large and his blonde hair matted and oily. He had pale blue eyes and skin stained with freckles. In his shadow stood a miniature version of him clutching his brother's shirttail.

Twenty paces away a man trembled in the knee-high grass as the boy pointed the pistol at him.

"Now I'm going to count down from ten," said the boy. "If you don't get outta here I'm gonna kill you."

"Go to hell, kid."

"Don't cuss in front of my brother, mister. His ears is too young for that kind of talk."

"Well he can go to hell then, too."

"Nine," said the boy.

"But he deserved it. He was trying to steal one of my chickens."

"Don't nobody have a right to lay a hand on him except our pa, and he never has."

"Well maybe he should."

"Eight."

"You ain't gonna do it, kid."

"Seven."

"At least give me back my gun."

"I'll leave it here. You can come back and get it. Six."

"I said gimme my gun, goddammit!"

"You better get movin', mister. I don't want to see you by the time I get to zero. Five."

"But there's nowhere to hide."

"Like I said, you better get movin'. Four."

"Jesus Christ, kid!" The man turned and ran.

"Three. Two." The man was now out of pistol shot range even with the boy's aim but the boy counted as if the man were still standing in front of him. "One. Zero." The speck of the man disappeared into the afternoon haze of the forest at the edge of the field and the boy took a few deep breaths to calm his quivering body. He lowered the gun and turned to his brother.

"You okay?"

"Yeah."

"Your ass ain't too sore to walk?"

"No."

"But it still hurts, don't it?"

"Yeah."

"You're tough, Billy. Don't let anyone tell you different."

"Okay."

"Come on, now. We better get goin'." He held out his hand. The little boy put his hand in his brother's. "Jake?"

"Yeah?"

"I wasn't trying to steal that chicken."

"I know't."

"I don't know why that farmer got so mad about me just looking at his chickens. It's not like I was goin' to take one or nothing."

"I know't."

"I mean, all I did was—"

"Billy?"

"Yeah?"

"You ain't gotta convince me."

"Alright."

"Just maybe next time you shouldn't take a look by grabbing one and putting it under your coat."

"Okay."

"You hungry?" asked Jake. Billy nodded. "But you ain't said nothin'." The boy shook his head. "I told you you're tough, little brother. Come on, let's go find ourselves some food."

"But we ain't got no money."

"No we ain't. But we got each other, and we got Pa's gun. We don't need anything else, do we?"

"My magic rock." In his tiny hand the boy gripped a gray rock, his fingers not quite able to reach all the way around it.

Jake smiled. "That's right. I almost forgot. Now we for sure don't need anything else, do we?"

The boy shook his head.

They walked for some time before the younger one spoke again. "Jake?"

"Yeah?"

"I miss Aunt Kate."

"Me too."

"How come she couldn't come with us?"

Jake thought of their aunt and the night they had left behind, her frail body framed in the dim light, her sad eyes colored with bruises. "I told you already. She's gotta watch the house while we go find Pa."

"When are we going to see Pa again, Jake?"

"I swear you don't listen to me. I said as soon as we get to California."

"And when are we gonna get to California?"

"As soon as you stop asking questions and start walking. Now come on." Jake tousled Billy's hair. "Race you to that tree over there." He pointed at a tree on the opposite end of the field from where the man had fled.

Billy smiled and took off for the tree, his bedroll bouncing up and down as he ran through the grass. Jake followed, looking back occasionally to see if the man was coming back.

Jake and Billy raced from tree to rock to stump to anything Jake could think of until early evening. When Jake told Billy to stop he did and after they caught their breath Billy collected firewood and Jake set out hunting.

The sun was just above the horizon when Jake returned. Firewood lay piled next to a rough ring of rocks. Billy's head popped up at his brother's arrival. "Sorry, li'l brother," said Jake. "Just nothin' out there to shoot."

"That's okay," Billy looked down at the ground.

"Here," said Jake, rustling into his bag and pulling out a shriveled piece of jerky. "Eat this."

Billy looked up at the jerky and then back down at the ground. "That's okay. I know we need it for later."

"Don't worry. There's more where that came from. Here, take it."

Billy pulled the jerky from his brother's grasp and walked over to a small rock and sat on it, tearing off pieces with his teeth as Jake built a fire. Soon flames were lapping at the larger branches. Close to the fire squatted Jake with his hands clasped and elbows around his knees and Billy got up and sat beside him. Jake passed him a metal canteen and Billy took a swig of water and then another and handed the canteen back.

"You did a good job collecting that wood, Billy."

"Thanks."

"You did real good. It was all nice and dry and everything."

"Thanks."

"You tired?"

"Yeah."

"Alright then. Roll out your blanket by the fire here."

Billy unrolled his blanket and lay down on one half of it and Jake handed him the bag stuffed with some clothes for a pillow. The boy took it and when he had rested his head on it Jake pulled the other half of the blanket over his brother. He sat there for a while staring into the glow of the fire, the one light in the darkness. It popped and hissed as the crickets and cicadas hummed and the frogs croaked in a nearby creek. There by the fire he sat watching as the flames lingered and died, the carcasses of the logs pulsating orange and casting a soft circle of dying light.

At his side his brother lay silent except the occasional stomach growl that echoed his own. The boy's hand lay atop his chest clutching his rock. Billy sniffled and in the fading firelight Jake saw the wet shine of his brother's cheek. With his sleeve he wiped off the moisture and placed his hand on his brother's shoulder, keeping it there until he felt the gentle rise and fall of slumber from Billy's chest.

Only then did he unroll his own blanket and lie down and wrap himself in it. The night was hot and muggy but Jake liked the feel of the blanket around him like a comfort from an old dream of a mother barely remembered. He lay his head on the ground next to his brother's and stared up at the sky. Bats swooped against the backdrop of stars. A lone whippoorwill called in the woods.

2

They woke early to the coo of mourning doves. Heavy dew covered every surface and the sun made the world's liquid coat sparkle. Next to them the fire smoldered, gray ash and smoke. Jake woke first and let Billy sleep a while before waking him. Silently they rolled their blankets and packed their bags. Then they slung all their worldly possessions over their shoulders and started walking along the forest edge.

When they got hungry they snuck into the forest looking for mayapples, careful to avoid the poisonous parts of the plant and eat only the fruit. By noon the sun was hot and they slipped again into the forest until they hit a creek. There they waded and wriggled their toes in the cool mud. They rinsed their socks and lay them to dry on the umbrella-shaped mayapple plants.

Thick bullfrog tadpoles and backward-swimming crawdads lazed in the shallows of the creek. The sun shone through the lacework of the trees and mottled the ground. Jake wanted to stay there for hours for eternity but knew they had to keep moving. Jake told Billy to put on his boots, and he laced up his own before climbing back out of the forest to walk its border. Grasshoppers and crickets in the tall grass jumped to avoid them. The boys tried to see how many they could catch and made their way over rolling fields until they stopped again for the night.

Billy set out for firewood while Jake hunted. The *crack* of Jake's pistol filled the air but was soon swallowed by the forest. Jake carried his quarry of rabbit back to the camp. Billy watched as Jake took out his knife and cleaned the rabbit, instructing Billy how to remove the skin without getting blood on it.

"Now normally we'd take the brains and tan the hide but we gotta keep moving so we don't have time. I hate to waste a good rabbit skin but it ain't even summer yet so we don't need it just now. You want the rabbit's foot? It's lucky. I don't know why but people say it is."

Billy shook his head and held up his rock. "That's right," said Jake. "You already got your lucky charm." Billy smiled and Jake smiled and continued cleaning the rabbit. There was a jingle and clang of metal as Jake pulled out his aunt's pot and spoons and handed the pot to Billy. "Fill this up with water, little brother." Billy stuffed his rock in his pocket and took the pot and walked toward the stream swinging the pot as he went.

When the rabbit was cleaned and gutted Jake built a fire and put on the pot of water. The water steamed and Jake cut the rabbit into pieces and placed them in the pot. The smell of fresh cooked meat wafted to their noses and the boys wiped the saliva from the corners of their mouths.

Jake pulled the pot off the fire with the two spoons. They said grace and spooned the hot broth into their mouths. The water burned their tongues so they blew on it. When the meat had cooled enough they lifted it out of the broth with their spoons and hands and picked the tiny bones clean. Then they took turns drinking the broth from the pot until it was gone. Jake took the pot and spoons to the stream and rubbed dirt on them and rinsed them. He filled the pot again with water and walked back to the fire and stoked it, putting the pot between two logs.

The sun was almost set when the water boiled again. Jake pulled the pot off and let it cool. When it had, he grabbed the pot and poured the water into their canteens. He made Billy drink as much as he could then finished the rest himself. Bellies full they lay down under the starry sky with clouds glowing white in the moonlight. *Tomorrow it'll rain* was Jake's last thought before he fell asleep.

It was still dark when Jake heard a thud and then a hiss as fat raindrops landed in the fire. He shook Billy awake and they crawled under the canopy of the forest under a big oak tree and watched and listened to the rain in the predawn darkness. The boys sat huddled and shivering, clutching their bags and blankets close to keep them dry. Black clouds turned dark gray as the sun behind them tried to push through. When there was enough light illuminating the clouds the boys started walking.

The rain continued for two days and by the third day the world was soaked. No fires. No meat. Mayapples for breakfast and lunch. Jerky for dinner. Cold even in the heat of the day. Late afternoon on the third day, exhausted and gaunt and shaking from the cold and wet the boys reached a small farm. Jake looked at his brother. Billy had not spoken all day.

Smoke curled from the rock chimney of the house. The chinking between the logs looked solid. Around the building was a well-built fence, and inside the fence a sturdy horse and Missouri mule were lazily grazing on pasture grass. A round woman with gray hair came outside to shake her rug and saw them. Jake's legs were swallowed by the tall grass, and only Billy's hunched shoulders and hanging head were visible. Picking up her skirt the woman hurried toward two boys, wet and gray as the day.

By the time she got to them the grass had wet everything from her waist down. "What in God's name—what are you poor little creatures doin' out here by yourselves? You look halfway to death's door. Come inside now!" The woman wrapped her arms around the boys, one under each arm and they walked that way back to the cabin. Her arms felt like warm pillows and her skirts the sheets of a bed.

A series of commands from the woman followed. "Stand by the fire. Take off those clothes. Put these on. Sit here. Drink this. Eat this." Jake said "Yes, ma'am" and "Thank you, ma'am" to everything the woman said. Billy said nothing but did what he was told and ate and drank more than Jake had ever seen him before.

As the boys ate the woman disappeared into a back room. After they finished eating she shepherded them to two made beds and told them to lie down. Jake thanked her and she said "Ain't no thanks about it." Not knowing what that meant he said "Thank you" again and she smiled and patted him on the head.

When the boys were in their beds the woman walked over to Billy's bed and pulled the sheets and blanket up to his chin and kissed him on the forehead and called him *poor baby* and *sweet child* and stroked his hair before leaving and closing the door. A tin pail full of hot coals from the fire warmed the room, and Jake lay in bed and watched his brother.

When he saw Billy wouldn't stop shivering Jake got out of bed and walked over and crawled into bed with him. He rolled Billy on his side and put his arm around his brother and watched his brother fall asleep as the light of day still shone through the curtain. Then he fell into a deep and peaceful sleep of his own as the steady breathing and the warmth of his brother lulled him.

In the morning Jake heard sounds from the kitchen. He left his brother sleeping and walked out. The floorboards creaked under his feet. The woman worked at the stove and he smelled the hominy grits cooking and bacon frying as he walked up next to the woman. She hadn't heard him coming and jumped back when she saw him. "Dear Lord! You scared the dickens out of me. What are you doing up?"

"I'd like to help if I could."

"You should be in bed."

Jake shook his head. "I'm fine, thank you ma'am. I'd like to help. I'm real good with horses. I can muck stalls and brush them and even shoe them. I can plant and weed in the field, too."

The woman stood with her hand on her hip. "Well you ain't doin' nothin' until you had a proper breakfast so set down right there." She pointed at a chair at the kitchen table and Jake sat down. At the stove she filled a bowl with grits and placed two strips of bacon across the top and brought them to the table. In front of Jake she placed the bowl and a spoon. He made sure to say grace before he ate.

Jake ate the bacon first and then the grits. They were still steaming hot, and he had to blow on each spoonful before eating. When he finished the woman asked him if he wanted more and he said, "No thank you, ma'am." She looked at him and grabbed his bowl and filled it again and placed it in front of him. He thanked her and ate that whole bowl and another one before stopping.

When he finished he asked to be excused. The woman looked at him and smiled and said yes. He got up and without asking took his bowl to the wash basin on the counter and washed his bowl and spoon. The woman stood and watched. Jake grabbed a towel hanging from the wall and dried his bowl and spoon and asked the woman where he should put them. She smiled and thanked him, taking them and placing them back in the cabinet and drawer as Jake watched.

Then Jake asked her if he could do anything else.

"What's your name, son?"

"Jake, ma'am. And my brother's name is Billy."

"Well Jake, my name is Mrs. McCready. Mr. McCready will be along in a minute. You can ask him."

"Thank you, ma'am." Jake sat back down at the table and waited until a man came into the kitchen dressed in a blue shirt and denim overalls. The man was older and the little gray hair he had left was pulled over the large bald spot on top of his head. He had a big barrel chest and arms like tree trunks and Jake thought he had never seen a man so big in his life.

Jake stood up and said, "Good morning" and the man looked at him and smiled.

"Morning, son." He went to his wife and placed his hands on her shoulders and kissed her cheek and said, "Good morning."

"Marshall, this here is Jake. Jake, this is Mr. McCready."

Jake walked over and stuck out his hand. "Pleased to meet you, sir."

The man grabbed Jake's hand and Jake felt like his hand had been swallowed by a giant paw. "And you."

"I'd like to help," said Jake. "I'm real good with horses. I can muck stalls and brush them and even shoe them. I can plant and weed in the field, too."

16

The man let go of Jake's hand and thanked him. "That won't be necessary, son. You can rest up if you like."

"I'm fine thank you, sir. I'd like to help." Jake stared at the man. His father always told him it was important to look people in the eye but with this man that was harder than he thought. He looked down at the floor ashamed but then looked back up at the man.

The man was smiling. "Very well then. Is it okay if I get some breakfast first?" He winked at his wife and she back at him.

"Yes sir. If you don't mind I'll just go check on my brother."

The man nodded. "Alright, son."

Jake went into the back room and found Billy sleeping. He went to his bag, which he had placed under the bed and pulled out his blanket and unrolled it. The outer layers were wet but by the time he got to the inner layers the blanket was dry. Inside it he found his father's pistol and took it out. Careful to point it away from his brother he ran his fingers over it feeling for water. There was none so he used the blanket to rub the oil from his fingers off the gun and then wrapped the gun back in the blanket and rolled it up.

Next he dug in his bag until his fingers reached a small piece of fabric. Jake took it out and unwrapped it. Inside was a small, folded envelope, and inside that were two letters. One was the last message from their father, describing his life in San Francisco. The other was from his father's last employer to Jake and Billy's aunt, explaining the untimely death of the boys' father. In it the man expressed his condolences, and he explained how he would hold onto the ashes and few possessions of Jake's father until someone came and got them. For a while Jake held the letters, as if in the holding he would somehow resurrect his father for some brief moment. But the moment fled, and he placed the letters back in the bag and the bag under the bed.

Jake walked back out to find Mr. McCready scraping the last of his grits out of the bowl. He waited patiently by the door as the man took his bowl and spoon to the counter kissed his wife and grabbed his hat. Jake's hat hung on the mantle where a fire newly stoked crackled. He went over and grabbed it and walked toward the door, careful not to put on his hat until he was outside.

"Jake, is it?" asked the man when Jake was by the door.

"Yes, sir."

"You ready to work today?"

"Yes, sir."

"Alright then. Come on." The man opened the door and went out.

Jake paused and turned to Mrs. McCready who was still at the kitchen counter staring at Jake. "Thank you for breakfast, Mrs. McCready."

"You're welcome, Jake." The boy nodded and turned and walked out the door before closing it behind him.

All morning Jake worked with the man, carrying water, digging holes. At first the tasks were easy but as the day wore on the tasks got more difficult. He chopped wood and helped fix the split rail fence. Each time the man asked Jake if he knew how to do it. Each time Jake said yes.

"You know how to hammer a nail in good and straight?"

"Yes, sir."

"You know how to milk a cow?"

"Yes, sir."

Jake worked without question or complaint. When Jake finished a chore the man would inspect his work and nod his silent approval. Then he would ask Jake if he knew how to do something else.

"Yes, sir."

As they worked the sun heated the earth and the water that covered it. The morning haze hanging low in the valleys burned off. Thick droplets of dew dripped from every surface and were sucked up by the warming air. The humidity made it feel like July when it was only May. Insects hopped and swarmed as man and boy worked. Both gave up on swatting them except for the big horseflies that stung when they bit. A choir of birds sang from the woods.

When the sun was high, Mrs. McCready called out to them from the door. They walked silently back to the cabin, Jake staring straight ahead and the man looking at Jake. At the door the man patted Jake on the shoulder. "Good job this morning, Jake."

"Thank you, sir."

The man and boy took off their hats and entered and greeted Mrs. McCready. Jake asked her about Billy, and she said he was still asleep and shouldn't be bothered. He said thank you but just as well he'd like to check on him.

"Alright," she said. "Just do it quiet."

Jake went into the room and saw his brother sleeping. He walked over to the bed, careful not to make a sound and felt his forehead. Warm, but not hot. He touched his cheek. It was dry. Billy moaned and turned his head, and Jake lifted his hand off.

Jake walked back outside and found the old couple sitting at the kitchen table. They had plates of food in front of them, but were talking not eating. A third plate of food lay in front of the chair Jake had used for breakfast. Jake sat.

"How is he?" asked the woman.

"Okay, I guess. Still sleeping. I felt his head and he ain't too hot or sweaty or nothin'."

"That's good. I'll check on him again this afternoon."

Jake looked at her and then her husband. He had been trying to get the courage to say what he had to say since they arrived but all morning he couldn't. But he knew he had to now so he cleared his throat. "Ma'am. Sir. It was real nice of you to take us in like this. Real nice. But I'm afraid we can't pay you for it. You see, my brother and me, we ain't go no money."

The McCreadys looked at each other and smiled. The woman got out of her chair and put her arms around Jake and the boy turned bright red. "You are just the sweetest thing," she said.

"Ah woman, get off the poor boy. Jake, you don't worry about paying us a penny. We're happy to have you."

"Besides," said Mrs. McCready. "Our house's been lonely since our boys done grown up and left and it's nice to have some company around here."

Her husband agreed. "Jake, if you keep working like you did this morning, you and your brother are welcome to stay here as long you like."

Jake thanked them both and bowed his head for grace. Mr. McCready said a quick grace Jake had not heard before. They ate in silence until Mr. McCready spoke again.

"Where you from, Jake?"

"Sainte Genevieve, sir."

"Sainte Genevieve! What're you doin' way up here?"

"Goin' to see our daddy."

"Your daddy ain't in Sainte Genevieve?"

"No, sir. He's in California." Jake heard the tinkle of metal and looked up and saw the man had dropped his fork.

"California?"

"Yes, sir."

The man chuckled. "And y'all just goin' to walk there?"

"Yes, sir."

Mr. McCready shook his head. "Well I'll be. Y'all ain't got no family in Sainte Genevieve?"

Jake stared ahead, chewing his food and his thoughts. His aunt was family and had taken them in. She was still there, but the man she had married was not family. The man who had smiled his way into their home before changing. The man who came home late smelling of whiskey. The man who took his anger out on their aunt and threatened to do the same to the boys before Jake stole away in the night with his little brother. Jake never wanted to talk about or think about him again. Ever.

"No sir," said Jake. "We ain't got no family down there anymore. That's why we're going to find our Pa."

They ate the rest of the meal in silence, and when they finished Jake tried to clean up, but the woman shooed him away. He and Mr. McCready went back outside after Jake checked on Billy and saw he was still sleeping.

They started the afternoon weeding the cornfield. The cornrows were so straight Jake could stand at one end and see the forest at the other end. Thistles were starting to overrun one corner of the field, and Mr. McCready cursed a quiet steady stream as they pulled the barbed stems from the ground. Jake said nothing even as the plants poked through

21

the pair of work gloves Mr. McCready had lent him. Both hands were stinging and starting to swell. Jake knew it would take several days for the pain to go away, but he kept pulling and focusing on his job.

Mr. McCready said Jake's name, and Jake stood up to see Mrs. McCready running toward them, her skirt bunched in her fists, cheeks puffing like a steam engine.

"Jake," she said. "You better come quick. Your brother's got a bad fever."

Jake followed Mrs. McCready through the cornrows but then ducked through a space between stalks and passed her. He took the three wooden steps to the door in one bound and opened the door when he landed. It slammed behind him as he ran to his brother's room.

Billy lay in bed shivering and wet with sweat. Jake ran to his brother's side and kneeled. The door slammed again. Heavy footsteps approached the room and entered. The woman barked orders and Jake obeyed.

"Help me take his clothes off. Run and fetch cold water from the spring. Mr. McCready will show you where. Tell him to fetch me some rags and rinse the washtub and bring it inside. Hurry now, move!"

When Jake returned with the water she told him to get more. Each time he dumped two pails of ice-cold water into the wash basin placed in the center of the kitchen. After four trips it was full and Mrs. McCready told Jake to soak the rags in it. Jake did and she disappeared and came back carrying Billy in her arms like a load of laundry and placed him in the tub.

As his trembling body hit the water Billy yelped. His teeth were chattering. Jake followed the woman's lead and took the rags out of the water and squeezed them onto Billy. Billy shivered and tried to push their hands away. But Jake knew they had to break the fever, so he fought through Billy's protestations. Mr. McCready stood watch, casting a big shadow over them.

When the water warmed, Jake grabbed the pails without being told and ran to the spring and brought them back and poured them in. Half the kitchen floor was covered with water and Mr. McCready soaked it up and carried the rags outside and wrung them out. All the while the woman tended to Billy, dabbing him with cold water, telling him how strong he was, saying he was going to be just fine. Jake kept looking for ways to help Billy, but Mrs. McCready was taking care of his brother. Jake felt helpless.

The sun went down and still Mrs. McCready and Jake tried to break Billy's fever. They fell into wordless work, the only sounds Billy's moans, the splashing of the water and the whippoorwill's sing-song call coming through the windows. At last Billy's shivering slowed. Jake didn't know if that was good or bad, but it must have been good because Mrs. McCready stopped putting water on Billy and told her husband to get a clean, dry towel. Mr. McCready brought it to her and lay it across her arms. Then he picked Billy up and placed him on the towel. He dried Billy with a tenderness impossible for his size, and his wife carried Billy back to the bedroom where Mr. McCready had already changed the sheets. She clothed Billy and lay him down on his bed.

Jake sat on the floor next to Billy's bed and leaned against it. Mrs. McCready patted him on the shoulder, walked out and closed the door. Jake sat there the rest of the night without sleep or food or drink and watched his brother. Billy had fallen into a deep sleep, and even though Jake believed he would be alright, he had to see it before he could go to bed.

In the middle of the night Billy woke and called Jake's name and Jake answered. Billy said he was thirsty and hungry, so Jake went to the kitchen and saw on the table two cups with a pitcher of water and two plates of food. Jake smiled. He filled one cup and brought it to his brother. When he saw Billy could sit up and drink, he brought the food and set the plate on the bed. He fed his brother until Billy couldn't eat any more, and then took the plate back to the kitchen.

Jake poured a cup of water and drank it in two gulps and then poured another. Plate in one hand cup in the other Jake walked back to the room, trying not to make the floorboards creak and wake their hosts. When he returned, Billy was already asleep again. Jake sat on the floor next to him and watched and chewed, and when he finished he took everything back to the kitchen and washed and dried it all and set it on the counter. Then he went back to the bedroom and sat on his bed. He took off his shoes and started to take off his socks when he fell onto the mattress and slept.

3

Light slanted through the window panes of glass, the latticework casting warped rectangles of yellow onto the floor. Motes of dust swirled and dipped and when Jake woke and sat bolt upright they scattered like frightened flies. Billy's bed was empty so Jake ran out into the kitchen with just his socks on and saw him sitting on the floor next to the fireplace reading. Billy looked up.

"Morning, Jake," he said.

Jake looked at Mrs. McCready who was at the kitchen stove and she smiled. His sigh of relief was audible. He walked back to the bedroom and put on his boots before going to the kitchen to eat lunch with the McCreadys and Billy. Billy's appetite had returned. After lunch Jake helped clean up, then walked Billy to bed and told him to rest. Billy protested but he was soon asleep. Jake went back out. Mr. McCready was outside and Mrs. McCready was in the kitchen. Jake whispered thanks to her, and she patted him on the head. It made Jake feel small and helpless, but he knew she didn't mean it that way.

Jake went outside to help Mr. McCready. For a while they spoke little save the necessary communication for the tasks at hand. It was cooler than the day before and the bugs not as bad. Moisture had been taken out of the air and off the land by a breeze from the northwest carrying songs of birds and the rise and fall of crickets. As they worked a two-man saw cutting logs for repairs on the house, they echoed the insects with their own strokes. Ebb and flow. Crescendo and decrescendo. The sawdust flowed in even streams from the teeth of the blade and fell into neat ridges on the ground.

The work was hard, and tough as he was Jake could not keep up with Mr. McCready. His arms burned. When the blade got stuck several times the man told Jake they would take a break. Jake knew why and told the man he was alright but Mr. McCready waved him off. "No shame in resting when you need to."

As they sat in the shade of the barn and drank water Jake stared at the ground in front of him. "Mr. McCready?"

"Yes, Jake."

"I want to thank you for all you and Mrs. McCready done for us."

"Well, Mrs. McCready likes having boys around. And I'm glad to have help around here."

They sat in silence again before Jake mustered the courage to talk again. "Mr. McCready? There's something else I gotta tell you.""

"What is it, son?"

The constant cadence of crickets rang in Jake's ears and for a while that was all the noise in the world. "I wanted to tell you I've got my father's pistol with me. I didn't want you to think I snuck it in your house or nothin'."

Jake stared ahead and Mr. McCready at Jake and the crickets continued their endless symphony.

"Jake?"

"Yes, sir?"

"You're alright with me, boy."

"Thank you, sir."

"I know you've got business in California but you stay here as long as you like."

"Thank you, sir."

"And don't you even think about leaving until that brother of yours is better. You hear me?"

"Yes, sir."

"Come on, now. We better get back to work before the missus calls us a couple of loafers."

The next few days Jake watched his brother's recovery closely, and Billy passed the days by Jake's side as he worked with Mr. McCready. Billy wanted to help, but each time he asked, Jake admonished him to take it easy. Slowly, though, the color returned to his brother's cheeks. So one morning after breakfast, when Mr. McCready was outside and Billy was in the kitchen helping Mrs. McCready clean up, Jake turned to his brother.

"Billy?" asked Jake.

"Yeah?"

"You ready to work? We need your help out there."

Billy jumped up and ran to the door.

"Hold on now," said Jake. "Put your boots on first."

Billy ran to the bedroom to fetch his boots. His feet pounded the floorboards as he ran to the door. He was out of breath by the time he got to Jake.

"Slow down there. We ain't even started yet and you're already breathin' hard." Billy looked up at his brother and smiled and Jake smiled back. "Alright, now follow me."

The two brothers walked to Mr. McCready who was standing by a missing section of the split rail fence. Several rotten posts and rails lay at his feet, and fresh ones green as the trees they were shaped from lay next to them. Billy ran two steps ahead of Jake and went to Mr. McCready. "Hi, Mr. McCready."

"Hello there, Billy. Feeling better?"

"Yup."

Jake cleared his throat. "Say 'yes, sir' Billy."

"Yes, sir."

"Good. You ready to work?"

"Yes, sir. I'm ready to work all day if you want me to. I won't even need a break."

Mr. McCready laughed. "Well boy, that sounds fine, but let's just worry about making it to lunch. Come on."

The man walked over to one of the holes got down on his knees and beckoned the boy. Even kneeling he was taller than Billy and his massive frame dwarfed the young boy's. "Now we've got to put these new posts in. The holes are already dug, so all we got to do is hold the new post in and fill the dirt around it. You see these piles of dirt here?"

"Yes, sir."

"You see that trowel stickin' out of that pile there?"

"Yes, sir."

"So I'm goin' to stick the post in and hold it upright. When I tell you, use that trowel to fill in the dirt nice and even around the post. Then your brother here will tamp it down using that pole. You think you can do that?"

"Yes, sir."

"Alright then, go get your tool."

Billy ran to the pile and grabbed the trowel. Mr. McCready stood and dusted off his pants, walking over to one of the posts. He lifted the heavy wood like it was a broomstick and carried it to the first hole, bringing it high before slamming it into the hole. The ground shook. After checking the post with a plumb line, he looked at Billy. "Okay, son."

Billy filled the trowel and put his other hand underneath. His tongue sticking out, Billy took three careful steps to the hole and bent over poured the dirt slowly into the hole.

Jake gave an impatient sigh and looked at Mr. McCready, who winked back. When Billy finished, he repeated the same motions with the same care. After the third time Jake was about to say something, but Mr. McCready cut him off. "You're doing a fine job there, Billy. Come here a second." Still holding the post upright he kneeled down until his eyes were level with Billy's. The man put his massive hand on Billy's shoulder.

"Now Billy you're putting that dirt in perfect. But don't worry so much about spilling. Your brother's gonna come through and put the dirt where it needs to be. You just gotta make sure it goes in more or less even around the post."

"Yes, sir."

"Just try to see how fast you can put that dirt in the hole."

"You want me to go fast? Well, why didn't you say so in the first place?"

Mr. McCready's eyebrows rose.

"Billy…" Jake drew out the last syllable of his brother's name.

"I'm just sayin'." Billy turned to Mr. McCready and patted him on the shoulder. "Don't you worry, Mr. McCready. I got it now. We'll be finished in no time." With new instructions he moved like a shuttle in a loom, snapping from pile to post and back, narrating as he went. "Okay, getting more dirt. Yes sir, gonna take it to the hole. Fillin' her up. Mr. McCready wants me to go fast. Easy as pie. Back for more."

Jake just shook his head, directing him to put more dirt here and there.

"Okay, Billy," said Mr. McCready. "Let your brother tamp it down now." Billy nodded went back to the diminished pile of dirt and sat down. His chest heaved as his lungs tried to catch up. Jake took a long pole and tamped down the dirt around the post. Then Mr. McCready told Billy to put more dirt in, and Billy ferried the dirt to the hole with renewed fervor.

When they thought they finished filling the first hole, Mr. McCready let go of the post and took the pole from Jake and tamped the dirt down some more. Without being told Billy filled in more dirt and the man tamped it down with the pole and then his foot. Jake was ashamed he had not completed the task but when he saw the force Mr. McCready was putting on the pole he knew he could not have. With each jab the thick metal pole vibrated like a guitar string.

When Mr. McCready finished, he told the boys to help him with the rails. Jake and Billy on one end and Mr. McCready on the other, they carried a rail toward the post. The man wedged one end into the bottom hole of the post. He told the boys to keep holding the rail, then walked toward another post lying on the ground. This he picked up and carried to the hole next to the boys. He spun it so the holes would match up and put it in the ground at an angle. Then he brought the post to the end of the rail the boys were holding.

"Watch your hands, boys." Jake and Billy shuffled their hands down the rail, still holding it parallel to the ground. Mr. McCready brought the post up just enough for the rail to rest in the bottom hole. "Okay boys, you can let 'er go. Billy, come here son. Now just hold this post here for me, will ya?" Billy put both hands on the top of the post and dug his feet into the dirt. His eyes were focused solely on the post, his body locked into place. "That's good, just like that," said the man. "Jake, give me a hand with this, will ya?"

Jake walked over to another rail and picked up one end as Mr. McCready lifted the other. The man wedged the second rail into the post, then walked to Jake's end. He tilted the post back and slipped the rail in the middle hole, slowly letting go as he made sure Billy had it. Then they repeated the procedure with the third rail.

When all three rails were in the loose post, Mr. McCready pushed against the post with slowly increasing pressure. The wood creaked and squeaked and groaned until the post looked upright. He pulled out his plumb line again, walking around the post to see if it was vertical from all sides. "Okay, boys," he said.

Billy filled the dirt in again, and this time Jake tried even harder to tamp it down. When they finished, Mr. McCready took the pole from Jake and tamped the dirt down some more. The pole didn't go down nearly as far as the last time, and he turned to Jake and smiled. Billy filled in the spaces with more dirt and the man tamped it and pushed on the post. It didn't budge.

"I ain't never seen nobody do it like that before," said Jake.

"No, I suppose not," said Mr. McCready. "Most men are too lazy to do it this way. They'll just put all the posts in first then slide the rails in after. I do more work on the front end, but then I don't have to worry about repairing it every time the wind blows. Go ahead and shake them rails, Jake." Jake walked over to the top rails and shook it with his hand. It didn't move. The man laughed. "Naw, Jake. Give it a good shake."

Jake put both hands and dug in, shaking it even harder. It did not move. He did the same for the middle and bottom rails, but they didn't move either. Mr. McCready chuckled.

"That's in there nice and solid," said Jake.

"Thanks to you two. Come on, let's get some water and rest a couple minutes. They walked to the barn and sat in the shade and drank water from the canteens they had brought. As they sat, Mr. McCready used his hands to demonstrate the techniques he had used to put the fence in himself, with Billy asking questions. Jake watched the man with his brother. He thought of the good fortune that brought them to this family, and his mind wandered to his aunt. A wave of guilt came over him. He felt bad they had left her, but he knew they had to. So did she, he thought.

"Jake? Jake? *JAKE!*"

Billy was tugging at his arm. "Come on, Jake. We gotta help Mr. McCready with the fence."

"Alright."

"You okay there, son?" A standing Mr. McCready towered over Jake. "You look like you saw a ghost."

"Yes, sir. Just daydreamin'. Sorry."

"Don't worry about it. Come on, let's get at it."

"Yes, sir."

The man turned and walked back toward the fence. Billy bounced alongside of him. Jake looked at the odd pair of the giant of a man and his tiny little brother. *Things are going to be alright*, he thought.

4

The earth soaked up the daily warmth the sun poured into it like a sponge. As May moved into June and July the sun's arc reached higher in the sky and the ground became saturated with heat. By August it could hold no more, so it tried to squeeze out the warmth. By then the sun was also overloaded, and as the heat leaking from the earth's pores met the sun's rays on the earth's surface, all those on it suffered.

Clouds brought the only brief respite from the heat. Great summer storms of thunder and light announced their presence from faraway hills, and residents breathed relieved sighs at their sound. Giant cumulus clouds dumped their cooling rain in hard, heavy drops that bent crops and scurried animals to shelter under barns and branches. But in the wake of the storms the heat grew more intense as the hot air sucked moisture from the earth before it could run downhill. Humid. Oppressive. Late summer in Missouri.

The boys and the McCreadys grew close. Jake was always looking for any sign they were overstaying their welcome, but none came. One night he lay in bed and overheard their whispered conversation and his ears perked when Mr. McCready said his name.

"That boy's somethin' else, Lizzie. I can't give him enough work. He keeps askin' for more. And I don't hardly have to show him how to do nothin'. It's like he's been doin' this his whole life."

"Probably has. How's Billy doin' out there?"

"He's just like his brother in most ways. A little louder. Little younger. He always wants to know why I do a thing a certain way. Jake just knows how to do it and knows that's the right way."

"Billy's always asking me questions in here, too. Especially when he's reading. I swear that boy knows more words than me now."

Mr. McCready laughed. "Yeah, I don't know why John gave us all those books. Guess he wanted his parents to learn something."

Mrs. McCready laughed too. "Guess living in the city he's got time to read, but he forgot how much work it is to run a farm. I ain't got time to read." She sighed. "I sure do miss that boy, though."

"Yeah, it's good to have these younguns around. Keeps us young too."

A long silence followed, and Jake thought they had gone to sleep until Mrs. McCready spoke. "You think we could let these boys stay?"

Jake tried to silence everything—even his breathing—so he could hear the man's response.

"For how long?" asked Mr. McCready.

"I mean *stay*, Marshall. You know they ain't got no place to go. Even if that story about his daddy's true, and even if he's still alive, you gonna let them travel to California all by themselves?"

"Of course not. I just wanted to be clear on what you were sayin'."

"Well?"

"Well, yeah. I think we can. We won't have to hire anyone to harvest if we've got these two boys around, and with that money we can last through winter. Easy."

Jake's thoughts ran. He imagined a life here. A home with the McCreadys far from the hard life of the road or the abusive home of his aunt. A home maybe like the one he knew as a small child before his mother died. Before his father left to find his fortune in California and the man who moved in after brought whiskey and fights and bruises on his aunt's face. Before he and Billy left to avoid the same. The McCreadys took care of him and his brother. And they knew the boys well, for they had guessed the truth that Jake was still too scared to tell his brother: Jake and Billy's father was dead.

There was a knock at the door. Then another knock came, louder and more insistent. Jake snapped back to reality. There was rustling in the McCreadys' bedroom, followed by Mr. McCready's voice.

"What the hell?" said Mr. McCready. There was more rustling, then the creak of bed and floorboard as someone walked down the hall. From the front door there was a click, and then the groan of hinges. "Saunders! What the hell do you want?"

"Hello, Marshall." The voice was a disembodied slick like silvery drops of oil in a puddle. A chill shot down Jake's spine. "It's been a long time. I was wondering if you had reconsidered my offer."

Mr. McCready snorted. "Reconsider? I did enough considering the first time when I told you no."

The other man's sickly, syrupy voice drew out each word, squeezing out all the sound before moving on to the next. "I thought you might change your mind. I've made a very generous offer for your land. You won't find a better deal, even though it is a lovely piece of property."

"It's nice because I've made it nice. You'd just turn it to dust."

"Now, that's not a polite thing to say."

"Polite? You're a helluva one to talk about being polite. Knocking on my door so late. Coming around after I've asked you not to."

"I'm a persistent man, Mr. McCready."

"So am I, Saunders. Now get off my property before I make you get off."

"No need to be rude, Marshall. I'll be on my way."

Without even realizing, Jake had gotten out of bed and walked out into the hallway. He was standing in there when Mr. McCready walked back to his room.

"Jake? What're you doing up?"

"Everything okay, Mr. McCready?"

"Everything's fine, don't you worry. Why don't you go on back to bed now?"

"If you need help protectin' this place you just let me know. I got my daddy's pistol and I—"

Mr. McCready interrupted him. "Thank you Jake, but I don't want you to do nothin'. Now go on back to bed before Mrs. McCready starts worrying about you."

"Yes, sir."

Jake went to bed, but could not sleep. He lay awake thinking of the two conversations he had overheard. The hope from one and dread from the other.

The next day Jake and Billy ate breakfast with the McCreadys. No one spoke of what had happened the night before. Billy had slept through the night's drama and Jake didn't think it proper to ask the McCreadys their business. Outside, large clouds black and gray and silver threatened rain. Mr. McCready said they needed to walk the perimeter, so he and Jake and Billy went outside despite the impending storm.

The edge of the McCreadys' property abutted a thick forest of oak and maple and walnut. Deer thrived in the wood but also ventured into the field to dine on Mr. McCready's crops. To prevent this Mr. McCready designed defenses belonging more to the battlefield than a farm. Long wooden pikes stood at regular intervals, pointing toward the forest and angled toward the tops of the trees, preventing deer from jumping over them and into the field. They were soaked in creosote to preserve them long after untreated wood would have rotted.

Somewhere along this pointed barricade was a hole large enough for a deer. The leaves of several plants were missing large chunks and other plants had disappeared altogether. Mr. McCready and the boys needed to find that hole quickly or face losing more crops. The three of them walked in silence, and Jake could sense Mr. McCready's mood was still soured by the visit from Saunders. Raindrops began falling, heavy but infrequent.

At the far edge of the field the rain started to fall in earnest. But Mr. McCready and the boys had not yet found the opening, so they plodded on. The rain came hard now as the sky emptied its moisture onto the earth. Soaking wet and still unsuccessful, the three reached a storage shed at the far corner of the field. Mr. McCready opened the door and let the boys in, removing his hat and shaking the water off. The boys did the same. They grabbed stools and sat in silence as the water of the world made its sounds. Pinging on the metal roof. Rushing from the roof's corrugated edges. Drip drip dripping from their clothes.

Jake saw Billy reach into his pocket and take out his rock. Billy stared at it like an object of meditation. Mr. McCready watched him, too. "Boy, what on earth is so special about that rock?"

Billy said nothing. He lowered his chin to his chest and slid the rock back in his pocket.

Mr. McCready softened his tone. "Hey, Billy. It's okay. I just wanted to know why you like that rock so much."

Billy pulled the rock out again. "It's my magic rock."

"Ahhhh," said Mr. McCready. "What's it do?"

"Protects me and my brother."

"Well, it's sure done a good job so far. You make sure you take care of that. I know what it's like to have something you don't want to let go."

"You mean like your farm?"

A slight smile crossed Mr. McCready's face. "Yes."

"It's a real nice farm."

"I think so. Trouble is, so do other people. Let me ask you something, Billy. What if I said I'd give you five cents for your rock, would you sell it?"

Billy shook his head.

"How about twenty-five cents?"

Billy shook his head again. "No sir, Mr. McCready."

"A dollar?"

"What are you going to use this rock for that you need to pay a whole dollar for't?"

Mr. McCready laughed. Jake was about to say something but the man waved him off. "How about five dollars?"

Billy's eyes grew wide. He stared at the rock and rolled it in his fingers, then shook his head and pulled the rock to his chest. "Now I know you think it has magic."

Mr. McCready let out a hearty laugh. "That's how I feel about my farm. No amount of money can replace it. You agree?"

Billy nodded and a small smile lit his face.

"Billy, you just set my mind right after it's been wrong all morning. Come on, you boys ready to get wet?"

Billy nodded and Jake said, "Yes, sir." They creaked out the door and headed toward the row of pikes. The rain was the same, but it seemed less now that Mr. McCready was talking again. He pointed out plants, talking about types of wood and which tools were best for certain jobs. All the while Jake tried to listen and remember.

At last they found the hole in the battlement, and while Jake and Billy waited Mr. McCready went back to the barn for two creosoted pikes. He carried one on each shoulder and looked more soldier than farmer. Jake had tried to remove the old broken pikes but they were secured and heavy. Mr. McCready pulled them out and put in the new ones. The boys tried to help, but Mr. McCready did not need any. Jake wondered why he had asked them to come, but figured Mr. McCready had just wanted company. His mind wandered more, wondering if Mr. McCready was training him to take over more of the duties of the farm so when Jake got older he could run it. He couldn't allow himself to hope that much.

5

Not long after Saunders's visit it started happening. At first it was little things, small events that by themselves could be explained away. A missing chicken yet no holes in the chicken wire. The barn door off its hinges after a windless night. A few bent stalks of corn even though there had been no hail.

Jake understood what was going on. He had seen it before when the man who married Jake's aunt had moved in, taken over. It was a slow dismantling, a breaking of wills. But Mr. McCready was not Jake's aunt.

Saunders came one night and when he did Mr. McCready was waiting for him. When Saunders knocked Mr. McCready cracked open the door and stuck both barrels of his shotgun through the opening. He talked from the other end of those barrels and called the man all sorts of words Jake had never heard before. Told him to stay off his property day or night and never to come back. Jake listened from his room and was surprised not by Mr. McCready's tone but by Saunders's. It was unchanged from the last time, devoid of worry. As if he were accustomed to speaking to gun barrels. His voice was like fermented honey, a rotten sweetness.

Saunders had cast a pall over the McCreadys. As the boys worked with him to harvest the crops for the coming winter, Mr. McCready spoke only when necessary. Mrs. McCready still smiled, but it was a cautious smile tinged with sadness. It felt like a storm was coming, they just didn't know when.

Autumn descended on the earth. First the nights became cooler, the earth losing the late summer heat it had stored. Then the rhythm of the crickets and cicadas and the croaks of frogs became slower, softer. Green turned to yellow, yellow to orange, red, purple, brown. The empty spaces in trees spring had filled became empty once more, and the wind blew rustling leaves in great, shifting piles like sand dunes.

Every able hand worked the land. Carefully tended plants grown full poured all their energy into their fruits and roots, their last dying effort. Farmers hastened to gather all they offered before it rotted on the vine or vanished in the mouths of deer and rabbits. Fields once high with corn were now shorn. Potato plants were upended, golden squash and orange pumpkins plucked plump from the ground. Apple trees and tomato vines strained to produce their last red orbs. Then the world fell quiet. Colors muted and disappeared in preparation for the stern white silence of winter.

One day after work Mr. McCready was sitting on the front porch with the boys and Jake got the courage to ask Mr. McCready about Saunders.

Mr. McCready said the man believed in quantity, not quality. "If he spent his time working his own land instead of trying to steal it from other people, he would have himself more than he could eat in three winters."

"Why doesn't he?" asked Billy.

Mr. McCready shrugged as he stared out over the yard. "Lazy. Lazy as a June bug born in July."

Billy snickered, but Jake shushed him. "You think he's coming back?"

Mr. McCready spat, and the saliva arced over the lip of the porch's floorboards. "I know he is."

"What you goin' to do when he does?"

Mr. McCready turned and looked at Jake. "Don't worry there, Jake. He ain't goin' to take my land."

41

"I want to help you."

"I know you do, Jake. But you help enough already. You and Billy both."

"But you and Mrs. McCready been real nice to us. You done more than you needed to. I don't want no one to take this farm from you."

Mr. McCready smiled, though he was no longer looking at Jake. "No one's taking our farm, Jake."

"Besides, we've already stayed too long. Now the harvest's over you don't need our help. We should just pick up and head—"

"You ain't goin' nowhere," said Mr. McCready, and while his voice held no anger Jake knew the conversation was over. "Come on," he said, turning to the boys. "Mrs. McCready's going to wonder if we want our supper hot or cold." The three stood up and opened the door, and when they did a current of warm air spilled out, filled with the smell of beef stew and pumpkin pie.

For a time the work on the McCready farm slowed. The harvesting was done but it was not yet cold enough to start winterizing the house. Aside from small chores—raking leaves into the barn for use as insulation throughout the winter, chopping firewood, clearing brush—the boys had their time to themselves. Billy spent most of his free time with his nose in books. Having finished all the McCready's library he was reading them all again, beginning where he had started. It was one of the few activities that kept him quiet.

Jake followed Mr. McCready like a hound begging for scraps. Whenever he got up to go somewhere, Jake would silently slip in behind him. They spent long hours together and formed an unspoken way of communicating. Jake would hand Mr. McCready a tool before he asked for it, do a chore without being asked. Jake saw a change in Mr. McCready. More than the usual autumnal letdown from a long summer's work. The man's mood hung low like November clouds. Jake knew without asking what weighed on Mr. McCready.

It was a clear, crisp November night when the peace they had enjoyed during and after the harvest was broken. The ground outside was cold but not yet frozen. Frosted dew formed on the brittle brown grass every morning. The few remaining leaves uncaptured by a rake were left to scutter soundlessly across empty fields, blown by the chill wind.

The McCreadys had allowed the boys to stay up late, sipping hot chocolate as they stared into the fire. Billy fell asleep with his face in a book, so Mrs. McCready picked him up and carried him to bed, chiding Jake and Mr. McCready not to stay up too much longer.

Jake became lost in the fire, the changing colors of the crackling logs. He was snapped from his reverie by a knock on the door. Mr. McCready and Jake looked at each other. He told Jake to go to his room, and then Jake heard Mr. McCready go to his own to get his shotgun. There were murmurs from inside, but Jake could not distinguish the sounds into words. A dull glow formed in the darkness and crept out through the crack in their bedroom door. Then Mr. McCready's heavy boots stomped down the hall as he held the kerosene lantern in front of him. As he passed their room the light of the lantern glared in Jake's eyes. Mr. McCready stared straight ahead.

Jake heard the lantern thud onto the kitchen table and the double click of Mr. McCready's shotgun. There was the clunk of the door bolt, and Mr. McCready's growl. The nasal voice of Saunders responded. Mr. McCready's voice rose to a shout, something Jake had never heard from him. It was followed by the unmistakable sound of guns clicking outside the door. Jake knew he had to do something.

As quietly as he could, Jake reached under his bed and retrieved his father's gun. Although he cleaned it regularly, it had been a while since he held it with an intention of using it. Resting in his palm it felt good, like it always had. Then he thought of Saunders. His hand started shaking slightly.

Jake heard footsteps coming down the hallway. Mrs. McCready's head popped through the door. Jake wheeled around and hid the gun behind his back.

"You boys be real quiet now," she whispered hoarsely. "And don't leave this room." Jake nodded and Billy moaned slightly but did not wake. As quickly as her head had appeared it was gone. Her footsteps went toward the door and she cocked her own rifle.

Cautiously Jake crawled to the open bedroom door. He stuck his head out and saw the soft light of the lanterns illuminate the kitchen, man and woman half lit half in shadow. The flickering firelight from the stone hearth cast long, wavering shadows on the wall by the door.

Mr. McCready and Saunders's verbal warfare escalated while the woman and Saunders's men stayed silent, but Jake's pulse was pounding too loud in his eardrums to understand all they said. In his stocking feet he slid across the living room floor to the far window, opened it and slipped out.

Jake slunk around the south side of the house. The cold from the ground seeped through Jake's socks and numbed his toes. The balls of his feet felt heavy and prickled with every step. Jake kept far enough away from the house to avoid the dry leaves gathered at its base, and as he crept closer he could see the light spilling from the front door. There was a line on the ground in front of him where light met dark. Although he could not see the McCreadys or their trespassers, he could hear their voices now, louder and more distinct.

Jake inhaled deeply, slowly letting out the air to calm his nerves and still his body. He withdrew his hands from his pockets and pulled the revolver from his belt. It glowed pale in the dim light of the crescent moon. The boy moved toward the house and pressed his shoulder into it. He took another breath and practiced the counting drill his father had taught him to clear his mind, then stuck his head into the light and the unknown.

Three silhouettes in long dusters and wide-brimmed hats stood in the triangle of light from the door, their shadows elongated into thin slices of darkness on the grass. Around them their breath lingered like tendrils of smoke, blurring their outlines. Saunders's hands were empty. The two men behind him held long rifles across their chests.

Jake waited while there was more talk between Saunders and Mr. McCready, their voices rising and falling with the wind. Then one of the men turned his head toward Jake. In an instant Jake's heart went from a trot to a gallop. He fought the instinct to hide behind the house and stood completely still, holding his breath as his racing heart depleted oxygen in his lungs.

The man spat a large wad of tobacco juice in Jake's direction. Saunders turned to the man and said, "Now don't go spittin' tobacco juice on my property." Jake's blood rose at Saunders's claim to the McCreadys' land, and before he realized it Jake had stepped into the light. The air went still, and in the quiet Jake could hear his heartbeat in his ears. He raised his gun. Jake glided silently across the grass as if it were ice. The three men on the porch stood silent and so did Mr. McCready.

"This ain't your property," said Jake. His voice rang shrill with nervous energy. Saunders and his men jerked their heads around, and the two men flanking Saunders raised their rifles. Mr. McCready saw this and took a step out the door. The man closest to Jake was moving faster, and soon would have his weapon aimed at the boy. In one smooth motion Mr. McCready raised his shotgun, spun it so the butt end faced the man and sent it cracking into his skull. Man and rifle crashed to the floor.

Jake became acutely aware of certain things. Their breaths hanging in the air. A cold drop dangling from his runny nose. The barrel of the other man's rifle rising as if slowed by the cold. Yet so focused was Jake on these details he did not notice his own hands trembling, taking aim. The sound from his pistol surprised him more than anyone else, and for a second he wondered who had fired. The crack of the pistol shot hung still in the cold air, and before it faded into silence the man fell off the porch. Only then did Jake realize where his bullet had struck.

Acrid gun smoke reached Jake's nostrils and jolted him from his daze. His hands still held his gun raised, now aimed at Saunders. Jake saw fear in the man's eyes, then saw Mr.

McCready stick his shotgun three inches from the back of Saunders's head. "Get your men and get the hell out of here," said Mr. McCready, "or they won't be the only ones on the floor."

Saunders kicked the man Mr. McCready had knocked in the head. He had been stirring, and groaned when the boot struck him in the ribs. "Get up and help him!" His voice was difficult to hear over the screams of the man who had been shot. "Get up!" yelled Saunders, his once calm voice now screeching in panic.

The man stood slowly and, despite the protestations of his partner, pulled him up and hobbled down the stairs with the man's arm over his shoulders. Saunders squawked from behind, telling them to hurry. As the men passed Jake they barely looked at him, too intent on staying upright. Saunders lingered though, and even in the dull light of the moon Jake could see his sunken gray features, wispy diminishing hair, pale, cold eyes. He looked half in the grave and Jake could not imagine how a man as frail as Saunders struck so much fear into the hearts of men. Saunders looked Jake up and down, snorted and followed his men as they disappeared into the darkness.

"Jake!" Mr. McCready grabbed the boy and turned him around. "Are you okay?" The boy looked down at the gun in his hand as if the answer lay in its metalwork. "Are you hurt?" Jake shook his head. "Come on, then. Let's get inside." Jake gave no response but followed Mr. McCready into the house.

"Boy, what in the *hell* were you thinking?" said the man as soon as Jake closed the door behind him. Jake hung his head. "You could've gotten yourself killed out there." Jake's face warmed and reddened, and though he tried to speak he couldn't. His eyes bore holes into the floor. Mr. McCready's face appeared in Jake's vision, and he put his enormous hands on Jake's shoulders. When he spoke his voice had softened. "What you did was also brave, Jake. Most men I know wouldn't have done that."

"Thank you, sir."

"No, thank you Jake. I've been wanting to do that for a long time."

"I...I..." Jake was starting to get his tongue back. "I just couldn't let him take your land, Mr. McCready."

"I know, Jake." Mr. McCready sighed and slumped into one of the kitchen chairs. "But now we got ourselves a real problem. Saunders has some powerful friends, or at least powerful people he pays to be his friends, and the sheriff is one of them. If I know anything, he'll be back tomorrow with the sheriff, and they'll be looking for you."

Jake's throat felt thick, and when he tried to breathe it felt like his chest was pushing in on his lungs. This life he had imagined here with the McCreadys had always felt tenuous, like it would crumble as soon as he believed it possible.

Jake cleared his throat and stuck his chin out. "I'm sorry I brought you trouble, Mr. McCready. Me and Billy'll pack our bags, and we'll be out of here in ten minutes.

A low chuckle emanating from Mr. McCready surprised Jake. "Boy, sometimes you're dumber than a Missouri mule. You really think we're going to let you and Billy walk out into the middle of a cold November night when there's a bunch of men with guns out looking for you?" Jake's smile was small and sheepish. "You're right about one thing, though. You two will have to pack your bags. If there's going to be trouble I want you boys far away from it."

Jake opened his mouth to speak, but Mr. McCready raised a hand to stop him. "I know what you're thinking Jake, but you can forget it. This here trouble's been coming for a long time, and I've been preparing for it. It ain't your fault it happened and it ain't your responsibility to keep more from happening. If you two was around here it would just make me nervous."

"Yes, sir."

"Now hurry up and pack your bags. Tell Billy to do the same. I've got a friend a couple miles away who owes me a favor. He won't mind hiding you out for a while."

"Yes, sir." Jake turned and headed to his room. When he got there the light was on, and Mrs. McCready was helping Billy pack his clothes.

"Jake?" said Billy. "You okay?"

"Course I'm okay. Don't you worry about me." He tried to calm his voice and limbs still trembling from the adrenaline running through his system.

"I heard a gunshot," said Billy. "What happened? Did you get hit?"

"No, Billy. I said don't worry about it." Jake's voice rose, so he paused and inhaled deeply before exhaling. He walked over to Billy's bed where his brother sat and Mrs. McCready sat stroking Billy's hair. Jake sat on the other side of his brother.

"Billy, we gotta leave here, at least for a few days."

"But why? I like it here."

"I do too, but we gotta go. Those men who came tonight'll come back, and when they do they'll be lookin' for me."

"But why will they be looking for you?"

Jake paused, staring at the floor before speaking. "Because I shot one of 'em."

Billy's eyes grew wide and when he spoke again it was with a whisper. "Did you kill him?"

"Naw. I just shot him in the knee."

"What'd you do that for?"

"If I hadn't a done it, he would've."

Billy thought about this answer and seemed to accept it because he changed the subject. "How long we have to be gone for?"

"We'll see. 'Til the dust on this one settles."

"How long do you think that'll be?"

"Dunno. Few days. Maybe a week."

"What happens if it don't blow over?"

"Well, we can just lay low until spring, then keep heading out to California to see Pa." A sharp, stabbing guilt pierced Jake at the mention of their father.

Billy's head hung low. "Okay," he said.

Jake patted his brother on the knee and hopped off the bed. "Okay, get your stuff packed up. We're leaving in fifteen minutes."

Billy sighed. "Okay."

It pained Jake to see his brother so sad, so he turned to his bed and started packing his own things. He had hoped it would distract him, so even when he finished he pretended to reorganize by unpacking and repacking, waiting for Billy.

Mr. McCready stuck his head through the door. "You ready, boys?"

Jake looked over at Billy and saw he was dressed but not packed. "Not quite, sir."

Mrs. McCready helped Billy pack the remainder of his things and hurried both boys out to the kitchen. They were wrapped in several warm layers of clothing, and their bags bulged with changes of clean clothes. The McCreadys had supplemented the boys' meager collection with all their children's clothes they had saved from when they were young.

Mr. McCready looked at Jake and Billy and nodded. They nodded back. He turned to his wife. "Will you be okay for a little while I take these boys over to John's?"

She waved her hand dismissively. "Please, Marshall. I could run this place without you. I just keep you around for appearances." Mr. McCready smiled and walked toward the door.

The woman kneeled in front of Billy. His chin was tucked into his jacket and pressed against his chest, so she gently pulled up his chin to look him in the eye. The light from the lantern's wick illuminated the moisture in her eyes, and when she spoke her voice cracked a little. "You be good, you hear Billy?" Billy nodded. "You listen to your brother and do what he says now. He's looking out for you." Billy nodded again. "And you keep reading them books, too. Some day it'll do you a lot of good."

Billy started to nod, but his lip began to tremble. His face scrunched as he fought the onslaught of tears but it was no use. One tear fell to the floor and then another. Mrs. McCready wrapped her arms around him and pulled him close and Billy sobbed as she clutched him. She whispered how it would all be alright and how this was just for a few days and not to be scared because they were going to a safe place and would be back home soon. When his sobbing ceased and breathing slowed she pulled away, held his face in her hands and kissed him on his forehead. She wiped the tears from his cheeks and kissed him again and stood up. "I'll see you in few days, okay Billy?"

Billy nodded, rubbed his eyes with the back of his hand and walked toward the door where her husband waited. Mrs. McCready turned to Jake and Jake felt an overwhelming desire to do just what Billy did, to fall into this woman's arms and cry for the loss of his own mother and father and for the loss of this new, adopted family. But he needed to be strong in front of his brother so he stuck out his hand. Mrs. McCready was already moving to hug him but when she saw his hand she looked in his eyes and nodded in understanding. She placed her hand in his and held it firm.

"I want to thank you for all you done for us," said Jake. "You saved our lives and that's the truth."

"It was our pleasure, Jake."

"Ain't no way we can repay you, ma'am. But I'd like to try."

Mrs. McCready smiled. "You already done it, Jake. Just having you boys here was real nice." She cleared her throat and for a second Jake thought she might cry but she shook her head as if to ward off the tears. "You take care of that brother of yours now. Mr. Jones, the man you boys'll be staying with, he's a real nice man. He'll take good care of you until you come back here."

"Yes ma'am. Thank you, ma'am."

"I'll see you in a few days, Jake. Don't you worry about that."

Jake nodded and thanked her one more time. He wanted desperately to believe her words. When Jake approached the door Mr. McCready opened it up, and the two boys stepped through it into a blast of cold air that struck them. Billy shivered. Jake put his arm around his little brother and they walked down the steps. "This way," said Mr. McCready as he passed them. His large boots crunched the brown, frozen grass, and his silvery breath hung in the light of the nighttime sky. Jake and Billy followed, their bags bouncing off their backs as they jogged to keep up.

They walked in the opposite direction of town and turned on a road cutting through a small cluster of trees that looked like gray skeletons lit by a pale moon. The houses were spaced farther apart over here, and soon Jake saw nothing but rolling fields and forests. He kept looking over his shoulder to see if anyone was following. No one was.

Soon Jake was able to make out a tiny house in the distance. It had no light within nor surrounding buildings save a small barn. When Jake saw the posts and rails of the perimeter fence lined up perfectly, he knew they had arrived. Any man with a fence like that would be friends with Mr. McCready.

The wooden steps groaned in the cold as Mr. McCready climbed up to the front porch. Before he even knocked on the door, a lantern was lit inside. Soon after the door opened and a long metal barrel stuck out. "What do you want?" said a voice from inside.

"Whoa, John. It's me, Marshall. Sorry to bother you so late."

The barrel disappeared and in its place emerged a face. "Marshall? What the hell you doin' out here this late? Everything alright?"

"Mind if I come in and explain?"

"Of course, of course," said the man. He opened the door wide.

"I've got company," said Mr. McCready. Mr. Jones looked past Mr. McCready and eyed the two boys. "I dunno, they look pretty dangerous. You'll vouch for 'em?"

Mr. McCready grinned, and Jake managed a smile. Billy just buried his face in his brother's coat. "I'll vouch for 'em," said Mr. McCready.

"Come on in, boys," said Mr. Jones. "It's too cold to stand out there."

Mr. McCready and the boys walked in, and as they crossed the threshold the warmth from the room enveloped them. They hurried inside. Mr. Jones walked to a cast iron stove in the corner of the room and set his shotgun in the corner. Then he grabbed two logs from the neat stack of split wood next to the stove and used one of them to lift the latch on the stove door. When the door swung open it creaked, and the man's face went from shadow to bright orange. He threw the logs in, grabbed another and used it to close the stove door.

After wiping his hands on his pant legs he walked over to a basin full of water. Next to it was a table, and from there Mr. Jones grabbed a metal teapot. He dipped the pot into the water and filled it. Then he walked over to the stove and placed the teapot on top. Water sizzled for a few seconds before it evaporated.

"Please, sit down," said Mr. Jones and he gestured to the chairs around the table. "This looks like a story I got to hear."

"Let's put the little one to bed first, if you don't mind," said Mr. McCready.'

"Of course," said Mr. Jones. "Follow me, son." Jake put his arm around Billy's shoulder and walked into a room with two beds. Mr. Jones left and Billy lay down in the bed. Jake put the blanket Mr. Jones gave over his brother and wished him good

54

night. He waited until Billy was asleep and then went back into the main room.

When Jake was seated at the table, Mr. McCready began to tell the story of the two boys, starting with their arrival at the McCready farm months before. Jake sat silently and tried to listen but all he could think of was the man he had shot. His young mind wove terrible stories of the man dying from his wounds and the sheriff coming after Jake and Jake hanging from the gallows or rotting in a jail until he was an old man. And of Mr. and Mrs. McCready suffering the same fate and their house being burned to the ground or Saunders taking over their land and living in the house or tearing it down cackling the whole time.

Mr. Jones's laughing brought him back to reality. The man slapped Jake on the knee and said, "Good for you, son. I've been wantin' to shoot one of them bastards for years." Jake's face and ears burned.

"So..." said Mr. McCready. His gaze lowered and he hesitated before continuing. "I was hoping to ask you a favor, John. These boys need to lay low for a while, and if they're at my house they might get found, even if I hide 'em."

"Hell, Marshall. You don't even have to ask. I'd be glad to have 'em."

Mr. McCready let out a huge sigh like the wind going out of a bellows. "Thanks, John."

The two men looked at Jake. His head was down but he willed his eyes to theirs. "Sorry for the all the trouble we've caused. Especially me. Mr. McCready, thank you for taking such good care of me and my brother." Jake turned to Mr. Jones. "Sir, thank you for taking my brother and me in. I'm sorry to say we don't got much to pay you, but what we have is yours."

Mr. Jones laughed. "Son, anyone who fired on that bastard Saunders or one of his men is welcome in my house. Stay as long you like, and keep your money."

Jake's head lowered again, and he shook it. "I shouldn't have done it. That weren't right."

Mr. McCready's enormous hand enveloped Jake's shoulder. It startled Jake so much he looked at it, and then Mr. McCready. "Jake, lemme tell you something. You need to take that weight there on your shoulders and drop it and never think about it again. You done right tonight. Hell, you done better than Mr. Jones or myself ever had. The first time that man showed up at my door I should've shot him. I knew what he was right from the start. Them men tonight came with guns and they meant harm. The only way to deal with them is the way you did. Don't try to tell yourself otherwise."

"Thank you, sir."

Mr. Jones spoke. "Don't you worry, son. You and your brother will be safe here. Sheriff won't think of looking for you out here, and like I said, you can stay as long as you like. I don't think it'll take too long. Saunders ain't a fighting man. Never was. He'll try to work out a *deal*." He spat out this last word like a thing to be despised.

Mr. McCready nodded and stood up. "I better get back, make sure my wife hasn't taken out all of Saunders's men. John, I can't thank you enough."

"Don't you worry about these boys, Marshall. They're safe with me."

Mr. McCready nodded. "I know. That's why I brought 'em here." He turned to Jake and when he spoke his voice wavered almost imperceptibly. "You take good care of your brother, and you mind Mr. Jones here."

"Yes, sir. Thank you, sir."

"I'll come and get you in a few days then." Just before the door, Mr. McCready stopped and put his hand in his pocket. He sighed and turned around and pulled his hand out. In it was a wad of bank notes.

"Jake, take this."

"No sir, I can't."

"Just in case, Jake. I'll most likely get it from you in a couple days."

"Mr. McCready, I--"

"Don't argue with me, son. Just take it."

Jake took the bills and folded both hands over them. Mr. McCready turned to Mr. Jones. They shook hands silently before Mr. McCready opened the door and closed it behind him.

Through the window, Mr. Jones watched his friend until he disappeared into the darkness. Jake stood there as if a soldier awaiting instruction. At last Mr. Jones turned around. "Alright, son. I imagine you're pretty tired."

The adrenaline from the night's happenings had dwindled, but Jake's mind was still churning. Only when Mr. Jones mentioned it did he feel the wave of weariness overtake him. His little body had consumed much energy in the standoff and the walk over to Mr. Jones's house, and Jake's knees buckled slightly. "Yes, sir."

"Well, come on and let me show you your bed."

"I know where it is, sir. Just next to my brother."

Mr. Jones nodded. "You need anything else before you go to bed? Trip to the outhouse? Some warm water?" The pot on the stove had steam coming out of it.

Jake shook his head. "No thank you, sir."

"You know you don't have to call me 'sir' if you don't want. Makes me sound like a general or something."

"Thank you, sir."

Mr. Jones laughed and again Jake's face turned red. "Suit yourself, son. I'm glad to have you here."

"Thank you, sir—I mean…thank you."

"Good night, Jake."

"Good night, Mr. Jones. You need help with that fire?"

"What's that? Oh, yeah. Good thinking, boy. Don't want to wake up in the middle of the night to feed the stove. Thank you, but I'll take care of it. You go check on your brother and then get yourself some rest."

Jake nodded and walked into the room on the left. His brother lay sound asleep, and Jake made sure the blankets were tight around Billy before taking off his boots and sliding under the blankets on his own bed. He kept his jacket on, unsure how cold it would get when the fire in the stove had died down. Not long after laying his head on the pillow, Jake fell asleep.

6

Jake's fears about the cold room proved unfounded. When he woke early in the morning he was drenched with sweat, and he unbuttoned his coat and threw it on the floor before falling back asleep. He awoke again and as he always did looked for his brother. Billy was lying in bed.

"Billy?"

"Yeah?"

"How long you been awake?"

"I dunno."

"You hungry?"

"Yeah."

"Reckon we better get ourselves something to eat."

"Okay."

The two boys got dressed and creaked down the wooden hallway to the living room. Mr. Jones was not there, but on the table there was a plate with a towel wrapped around it. Jake walked over to the table and put his hand on the towel. "Still warm," he said.

He peeled off the folds of the towel and grabbed two bannock cakes, covering the remaining one with the corners of the towel. One he gave to Billy and the other he took himself. Still standing, they ate in silence. When Billy had finished half of his he handed the rest to his brother.

"No, go on and eat. You need it to get big."

Billy took two more bites and slowly chewed each one before handing the cake back to Jake. This time his brother took it and finished it. After that they swept their crumbs off the table, opened the stove and threw the crumbs into the fire. Jake closed the stove door.

"Let's go make our beds and clean up. Mr. Jones is bein' real nice to us and we oughta do what we can to let him know we're grateful."

"Okay."

In the corner Jake found a broom, and the two boys walked back to their room. Soon the beds were made, shelves dusted and floor swept. When finished they did the same to the hallway, living room and kitchen. The only place they didn't touch was Mr. Jones's room, and they were careful not to even look in even though the door was wide open.

"Well little brother, what you wanna do now?"

"Wanna see if he's got any cards?"

Jake shook his head. You and your cards. Aunt Kate used to say that was a devil's game."

"Is not. Daddy taught me before he left."

"Well, that don't mean you gotta do it, too. Besides, I don't feel like it just now. But seeing as how we're in hiding and can't just stick our heads out the door, what say we—" Just then the door opened. Jake lunged for Billy and shielded his body.

Mr. Jones stood framed in the doorway. "Whoa, easy son. It's just me."

Jake's body relaxed. "Sorry, sir."

Mr. Jones waved Jake off and closed the door. "What you boys been up to?"

"We ate breakfast and then cleaned up a little."

Mr. Jones looked around the room and nodded. "So you did. You didn't have to do that."

"Yes sir, we did. We're mighty grateful for you taking care of us, and we want to help out any way we can."

The man's heavy boots thudded on the floor as he walked over to the table and sat with a sigh. "Son, it's goin' to get awful tiresome if you keep thankin' me every time you see me. I appreciate it, but there's no need to keep sayin' it. I know you're grateful."

"Yes, sir. Thank you, sir." Mr. Jones laughed and Jake's cheeks flushed. He cleared his throat. "Any news on Mr. McCready or Saunders?"

Their host shook his head. "Afraid not. That's where I just been, but Marshall ain't seen or heard nothin' yet. He didn't want to go into town, so I did just to see if I could stir up any news. Nothing."

"So you don't think they're going to do anything? I mean, they was trespassing."

Mr. Jones's low, rumbling laugh chilled Jake. "I wish that was true. Saunders is a snake in the grass, but I will say this for him. He is one patient son of a gun. He'll do something alright, but he'll wait till we're settin' on our heels a bit."

"What should we do then?"

"Just wait and watch. And be ready when they come." Billy moved closer to Jake, and Mr. Jones noticed. He smiled. "Don't worry, little fella. They don't know y'all are here. As long as you two stay inside there ain't no way they're gonna know, either."

Mr. Jones slapped his hands to his knees and stood up. Jake wasn't sure if the creaking was from the chair or the old man's joints. "Well, most of my chores are outside chores, and you already done all the inside ones. I got some split wood I can haul inside and you boys can stack it by the stove."

"Yes, sir."

"And there's some leftover stew in that pot hanging from the stovepipe there. Why don't you put it on the stove so we can have ourselves a hot lunch."

"Tha—" Jake caught himself and the man smiled.

"For supper we might go hungry unless I can find us some meat running around out there." Mr. Jones noticed Jake's eyes widen at the mention of hunting, and smiled. "You like to hunt?" Jake nodded. "Well, alright then. No wonder. Now I know how you coulda made that shot at Saunders's man. In the dark at twenty paces ain't easy." Mr. Jones laughed so hard his lungs wheezed to catch breath. "You alright by me, boy. You alright."

The man left and closed the door behind him, but soon the door opened and three pieces of wood skidded across the floor before it closed again. Not long after the same thing happened, an open maw spewing wood and closing again and again. Each time Jake and Billy gathered the wood and stacked it neatly in the iron wood holder. Billy started to sweep the floor again but Jake stopped him. "Just wait 'til he stops bringing wood."

As they gathered and stacked, Jake periodically stirred the stew. It was mostly potatoes but there was some meat. He couldn't tell the kind but it smelled like squirrel. Maybe rabbit. When the holder was full, Mr. Jones came back into the cabin. They sat around the table and ate the stew. It was simple but good. When they finished Mr. Jones licked his bowl clean so the boys did the same. Then Jake took the bowls over to the wash basin and poured some water from the pitcher next to it. Jake rinsed and Billy dried, and Mr. Jones took the dirty water outside when the boys had finished.

He disappeared down the hall and into his room, and when he came out he was carrying a rifle. It was old but well cared for, the metal nick-free and the worn wooden stock freshly oiled. The sun was just starting to descend from its apex but Mr. Jones put on two coats grabbed his hat, gloves and rifle and slipped out the door.

It was long after nightfall when the boys finally heard the door open. In one hand Mr. Jones carried his rifle and in the other was a piece of thin rope. Hanging from it were seven rabbits, their legs tied together so tightly it looked like one mass of fur. He stood in the doorway and set his rifle just inside the door, holding his quarry outside so blood wouldn't drip on the floor.

"Jake, grab that lantern over there, would you? I'm gonna need some light out here. I suppose it won't do no harm to have you out here when it's dark and nobody can see. Billy, you stay here and tend that fire. Careful not to burn yourself on that stove." Billy nodded.

Jake took the lantern and followed Mr. Jones outside and around back. When the man gave him the rope, Jake tried to hold it away from his body but the weight of the rabbits pulled down. His arm shook with the effort. In the small dim circle of kerosene light Mr. Jones worked quietly and quickly. The moon had not yet risen and the pinprick starlight did little to illuminate the world. Beyond the light of the lantern were ghosts of shapes glowing pale gray, tops of trees barely discernible from the sky above.

From the side of the cabin Mr. Jones pulled a table and wash basin and carried the basin out of the light. The darkness swallowed him whole. Jake could hear the pump of the well and the metallic flow of water into the basin, the water sloshing against the sides as it came closer. Basin then hands then face regained shape as they moved into the light.

After he put the basin on the table, Mr. Jones beckoned Jake. "Set 'em here, son," he whispered. "Hold that light just above the table." Relief washed over Jake's arm when he put the rabbits on the table, blood flowing back into his hand. He let it hang loosely at his side.

The table was scored and blood-stained, its markings a written history of carnage. With easy, efficient knife strokes Mr. Jones skinned and gutted and cleaned the rabbits. The only sounds were the slicing and ripping and gentle thuds as he turned the carcasses over, the washing of water over the knife and cleaned animals.

Several times Mr. Jones disappeared into the darkness with the basin and reappeared with fresh water. When he was finished, he tied the rabbits up again and gave them to Jake before putting the table and basin back against the cabin. He took the lantern from Jake and led him back to the door. Beyond the light the world was invisible.

Once inside, Mr. Jones took the rabbits from Jake and set them on a table in what served as the kitchen. He grabbed a bowl from the cupboard and butchered the rabbits, throwing the small chunks of meat into the bowl. When finished he reached into the cupboard below and pulled out two potatoes and cut them and threw them into the bowl. From the pitcher he poured water into the bowl and carried the bowl. Without being asked Jake put the stewpot on the stove and Mr. Jones walked over to it and poured the contents of the bowl in.

After dinner they cleaned up and sat by the fire for a while in silence, unable or unwilling to talk away the time, each in his own thoughts. Mr. Jones broke the silence by announcing he was going to bed, and the boys did the same.

The next few days saw the same routine. When the boys woke up, their host would already be gone but would leave breakfast on the table. Every day Mr. Jones came home before lunch with news from the town, although there was little to report. He always stopped by the McCreadys and sometimes brought a book or piece of pie or leftovers. Jake and Billy shared everything except the books. Those were Billy's, although Jake got so bored he started asking Billy to read the stories to him.

During these days the boys rested and recuperated. Their bodies had been worn to the bone, first on their journey and then keeping up with Mr. McCready's work schedule. Now they were recovering. The food was not as good as Mrs. McCready's but it was sufficient, and the hours of rest they got built their bodies back up, even gave them a thin lining of fat to protect them from the winter chill.

One day the boys fell asleep while Billy was reading Jake a story. When the boys woke the sun was already well into its descent, but Mr. Jones still had not come home. Wanting to be polite, they waited to eat. But as the sun crept toward the horizon their hunger got the best of them and they ate some of what was in the stewpot, careful to save some for Mr. Jones when he returned later that evening. He did not. They stoked the fire one more time before going to bed, sitting next to the stove to make sure the logs caught fire.

"Jake?"

"Yeah?"

"Where do you think Mr. Jones is?"

"Probably out huntin'."

"Do you think something happened to him?"

"Something like what?"

"Like maybe those men got him?"

Jake turned to Billy. "Now don't you go worrying about that, you hear? If anybody can take care of himself it's Mr. Jones."

"What about Mr. McCready?"

"Him too. I'm sure Mr. Jones just had some business to take care of, and he doesn't have to worry about telling us nothing." Jake tried to sound reassuring but worry made his voice tense and curt. Billy said nothing.

They went to bed, and as Billy slept soundlessly Jake ran over and over in his mind any reason why Mr. Jones would not come home. He tried to keep his mind from imagining the worst, but his fears kept creeping into his thoughts like cold air through the cracks of a door. His sleep was fitful.

Morning brought no answers. The cabin was empty except for the two boys. There was no breakfast on the table. The logs in the stove dwindled to ashes overnight, its door now cool to the touch. Jake opened it and placed small split logs on the old wood's remains. Then he blew on them, and the gray powder flew off to reveal glowing orange coals. When the fire was crackling he put the frying pan on it. In a bowl he mixed flour, water, salt and lard and made flat cakes that he fried in the pan with more lard and he and Billy ate breakfast wordlessly.

They sat by the stove, and Billy read to Jake. When the room grew cold, Jake got up to put more wood on. The pile was low. He turned to his brother.

"You cold, Billy?"

Billy shook his head. "It's alright to say, Billy. I'm cold. Are you?"

Billy nodded.

"Well, we ought not have a fire in here if Mr. Jones isn't here. We can save the wood for when it's dark. Then maybe I can go out and get more from the pile outside. Come on, let's get under the covers and get warm."

The boys walked back to their bedroom and got in bed. They spent the rest of the day there. After nightfall they stoked the fire and sat in the dark, sharing the last of the stew they had saved for Mr. Jones before washing the stewpot. Jake fetched more wood from the pile outside. With nothing to do and no light to do it with they crawled back into their beds. Neither could sleep or had much to say, so the beds groaned as they tossed and turned.

By the next morning the cabin had become very cold, and Jake told Billy to stay in bed while he checked the fire. It was lower than the day before, and when Jake stuck his hand in the stove he felt only faint heat coming from coals buried under the snowy ashes. As he squatted in front of the last of their heat, he did not want to think of what to do if Mr. Jones didn't come back. They would only have one option and he didn't know if he could survive the journey outside in the cold of winter. He knew Billy could not.

Billy stirred. Jake went back to the bedroom. His brother was still under the covers, so he sat on the edge of Billy's bed and put his hand on Billy's shoulders like their mother used to. Normally the tension drained from Billy at his brother's touch but this time it did not. "Come on, let's get up and make the beds. We want 'em lookin' nice when Mr. Jones comes home."

Jake stood up and walked over to his bed. Billy didn't move at first but one look from Jake motivated him to get up and start making his bed.

Jake sighed. "You tired of waiting?"

"Yeah."

"Me too." When they finished making their beds, it took a while for Jake to find the right words to comfort his brother. "But we just can't do anything else. Mr. Jones and Mr. McCready--"

The sound of the front door opening interrupted Jake. He didn't know why but instead of running for the door he slipped over to Billy put his hand over Billy's mouth and held perfectly still. One voice was talking to another. Both male but unfamiliar. Jake looked at his brother and knew he understood. Billy's eyes were wide with terror.

A third voice joined the first two and Jake thought he recognized it from that night outside Mr. McCready's door. "Anything we can use?"

Still covering Billy's mouth, Jake used his other hand to point under the bed. Both beds were so low to the ground no one would suspect a person could fit under them. As Billy slid under it, Jake grabbed both their bags and took them with him under his own bed. Not as small and frail as his brother but still skinny, he could fit but only if he turned his feet. Before he wedged himself underneath he reached into his bag and felt the cold comforting steel of his father's gun. He fumbled for the wooden handle and when he grasped it he pulled it out and wedged himself all the way into his hiding place.

Two pairs of boots came walking down the hallway. One stopped in front of their door and the other continued to Mr.

Jones's room. The pair that stopped closest to them spoke. "Looks like we got ourselves a fancy guest room."

The other pair walked back. "Them mattresses look nice. We should take those."

"I ain't fixin' to carry them big mattresses all the way back to Saunders's house."

"But he said to take anything valuable."

"He means like money and tools and stuff. What the hell is he gonna do with a coupla beat-up old mattresses?"

The second pair of boots shrugged away and the first pair followed. Jake heard clangs and thuds moving from Mr. Jones's room to the living room.

"What'd y'all get?"

"Just a couple old rifles that ain't worth much."

"Gimme those. What you mean they ain't worth much? They're old, but looks like he knew how to take care of 'em. What else?"

"That's it. We couldn't find no money or nothin'. You want us to tear up the floorboards?"

"Naw, that'd just be a waste of time. Doesn't look like he had much other than this old cabin and his land. Come on, let's skedaddle."

Jake heard the door close. Despite the cold he was sweating. Large beads trickled from his forehead into his eyes but his arms were trapped at his sides, so he had to endure their salty sting.

"Jake?"

"Shhh, not now Billy. Don't talk until I tell you to."

As the two boys lay there silent and unmoving the warm terror of the moment dissipated. Soon Jake was shivering, and he knew no matter what was outside he had to get up.

Hopefully the men had left. His muscles protested the movement as he slid out from underneath the bed. He checked on Billy, and his brother was shivering worse than he was.

"Come on out now, Billy." Reaching under his brother's arms, Jake pulled until Billy was leaning into his lap. His instinct was to draw his brother close to warm and comfort him, but he knew no comfort was coming.

Jake stood up, grabbed both blankets from the beds and wrapped them.around his little brother. "Stay here until I tell you to." He whispered as if the men were still in the next room. Then he took off his boots and walked along the edge of the room, hoping the floorboards would make less noise.

The door to the room was already open, and he slipped into the hallway toward the main room. No one was there. Jake's pulse slowed a little but he still had to check outside. From the small warped window he could see nothing besides the front yard and the narrow road separating the yard from line of trees beyond.

With surer, stronger strides he went back to the room. "Billy, I think we gotta go."

Billy was curled up in the corner with both knees pulled to his chest and the blankets wrapped taut around him, trying in vain to keep out the cold. "You think those men are going to come back?"

"No."

"Then why do we have to go?"

"We just do, Billy."

"Are we going back to the McCreadys?"

Jake's heart sank. "I don't think so."

"But then where we going?"

"I don't know just yet. All I know is we gotta get outta here."

"But why?"

"Billy..." The edge on Jake's voice sharpened, but he couldn't look directly at his brother. Jake sighed in relief when Billy got up. "Come on now, let's put those blankets in our bags and grab what food we can. I don't think Mr. Jones would mind."

Billy obeyed his brother but with a silent, slow protest. They grabbed a small sack of flour, a tub of lard and some matches. Jake put all the heavy items in his own pack and filled Billy's with clothes and one of the blankets. Jake inspected his father's revolver, wrapped it in rags and put it at the top of his pack just above the box of shells. Soon the boys were at the door, bulging bags slung over their shoulders, their faces dwarfed by layers of clothing, heads of children on bodies of men.

Jake struggled to conjure words of comfort or inspiration, but he had none. Without a word Jake opened the door and Billy followed, the brunt of the Missouri winter on the horizon.

7

The whole day they saw no one on the road, but they still didn't dare walk on it for fear of having nowhere to hide. Instead they moved along the edge of the forest the road cut through, so shaken by that morning's events that neither spoke. For a while the rising sun and permeating fear kept the boys warm, but as the pale sun sank so did the temperature. A light afternoon wind from the north chilled them even more as they headed into it, Jake leading and Billy staying in the lee of his brother.

By dusk their bodies were nearly heaving in shivers, and Jake ducked into the forest along a deer trail. Billy followed. Brittle branches dead and dry from winter's cold snapped underfoot, and there was the crisp crunching of leaves as they walked. When the boys were far enough in from the road, Jake stopped. They fell into their old routine, so far removed from their time on the road and yet not. Billy gathered wood. Jake cleared a ring on the forest floor of leaves and twigs, then used a pointed rock to dig into the hard earth. Its jagged edges rubbed his hands raw and red, and he soon gave up.

There had been no rain or snow for days and the dirt was dry and hard. Jake pulled a small piece of bark from the earth and brushed it off, placing it where he wanted the fire. Billy had found some dried grass for tinder and armfuls of small branches. Twisting the dried grass into compact knots, Jake set them on the bark and began snapping the smallest twigs from the dried bones of trees Billy had collected. These he rested against the tinder, tips crossed. His hands shook so badly he knocked over his structure three times before he was able to form a small teepee.

Once it was done he leaned back onto his haunches. A slight wind wound through the tops of the trees and they creaked and swayed, but the air on the ground lay still. Jake rocked back and forth and blew on his hands. He could not feel his fingertips. That didn't work so he stood and jumped up and down, swinging his hands down hard like he was trying to dry them, sending the blood to his frozen digits. The motion brought painful pinpricks of warmth.

Once he could move his fingers well enough, he reached into his bag and pulled out a box of matches. They rattled as he slid open the box and pulled one out. He pushed the drawer back and turned it over, eyeing the striking surface. Long scores ran along it and Jake looked for any unused stretches. His hands shook.

Moving closer to the fire, he kneeled in front of it. The cold pierced his pants where his knees touched the ground. He tried to steady the match against the box but it slipped, losing some of the red coating on the end. Jake turned the match over and too quickly pushed it into the box instead of along it. Its decapitated head somersaulted away. By now the woods were growing dark, and it flew out of his sphere of sight.

"Goddammit!"

Billy's footsteps stopped and Jake knew his brother had heard him curse. He had broken his own rule but did not care. All that mattered was bringing light and warmth to this cold patch of forest. Jake reached in and grabbed another match and tried again, this time smelling sulfurous smoke but seeing no spark. Rotating the match he tried again with the same result. This match he put into the tinder and he pulled out another. There were plenty left but their journey was long and uncertain, the light waning.

By now his anger at himself had warmed him a little, and his hands were more confident. The third match blazed bright in the near night and he held it steady for the flame to catch the wood of the matchstick. When it had, he lowered it slowly into the opening of the twig teepee and held it to the tinder until it singed his thumbs.

A blue flame burned slowly under the matted grass and Jake worked quickly to reach behind him and grab more fuel. As the flames consumed twigs he replaced them with ones the same size until the glowing orange threads cast a small ring of light, heat and fuel and oxygen combining. He increased the size of the sticks until they were as big around as his thumb. By now a clump of young coals the size of his fist pulsated under the fresh fuel. Jake leaned in and began to blow a soft steady stream of air. It began to make noise, a low purr increasing to louder growls and pops and Jake blew harder. Bigger flames and more sticks. Heat and light brought forth into the world from the darkness.

Fire.

The brothers huddled around it and stuck their hands so close to the flicking yellow tongues they had to jerk back when the flames reached their outstretched fingers. Both boys continued to pile wood on. There would be no food tonight but there would be fire, and when they had thrown on two large logs and the flames wrapped around, Jake grabbed Billy's bag and rolled out the blanket. Once his brother tucked in, Jake did the same for himself.

The wind in the trees and the growls from their empty stomachs lulled the boys into a cold sleep. Jake woke periodically and threw more wood onto the fire, always checking Billy before pulling his own blanket back over himself. Each time he drifted to sleep only one thought entered his mind. *We can't do this for long.*

The boys broke camp before dawn, covering the smoldering coals with rocks and whatever dirt they could scrape from the nearly frozen earth. When they emerged from the forest and onto the road a panoply of stars greeted them. Low on the western horizon lay a fat full moon. The crowns of the oaks and maples speared it from underneath, their skeletal branches tracing thin lines across its surface like cracks on a dinner plate.

"Hunter's moon," said Jake. It was the first words either had spoken since they left the cabin.

"Reckon we'll get to hunt tonight?"

"Maybe. I'd like to get some more distance between us and the town before I start shootin'."

The loose rock and dirt of the road slid slightly as their feet landed, and the sounds echoed off the walls of forest on either side.

"Jake?"

"Yeah."

"Where we goin'?"

"St. Louis. I figure we can try to catch a train from there to get to California."

Billy paused and the silence rang in Jake's ears. "How come we can't go back to the McCreadys?"

"You know why."

"What, you afraid of the law?"

Jake stopped. "I ain't afraid of nothin'." His breath hung suspended in the air. He started walking again and the thin cloud vanished. Billy ran to catch up, his shorter legs struggling to keep pace with his brother's.

"You and me can take 'em, Jake. Everyone knows you're the best shot around, and you taught me enough. All I need is a gun."

"You and what army?"

"I'm just sayin', it don't have to be like this. We can stay with the McCreadys and be nice and warm instead of freezin' out here. I'm sure they would let us stay."

Jake's boot skidded as he stopped again and looked at his little brother. Billy was now out of breath and the boys' condensed exhalations clouded the air between them. "Billy, I know this is hard for you. It's hard for me, too. But we can't go back to the McCreadys. We just can't. I want to, too, but they been real nice to us. If we went back we'd bring nothin' but trouble. Do you want somethin' bad to happen to them?"

"Course not."

"Well, then we just gotta move on, then. They got enough trouble without havin' to deal with us. Besides, we were goin' to up and leave in the spring to go see Pa in California. Might as well get a head start."

The brothers stood looking at each other as Billy's breaths slowed. The sky was lightening, the stars slowly disappearing. The woods were quiet except for early rising birds. A crow cawed in a distant field.

"Come on," said Jake. "We better get movin' or we'll get cold. We got a lot of miles between us and that city."

They started walking and Billy spoke again. "You ever been there?"

"Saint Louis? Nope."

"You think they'll be looking for us there, too?"

76

"Probably not. But we still need to be careful."

"Jake, are we outlaws?"

Jake shrugged. "I guess."

"I always wanted to be an outlaw." Billy's voice was tinged with awe.

Jake laughed, and the tension between them finally broke. "Well, careful what you wish for."

The rising sun revealed a cloudless, pale blue winter sky. No travelers were on the road and the air was still, the north wind having died some time during the night. By midmorning a new breeze came from the south, its currents like warm puffs from a bellows. The boys even shed some of their layers and put them in their overstuffed packs.

For the rest of the day they only saw one other person, an old man with grizzled hair resting with his mule by the side of the road. As the boys walked past he had looked up and nodded but said nothing, chewing in unison with his mule as if two young boys miles from anywhere was normal. Or maybe a sign of the times.

That night the boys stayed in the forest again, this time stopping early enough to set up camp before dark. The warmth of the day lingered, and although the boys needed the fire they sat a comfortable distance.

"How come it's so warm now, Jake?"

"That's Missouri weather, for you."

"But how'd it get so warm so fast?"

"Pa used to call it Indian Summer."

"What's that?"

"I dunno. I guess 'cause the Indians are poor they only get a little bit of summer."

Billy laughed, which made Jake laugh. It felt good, like water after a long, hot walk. "Tell me about Pa again," said Billy.

"What you wanna know?"

"Tell me what he said the last time we saw him."

"You was there."

"I know, but I like how you tell it. You can make your voice sound like Pa's."

Jake stared into the fire as if remembering some half waking dream. As if the telling of it made it real. Each time the story was different, the years blurring the true version into an amalgam of its best parts. "Pa was standing in the doorway of Aunt Kate's house, and he said—" Here Jake cleared his throat. When he spoke again his voice was artificially low. "'Boys, there are times in a man's life he has to make a sacrifice to take care of his family. I ain't been making much money here, so I'm going to head out to California. There's a job waiting for me out there.' Then he put on his hat and squatted down real low so he could look into both our eyes."

"What he say to us then?"

"He said, 'Jake you're the best son I ever had. Billy, stop eating worms. It's disgusting.'"

"He did not!" Billy tried to sound mad but he was laughing. "Don't ruin the story, Jake. Tell it like it was."

For an instant the image of his father framed in the doorway, face weighted with sorrow and shame flashed in Jake's mind. A mumbled apology before turning and leaving. And then it was gone. In its place was his father's face the way he chose to remember it, the way it was before their mother died.

"He placed one hand on your shoulder and the other on mine and said, 'Jake, you be a good boy. Obey your aunt and take good care of Billy. Billy, make sure you keep reading them books. You have a gift and some day you are going to use it to help this family move up in the world.'"

Jake paused to let Billy savor those words. In all his various retellings Jake made sure to say that last line the same. Billy was now staring up through the trees at the last light of day. "To help this family move up in the world..." he echoed.

"Only place you're helpin' us move is Wormville. So you can eat all the worms you want."

"Shut up," said Billy. He pushed his brother, but his laughing made him fall on his face.

"See, you trying to eat some now. I done told you to stop. That's disgusting." Jake dug his fingers into his brother's midsection and Billy shrieked. "Now you got worms in your belly. Worms in your belly!" Billy squealed and Jake tickled him until both were exhausted and out of breath. "Come on," said Jake. "Let's go to sleep."

For the next two days, Indian Summer brought respite from the cold. The road they walked rose and fell with the rolling bluffs. Sometimes the boys saw only thick hardwood forests. Other times when they reached some farmland or stood atop a hill where they could see for miles, brown fields dotted with clumps of gray forests or forest with the fields carved out. Hard to tell which.

On the third day the wind shifted once more and the north brought cold and despair. Even when they could see to the horizon there was still no city. In their minds Saint Louis would be an immense thing, towering over all else and visible from hundreds of miles.

They saw few travelers, but farmers were often out in their fields. No crops were left to harvest so it was fence-mending time, and neighbor worked with neighbor to pile earth and rocks along property lines. Those with means walked their fences with mule-drawn carts laden with posts and rails, replacing rotten ones and casting them to be consumed by the earth.

Near dusk on the third day the brothers came across a cluster of structures clinging to the road like clumps of berries on a vine. Three one-story houses. Small but well built. A blacksmith shop. At the far end of the offices, there was a small lumber yard. In the middle stood a building larger and older than the rest, with gray boards on the porch. One of the steps leading up to it was lighter than the others, a replacement for a broken plank.

A sign hanging from chains attached to the awning swung lazily in the dying wind. DAVIS GENERAL STORE. In the failing light the kerosene glow from inside beckoned.

The door squeaked as the boys entered and a man sitting at a long counter looked up. He looked at the boys with neither joy nor malice but did not say a word or look away. On his hawk-like nose sat a pair of half-moon spectacles. A few long wisps of hair were all that remained on his head, but he made up for it with a prodigious beard that dwarfed his small head and frame. His beady eyes bore into the boys.

Suddenly Jake was aware his hat was still on his head so he quickly removed it. Billy followed suit.

"Evening, boys. What brings you into my store?" His expression did not change.

"Sir," Jake nodded. He held his hat over his heart. Billy was silent. "We're headin' to Saint Louis."

"Well, you're a little early to catch the train."

Jake's heart leapt and mouth dropped. "There's a train?"

"Sure, if you don't mind waiting twenty or thirty years. I'm sure they'll lay tracks down to here someday." The man cackled and Jake shifted uneasily from one foot to the other. When the man finished and realized the boys hadn't laughed he cleared his throat. "Where you boys coming from?"

"Sainte Genevieve."

"Ain't you got family with you?"

"No, sir. We got family up in Saint Louis. That's why we're going up there."

Billy gave Jake a curious look. Jake shot him a quick glance and shook his head. The man at the counter looked back and forth at the two with furrowed brow. "How you plannin' on getting there?"

"On foot," said Jake.

"Walkin'?" This he shouted more than said, and he slapped the counter. "Well, I'll be. You walked all the way from Ste. Gen?"

"Yessir."

"How long that take you?"

"A couple weeks." This time Billy didn't look at Jake.

"A couple weeks? Well, I'll be. Ain't you tired?"

"No, sir. Well, maybe a little."

"I'm tired," said Billy. Jake looked at him. "Well, I am. Ain't no use sugarcoatin' it, Jake."

The man cackled once more. Jake shivered at the sound, no more accustomed to it than the first time he heard it.

"You got that right, son. Well, you boys are in luck. I've got a room in back I normally rent out to travelers. It's only got one bed, but I imagine you both can fit on it."

"Thank you sir, but--"

"I normally charge twenty cents a head, but I like you two. I'll only charge two bits for the both of you."

"Uh..." Jake looked at Billy then toward the door. As if in answer a gust of wind rattled it. "Thank you, sir. We accept your offer."

The man hopped off his stool and came around the counter. "Okay, boys. Let me show you where. You need help with those packs?"

"No, sir. Thank you," said Jake. Billy opened his mouth to speak but one look from Jake shut it. They followed the man past aisles of grains and iron tools and warped glass bottles full of strange-colored liquids to a small door in the back. After a short hallway they reached another door, and the man took out a long key.

It opened to a small windowless room with a cot against the far wall. Save for a small table with three books on it and a small porcelain bedpan underneath the cot, there was nothing in the room.

"Living like kings, you'll be!" said the man. "You probably been sleeping in the woods up till now, I suppose. Let me get you a basin and some hot water so you can wash up."

Before Jake could thank the man he was out the door, but before it could close his head popped back in, beard first nose second and the rest after. "Say, you boys might want to talk to Steve tomorrow. He comes down here twice a month from Saint Louis bringing supplies. He usually drops them off and spends one night, then goes back up to the city the next morning. Maybe you all could catch a ride with him."

Again before Jake could speak the man had disappeared. Jake and Billy unpacked their bags and unrolled their blankets onto the cot. The man came in with a washbasin and put it in the corner. Jake motioned Billy to go first.

When washed they walked out to the front of the store where the man still sat at the counter. He offered them dinner and they accepted, and as they ate silently he told stories and laughed at his own jokes and kept going without need of response from the boys. Only when they were cleaning up did Jake speak to the man. As he did, Billy quietly slipped back to the room.

"Thanks for your help, sir."

"No problem, boy. Business is slow this time of year anyway. Happy to have some company."

"Do you mind if we wait here tomorrow for the supply wagon? We'd be glad to help out around the store if you like."

The man stared down his nose at Jake, the glasses making his eyes look like saucers. He smiled, but it looked more like a grimace. "Well, I think I can find something for you to do."

"Thank you, sir."

"Go ahead on back, boy. I can finish up here. I imagine you're tired from all that walkin'." He started to cackle again, but the effort failed like he had run out of breath. "Walkin'," he mumbled, shaking his head.

"Thank you, sir."

Jake wiped his hands on his shirt and walked to the room. Billy was already in bed reading, but when he saw Jake he got up and put the book back on the table before going under the covers again. Jake joined him.

They lay in bed next to each other. Despite their blankets and the coals in the pan next to the bed giving heat, they were still cold and pressed into each other for warmth.

"I don't like him," said Billy.

"He's alright."

"He talks too much."

"You talk too much."

"Well, that don't make it right."

"Listen to yourself."

"Besides, when I talk people like it."

"You keep telling yourself that."

There was a long silence before Billy spoke again. "You think we'll get a ride with that man comin' tomorrow?"

"We'll see."

"It'd be awful nice to ride up there instead of walk."

"Yes it would."

"What are we going to do when we get there?"

Jake said nothing, thinking as the silence grew heavy.

"Jake?"

"Don't you worry about that now. Just try to get some sleep. We got work to do tomorrow."

Billy's tossing and turning slowed until he fell asleep. Jake lay awake long into the night staring at the ceiling, the warm weight of his brother beside him sinking into the mattress.

The boys spent the next day scrubbing and sweeping and cleaning and waiting until the supply wagon arrived. When it did, they helped unload flour bags, coffee, dried fruits and vegetables and salted meats. As they shuttled from the wagon to the store and back, Jake tried mustering the courage to ask the driver for a ride to Saint Louis.

Mr. Davis saved him the trouble as they were standing around the wagon waiting for the driver to give them more goods. "Steve, these boys want to go to Saint Louis."

The driver grumbled.

"You think you might be able to take them?"

The man stood hunched inside the arched canvas of the wagon cover. He eyed the brothers up and down like it was the first time he had seen them. "You boys runaways?"

A cold gust of wind blew dust into Jake's eyes, and he squinted and turned away. It died down. "No, sir," said Jake. "We got family up in Saint Louis."

"Where they live?"

Jake's body froze momentarily, his mouth incapable of moving as his mind whirred. "Uh...near the train station."

The man pursed his lips and put his hands on his hips. "Which one?"

"Um...the main one." Jake said it more as a question than answer, but he hoped the man wouldn't notice.

The man shrugged. "I'm heading back to my warehouse down by the river. You can walk to the station from there." After a moment he added, "It's not far."

"Thank you, sir. Much obliged." The tension that had held Jake's limbs hostage dissipated. He grabbed a bag of flour and walked into the store before the man could change his mind.

8

The wagon groaned in protest as it swayed drunkenly over the rocks and ruts of the road. Jake and Billy sat under the canvas, staring out the back, a moving window into their past.

They had left early that morning and lunched huddled against the wheel spokes to shelter from the wind and cold. It was now mid-afternoon, and although the driver had promised they would arrive before supper, nothing in their view had changed. There still seemed to be only the endless rise and fall of field- and forest-covered bluffs, green and brown covered by a gray sky.

The driver's voice broke a long silence. "Hey! You boys ever seen the city before?"

Jake stuck his head through the canvas flap separating them from the driver. "No, sir."

"Well, you might want to climb out here. A good view of it's comin' up."

Jake turned to tell his little brother, but Billy was already clawing past Jake to grab a seat to the left of the driver. As Jake was trying to maneuver around the driver to the right, a rock jolted the wagon and threw Jake headfirst into the man's sizeable rump.

"Quit horsin' around back there and come up here!" A flush of embarrassment warmed Jake as he scrambled to sit down. "Now just around that clump o' trees there is your first good view. If y'all are from the country you ain't never seen nothin' like it. Buildings as tall as the tallest trees in the Ozarks."

"I've read lots of books and they've told me about faraway places and had pictures and everything," said Billy. "I'll bet Saint Louis ain't nothin' like New York City or London or Paris. I—"

"Billy…" Jake tried to get his brother to stop talking for fear of insulting the driver, but to his relief the driver laughed.

"Well, I don't know nothin' about those cities, but this one here is a sight."

"We'll see about that. I—" As soon as they rounded the corner and were afforded the first glimpse of the city, Billy stopped talking and his mouth dropped. He gasped. Jake's eyebrows rose but he said nothing. The driver simply chuckled.

Out of the landscape before them stood strange and wondrous geological formations unlike anything the boys had seen before resembling rocks, but neither colored nor shaped like ones. They were buildings but not made out of wood, and larger than any structure they knew.

The boys gaped for a while in silence before Billy spoke. "Those look much bigger than the ones in the books."

The driver laughed again. "I suppose they do. You two see the boat crossing under the bridge over there to the east?"

"That's a boat?" said Jake.

"That's a bridge?" added Billy.

"Yup. Just finished it last year. Now the trains can cross the Mississippi and they don't have to ferry all the stuff across. A couple years ago I was working on them ferries but I seen the writing on the wall. That's why I got me this job. Don't need those ferries anymore except for people, and more goods across the river means more goods that gotta be hauled down thisaway."

"You think they'll bring the railroads down south?" said Jake.

The man turned to Jake. "Here?" He laughed and shook his head. "No, not now anyway. Everybody's thinking go west, go west. That's where all the money and land is. By the time they build rails down here I'll be dead and gone."

As the driver continued to talk, Jake learned how far the railroad went and how so many people were trying to—in the driver's words—cheat their way west by hopping trains.

"Most of the time they don't get noticed until the cars get inspected, and even then there's so many people on them they can't catch 'em all. Even them they catch don't stay in jail more than a day and then they're one step closer to where they wanna be. Damn cheaters, I say. My daddy came out here with nothin' but my ma and a wagon, and these bums just ride along someone's else's train." The man paused before adding, wistfully, "Hell, I'd probably do the same thing if I was younger."

Jake had no more to say and neither did Billy, so they listened to the driver's thoughts on rails and ferries and cargo as long as they could before their minds drifted and his voice became another noise along with the wind. As they drew closer to the main part of the city, the size and number of buildings along the road increased. Now it was not just cabins and farms, but stores and lumberyards and mills and warehouses, iron yards and large houses. The people and traffic increased too, and those on the streets paid little mind to a man and two boys on a wagon.

When they got to the city, the man pulled into his warehouse. The boys offered to help with the horse, but he waved them off and said goodbye. Before they left he pointed the boys toward the railroad station and wished them luck in finding their family.

Billy and Jake walked among the large warehouses crowding the water. Utilitarian buildings constructed for function not form were drab and gray and oppressive. In the dying light their immense shadows covered the boys in darkness, and without realizing the brothers moved closer together as they walked.

Jake spoke just to break the silence. "You hungry?"

Billy shook his head.

"You scared?"

Billy did nothing for several seconds before shaking his head again.

"Yeah, I don't like it here, either. Come on, let's head over to that building by the water. At least it gives us some open space to look at."

In contrast to the other parts of town they passed, this area was deserted. The wind blowing through the narrow spaces between buildings whistled, and dust kicked up in thin plumes. The boys shielded their eyes. The sun had not quite set, and when the brothers reached the last structures lining the riverbanks the dark and colorless world was transformed into something else, a new world full of color and light and hope. Though the wind still blew cold, it seemed less so in the remaining orange warmth of the sun. From their feet the levees sloped slowly down to the sides of the river where the water lapped in easy waves against the shore. Brown stalks of cattails dry and fragile yet unbroken by winter's cruelty stood defiant in the shallows.

A lone tugboat plowed upstream to its moorings. A small V of geese pointed southward, silent at first but then one honked and soon their cacophony echoed off the warehouses, hurrying to catch up with the birds as they disappeared downriver.

"Come on," said Jake. He put his arm around his brother and rubbed his shoulder to warm him. "Let's find a place to bed down for the night."

"I don't want to stay in one of those buildings."

"Me neither." Jake looked to his left. "Let's head over there past the warehouses. Those trees look like they'd give us some good shelter."

Billy looked around his brother and nodded. Then he dug his hands deeper into his jacket pockets and walked toward the trees. There they opened their packs and ate some jerky. As soon as the sun dropped so did the temperature, and quickly they were digging out their blankets and burrowing into the dry leaves trying to get warm.

Before long Billy fell asleep, but Jake could not so he took his blanket and left his brother sleeping. At the edge of the small forest he stopped and stared out onto the river. By now the wind had died and Jake was not cold. A great hulking mass of a ship approached from the south, and the sounds of reverie carried across the water. Clinking glasses. Loud music from a band. Cheers and laughter.

As it drew nearer, Jake could see the boat more clearly. Two layers of lights between bands of blackness looked like a chocolate cake with fire for frosting. A thick billow of steam like an ink stain spilled across the starry sky. The boat cut a path through the dappled moonlight rippling on the water, and in its wake it left a churning trail of darkness. Before it came closer, Jake retreated into the woods to lay next to his brother, and shivered himself to sleep.

The boys left the trees before dawn and skirted along the outer edge of the warehouses. Already some men were arriving for work, and Jake wanted to be well away before the rest showed up. By the time the sun rose, the boys reached the edge of the warehouses. Large buildings gave way to smaller stores and apartment houses where the more industrious were already sweeping stoops or cleaning windows.

The sounds and smells of morning meals being cooked reached the boys. Slumbering stomachs used to hunger now awakened and growled their displeasure.

"Oh, Jake." Billy clutched his stomach and sniffed the air.

"I know, little brother."

"It smells so good."

"I know. Come on, ain't no use sufferin' any more than we have to."

"But it smells so good."

The buildings got bigger. Small stores and dwellings gave way to larger commercial buildings and tenements. More than once the boys bumped into people on the sidewalk because they were gazing up.

"Gosh, Jake. Would you look at those?"

"Pretty big, huh?"

Billy stopped staring up to turn to his brother. "Don't pretend like you seen somethin' like this before. I know you ain't. Hey!" Billy ran over to a window and pressed his hands and nose against the glass. When Jake caught up Billy detached himself. "You ever seen anything like it?"

On the other side of the glass was an entire window display devoted to candy. Neat little rows of lemon drops and horehound drops and peppermints and chocolates lined up on shelves covered in white lace doilies. Down Billy's chin streaked a dab of saliva, and even Jake was left speechless.

Jake cleared his throat. "They ain't open yet."

"Can we come back, Jake? Can we?"

"We ain't got no money."

"Aw, goddammit Jake. We got money. You just don't want to spend it."

"What'd you say?" The harsh tone of Jake's voice surprised both him and his brother. He immediately regretted it.

"I heard you say it." Billy tried to stick out his chin defiantly, but his voice trembled.

"When?"

"When you was makin' a fire. That first night after we left Mr. Jones's."

"Well that don't make it right. Besides, that was extreme circumstances."

Billy opened his mouth in mock shock and pointed his open hand toward the window. "So is this, Jake. So is this."

Jake laughed and shook his head. "Alright, but just one piece, you hear? We can get it after we come back from the station. I gotta see about us catchin' a train."

The two brothers renewed their walk. "How much you think it costs to get to California?" asked Billy.

"I ain't got no idea."

"How come we can't just hop on the train like that man said?"

"Cause it ain't right. You heard what the man said. It's like stealin'."

"But I don't get it. How's it stealin' if we don't take anythin'?"

Jake's face pinched in concentration and he stared at the sidewalk as if he could divine the answer from it. "I don't know. It just is."

The boys kept heading east. By now more people were about, although most stores were still closed and those open had few customers. A train whistle blew. "Over there," said Jake.

A few blocks farther west they looked down to discover long steel rails running along a street. The boys followed them until they came across the station. The brick building was squat and worn. Several lines of tracks lay perpendicular to the edifice. One held a few rusting cargo cars, another a shiny black engine with triangular cattle guard and mushroom smoke stack. The rest of the tracks were empty. Despite the early hour and lack of people on the streets, those waiting for trains or travelers were spilling out of the station.

Jake pulled Billy closer. "Hold on to your bag."

Billy looped his thumb through the shoulder straps and gripped them tightly. He followed Jake as they entered the building. Inside, the walls were lined with ticket windows. Long lines of customers waited at each one. In the middle were rows of benches where people sat elbow to elbow. There were grime-covered prospectors and ladies in colorful dresses and white gloves, stoic black-suited businessmen and snot-nosed children running through the aisles.

The boys got in back of one of the lines and stood waiting. Jake scanned the other lines, but none seemed to be moving.

"Jake, can I go sit over there?" asked Billy.

"Where?"

"On that bench."

"Just make sure I can see you from here."

Billy walked over to a small spot on a bench next to a young couple who sat close together. The woman wore a boxy gray dress covered by a black jacket with a wrinkled collar. The man had on brown wool pants and an unironed shirt. His hat and jacket lay in his lap. Both stared straight ahead without speaking, eyes darting back and forth as people passed.

The line moved, and Jake took one step forward then looked back at Billy. His little brother was still on the bench and so was the couple, all three now following the crowds with their eyes. Wait. Step forward. Check back for Billy. Billy fidgeted, turning to look around the building. Jake tapped his foot nervously.

He was almost surprised when the man in front of him disappeared and in his place sat the ticket agent at the window.

"Where to?"

"Uh...sorry?"

"Where to? Where you headin'? Come on, boy. People are waitin'."

"Uh, San Francisco."

"How many people traveling?"

"Just me and my little brother."

The man raised one eyebrow. "You travelin' alone?"

"Yes, sir." Jake felt his tongue swell and heart rate quicken.

"Where are your parents?"

"We're goin' to see our Pa in San Francisco."

The man stared, and Jake shifted from one foot to the other. He tapped his fingers against his leg and tried to meet the man's gaze.

The man shrugged. "Well let's see...first you gotta take the train to Topeka, then switch there to go toward Santa Fe. From there you take the train to San Francisco." As he talked he tallied the numbers on a piece of paper. "All told for two people that would be…"

When the man said the price someone in the waiting area shouted, and Jake thought he had heard incorrectly. He asked the man to repeat it. Jake could not hide his disappointment when he heard the total. He had hoped the money they had from their aunt plus that from the McCreadys would be enough. For a while he stood there, and all sounds muffled as his world narrowed. He heard his breathing slow and deliberate and his heartbeat and saw only the soft blur of light from the window. Even his mind quieted as the flood of thoughts threatened to overwhelm it and for a moment he thought nothing.

"Boy! Boy!"

Jake jerked his head up.

"Are you goin' to buy the tickets or what?"

He looked at the man and searched for some feeling some hope this man might take pity on their plight and give them the tickets.

"Come on, kid!" A voice came from behind him. "We ain't got all day."

"No, sir." Only able to drag his feet, Jake shuffled out of line and stopped to take a deep breath and collect himself before telling Billy. Then he looked up.

Billy was gone.

Jake's senses came roaring back and he rushed over to the bench where his brother had been. The couple was still there.

"Have you seen my little brother?"

The man looked at Jake, and the woman buried her face in the man's shoulder. "*Bitte*?" he said.

"Aw, hell." He said it more to himself than to the man. "You don't speak English?"

The man smiled and shook his head. *"Englisch nein."*

"Damn! Uh…" Jake frantically pointed at the empty space where his brother had been and held his hand the height of Billy's head. "My brother?"

The man's face furrowed in concentration and he looked at the bench and back at Jake several times.

"The boy who was sitting there?" Jake made several more gestures unintelligible even to himself. "My brother?" Here he pointed at his chest.

The man's eyebrows lifted. *"Dein Bruder?"* He pointed at Jake.

"Yes! Yes! My brother. Do you know where he went?" Jake's arms flailed as he tried to indicate every direction at once.

The man shrugged and smiled again. *"Ich weiss nicht."* He shrugged again.

"Dammit!" Jake checked under the seat for Billy's bag and saw nothing, so he headed toward the door. As he walked his head swiveled, eyes scanning at the level of Billy's head.

He moved toward the row of doors, bumping into people as he went. One man knocked him so hard Jake fell to one knee.

"Watch where you're going!"

"Sorry, sir."

"You should be." With his hand the man brushed his black suit where Jake had touched it. He walked away, mumbling something about a street urchin. Jake stood, almost bumping into a woman before catching himself.

"Excuse me, have you seen a little boy? About this tall?" The woman shook her head. "Sorry, dear."

As he watched the crowd swallow her up, Jake backed slowly toward the far wall. Once he reached the door, Jake put his back to it and scanned the room again. There were so many people, all he saw was an ever-shifting mass of colors. Every time he thought he saw the dark blue of Billy's coat or the faded canvas of his bag Jake's heart leapt, only to sink when he saw it wasn't his brother. His head moved back and forth like a metronome until his neck was sore.

One minute stretched into five into ten. He debated whether to stay put and block Billy's exit or immerse himself in the crowd to try to find his brother. Though he couldn't see it very well from his vantage point, Jake's eyes kept returning to the bench where Billy had been waiting. Different people came and sat and left but not his brother.

When his limbs felt like they would move on their own if he did not look for his brother Jake dove into the crowd looking over and around people as he ricocheted off them. Tides of people came and went in the intervening hours with still no sign of Billy. Each time the building cleared, Jake was sure he would see him. Each time he was wrong. Finally there was a large ebb of people, and only a few remained in the station. Jake ran along the walls of ticket windows, down the aisles of benches. He bent down to see if his brother had fallen asleep under one. Nothing but bags and dust.

Tears welled and he fought them back, swallowing painfully. His body began to tremble and he knew if he stayed he would lose it so he left. Like a leaf drifting in an indecisive breeze Jake fluttered in and out of the building, along the tracks and back, toward the streets beyond and back to the station for one last look, his movements as scattered as his thoughts.

Jake wandered in the direction of the river, trying to recall every word spoken between them that day. His explicit instructions in the station. The dialogue before. Then it came to him, and his legs started running before he became completely aware of why. He wound through several streets, and when he turned the corner he saw Billy sitting on the sidewalk in front of the candy store.

"Hey, Jake. Where you been? I've been waitin' here for hours."

Jake didn't respond while he tried to catch his breath.

"The owner here's real nice," continued Billy. "He saw me and let me come inside and even gave me some candy to suck on while I waited. I was—"

Hands on his knees and gulping air in great heaving breaths, Jake was able to utter only two words. "Let's go." He grabbed his brother by the wrist and yanked him up.

"Ow!" said Billy. Jake pulled harder and said nothing, lengthening his strides as his brother's small legs struggled to keep up. "Hey, slow down!"

Only when they were back at the warehouses did Jake let go of Billy and slow his pace. But he remained silent. So did Billy. When they reached the water, they turned north and kept walking past the last warehouse past the small boathouse past the last houses of the city until they reached forest. Billy gathered wood and Jake prepared the fire, and soon they were sitting silently staring into the flames.

Finally Jake broke the silence. "You gotta listen to me, Billy. I told you stay put. I didn't know where you were."

"I'm sorry. I just…"

"I looked for you everywhere."

"I was glad to see you when you came to the candy store."

"Me too."

"I ain't never seen you so mad."

"I ain't never had cause to."

A log in the fire fell, and sparks flew up in a cluster like fireflies, bright and ephemeral.

"The man gave me a couple pieces a candy. I still got one left. You want it?"

"You keep it for yourself."

"You sure?"

Jake nodded in the wavering light. "Thanks Jake."

"We got to stick together, little brother. We're all we got."

"I know." A long period of quiet passed, punctuated only by the popping fire. "Did you get the tickets?"

Jake let out a long sigh. "We'll talk about it in the morning. Get some sleep."

He waited as Billy curled up in his bedroll and his breathing slowed. When it did, Jake wrapped himself in his own and was asleep as soon as he lay down his head.

9

Over breakfast Jake broke the news of the tickets.

"That's a lot of money, Jake."

"I know't."

"What are we going to do?"

Jake sank his teeth into a stale bannock cake and tore off a bite. It took a minute of chewing and several swigs of water just to get it down. "I haven't figured that out quite yet."

"We could do what that man said and hop on the train when no one's lookin' and—"

"I know, I know. You don't need to remind me."

"But why can't we?"

"Cause it just don't feel right."

"Well, neither does sittin' here and waitin'."

Jake sighed and threw the rest of the bannock into the fire. "You done eatin'?"

Billy nodded.

"Help me put this fire out then."

The boys grabbed rocks and dirt and piled them onto the flames until not even a trickle of smoke escaped. Then they rolled their blankets and stuffed them into their bags and slung the bags over their shoulders, a motion now all too familiar.

"Let's go," said Jake.

"Where we goin'?"

"Scoutin'. Just remember to stick with me this time."

Billy made an elaborate gesture of crossing his finger over his chest twice. "I swear."

"Good. Maybe next time I won't come lookin' for you."

"Would not."

"Would too. Be nice to have some peace and quiet for a change."

Billy's chin started to drift downward. "You're just playin'."

Jake tousled his brother's hair. "Course I'm just playin'. Now come on. We gotta find ourselves a way to get on that train." He began walking and Billy fell in step behind him.

"We're on an adventure, Jake."

"We sure are."

"Just like in the books."

Jake smiled and inhaled deeply. "You would know."

When they got to the train station it was as busy as the day before, but this time the boys didn't bother going inside. Instead they sat against the outside wall of the station and watched.

For most of the morning all they saw were passenger trains. Some were headed east but most went west toward Kansas and beyond. It was Billy who noticed the system of how the destinations of the trains were identified. Look, Jake. That one's goin' to Topeka…That one's goin' to Kansas City…That one's goin' to Santa Fe…Where's Santa Fe?

For lunch they had jerky from the waning supply in their bags. When they got too cold sitting outside, they would go inside and soak up the warmth from all the people filling the room. The rest of the afternoon was uneventful as the boys continued to watch.

"Jake?"

"Yeah?"

"Can we go back to our camp now?"

"Not yet, little brother?"

"What are we waitin' for?"

"I don't rightly know just yet."

"Jake, I'm cold. Can we go back inside again?"

Jake looked at his brother and saw his lips were purple moving to blue. "You go on. Just go inside the door and wait."

"Okay." Billy got up stiffly like an old man and stumbled toward the door.

"Billy?"

His brother stopped and turned. "Yeah?"

"Don't make me come lookin' for you."

"I know."

Night was falling and the people dwindling. Only then did Jake see something out past the cars on the other side of the tracks. At first he thought it might be a trick of light, or a stray dog. But the shadow moved with the clumsiness of a human, even if its owner was trying to be stealthy. It disappeared behind a car.

Jake sat for some time before seeing another. Same stilted movement. Same disappearance. In the eastern distance Jake heard a plaintive train whistle. Then nothing. Then the soft exhalations of the steam engine. Not long after came the rattling of wheel on rail, groans and creaks shimmying down the metal miles of track.

A big black engine pulled into the station tugging a train. Jake tried keeping track of the cars, but lost count somewhere around forty. Billy came back out and sat next to Jake.

"Wow."

"Yeah."

"What's in all those cars, Jake?"

"I don't know. Maybe stuff for the people out west."

"Like what kind of stuff?"

"Stuff for eatin'. Stuff for buildin'. Just stuff, I guess."

"Gosh. That's a lot of stuff for a lot of people."

They sat a while but the cold did not allow them to stay motionless much longer. "Come on. Let's head back."

Billy stood up and dusted off his pants. "What're we goin' to eat for supper, Jake?"

"You hungry?"

Billy nodded.

"I know you are. We ain't had a good meal since we left that store." Jake sighed. "Come on, we still got some money. Let's go get us some real food."

A layer of light hung low over the city like fog. The two boys headed away from the station. Gas lamps hissed as they walked by. Men and women bundled in furs and long coats and top hats hurried into their houses, their restaurants, their worlds. No one noticed the boys. Once when passing an open door the warmth and welcoming smell drew Jake and Billy in. The maître d' dressed in a starched white shirt and black bow tie shooed them away before they were three steps in. At the next block they turned to walk down a different street.

Here the customers and establishments were louder and dirtier. Clinking and singing and shouting spilled into the streets along with the smells. Billy moved closer to Jake.

Then they reached a stretch with only residences. Even the night absent of street lights could not hide the fading facades of the sagging structures. Each building was a moribund patient, sick beyond cure but still struggling to survive. No one was about. The noise up the street faded to a memory.

At the end of the block a small hope of light eked out of a window. Too cold to walk more the boys entered, hoping to catch a bit of warmth even if they were kicked out soon after.

Inside the light was not much brighter, and slow sounds of sadness strained to fill the room. Whispers in a corner. The slosh of liquor into a glass. The dulled din of forks on plates. Almost all the customers were lone old men, tired eyes staring into drinks to divine some meaning from the brown liquid within.

Only the man behind the bar turned when they came in, and quickly afterward he turned back to wipe the counter. As casually as he could Jake strolled up to the long wooden plank separating the men from the bottles. His chin just cleared it when he looked up, but Billy's head did not even reach it.

The bartender looked up and raised an eyebrow. "Can I help you boys?" The man sitting next to Jake turned and pulled his wispy white beard but said nothing.

"Yes, please. Do you still have food?"

"We don't take beggars here. Go on an' git."

He looked the boys up and down. "We have money, sir."

The man stuck out his lower lip. "How much?"

Jake cleared his throat and drew in a slow, deep breath. He looked the man in the eyes and tried to hold his gaze. "What you got?"

"Hmph. For you? Beef stew for twenty-five cents each."

"You got bread with that?"

The man's eyes narrowed. "Two cents more."

"That's fine."

The man grunted again and disappeared through a door in the back of the bar. Jake let out his breath and motioned to Billy to sit on a stool and did the same. The old man next to them turned his attention back to his drink and took a long, sad draw from the glass before setting it back on the bar, staring into it as he swirled the liquid.

The bartender returned with a blue bowl and a green one, both filled with stew and topped with a small piece of bread like a sad cherry on top a melting sundae. Before he set the bowls down he looked once more at Jake. "Let's see your money."

Though he had never before been in a restaurant, Jake knew he was being insulted. The back of his neck got hot but he dug into his bag and pulled out enough coins to pay for everything plus a little extra and set them on the counter. The man stood back and peered over the bowls to count the money. His scowl disappeared. "Oh," he said before setting the bowls down and sliding two quarters and a dime into his hand. "Well, enjoy your meal."

Jake looked up to say something but the man cleared his throat and headed toward the other end of the bar before he could. He grabbed the spoon stuck in the bowl and looked over at Billy who was already shoveling the stew into his mouth. Jake did the same, and as he focused on his bowl the bartender placed two glasses of soda water in front of them.

When Jake had finished, he looked over at his brother. Billy was using the bread to mop up the last of the stew and chewing thoughtfully, like he had only now realized they would have to leave when he finished and wanted to hold on to the warmth as long as he could. Jake sipped his water.

No one had entered or left since they arrived. If possible the room had dimmed and slowed. Jake stared straight ahead, afraid of making eye contact with any of the solitary figures or even striking up a conversation with Billy. Like the little joy they had in their hearts would be sucked out if they opened their mouths.

Despite the cold outside, the boys soon found the dreariness oppressive. Billy had not even taken off his coat, and his head had retreated partially into his collar like a wary turtle, glancing nervously over his shoulder.

Jake patted him on the shoulder and Billy understood before his brother said a word. Though the bartender was near they did not bother to say goodbye and opened the door to enter the cold and the dark.

The next day, they got to the train tracks in the late afternoon. Their morning had been filled with aimless wanderings around the city, staring at large buildings and crowds of people. The dinner the night before still filled their bellies, but they stopped by a dry goods store to stock up on jerky and bread and some dried fruit. Billy even convinced Jake to swing by the candy store and buy lemon drops for both of them.

Instead of heading to the main station, they wound around the alleyways leading to the other side of the rails. Giant warehouses and industrial buildings loomed over the boys, their massive gray walls obscuring the sun. The narrow corridors between them were shadowy and cold, the air still. As the boys walked, their breaths hung suspended.

Some of the buildings sounded active, the din of machines or men yelling reverberating from within. Others were silent, hulking ghosts, where pigeons roosted in the window sills of their cavernous shells.

"What are we doin' on this side, Jake?"

"Shhh."

Billy's voice dropped to a whisper. "But it's cold over here."

Jake whispered too. "We gotta figure out how to get on that train."

"How come we can't buy tickets?"

"You know why."

"But maybe we can earn the money."

"How we goin' to do that?"

"I dunno. Work in a factory or somethin'."

"No way. I ain't lettin' you work in one of those places. That ain't no kind of life. Besides, we're country folk. We don't know the first thing about city livin'."

"I'm just sayin', Jake."

"I know. Don't worry about it. We'll find a way."

They were getting close to the edge of the last building before hitting the tracks. Jake stopped, and Billy almost ran into the back of him

"You got your magic rock?"

"Yeah," said Billy.

"How's that thing work, anyway? You gotta wish for somethin' or it just makes up its own mind about what to get you?"

"Well, usually it just keeps us safe. But sometimes if I really want somethin' I might ask it. I turn it over three times in my right hand then two times in my left then once in my right and then I hold it tight and close my eyes and make a wish."

"Well, make sure you hold onto it. We're goin' to need it."

"What for?"

"Billy, what we're doin' is gonna start to get dangerous. And I don't mean just gettin' on trains."

"What you mean?"

"Well, we ain't exactly doin' somethin' that's legal, and when you do that you're bound to run into people that're a little…"

"Suspicious?"

"Where'd you learn that word?"

Billy shrugged.

"Well, yeah. Suspicious. You need to stay close to me and do exactly as I say."

"I know, Jake."

"Not like before where you took off. I mean you need to be right by my side."

"I *know*, Jake."

"Well, I thought you knew the last time and look what happened."

"I said I was sorry."

"You know what I mean, Billy. Just stay close. Now hush, we gotta be quiet."

For a while the boys waited in the lee of the building, Billy huddling close to his brother as the cold seeped through his clothes. Jake was still. The shadows grew longer and the air colder but both remained silent. Billy's only protests were the occasional dramatic sigh. The sun's rays faded to let the weak light of the stars populate the sky.

Jake's body tensed and Billy looked up. A man emerged from behind the next building and squatted, black and shapeless, a form indistinguishable from those around him save a slight rocking motion. Billy craned his neck to see, but Jake pulled him back.

In the distance a train whistle wailed. Jake looked down the line of buildings and saw shadowy figures moving in the darkness. Men but not quite. Animals in wait. The hairs on the back of Jake's neck rose. He nudged his brother and turned to go.

They took one step and Jake pulled his brother in. The gravel crunched as his foot slid to a stop. His right hand moved toward the inside of his coat as he peered into the dark. His left hand covered Billy's mouth.

There was movement in the shadows. Jake looked up. Horsetail clouds of breath almost too thin to see rose into the light streaming from one window. In one movement, Jake drew his gun and threw Billy behind him.

"Whoa, easy there sonny. I ain't tryin' to hurt you."

Jake held his gun up but said nothing.

"Just tryin' to get on the train, same as you."

There was a pause before Jake spoke. "Why you think we're tryin' to catch a train?"

The darkness began to wheeze laughter like a bellows with a hole in it. "I'm old, but I'm no fool. Why the hell else would you be out here at this time of night?" The scuffing sound of gravel bounced off the close walls.

"Don't come any closer!" To Jake's dismay, his voice cracked.

The sound of gravel stopped but they could hear the man mumbling curses under his breath. "Aw hell, boy. Go ahead and shoot me if you want. But if you're not goin' to use that thing then just put it away. I'm too tired to be scared anymore."

Jake's hand loosened its grip on the gun, and he slowly lowered it.

"That's better. Now what are two young boys like you doin' out here? Where you headed? Ain't you a little young to be hoppin' trains?"

"Aren't you a little old?" asked Jake.

The man laughed again, this time longer and louder. "Hoo boy, you got that right. It's hoppin' trains that makes you old. I'm really only twenty-seven." His laughter devolved into a coughing fit. Billy pulled himself close to Jake again.

When the man stopped coughing, Jake spoke. "Mister, we don't want no trouble."

"Me neither."

"We just want to go in peace."

"Me too."

His brother tugged on Jake's arm and Jake leaned down. Billy cupped his hand over his brother's ear and whispered.

Jake listened then sighed, but did not speak for some time. "Mister?"

"Yeah?"

"Can you tell us which train to catch if we're tryin' to get to California?"

This time his laughter was even louder, producing even more wretched convulsions of coughing.

"California? You serious?"

"Yeah."

"Why you wanna go there? Ain't nothin' there but desert and deserted mines." He laughed but the boys didn't, so he repeated the joke in the hopes they would.

"You been there?" asked Jake.

"What's that?"

"I said if you've been there."

"Me? Oh, yeah. Lots of times. Just got back from vacation there last week. Had to visit my mansion make sure everything's still there."

110

"Come on, Billy. Let's go." With his arm still wrapped around his brother's shoulders, Jake started walking away from the tracks.

"Now hold up just a minute," said the man. "I'm just jokin' around. Y'all ain't got no sense a humor. You wanna get to California?"

They stopped walking. "Yeah," said Jake.

"Well, the first thing you gotta do is get on the train to Kansas City, make the transfer to Council Bluffs, then take the Pacific line all the way west. Easy peasy."

"How do we get to Kansas City?"

The train whistle blew again, this time much closer. It pierced the silence once more before the groan and squeal of metal brakes on metal wheels filled the night air.

"There's your answer."

Jake turned around to look at the train, but quickly turned back. "That train goes to Kansas City?"

"Yup. Stays in the station for about a half an hour then heads out."

"How do you…"

The man took three steps forward and his face became partially illuminated by a stripe of moonlight slicing through the narrow canyon between buildings. Its craggy features were elongated and deepened by dark lines of shadow. Even at this distance his ripe odor reached the boys. Billy scrunched his nose and buried it in Jake's jacket. "You sure you wanna start runnin'?" The tone of his voice was stripped of all its humor, barren.

"We ain't runnin'."

The man emitted a low grunt. "Course not. Just be careful. Once you start you might never stop." The boys did not move

111

as he walked past, but Jake's eyes followed him until he stopped and turned back. "Well, you boys comin' or what?"

A deep sense of foreboding prevented Jake from answering. He did not like this man. But then he thought of their makeshift camp by the river, of hiding in the cold copse of trees and waking before the sun rose. He thought of the dismal restaurant where they had eaten, and the forlorn faces of the men there.

"Shit or git off the pot, boy."

Jake's hand squeezed Billy's shoulder even tighter, and he turned around with his brother attached to his side. The man nodded and walked forward, following him silently into the darkness.

On either side of them, Jake saw men moving toward the tracks. Staring into the light from the station made it difficult to see this side of the train, but Jake could make out the silhouettes of freight cars black against the bright yellow glow.

"Stay close, boys. Don't want the engineer to see you. Look out for these rails here." The old man's bowlegs tiptoed over the ties and rails. Billy stumbled, and Jake caught him before he fell.

The man brought his finger to his lips and slowed his gait, looking left and right as he lowered into a crouch. Jake and Billy did the same. All three froze there, waiting for what Jake did not know.

In a jerk, the man motioned forward with his hand and took off. Before the boys realized what happened, he had almost disappeared. Jake grabbed Billy's coat and started running. Ahead they could see the man going toward one of the cars, so they ran faster to catch up. As they got closer to the car, an even darker part of it appeared in the middle of it, a large black mouth shaped like a rectangle. The man seemed to float into it and disappear.

At the car Jake turned around. Putting his hands underneath Billy's arms, he hoisted him and turned back toward the open door. A large pair of boots stared back at him.

"Whaddaya think you're doin'?" a man's voice growled.

A voice came from behind the man. "It's okay, George. They're with me."

"You gonna pay for them, too?"

"They're just kids, George."

The boots grunted then disappeared. In their place was the old man's wrinkled hand. Jake lifted Billy and the man grabbed him, then Jake climbed up into the car.

Beyond the dim light from the door, inside was complete darkness. With one hand on Billy's shoulder and the other on the old man's, Jake shuffled toward the far right corner of the car.

"Sit here and don't make a sound," said the man. He jerked free of Jake's hand and the boys fumbled forward until Jake found a wall. He and Billy sat leaning against it. They could hear the breathing of someone to their right. The crunch of gravel outside. Hushed voices at the door. Then voices from the station side of the car, louder but indecipherable. The breathing next to them stopped, and unconsciously they both held their breath.

For a while there was nothing, no sound, no movement, the slow painful ticking of time. Then there were a few yells from far away, audible only in the stark silence. A train whistle blew so loud it shook the car. Jake pressed one hand to his ear,

113

the other to Billy's as he drew his brother's head close to smother Billy's other ear in his jacket.

The car lurched forward and the boys fell on their sides. Just as they pushed themselves up it lurched again, but this time their arms prevented a second fall, palms digging into the cold steel floor. Slowly the train increased speed, each successive surge forward less and less until the train reached a smooth rocking motion. There was the clink of steel on steel underneath. Someone closed the door, and blackness enveloped them. Cold air still leaked through, and Billy curled into a fetal position and pulled himself next to Jake.

Above the clanging of the rails, conversations began. Men talked low in the corners of the car. Bright yellow flashes followed by small orange circles of light gave elusive form to their faces, and the smell of tobacco smoke stung Jake's nostrils. Jake moved his hand toward his waist, hooking his thumb on his belt buckle. His knuckles brushed against his father's revolver.

Billy's shivering slowed and so did Jake's as the vague warmth of the denizens within tried to fill the car. Jake felt his brother's breathing slow, and he leaned his head back into the wall. It rocked gently back and forth with the rhythm of the train. He struggled against the sleep that pulled his eyelids down, but the heat from Billy's body and his own weariness and the lullaby of the train wheels overpowered him and he slept as the train headed west.

10

A slam of metal and a blinding white light jarred Jake from his slumber. The walls seemed to come alive as people began pouring out the door. In the harsh light of day Jake saw how many men had hidden in the bowels of the container. They ran past three men dressed in long brown dusters standing at the door. The man in the middle had a silver star pinned to his chest. Each time someone passed one of the three tried to grab him and look into his face. Most were caught, but some slipped by before being examined.

Jake's heart hammered out of his chest. He looked around for another exit, but the men were blocking the only one. More men jumped out the door. Now only a few remained, yet the sheriff and his deputies were still there waiting.

Billy pulled hard on Jake's arm, and Jake looked down. The sunlight made the whites of Billy's eyes glow bright in the darkness of the car.

Commotion came from the opening. Shouts and grunts. The rustling of leather. A hard *crunch*. When Jake turned the men were gone, the square of light free of silhouettes. He grabbed Billy's arm and ran toward the door. At the edge of the floor they skidded to a stop. Jake peered over, let go of Billy and jumped. Quickly he turned back and held his hands up for his brother.

"Move!" said Billy.

"Not now, Billy."

"I can do it."

"I know't. But I ain't got time to see. Let's go now."

Billy rolled his eyes and leaned into his brother's hands. Jake lowered him, turned and ran with his brother's coat sleeve firmly in his fist.

Before them an enormous cloud of dust rose from the earth like steam from a boiling pot of water. Despite the cold, dry air Jake was sweating. The three officers were now wrestling with another man. Most of those from the car were fleeing toward town, but some stood transfixed as the officers tried to subdue the man. One flew out of the dust and fell onto his back, smacking his head against the packed dirt. He rolled onto his side and shook his head, rising woozily before wobbling back into the fray.

Inside the cloud, the man bounced back and forth between the sheriff and the deputy, pushing off one only to fall into the other. When the fallen deputy charged, he was parried and thrown back onto the ground. This time he did not get up.

In the man's hesitation to stand over the deputy, the other tackled him from behind. Quickly he got back on his hands and knees and bucked before elbowing the deputy in the face. The deputy stumbled backward and clutched his nose with both hands. When the man turned to face the sheriff he was greeted with a boot in the face.

Droplets of blood traced an arc through the air, and when they landed they became black, dust-covered globs. The man turned back and the sheriff's gloved fist struck him in the cheek. His flailing arms could not deflect the blows and soon he was face down in the dirt, hands cuffed behind him.

The sheriff grabbed him by the collar and pulled him up. Drops of blood fell from his mouth and nose to stain the earth below. His face was coated with dirt frosting the blood, dark red and sticky underneath. His chest heaved and his raspy,

116

rapid breaths grated Jake's ears. Jake forced his eyes to look away from the spectacle.

"Come on, Billy."

Billy stood staring at the man.

"Billy, let's go."

Still his brother gaped, and as he caught his breath the man took note of the small boy with a hat too big for him staring back. They held each other's gaze for a time and then the man's mouth curled into a gruesome smile. Its corners pulled back, causing cracks to form in the dust on his cheeks.

"Welcome to Dodge City, kid." The man laughed, but soon began coughing and spitting up more blood onto the earth. Jake looped his arm around his brother and dragged him away.

For a while Billy was silent and so was Jake. The dirt road ahead of them was lined on one side with a long row of modest wooden buildings. In the street, horses and wagons and cattle moved up and down. As they approached, they heard noises coming from several of the buildings. Rowdy cheering. Piano playing. The crash of a bottle. Laughter. A shout. Singing.

Jake stopped and Billy too, and they scanned the area outside of town. There were no discernible landmarks or geographic features, just one endless stretch of land stretching toward the blue sky almost white in the winter sun. Dust and air.

"Where are the trees, Jake?"

"I don't know."

"Where are the hills?

"I don't know."

Billy paused before speaking again. "Who'd want to live here?"

"Quiet, Billy. Someone might hear you."

"Well maybe they could answer the question, then."

Jake tried hard to repress a smile. "Hush, Billy. Come on and keep walking."

"What're we goin' to do?"

"I don't know just yet."

"Why not?" ·

Jake stopped walking. "You and your questions. Let's just go over there behind that building so we can get out of the wind. Then I can set and think on it before we do anything."

Billy said nothing.

"Is that alright with you?

Billy nodded.

"Alright, come on then."

When they got into the lee, the wind could not reach them save for pale puffs that curled around the corner of the building. They sat huddled close to the wall in silence for a while before Jake spoke.

"I don't want to do that again."

"What you mean?"

"We can't hop trains all the way to California."

"Why not?"

"You saw what happened. It's too dangerous."

"But—"

"No buts, Billy. We ain't gonna do it."

"But how will we get there?"

Jake stared out toward the street. The wind whistled through the open spaces and kicked up a small whirl of dust on the road. "I guess we'll find work."

"What kind of work can we do? Can't do no farmin' in the winter."

"I know't."

"Well, what then?"

Jake sighed. "I dunno, little brother. But all these people gotta do somethin'." He stood up and brushed off his pants and Billy did the same. They grabbed their bags and cleaned them, slinging them over their shoulders before heading out onto the street. When they cleared the corner, the wind hit them square in the face and hurled the dry earth into their eyes. Both boys raised their hands to shield their faces. At the first open door they went inside.

All morning they asked anyone who would speak to them if there was work to be found. Some laughed and others poked fun, but some just shook their heads apologetically and wished the boys luck. No one asked where their parents were. From what Jake could gather it was a cattle town and work in winter was scarce. What work could be done was done by grown men experienced in the ways of herding and roping and riding.

The old man working the general store thought for a while about hiring them, but he said he would only need one person if that. He sat stroking his long white beard, occasionally pushing up his wire spectacles as Jake made his pitch. Jake said he could work all day and not get tired and Billy was really good with books and with math and could help him with orders but then the man just shook his head burying his chin in his chest.

"Sorry, boys. I just don't know right now. Check back in a week and I'll have a better idea."

Billy was about to speak, but Jake put his hand on his brother's shoulder. "Thank you for your help, sir."

"Anytime. Here." He slid two pieces of candy across the counter to them. "You look like you could use these."

Before Jake could refuse, Billy swiped them off the counter and handed one to Jake. "Thank you, sir," said Billy.

Jake smiled painfully. "Yes, thanks."

"You boys need anything else you just let me know. Name's Wilkins."

"Thank you, Mr. Wilkins. My name is Jake and this here's my brother Billy."

"Jake, Billy, a pleasure."

Jake tipped his hat and the boys walked back outside. By now it was mid-afternoon, and the boys had not eaten breakfast or lunch. The candy Mr. Wilkins had given them was already in their mouths and half gone.

"I'm hungry, Jake," said Billy.

"Me too."

"Can we eat?"

Jake's stomach growled. "We ain't got much money, and we need to save it."

"Save it for what?"

Jake looked at Billy. The sad, hungry eyes.

"Aw hell, let's get us some food. If we run out we run out."

"I don't want to waste it, Jake. If you say we can't spend it we can't."

"It'll be alright, Billy. Don't you worry." They walked into the wind a little way before the smell of cooked meat from one of the buildings drew them in. By the time they reached the door, their mouths were watering.

Several people looked up when the boys entered, but they all quickly returned to their meals. The cook standing in the doorway to the kitchen saw them and nodded in the direction of one of the tables. The boys sat and he came over.

"What'll it be?"

Jake looked over at the next table. A man's weathered face hovered over a steaming bowl of something, steam blurring the hard lines and dirt-filled crevices on his cheeks. "Whatever he's having. Please."

"One for each of you?"

"Yes, sir."

He disappeared into the kitchen and returned moments later with a bowl in each hand. Steam rose in large stripes from each extended arm as he walked toward the boys. He set the bowls down then pulled two spoons out of his apron, wiped them on his sleeve and placed them on the table.

"Thank you, sir," said Jake. He elbowed Billy, who had already grabbed his spoon and was staring into the bowl. Billy looked up.

"Thank you."

The man said they were welcome but continued standing next to the table and looking at the boys. The practiced smile on his face still held but seemed to be falling at the corners.

"Sorry," said Jake. "How much we owe you?" He began digging in his bag.

"One dollar even please."

Jake tried to hide a wince as he reached into the small leather pouch that held all the money they owned in the world. The coins inside rattled instead of jingling, and when he pulled out a dollar's worth the sound from the bag grew quieter. Jake placed the coins in the man's hand. The man held his palm open and stared at it before closing it swiftly like the jaws of a snapping turtle. "You boys enjoy your meal now. Let me know if you need anything else."

Jake picked up his spoon again and started eating. Out the corner of his eye he saw Billy shoveling spoonfuls of stew, then holding his mouth open to cool it down.

"Why don't you just wait 'til it cools down some?" asked Jake. His brother ignored him.

When both boys had finished they sat there trying not to notice the sidelong glances from the man behind the counter. After a while, Jake could not take it anymore.

"We gotta go."

"But it's cold outside. Can't we stay a little longer?"

"Now, Billy."

The wind had picked up and now the cold pinched them in the face as they walked back out. They kept heading west, staying behind the buildings as much as they could. All the buildings looked the same with their gray-brown walls buffed and faded by wind and dirt. Residences and stores lined the street, but more than anything there were saloons. Though it was just after noon, the noise from them spilled out onto the dirt streets. Forgotten horses tethered to rails stood outside squinting and turning from the dusty wind.

The boys huddled and hunched as they walked and before long they had reached the end of town. They headed back east with the wind at their backs, but still the dust kicked up in eddies around them and found its way into their eyes and mouths.

They took shelter in a narrow space between two buildings. Jake slumped to the ground, and Billy slid down and sat next to him leaning into his brother for warmth. They sat a while, staring at the dirt in front of them. At the weathered wooden planks on the side of building. At the small whorls of dust dancing between their feet.

Billy started shaking and Jake looked at him, his brother pale and cold, teeth chattering and lips blue as the wind buffeted the town. Jake shook his head.

"Come on."

"Where we goin'?" The effort of speaking brought only a brief pause to the quivering of his jaw.

"I don't care, as long as it's warm." Jake held out his hand and Billy grabbed it and pulled himself up. "Where's your magic rock?"

"In my pocket."

"Well hold on tight to it and let's see if it works."

They walked across the street, Jake pulling his brother close. The first saloon they saw had only one horse standing outside. Its long winter coat was tangled and splotched with mud. The skin on its underside had been rubbed raw where the girth hung loosely beneath the saddle. When they approached, the horse shied but Jake walked up slowly and spoke in low tones as he put his hand on the animal's shoulder. Its skin shivered, but still Jake talked and soon the horse was nuzzling Jake's neck.

A bubbling fear rose in Jake's throat as he creaked up the steps toward the saloon door. He felt a gentle tug on the back of his jacket as Billy latched on. Inside the few tables still standing were sparsely populated. There was no obvious source of heat save the warming liquid in the glasses and the heavily wrapped men hunched over them. Some were even slumped over their drinks and snoring loudly. No one was behind the bar, and no one looked up at the boys as they entered.

A noise came from the back of the room and out of the shadows emerged a man in a stained white shirt. His black string bowtie was one loop short of full, and he stumbled more than walked to the edge of the bar. There he steadied himself with one hand and took two deep breaths before continuing his journey behind the wooden counter.

Jake had grabbed Billy's elbow and turned to go when the man spoke.

"Hey!"

Still facing the door, Jake looked back but said nothing.

"What're you doin' here?" asked the man.

Jake cleared his throat. "Sorry, sir. We were just leaving. Wrong address."

The man's head and eyes bobbed and weaved independently of each other as he struggled to focus on the two boys in front of him. "Well, stay and have a drink if you like. We don't mind." He tried to laugh but it came out more as an attempt to rid his throat of phlegm. Another more sickly, wheezing laughter came from somewhere behind the boys.

"No thank you, sir. We gotta get goin'."

The man waved his hand clumsily. He said, "Suit yourself," but it sounded more like *Shoot yourself*. As Jake opened the door, he saw the man reaching for another bottle behind him.

The air outside almost seemed warmer as the boys descended the steps. Jake walked over to the horse once more and rested his hand on its neck. The horse snorted and reached forward to pull against the bridle.

"I got half a mind to take him and take care of him myself."

"I dunno, Jake. What if his owner finds out who took him?"

"You think he's sober enough to find us? He probably wouldn't even notice his horse is gone. Sure as hell don't notice he needs a good brushin'." Jake shook his head, hand still on the horse. He patted it and leaned in and said something in the horse's ear. The horse jerked his head and snorted in reply and Jake let go and started walking down the street.

The customers at the next saloon greeted the boys with cold stares that made them turn around before taking three steps inside. At the next, a man flew headfirst out the double doors and tumbled down the stairs into the street. Before the boys even entered they backed away and kept walking. And so it went. At each place they found only hostility or drunken indifference.

"You think we should go back to that first place? I don't think they'd even notice we was there," said Jake.

Billy shook his head.

"What about that other one? The one with the bear out front? That wasn't so bad."

Billy shrugged his shoulders, but Jake saw his brother's eyes widen.

"Not that one neither, then?"

Billy waited before shaking his head again.

"Well, you got any better ideas?"

Again Billy paused before responding with a shrug. By now the winter sun was setting, and whatever pale warmth it had given during the day was rapidly disappearing. A moving wall of wind thumped the boys and was gone before they could brace themselves. Jake pulled up his collar. "Let's get close to one of these buildings at least. Don't make sense standing out here in the open."

125

The street and saloons lining it were beginning to fill with more people, almost all men. Sounds emanated through the doors and windows and thin walls. Clinking glasses. Shuffled cards and gambling chips. A woman's laughter. The canned music of a player piano. The scuff of chair legs on wooden floors.

Even in the long shadows of dusk there was nowhere to hide. Spaces between buildings were narrow and cold during the day. They would be unbearable at night. The boys hid behind the corner of one saloon. Most people coming through the doorway didn't even look in their direction. Those who did either didn't care or were too drunk to notice.

As the night wore on, the noise from the inside grew. Warmth leaked out through the pores of the building, not enough to counteract the cold but as long as they pressed themselves against the sideboards it stopped them from shivering.

Jake and Billy played a game by telling stories of what was going on inside. Any time a new sound came the boy speaking had to add a detail. Jake always flubbed early, but Billy wove wild tales filled with fanciful descriptions of men and monsters locked in mortal combat.

"You win," said Jake. "Must be all those books you read."

Billy smiled. "Honest Jake, it's not that hard. You just gotta—"

"It's okay, little brother. I know you're better than me at it."

"I'm just sayin'."

The door banged open and three men stumbled out. Another group of men inside had started to sing, a warbled, off-key gurgling.

"My hands are gettin' cold, Jake."

"Swing 'em around like this." Jake held his arms straight and swung them in large circles. Billy did, too.

"It tingles in my fingers."

"It's supposed to. That means it's workin'."

"My feet are numb, too."

"Jump up and down then." Again Jake demonstrated and Billy mimicked. They looked like bouncing windmills, and when they looked at each they started giggling. When they stopped laughing they looked up. The light that shone through the window had been blocked out, and a large man with no jacket was standing over them.

"What are you boys doin' here?"

Both boys quickly got up and dusted themselves off. "Sorry, sir," said Jake. "We was just tryin' to stay warm."

"Ain't you got a home?"

"Yes sir. But we was just—"

"Then why don't you go there?" The man's voice had risen.

Just then the door swung open again. "What's going on, Henry?" It was a woman's voice.

"Just a couple boys up to no good."

"Boys?" The woman's head peered from behind the man's shoulder. Light from the window illuminated only half her face, and the heavy makeup and shadows combined to create a ghoulish, clown-like effect. It made Jake tense, but when he looked over at Billy his brother was transfixed.

"Oh, my poor sweet little babies! Henry! What are you doing out here with these boys? They should be inside where it's warm."

"But—"

"Don't you 'but' me. Come on in, boys. You must be freezing."

127

Billy looked at Jake and Jake looked at his brother and knew he could not tell him they shouldn't go in. Something about this woman didn't feel right, but he couldn't tell his brother to stay out in the cold any longer. He couldn't even say that to himself.

They followed the woman to the door with her husband behind all of them, and when she opened the door the warm air enveloped and beckoned them. There were some customers left, but they mainly paid no mind to the two boys walking in. The boys walked past the tables, past the bar to a door in the back of the saloon. As they walked, Jake looked around while Billy trailed so close behind the woman he almost got tangled in the folds of her voluminous blue dress.

They had visited this place earlier, but been run off by the man the woman called Henry. Jake saw the place was cleaner and bigger and better kept than most of the other saloons. The walls were mostly unadorned, but there was a large bison head mounted above the player piano at the far end of the room. The head was larger than that of any bull Jake had seen, and great brown curls of hair made the head appear even larger. The bison's black beady eyes seemed to follow Jake as they made their way through the room.

The door opened to the kitchen and they walked through as several men scrubbed large pots and swept floors and dried and stacked dishes. Past the kitchen there was another door and they went toward it. Jake looked back. Henry was gone, but the workers stood staring at Jake so he hurried to catch up with his brother and the woman.

Before they entered the room, the woman grabbed a lantern lying on one of the kitchen shelves and opened the door. Its yellow light struggled against the darkness, but after Jake's eyes adjusted he could see the dim shapes of two beds pushed against the side walls. Between them was a small table and the woman set the lantern on it, grabbed a stick from the table and used the flame to light the wick of another lantern on the table. The new light started low at first, but once she raised the wick a warm light filled the room. She grabbed the first lantern and hung it on a hook above her head. The light filled the room.

"You boys lie in bed there and get under the covers. I'll bring you some hot water to wash up with." She sounded sweet enough, but Jake couldn't help thinking her voice reminded him of Saunders much more than of Mrs. McCready. Without saying another word, she went back out into the kitchen. Jake couldn't hear what she was saying, but her voice was sharp and loud. When she came back it was soft and low again.

"Here you go, boys." She placed a chipped ceramic wash basin on the floor. The water sloshed over the sides a bit and onto her hands, and she wiped her hands on her dress and mumbled a curse under her breath. Before Jake could thank her she left and closed the door.

There was more talking from behind the door, and this time when someone entered it was one of the men from the kitchen. In his gloved hand he carried a bucket of coals. He swung it down into the corner at the foot of Billy's bed.

"Don't burn yourselves," he said without looking at them, and then he left.

Jake looked at Billy and was about to tell him to wash up when the woman came in again. "I gotta go now boys, so I'll see you in the morning. Wash up now and get some sleep. If you need the outhouse it's through the kitchen and out the door to the right. Good night."

Again the door slammed closed. For a while the boys stared at the door waiting for it to open again. Slivers of light leaked in around its edges. The coals in the bucket glowed a wavering red so the walls appeared in motion. Like the slow lungs of some animal. Its breath the odor of burning wood and of kerosene from the lamps.

Jake reached down into the basin and dipped his fingers tentatively, then a little more. "Go ahead and wash up before that water gets cold."

Billy sunk his hands into the water and rinsed the dirt off them. Even in the yellowed darkness the brown ribbons of dirt swirling in the water were visible. He laved the water over his face and used his shirt to dry off. When he finished he lay down on his bed while Jake washed up. Then Jake dragged the basin under his bed and reached up and grabbed the lantern from the hook on the ceiling. When the fire on the wick had extinguished from the turning of the key, Jake made sure Billy's blankets were pulled up tight around his neck. Then he got into his bed and under the blankets and lay staring at the red and yellow patterns of light on the ceiling.

"Can we stay here?" asked Billy.

"You mean tonight? Yeah."

"No, I mean stay. It's nice here."

"You don't know that. You're just sayin' that 'cause it's warm in here." ·

"Naw, it's 'cause that lady's nice."

"You don't know her, Billy."

"Well you don't either."

"I know enough."

"Jake?"

"Yeah?"

"I know you're just lookin' out for me but sometimes it's like we can't trust no one."

Jake felt the familiar pang of guilt when he thought how Billy couldn't even trust him. That Jake hadn't even told him the truth about their father. "I got a bad feeling, Billy. I got a bad feeling about this whole city. I just don't know about her yet. That's all."

"I know, Jake, but I think she's a nice lady."

"We'll see, little brother. Right now I ain't sure we got much choice."

There was a long pause and Jake thought his brother had gone to sleep. His own eyelids had started their heavy path downward when Billy spoke. "Good night, Jake."

"Good night, Billy."

11

The boys lay awake listening to the sounds outside the door. Night and morning had long since passed, and although they had both gone to use the outhouse just before dawn they had quickly gone back to sleep. Now the muffled clanging of pots and pans and voices came through the door. There was no clock, but Jake reckoned lunch was being prepared by the savory smell of stew seeping into their room.

After getting dressed, the boys approached the door. Billy stood behind him, hand resting gently on his brother's elbow. Jake turned to look at Billy.

"It's alright. They sound loud but they ain't gonna hurt you."

"I don't hear the lady."

"She's probably out front. Come on, let's go see."

Jake opened the door and poked out his head. No one in the kitchen turned to look at him, so he opened the door fully. Only one person stopped what he was doing to sneak a look but he quickly returned to his chopping, shooting a nervous glance over his other shoulder.

As the boys walked through the kitchen no one spoke to them or offered them anything to eat. Even when Jake said good morning to a man washing dishes he received no response. Down the narrow aisle they wedged past the working men to the double doors that led to the main room.

On the other side they heard laughter. Jake looked at Billy and forced a smile and Billy forced one in return but looped his fingers into his belt and hung his head. Jake pushed the door open.

Another round of laughter rang in their ears as soon as they entered the room. A few people turned to look at them, and out of the crowd emerged the face of the woman from the night before.

"Here they are. Here are the darlings I've been telling you about. Come here, little ones."

Jake's ears reddened at the phrase 'little ones' but Billy removed his fingers from his belt and walked ahead of his brother toward the woman. A crowd of people stood in a semicircle around her, all eyes on Billy as he approached. When he reached the woman she put her arm around him and pulled him so close half of him was lost in the folds of her dress.

"Tell them your name, sweetie."

"Billy. And that there's my brother Jake."

Jake took a couple steps forward but the woman only glanced at him sideways before turning her attention back to Billy.

"Ah, yes. And where are you from, Billy?"

"Ste. Genevieve."

She looked at her audience. "Can you believe it? I found these boys sitting on my porch last night. They were huddled up without anything but their shirts on trying to stay warm by pressing up against the wall just over there. Henry tried to kick them out, but I came out and rescued them from the cold. Poor babies. They spent the night in the back room."

"You gonna let 'em stay with you, Alice?" asked a man in the crowd.

Jake was now at his brother's side, resting his hand on Billy's shoulder. The woman looked at them quickly before responding. "Why yes, of course. You know Mama Alice always takes care of everyone. Henry?"

For the first time, Jake noticed her husband drying out glasses behind the wooden counter of the bar. On his slumped shoulders hung a head that seemed too big for his bony frame. Small white wisps like ghost plants on a fallow field were all that was left of his hair. He looked a far cry from the fierce man Jake had encountered on the porch the night before.

"Yes, dear." Henry's voice was weary.

"Get these folks a drink."

"Yes, Alice."

The customers sidled up to the bar, and Alice turned to face the two boys. "Well, you must be hungry. Come back to the kitchen and I'll have the boys fix you something." She put one arm around each boy and walked with them toward the double doors leading to the kitchen. To open the door she kept her arm around Billy and removed the one from Jake's shoulder. After they went through, she didn't put it back.

Once on the other side her pace quickened, footsteps falling harder on the floor. Gone was the sweet tone in her voice. She barked orders to the men in the kitchen and they nodded silently or responded with a quiet "Yes, ma'am." Hands that were already moving quickly worked even faster, and soon there was a bowl of steaming mush in front of each boy. The woman instructed the boys to take them to the room to eat. Then she spun on her heel and disappeared through the double doors. When she did, the men's pace slowed, and several began to eye the boys with a mixture of pity and contempt.

Jake said, "Thank you, sir," to no one in particular and Billy did the same. Pulling their sleeves down to hold the bowls without burning their hands, they took them back to their rooms. They sat on their beds and ate and when they were done Jake got up and grabbed Billy's bowl. As Billy followed, Jake took the bowls to the sink and asked the man working there if he could wash them himself. The man's eyebrows rose a little at the question and he nodded. When Jake finished he asked where he should put them to dry.

"I'll take them."

"Thank you, sir."

A slight smile broke the stern look on the man's face. "It's alright, kid."

Jake turned to Billy. "Go back to the room."

"But why?" asked Billy. "I wanna go back out there."

"I said go. I'll be back there in a minute."

Billy opened his mouth, but when Jake gave him a look he closed it hung his head and went back to the room. When Jake saw his brother close the door behind him, he turned back to the man who was still standing at the sink looking at Jake. He nodded and the man nodded back and Jake went out through the double doors.

In the main room of the saloon, Mama Alice was standing next to a table of men. They were all wearing hats whose faded rims drooped and undulated in uneven waves around their heads. Their faces were covered with layers of dirt and grime so thick it made the wrinkles in the men's faces look like deep ravines cut through some unholy black earth, the patient carving of features over the years.

Jake approached quietly until he was close enough to hear, but not so close he would be noticed by Mama Alice or anyone at the table. There were many tables but most of them were still empty at this hour, and the ones Jake stood between were empty. He waited, hands at his sides, and stared at the legs of the chairs where the men sat.

Mama Alice was instructing the men on the rules of the saloon. She kept saying *my* saloon whenever talking about the establishment and the men kept responding with, "Yes, ma'am," and "Yes, Mama Alice." At one point one of the men said, "Yes we know, Mama Alice. We've been here before. Many times."

"Well I know you've been here many times. But some of those times you gentlemen don't always follow my rules. That's why I'm telling them to you again. It would be awful if you boys couldn't come back in here because you kept breaking my rules."

The front door opened and she looked up to see who was coming in. When she did, she noticed Jake in the corner of her eye. "Why, hello."

"Jake, ma'am."

"Yes, of course. I know your name, boy. I know the name of everyone who comes in here. How was your breakfast?"

"It was nice, ma'am. Real nice."

"I imagine. Poor things waiting out there in the cold for someone to rescue them. Good thing I came along."

"That was real nice of you, ma'am."

"Think nothing of it." When she said this she waved her hand dismissively. "Mama Alice always takes care of everybody. That's why they always come back to see me. Isn't that right, boys?" She patted one of the men on the shoulders and they all murmured assent. "So what can I do for you now, Jake?"

"Well, that's just it, ma'am. You see, my brother and me would like to repay you if we could."

"Oh, that won't be necessary. It was nothing, really."

Jake swallowed. A knot of apprehension was forming in his gut, but despite his misgivings about this woman he felt he had no other choice. "Ma'am, my brother and me ain't got much money, but we're good workers. We'd like to help you out any way we can."

Mama Alice's eyes widened and a slow smile stretched across her face. "Would you now? Well, I can probably think of a couple things for you boys to do." She paused and Jake shifted back and forth on his feet, trying to look at her without actually looking into her eyes. "Follow me, Jake."

Her boot heels shook the floorboards as she walked toward the kitchen. She burst through the doors so hard they almost hit Jake in the face as they swung back. Without greeting anyone she headed straight for the sink and stopped. The man Jake had spoken to earlier was there. As Mama Alice stood there hands on hips, his entire upper body slumped. Head, shoulders and spine deflated in succession until he was bowed before her.

"Harris, we need to make a change," she said. "You've been showing up late every day and working less and less even when you're here."

"But I'm always here fifteen minutes early. And I—"

"Hush now. You know I'm right." Mama Alice reached into the pocket of her dress and pulled out some coins. She counted them carefully and put the remainder back before handing the coins to Harris. All the while that eerie smile stayed plastered on her face. "Here's your pay. Now don't be a stranger."

"You heartless—"

Mama Alice put up her hand. "Now, now, Harris. Don't start going there. You know Mama Alice always treats people fair."

Harris glanced around the room. The other men in the kitchen stayed at their stations, silent, unmoving. They did not work, but they also did not look up. Harris called a couple of their names but no one responded. Then he looked at Jake.

Jake tugged on Mama Alice's sleeve. "Ma'am, that's not what I meant. This man here ain't done nothin' wrong. I don't want to—"

"Hush now, Jake. Don't you worry about this at all. It's none of your concern."

"But, Ma'am—"

"I said hush." She fixed Jake with a stare that seemed to freeze all movement, squelch all sound in the kitchen. Jake was afraid she could hear the beating of his heart pounding his eardrums from the inside. Mama Alice saw his fear and pounced. "Are you telling me how to run my business, boy?"

Jake searched for the courage to speak. When he found it, his words were wheezes from a deflating balloon. "No, ma'am."

"This man here hasn't been pulling his weight since he started here. Do you want to pay him for doin' half-assed work?"

Jake could no longer speak, so he shook his bowed head.

Mama Alice turned back toward the man. Some of the malice had drained from her voice, but the sweetness that replaced it belied the message. "Get your things and go, Harris."

The man stood staring at her, as if the force of his glare could move her. Every other soul in that kitchen stood still, watching in the waiting silence for the inevitable. A pulsing vein protruded from Harris's neck, and his whole body trembled slightly. He said nothing. Mama Alice stared back, a deceivingly placid smile on her face. Then, in an instant, all tension in his body drained. His gaze dropped to the floor and his chest collapsed like a compressed bellows. When he looked up it was not at Mama Alice but at Jake, and the faint flickers of hatred that lay buried underneath the man's sorrow like coals under layers of gray ash burned their way into Jake. The boy looked away.

Harris shuffled toward the door and took off his apron. He hung it on a hook before grabbing his hat and coat. Staring at the wall, he slowly slid his arms into the sleeves. Gravity seemed to be pulling his shoulders and arms down, and it took all his strength to plop his hat listlessly on his head. Without so much as a nod goodbye to anyone in the kitchen, he grabbed the knob and walked out into the cold.

As soon as he did, Mama Alice scanned the room. "What're you all looking at? Back to work!" The men in the kitchen resumed their chopping and wiping and sweeping even if they had already cleaned the area. She looked at Jake. Welcome to my saloon, Jake. Roger here will help you get familiar with how we do things. Roger!"

A stout man with short gray hair and a bushy moustache snapped to attention next to her. "Yes, Mama Alice."

"This is Jake. Make sure he knows exactly what to do and what not to do."

"Yes'm."

"Jake, you make sure you listen real good to Roger and do exactly what he says."

"Yes, ma'am," said the boy.

"You have any questions you just ask him."

"Yes, ma'am."

"Now where is that brother of yours?"

Jake's heart leapt into his throat, but he tried to make his voice sound calm. "In the room over there, ma'am."

"*Your* room, Jake. That's your room now. I told you I was going to take care of you. Now I'll just go get Billy while you get to work."

Jake fought the urge to run ahead of her to the bedroom door and grab his brother. Grab him and their bags and run out the door. But she had already opened the door without knocking and entered. Through the partially open door, Jake could see her knees next to Billy's on the bed. They did not sit there long before she emerged with her arm around Billy. As they passed Billy greeted his brother, but before Jake could respond Mama Alice had steered his brother toward the double doors and into the main room of the saloon.

The moment they were gone, all the men stopped working and turned to look at Jake. Roger grabbed under Jake's arm and pulled him close, bending down so his moustache scraped Jake's ear. His breath smelled of stale chewing tobacco, and when he spoke it was in a whispered growl.

"I don't know what kind of game you're pulling here, boy, but if you pull that shit with anybody else we're going to string you up by your nuts and hang you from the clothesline."

Jake swallowed hard and nodded. "I swear, Mister, I didn't know that was going to happen."

"Well, what the hell did you think was going to happen? Did you ask the old lady for work? You think a woman like that would pay someone for something she could get someone else to do for free? You think there are lots of jobs at a cattle town in the winter? Or are you just too stupid to think?" As he spoke he punctuated his statements by pulling on Jake's arm with increasing force. It took all Jake's will not to wince.

"Now in case you ain't realized already, Mama Alice is a hard woman. She's got the whole town thinking she's some sweet lady who takes care of everyone. But really she'll toss you out on your ass the moment she don't need you anymore. So I suggest you do what we do: keep your nose clean and don't say nothin'. In this saloon on time means early, clean means spotless, and one mistake means you're gone. Mama Alice runs the best damn saloon in Kansas, and if she thinks you done somethin' to tarnish that reputation you won't never work for her again. You got it?"

"Yes, sir."

"Then you best start washing those dishes 'til you can see your face in every one."

"Yes, sir."

"You do know how to wash dishes now, don't you?" For the first time Jake heard noise from the other men in the kitchen. They were laughing.

"Yes, sir."

Roger grunted and walked back to his station. Soon the others fell into the rhythmic quiet of their chores. No one spoke or stopped their work. Even though Jake could not see them, he could hear the faint noises coming from each part of the kitchen. He scrubbed furiously to keep his mind off what had just happened, but the oppressive silence of the kitchen bore down on him. And in that weighted silence Jake knew he had set in motion something which could not be undone.

For the rest of the day, Jake saw little else but the sink. The pile of dishes to his left steadily increased throughout the day, and no matter how fast he washed the dishes and put them on the drying rack to his right, they disappeared as soon as he placed them there. Occasionally Roger would come over and yell at him for going too slowly or not washing a pot that was needed immediately or for missing a spot on a dish he pulled from the rack and put right back in the dirty pile. The only respite Jake got was the occasional glance out the window above the sink. Lunch and dinner were eaten while working, and the few times Jake went to the outhouse, the pile of unwashed dishes got so big he figured it was better to just hold it.

Through the window he could gauge the time of day, and as the light went from pale white to reddened hues to pitch black the work was the same. Only after a gibbous moon rose high in the sky did the steady march of dishes and pots and silverware start to wane. The sounds behind him slowed as well, and soon he was able to take a break and look around the room. Men were cleaning their stations or putting away foodstuffs. A brave few were even standing around and talking.

Jake's entire body was sore, from his aching knees to his hunched back. When he straightened himself up and pulled his shoulders back, his vertebrae popped in several places. His hands were so white and wrinkled they resembled raisins dipped in powdered sugar. He had cut himself twice with knives, and punctured himself so many times with the tines of forks he had lost count. Where his flesh was scored, pale white flaps of skin peeled away.

Suddenly Jake realized he had not seen Billy the whole day. He dared not leave the sink, but he kept checking the double doors for any movement, any sign of Mama Alice or his brother. Finally she burst through the doors, and with her came the sounds of laughter and music from the main room. As the doors swung back and forth, the saloon sounds ebbed and flowed until their volume was muted once more by the heavy wood. Some men still worked to clean their areas, but most stood by them in silence as Mama Alice walked around the kitchen inspecting. Jake spun around and checked the sink, cleaning or wiping anything that looked like it needed it. He dumped the contents of the food trap at the bottom of the sink into the trash can below, and even rinsed and wiped the trap until it was shiny.

Behind him he could hear Mama Alice's comments. *Good work, Walter. You missed a spot there, Jim. Lucas, I've told you a hundred times those pots should all go upside down.* When Jake couldn't see anything else to clean, he turned around and waited for Mama Alice to come. He saw each man who passed inspection receive several coins or bank notes from the roll Mama Alice pulled from the pockets of her dress. And each time the man thanked her before leaving.

Roger stood in the center of the kitchen, watching and waiting. Once everyone else had been cleared and paid she walked up to him. She did not inspect his station but instead began debriefing him about how the night went. Who lagged, who pulled his own weight, who worked especially hard.

"We had a good night out there, Roger."

"That's good news, ma'am."

"Very good news. Seems you have your boys working well."

"Just trying to keep 'em up to your standards, Mama Alice."

Mama Alice smiled. "Oh, I doubt that's all of it, Roger. I see good things from you."

"Thank you, ma'am."

She pulled out a roll of bank notes and peeled off several. "Here you go, Roger. Your normal pay."

"Thank you." He took the money without changing expressions.

Mama Alice peeled off two more notes. "And here's your bonus pay for doing such a fine job tonight, especially with the new hire and all."

"Thank you, ma'am." Again his expression did not change.

"Speaking of which," at this point she turned toward Jake, "how did our boy do?"

Roger looked at Jake, too. "Not bad, ma'am. No broken dishes, cleaned most of 'em right the first time."

As he talked, Mama Alice walked over and inspected the sink, running her finger over several places. "Did he keep up?"

"Not at first, but he learned to speed it up pretty quick."

"No complaining?"

"Quiet as a church mouse."

"Did he take any breaks?"

It unnerved Jake that they were talking about him as if he weren't there, but he said nothing.

"Not more than a couple," said Roger.

"Good, good." She nodded, then looked at Jake. "Well, you've earned your night's keep, Jake. Good night."

"Thank you, ma'am," said Jake.

Though Mama Alice moved back toward Roger and began speaking with him again, Jake remained in his place by the sink. When she noticed, she turned back toward the boy. "You waitin' for something else from me, boy?" Whatever pleasant tones she had in her voice had vanished.

"Ma'am, my brother?"

"What about him?"

"Where is he?"

Her eyes squinted and lips pursed. "What do you mean?"

Jake cleared his throat as he contemplated her question. He thought he had been clear. "I mean, he was with you out in the saloon last I saw, but now he ain't with you."

She took a couple steps toward him. "You mean you don't remember?"

"Remember what, ma'am?" Jake's heart was now pounding as he tried to figure out what she was talking about, tried to guess where he might be.

"Child, he went to bed hours ago." Jake's brow furrowed, but he said nothing. "He even came by with me to say good night to you." She stared at Jake for a while as his eyes moved from the door to the sink and back, eyebrows still pressed down in concentration.

Mama Alice broke the tension with a hearty laugh. This one sounded like the one she reserved for the patrons partying in the main room of the saloon, but more genuine. "Boy," she said, "you were working so hard you didn't even see your own brother come and talk to you." Jake's face burst into a dark shade of red, and Mama Alice put her arm around him. "You're alright with me, Jake. I can't get most of my men to work that hard for me, and here you go working that hard

145

on the first day." She made a clicking sound with her tongue. "Go check on your brother and get some sleep, sugar."

Jake managed a weary smile. "Thank you, ma'am. I really appreciate what you're doin' for my brother and me."

"Don't mention it, Jake."

As soon as Jake started walking toward the bedroom, the soreness and fatigue in his whole body set in. With each step he felt like someone was pulling him down harder and harder until he could barely stand by the time he got to the room. Without looking back or saying good night to Roger and Mama Alice, Jake opened the door. His brother was fast asleep, illuminated slightly by the dim lantern light that made its way in from the kitchen.

Jake closed the door slowly so as not to wake Billy, and walked with his hand low in front of him until he reached his own bed and sat down. He pulled off his soaking wet boots and socks and put them close to the pot of coals on the floor. He wanted to put on dry clothes too, but the soft feel of the mattress changed his mind and he lay down and wrapped the blanket around his sore shoulders.

12

Jake stared at the window above the sink. Behind the glass, the thick blackness of night gave no light and the flickering lanterns in the kitchen made the reflection of his face waver in the warps of the panes. Even in that dim light he saw the difference. No longer was his the face of a farm boy, its color leeched by endless hours indoors. His only ventures outside were to the outhouse, and even those trips were infrequent.

He looked down at his hands. At the end of each night they looked as they did now. Pruned pink with white patches of dead skin peeling off. Wounds from washing. A cut from the slice of a knife. Small holes from the punctures of fork tines. Jake wiped the sink down one last time, throwing any stray bits of waterlogged food into the trash bin.

"Jake, come here a second."

Jake sighed, weary hands braced on the sink edge. When he turned he saw Roger at his station. Wiping his hands on the only dry spot on the back of his pants, Jake walked toward Roger. As he did the men at other stations teased him under their breath. *Yes, sir. No problem, Roger. Anything for you, sir.* Jake's face was too tired to change expression, but inside the remarks still cut.

"Good job tonight, Jake," said Roger.

"Thank you, sir." Jake heard a couple snickers behind him.

"Mama Alice said tonight was good. She wanted me to give you this." Roger handed Jake a small wad of bank notes.

"Thank you." Jake pocketed the money, knowing later he would count and place it in the secret compartment he had made under the floorboard in the bedroom. Mama Alice had begun to pay him on good nights, and he was hoping to save enough to take Billy and leave. But he didn't have enough. Not yet at least.

"I've got a job for you tomorrow. Something different."

Jake cringed. Any time Roger said that, he meant something no one else wanted to do. Cleaning grease traps. Crawling under sinks to clean food off the floor. Scrubbing rust off old knives until they were polished and shiny. "No problem, Roger."

"I want you to go to the general store."

Jake looked up. "Sir?" He could hear the men behind him stop working.

"You heard me. I said I want you to pick up some things at Wilkins's store tomorrow. That alright with you?"

"Yes, sir."

"Alrighty then. Here's the list." Roger placed a scrap of paper on the wooden counter. "Just take this to Mr. Wilkins and he'll take care of the rest."

"Okay. Is that all, sir?"

"That's all, Jake. Go get some rest. You look like you ain't slept in a month."

Without responding, Jake shuffled back to the bedroom where Billy already lay fast asleep. He heard Roger say, "What? If you all worked half as hard as him maybe I'd give you the easy job, too." Tonight Jake bothered only to hang his apron on the hook inside the door before crawling under the covers with wet clothes and the money still in his pocket.

The pale winter sun warmed Jake's face as he walked to the store. He squinted as its harsh white glare reflected off the bleached gravel of the main street, the brightness of day contrasting with the dinginess of the buildings. The bones of trees cobbled together for shelter and sustenance. Man's attempt to remove himself from the elements, from his own nature. But here in this desolate place in doing so he shut out the good and kept the bad behind the doors.

Jake knew Roger needed the goods from Wilkins quickly, but he took his time to breathe in the cold, dry winter air. He shivered and it felt good, like he was still alive. The long, hard days indoors had begun to eat away at Jake, slowly corroding the self that was.

A bell jingled when Jake opened the door to Wilkins's store. At the counter stood Mr. Wilkins, appearing exactly as he did when Jake met him weeks earlier. The man looked up at the sound of the bell, and Jake walked up to the counter.

"Good morning, son. How can I help you?"

"Morning, Mr. Wilkins. How do you do?"

Mr. Wilkins furrowed his brow. "I'm sorry, have we met?"

Jake took off his hat. "Yes, sir. My name's Jake. I was here with my brother Billy a few weeks back." The man's eyes examined Jake but he said nothing. "We was looking for work."

Mr. Wilkins's eyes widened. "My god, boy, what happened to you?"

"Sir?"

"I'm sorry." He waved his hand as if hoping the action would erase what he said. "It's just...where you been staying?"

"With Mama Alice at her saloon."

"Ahhh," said the old man. "No wonder you look so tired." He looked over his spectacles at Jake. "You been staying on her good side?"

"So far."

Mr. Wilkins laughed. "You've probably already figured out that's the only place you should be."

Jake managed a smile. "Yes, sir."

"Well now, what can I do for you?"

"Roger gave me a list of stuff to get."

Jake placed the list on the counter, and Mr. Wilkins picked it up. His glasses made his eyes look like giant painted eggs that protruded some distance from his face and moved as he scanned the list. He brought the paper back down to the counter and slid his glasses down his nose to look at Jake. His eyes looked normal again.

"I've got everything except the nails. Half of old Jaffrey's barn collapsed last week in the winds, and he bought up my whole supply of nails to fix it. I don't suppose Mama Alice is going to be happy about that."

"I don't suppose so."

"Well, that old witch could stand to learn a little patience. Hell, I wouldn't even do business with her except she's my biggest customer and always pays her bills on time." He picked up the list again. "Here boy, start helping get some of this stuff. You didn't come here to listen to me complain."

As Mr. Wilkins told Jake where to go, the boy plucked the items off the shelves and placed them on the counter. The larger items like bags of flour he placed on the floor. Soon there was so much on the counter Jake could only see the top of Mr. Wilkins's head.

"Mr. Wilkins?" Jake asked over the stacks.

"Yeah?"

"It might take me a while to carry all this stuff back to the saloon."

The old man poked his head around the piles of goods and laughed. "Don't you worry about that, Jake. I got a couple wheelbarrows in the back. I'll help you bring it all over."

"That's kind of you sir, but I can take care of it."

"I don't mind at all, Jake. I spend most of my days cooped up in this store, it'd be good to get out and stretch my legs. Okay, last thing. Go over to that far shelf and fetch me three bags of buckwheat flour."

Jake brought over the bags and placed them by the others on the floor. Then Mr. Wilkins reached around the stack on the counter and put down two candies.

"For you and Billy."

"Thank you sir, but we can't—"

"Jake, don't tell me you can't accept a gift from me. You're bound to hurt my feelings."

Jake's ears grew crimson. "Yes, sir. Thank you."

Mr. Wilkins walked to the back of the store, and Jake followed through a large door that led to a storage room. The room was half the size of the store but much darker. Only one four-paned window let light in from the north, and the sun lying low on the southern horizon had to work to reach its rays through the glass. The shelves were made of unfinished boards nailed neatly together, more utilitarian than the polished ones in the store. In the corner, two wheelbarrows were parked parallel. Man and boy grabbed one each and wheeled them back out into the main room.

When they had loaded all the goods, Mr. Wilkins went back into the storage room and emerged a short time later wearing a coat and hat. He went to the front door and locked and bolted it before grabbing the handles of his wheelbarrow. "Come on, follow me. There's a ramp out the back door."

Soon the two were walking down the street back toward the saloon. The dirt and gravel crunched under their feet and under the weight of the wheels and several times they had to stop to rest their arms. At one of those pauses Mr. Wilkins asked Jake how Billy was doing.

"Fine, I guess. I don't see him much."

"Why not?"

"Well, I'm usually in the kitchen and Mama Alice usually has him up front with her."

"In the saloon?"

"Yes, sir."

"That ain't no place for a boy his age."

"I know't, sir. But I can't do nothin' about it. She's been real kind to us takin' us in and all, and I don't want to seem ungrateful askin' her to keep him away from there."

"Wait a minute." Mr. Wilkins was stroking his beard. "You mean to tell me Billy's the boy she's been telling everyone about? How she rescued him starving and naked and alone from her front porch?"

"I guess so. I know she's mighty fond of tellin' that story."

"I'll say. I ain't set foot in her saloon since you boys got to town, and I've heard that story a dozen times. It gets more amazing and heroic every time I hear it." He paused to greet a man who hailed him from the far side of the street. "So you were the boys she took in. I didn't put two and two together since the story was usually only about Billy."

"Yeah, she seems to like havin' him around."

"Mind if I give you a word of advice, Jake?"

"No sir."

"Be careful with that woman. I've seen her do this before. Some mangy mutt kept hanging around the saloon. People

152

always thought it belonged to one of the men who came there, and maybe it did at first. But after a while it just sort of started staying the night even after everybody up and left. Just curled up by the fire and slept.

"Well, Mama Alice took this dog in like it was her long lost son. Made the men in the kitchen feed and bathe it and comb it every day. She told everyone she could how bad it was when she first got him. Made like it had three legs and she grew him the fourth. After a while the people got tired of the story and as soon as they got tired of it so did she. By then the dog was used to being pampered and got all uppity if it didn't get its food or its bath.

"One night it howled all night, and Mama Alice got so sick of it she threw it out the door. The dog didn't take too kindly to that, especially being the dead of winter and all. So it kept howling and howling and howling outside that door all night. Whining and carrying on like its ancestors were princesses not wolves."

"What'd Mama Alice do?"

"What'd she do? She come out in the middle of the night in her nightclothes carrying a shotgun. Then woke up one of her men and made him clean up the mess before people come in the morning. Even made him replace the boards she put the buckshot in."

Mr. Wilkins walked toward Jake and put his hand on the boy's shoulder, bringing his face so close Jake could smell the remnants of pipe smoke on his breath and beard. "I don't mean to say your brother's like a pet, but do you get my point?"

"Yes, sir."

153

"If that woman ain't got no use for you and your brother, she'll put you out fast as she took you in. It sounds like you're in good, but you'd best make Billy useful as quick as you can."

Jake nodded. "Thank you, sir."

Mr. Wilkins stood up. "Don't mention it, boy. Now come on, let's get out of this cold and over to the saloon before Roger wonders what happened to you."

When they reached Mama Alice's, they wheeled their loads around back and brought them to the kitchen. Roger opened the door.

"There you are. I was beginning to wonder if you got lost," said Roger.

"Sorry, sir."

"It's my fault Roger," said Mr. Wilkins. "I was talking the boy's ear off."

"Well, that's a surprise," said Roger. Both men laughed. "Now let's get this stuff unloaded quick. Train's supposed to be bringing a lot of people today."

Soon all the goods were in their proper places and Jake and Mr. Wilkins were pushing the wheelbarrows back to the store, but not before an admonishment from Roger for Jake to hurry back. The two walked in silence save for the crunches and squeaks from the wheels, and Jake was content to drink in the fresh air and move his legs. They arrived back at the store all too soon for his liking, and he said goodbye to Mr. Wilkins and headed back to the saloon.

When he got there he went into the bedroom to hang up his coat. A groan coming from Billy's bed startled him.

"What're you doin', Jake? Close the door!"

"What you mean, what am I doin'? I'm workin'. You should be doin' the same."

"Aw, don't get mad at me just 'cause Mama Alice likes me better. You're just jealous."

Jake closed the door and sat on Billy's bed. He could see nothing beyond the small sliver of light coming from the door, but he could feel his brother's movements under the blanket. "Billy, we need to talk. I don't think it's right for you to be spendin' time out there in the saloon."

"You don't know what's right for me." Billy's disembodied voice came from somewhere in the darkness.

"Billy..."

"I'm tired of you tellin' me what to do all the time, Jake. You ain't got no right to tell me what to do. I'm growing up, and I can make my own decisions."

Jake said not a word but sat on the edge of the bed and waited. The silence in the room grew until both boys were still. Even their breaths slowed, and Jake could hear his own heart beat. He thought he could even hear Billy's. Then Billy stirred and sat up. Jake's eyes had adjusted, and he could see the outline of his brother's arms propping him up on the mattress.

"I'm sorry, Jake. I didn't mean it. You know I didn't."

"I know't, Billy."

"It's just that I don't know what to do. I'm feelin' trapped."

"What you mean?"

"Jake, she wants me there next to her all the time. She keeps tellin' that same story about rescuin' us off the porch, only now it's changed so much I don't even recognize me in it. And she tells me to smile all the time and help her tell the story. I got so I know exactly what she wants me to do when she gets to certain parts of the story. Shiver here, smile there. I even

155

have to talk like her husband, say what he said to us when we were out there."

"What'd he say to us?"

"Tell you the truth I don't even remember. I just say what she told me to say."

"Well Billy, sounds like you and me got the same idea. I don't want you out there and you don't want to be out there neither."

"But where we goin' to go? It's still winter and I don't want to be out in the cold again."

"We'll still stay here, little brother. Don't you worry about that. I'm just proposing we find you a job to do around here that don't involve storytelling."

"But what can I do? You all got a spot for me in the kitchen?"

"Maybe, but I had somethin' else in mind. You still good with numbers and figurin' and all that?"

"Of course, Jake. You know I was always good at that."

"Yeah, but this time you got to be real good. Can't make no mistakes. You think you can help Mama Alice take care of the numbers for this place?"

"Whoa, I don't know Jake. She takes them real serious. I always see her yellin' at her husband about 'em."

"Yeah, but doesn't she yell at him for everything?"

Billy laughed. "Yeah, I guess so. But I don't want to take away his job."

"You won't be takin' away nothin'. You're just goin' to be helpin', that's all. That's what we'll tell her. Help her out so she don't got to worry about the money all the time."

"Jake?"

"Yeah?"

"I think she's always goin' to be worryin' about the money."

Jake laughed. "You're probably right, little brother. Come on, get dressed and head on out there. We'll try to talk to her about it tonight. Don't you say a word about it. You let me bring it up, you hear?"

"Okay."

That day and the next the saloon was so busy the boys didn't get a chance to speak to Mama Alice. While Billy slept, Jake worked long past his usual stopping time to wash all the dishes. The voices from the saloon kept trickling in long after they normally did. It was late winter, and though spring was still far off a few brave souls had come to get an early start on their trips out west.

Every morning now, Jake also had to run to Wilkins's store. At first he thought the job would give him a break from his regular duties, but he still had to keep up with his regular workload. That made him even more tired than before, but he didn't mind. He liked the walk and Wilkins's company.

On the third day the work dipped back down to normal. Most of the travelers had caught trains farther west, so only the locals remained. At the end of the evening Mama Alice came in to talk to Roger, and Jake walked over to her.

"Mama Alice?"

"What is it, Jake?"

"I was wonderin' if I could ask you a question." She stayed silent, so he continued. "I'm worried about my brother."

"You think I'm not taking good care of him?" Her eyes had narrowed, and Jake knew he had to speak quickly.

"No, ma'am. It's nothin' like that. Me and Billy, we're real grateful for all you done for us. All you do for us. It's just-"

"Just what?" Mama Alice's voice was rising.

"It's just I'm worried about his education."

This must not have been the response she expected because her voice softened noticeably. "Education?"

"Yes, ma'am. You see, before our mom died—"

"Oh child, I didn't know she died. Why didn't you tell me before?"

"Well Mama Alice, I didn't want to bother you with that. You already been so nice to us, I didn't want you to feel sorry for us at all." Jake hated calling her Mama Alice, but he knew she liked to hear it.

"Is that why you boys ended up here? You don't have any place to go?"

"No, ma'am. We got a place to go. We're headin' to see our father in California."

Mama Alice's piercing laugh startled Jake. "California? Jake, you sure got some nerve."

"I'm sorry, ma'am. Did I say somethin' wrong?"

"Not at all, Jake. I was just saying I like your spirit. Now what is it you were saying about your momma?"

"Well, when we was young it was real important to our momma for Billy to learn. Every penny we had we'd buy more and more books for him to read. I liked 'em well enough, but Billy really took to 'em. If we didn't have money for new books he'd just read the old ones again."

"Well, I've got some books he can read. I do a little reading myself, when I have time." She sighed dramatically.

"It's not just that, Mama Alice. He also learned stuff like history, and he especially liked figurin' with numbers."

Mama Alice waved her hand. "That's all I do all day."

"Well that's just it, ma'am. You see, I was thinkin' Billy might be able to help you with the numbers here."

She scoffed. "But he's just a boy. He can't add and subtract the numbers as fast as he needs to. Lord knows I yell at Henry about them, but I must admit he's the only one I know who can keep track of the money as fast as it comes in."

"Does your husband serve the drinks and take the money and count it?"

"He does it all."

"You see, I think Billy could help. Your husband could still serve and handle the money, but once it needed counting Billy could do it."

"Well, even if Billy could do it, what makes you think I'd trust him with my money?"

Jake felt the heat of anger warm his cheeks, and he had to pause before speaking to control his voice. "Ma'am, no one in my family ever stole nothin', and we sure ain't goin' to start now."

"You're absolutely right, Jake. I apologize. I didn't mean it like that. It's just an important job, and I don't want Billy to make mistakes."

"He won't."

Mama Alice paused, pursing her lips. "You really think your brother can do it?"

"Just try him out, that's all I ask. I know he loves numbers, and it'd be real good for him to start using 'em again."

"Go get him then."

"Well, he's asleep right now."

"You said he wanted to work, Jake. This is when we work. If you want him to do this, go get him now."

Jake walked over and opened the door. A growing wedge of light slowly illuminated the floor, bed and wall until the room glowed a pale yellow. Billy was lying in bed, and Jake stood over and nudged him.

"Billy?"

His brother groaned but did not move.

"Billy? You got to get up. Mama Alice wants to talk to you."

"About what?"

"About doing the numbers for this place. Billy, you got to get up now." Jake leaned down and whispered into his brother's ear. "Billy, remember what we talked about. This is somethin' you got to do if we want to stay here. Come on now."

Billy let out a long sigh and rolled over onto his side. He pushed himself up then put his hand on Jake's shoulder and pulled himself to his feet. With his free hand he rubbed his eyes and he wobbled and leaned hard on his brother and regained his balance and opened his eyes.

"You awake now?" asked Jake.

Billy nodded.

"Alright, I'll let you get dressed."

Jake went back out to Mama Alice and Roger, and a few minutes later Billy emerged. A large cowlick stuck up from the back of his head and he bumped into the counters a couple times before reaching where the others waited for him.

"Sugar, you sure you're ready for this?" Mama Alice looked sideways at Roger and they both smiled.

"Yes'm."

"We can do this tomorrow if you like."

Billy knew that wasn't true, that if Jake said he had to do it now this was his only chance. "It's alright, Mama Alice. I'm ready."

"Okay, honey. Here's how we're going to do this. I'm going to give you a sheet of paper and a pencil, and I'll start giving you numbers. You write them down on the paper and add them all up."

Billy looked up at her. "That's it?"

"Yes, that's it. We'll start with just a couple numbers, then work our way up to doing more." She slid him a piece of paper and a pencil, and did the same to Roger.

Billy nodded.

"You ready?" she asked.

He nodded again.

"Okay. Two, three, four, one."

Billy wrote quickly then yawned, answering on the exhale. "Ten."

"Okay, good. Next one. Five, two, minus three, four, three."

This time Billy didn't yawn, and his eyes looked a little brighter. He didn't even look up from the paper before saying, "Eleven."

"Right. Next." She gave him a longer list and he gave the correct answer as soon as she finished. Then she starting mixing things up, using decimals, then using actual amounts they charged for food and drink. The lists of numbers got longer and more complicated. Each time he got it right. Each time he answered as soon as she finished talking. His eyes soon glazed over, writing the numbers while his mind added and subtracted each figure as it came.

Roger was writing the numbers too, but Billy was answering faster than Roger could calculate, faster than even he himself could write down the numbers. After a couple times where Roger got the wrong answer and Billy had to wait patiently while Roger redid the problem, even pointing out where Roger forgot to carry a number or added instead of subtracted, Mama Alice acquiesced.

"Okay Billy, I give up. You got the job." She stuck out her hand. "Congratulations."

Suddenly shy, Billy placed his hand in her palm but didn't squeeze. Mama Alice wrapped her fingers around his and moved their hand up and down once, going through the motions with a reluctant partner.

Billy pulled his hand away. "Can I go to bed now, ma'am?"

Mama Alice laughed. "Of course, Billy. You go right ahead. Jake will wake you in the morning when he gets up. Won't you, Jake?" She looked at him out her eye's corner.

"Yes'm," said Jake. Billy looked up at his big brother. "You go on to bed, now. I'll be there in a minute."

After she watched Billy shuffle back to the bedroom, she turned her full gaze onto Jake. "You two are something else. One brother who doesn't stop working and the other with a mind faster than a thoroughbred."

Jake tried to smile, but the weight of her stare kept the corners of his mouth down. His face flushed. All he could manage was, "Thank you, ma'am."

"Here I thought I was doing you a favor taking you in, but maybe you all will be the ones helping me." She put her hands on her hips and blew out a melodramatic sigh. "Well, I'm going to have to tell Henry."

"Are you sure it's okay, ma'am?" asked Jake. "I mean, I don't want to take his job or nothin'."

162

She waved off the comment like she was shooing a fly. "Nonsense, boy. He'll be happy to have less work to do. Now go to bed."

Jake nodded and bid them good night and they bid him the same, turning the keys of the wicks until the lantern flames were thin slivers of orange casting their dull flickers on the sooted glass globes.

Henry was yelling at Mama Alice when Jake left with Billy for Mr. Wilkins's store the next morning, and he was still yelling when they came back. As the boys were helping unload the daily supplies, Henry burst into the double doors and into the kitchen.

"If I'm going to be replaced by a *boy*, at least let me talk to him first," he said.

"How many times do I have to tell you, Henry? He's not replacing you." She was not yelling, but her voice wavered wearily. Jake had never heard her like that.

"Billy? Billy where are you?" asked Henry. The boy's feet rooted themselves to the kitchen floor, and his whole body tensed. Jake put his hand on his brother's shoulder, but Billy was still rigid. He opened his mouth to speak but could not.

Henry walked up to Billy and bent at the waist so his nose almost touched the boy's. Small rivulets of sweat streaking his face fogged his round spectacles, and his quivering nostrils caused his glasses to shake. "So boy, you think you can do my job?"

Billy shook his head but still said nothing. Jake squeezed Billy's shoulder.

"You and your brother come in here, we feed you, give you a place to sleep, even give you a little extra money, and this is the thanks I get?"

This time Jake squeezed his brother hard, and Billy let out a little yelp. "I'm just tryin' to help out, sir. I don't mean no harm by it."

Henry stood up and took in a deep breath. A drop of sweat that had been hanging precariously from the tip of his nose sailed just past Billy's and splatted on the floor. "Is that so? Well, be careful what you wish for. In that case we start today. I'll give you five minutes to eat your breakfast and get out there. We'll see how much you can help."

The man whirled around and stomped back out the doors.

The kitchen was silent until Mama Alice spoke. When she did her voice was little more than a graveled whisper. "Come on, Billy. Let's get you something to eat."

The boys followed Mama Alice as she barked orders at one of the cooks. She directed the boys to sit at the long table running down the center of the kitchen, and soon after they were looking at two plates piled high with potatoes and eggs. Steam rose in warm wisps from the plates. Billy grabbed a fork and scooped food into his mouth. Plumes of steam poured from his lips as he blew on the food and rolled it around on his tongue.

"Sorry I got you into this, little brother."

Billy spoke through his food. "Don't worry about it, Jake. I'll be alright."

"Just do what he says and don't backtalk, even if he's cross."

"I know, Jake. I said don't worry." He shoveled another bite into his mouth.

164

Jake stared at his brother for a while before starting to eat. Even then he watched his brother from the corner of his eye.

Mama Alice came over to them. "Billy, you all done?"

Billy stared at a mostly full plate and nodded, cheeks puffed with food.

"You better get into the office, then. Don't want to keep him waiting first day on the job."

Billy hopped off the stool and walked toward the doors to the saloon. Jake held his full fork halfway to his mouth and watched Billy push through the doors and disappear as they swung closed. He sat in silence until Mama Alice cleared her throat. Jake looked at her. She eyed his plate then him. Lowering his head and raising the plate he poured the rest of its contents into his mouth and finished chewing as he washed the plate and fork.

Jake spent most of the morning at the sink, his neck sore from looking over his shoulder at the doors to the saloon. But Billy only appeared at lunch, and even then only to grab a plate of food and head back to work. He didn't say a word to Jake or anyone else but the cook who served him. Day wore on and night came without warning or announcement but crept in through the window until Jake looked up and was surprised to see blackness framed in its panes.

The pace of work had picked up with the nearing of spring. Though the Kansas prairie still lay hard and frozen some people hoped to get an early start on their pilgrimages west to the green lives they dreamed up in gray cities. But here they met the harsh realities of late winter and stopped to spend the little savings they had on food and shelter in this sparse outpost.

With all the extra customers the kitchen was busier than ever, and that day Jake was so consumed with work he had no time to check in on Billy. He didn't even notice when his brother walked past him to their small bedroom in the back. Only when he went to bed did he see his brother face down on top of his blankets, still wearing his clothes and shoes, a small puddle of drool by his open mouth. He groaned as Jake took off his shoes and rolled him to the side so he could cover him with the blankets, but he did not wake.

The next morning it was Billy who woke Jake. Jake called to him as his brother was reaching to open the door.

"Hey," said Jake.

Billy stopped but did not respond, his hand resting on the doorknob and chin resting on his chest.

"How was it?"

"Alright."

"He's not too mean to you?"

"He's alright."

The room was silent, Jake struggling to find words of comfort. Whether the words were for Billy or himself he did not know. "I'm sorry I got you into this."

For a while Billy said nothing, and Jake wondered if his brother had heard him. Then he drew in a deep breath and let it out slowly. "It's alright," said Billy. He opened the door, and for a moment the light from the kitchen illuminated the rumpled blankets on Billy's bed before the door closed and the room fell dark once more.

That morning at the first opportunity Jake snuck out to the front room. He stood outside the door to the room where Henry usually did the books. There were a few customers eating silently in the early morning stillness. The smell of pork sausage and bacon and eggs and hash brown potatoes filled the room, and Jake's stomach growled. He had been so worried about Billy his breakfast lay uneaten by the sink.

He brought a broom and rag, pretending to dust and sweep as he moved toward the door on the other side of the bar. Mama Alice was still in the kitchen, but Jake kept an eye on the entrance. When he got closer he could noises from behind the door. Shuffling papers. A thud. A muffled shout.

"Godammit boy!" It was Henry. "Don't you know how to add?"

No response from Billy, at least none Jake could hear. Jake craned his ear closer.

"Godammit boy, you did it again!" Jake leaned even closer and without thinking or even realizing his hand moved slowly toward the doorknob.

"Jake?" Mama Alice's admonishing voice made him jump.

"Yes?"

"Don't you have work to do?"

Jake fumbled the broom as he bent to pick up the rag he had dropped. "I was just cleanin' up out here."

Mama Alice squinted down at him. "You think a lot of dust gathered since last night's cleaning?"

"No, ma'am. I mean, yes. It's just—"

"It's just you wanted to check on Billy and wanted to look sly doing it."

"I wasn't tryin'…I mean I didn't mean to-"

"Go back to the kitchen, Jake. You're not needed out here."

Jake's head bent low. "Yes'm." He dragged the broom behind him as he walked toward the double doors. When he was almost there Mama Alice called to him and he turned.

"Jake, you made your choice and so did Billy. Now you let him grow up."

Jake's ears burned red. Her words sounded wise but Jake could not shake the feeling the wedge she had put between him and his brother was pushing Billy further away and closer to her. That by trying to secure their place at Mama Alice's he had merely secured Billy's and made himself more expendable.

That night Billy said nothing despite Jake's pleadings, and the next morning Mama Alice again caught Jake listening at Henry's door. That pattern repeated the next day and the day after and the day after that. Finally Mama Alice gave up and moved Jake to clearing tables and hired someone else to wash dishes. She said she needed the extra help anyway with the increase in customers, and although she said she had acquiesced Jake did not trust her or her motives.

13

Spring came slowly on the plain. Its first whispers were warmer breezes seeping into the frozen cracks of the earth. Then a few hard rains, the first precipitation that was not snow or ice, turned that earth to a thick mud that Jake spent hours scrubbing off the floors at Mama Alice's. At last the first shoots of green emerged from the ground, freed from their icy cocoons.

With warmer weather came wagons. The once desolate main street now thronged with speculators and prospectors and families and cattlemen and carpetbaggers all trying to restock before heading west. The saloon was busier than ever, and most nights Jake and Billy only got a few hours sleep before Mama Alice's hard knocks woke them.

Billy was speaking again to Jake and they were more or less on good terms. After fighting it at first, Henry had come to realize he could let Billy do most of the paperwork and spend more time tending bar which he preferred. Henry still checked Billy's math every night but it was never wrong. And Billy seemed to enjoy the job although Jake saw in him a loss of something, a diminishment of the wide-eyed enthusiasm his brother had once had and it broke Jake's heart every time he looked at Billy.

One afternoon, still in the early part of the Kansas spring, Jake was coming back into the main room of the saloon to clear more plates when he heard the groan of chair legs being dragged hard across the floor planks. Then there was a clatter and crack of the chair back as it fell. A man stood at his table close to the bar.

Jake had not seen this man before, but he had seen his type. Leathered skin from years on the trail and dirt in every crease and crevice of his face. A long faded brown duster and hat of the same shade that seemed permanently attached to his skull. Worn boots and teeth. The rank smells of body odor and alcohol that seemed barely distinguishable from each other.

"Barkeep!" The man shouted.

Henry winced, then looked around for Mama Alice but she was in the kitchen. He cleared his throat. "Yes?"

"I gotta go. How much do I owe you?"

Henry nearly knocked over the glass in his hand as he tried to set it on the bar, and he cleared his throat again. "Billy? Billy? How much does this man owe?"

Billy emerged from the room and brought the book out and placed it at the end of the bar. His eyes tracked his finger down the page of the book in front of him. "Five dollars."

The man grabbed the plate in front of him and slammed it on the floor. When it shattered, whatever patrons had still been talking were silent now and all eyes were on either the man, Henry or Billy standing next to him. "That's horseshit. How you figure that, boy?" He looked down at the white ceramic shards covering his boots and tried to shake them off, but nearly lost his balance in the effort and gave up.

Billy tallied the list of food and drinks—mostly drinks—the man ordered. Then Henry added ten cents, whining that the man would pay for the plate he just broken. The man took one of the many shot glasses on his table and hurled it at Henry. "I ain't payin' for nothin'." Then he stumbled over to Billy. "Let me see that book here." His hand wavered in front of Billy, and Billy closed the book and clutched it to his chest. He shook his head silently. Jake moved closer.

170

The man slammed his fist on the bar. "I said gimme the goddamn book, boy!"

Billy shook his head again and said, "You owe five dollars."

The man scoffed. "Five dollars? I didn't even drink half those drinks you said. Count 'em again."

"You bought drinks for all those men. You owe five dollars."

"Now don't get smart with me, boy. I know how much I bought and it weren't five dollars worth. Be careful you don't call me a liar."

Billy repeated the amount again as if the saying of it would somehow convince the man, would protect Billy from his ire.

The man slammed his fist again and lowered his face toward Billy's. Jake moved closer. "You better not say that again or I'm gonna knock those words right out of your mouth. Now tell me again how much I owe."

Billy pulled the book even tighter to his chest and stood frozen, saying nothing.

"I said tell me how much I owe."

Billy's nose scrunched as the man's breath reached his nostrils, but still he said nothing.

"Godammit boy, I'll show you how to respect your elders." The man raised his hand in the air and brought it down on Billy's face.

The sound of slap filled the quiet room. Quickly, moved by some uncontrollable engine of anger, Jake rushed toward the man. He did not even remember grabbing a bottle from the bar, or raising it and bringing it down on the man's head. He only remembered standing over him gripping the broken bottle, the man clutching his face and wallowing in a pool of

171

blood and alcohol, the smell of cheap whiskey and screams of the man rising from the floor.

Jake looked up and rested his eyes on Billy, and Billy's eyes stayed stuck on Jake. Whatever distance had come between them disappeared. At first Jake did not hear Mama Alice making her way through the crowd of men, but when in his periphery he saw movement his senses returned and he heard her calm yet forceful voice persuading the customers to sit down, that everything was fine.

For a moment silence and stillness hung in the air. Even Mama Alice had stopped speaking, as if she too were wondering what would happen next. Then Jake felt a rush of air by his ear, followed by a crash of glass against the wall behind the bar. From behind him a man let out a yell, wild and almost celebratory. Jake turned and saw him glaring back, a maniacal grin on his face.

"Damn, I missed," said the man.

Someone next to him sucker punched him from the side, knocking him to the floor. "Don't go after a kid, asshole."

Another man threw a glass, and the man who had thrown the punch ducked out of the way. The glass flew past his shoulder and hit another man square in the face, breaking as it bloodied him. The man who threw it laughed.

"No, no, no," said Mama Alice weakly. Jake looked at Billy. His little brother's eyes were wide, his cheek a bright red where the man had struck him. He reached for Billy and wrapped both arms around him, bringing him to a crouch by the bar. "Stay with me," he said.

The saloon erupted in violence. Chairs, glasses, bottles and punches were all being thrown as Jake tried to drag Billy through the melee and into the kitchen. Several times flying shards hit him, and he had to cover his brother to protect him from the shrapnel.

Close to the end of the bar, Jake stopped. In the unsheltered gulf between there and the double doors leading to the kitchen, several men were fighting. Jake waited for them to move on.

"You okay?" he asked his brother.

"Yeah," said Billy. "You?"

"Yep. Just want to get out of here. Hold on tight."

Just then Jake felt a grip like iron around his leg. He looked at Billy and Billy at him, but before Jake could speak his leg was yanked out from under him. His shoulder slammed into the floor, and he was dragged into the fray.

As he slid across the floor, he turned onto his back to see who was pulling him. The man's face was covered in blood, but Jake recognized him. It was the man he had hit. Frantically Jake tried to claw at anything he could use to pull himself away. He grabbed a chair, but it crashed to the floor and came with him. Then he wrapped his arms around a man's leg, but as soon as the man's foot came off the floor, Jake lost his hold.

Jake bounced off an overturned table, skidding into a man's leg. The man yelled and kicked Jake in the ribs, but before Jake could even register the pain he was pulled into a small clearing in the middle of the mass of men. The man he had hit grabbed him by the shirt and yanked him upright.

His face was streaked with red, his breath so heavy with alcohol Jake coughed on the fumes. He held Jake close, and Jake could see the lines in his yellowed, bloodshot eyes.

"You little shit," said the man. "I'm gonna give you a hurtin' like you ain't never had." He shook Jake hard, and Jake felt his head whip back and forth. "You feel brave now?"

Jake clutched at the man's large hands, trying desperately to pry the man's fingers from his shirt. But his grip was iron. The man set Jake down and let go with one hand, balling the other in a fist and cocking it back. Jake's boots slid on the slick wooden floor as he tried to pull himself free.

The loud boom of a shotgun thundered over the din of shouts and crashes, and the saloon fell silent. Momentarily the man's grip on Jake slackened, and Jake jerked himself free, crashing to the floor. Above him all the men stared toward where the sound had come from, hands on their holstered pistols.

"Get out! Get out of my saloon and don't come back!" Mama Alice's voice was shrill. Jake had never heard her sound like that. Her voice had lost all power, all semblance of calm. To Jake she sounded like a terrified ewe defending her kids.

In the stunned silence Jake began to slither through the legs of tables and men. No one else moved until Mama Alice yelled again, and even then the exodus was slow. Jake's heart pounded fast as he crawled through the crowd to get to Billy. He could not see his brother, and hoped he was still hiding underneath the bar.

At last he broke free of the crowd moving toward the door, but when he got to the bar his brother was not there.

"Billy!" Jake looked around frantically. "Billy!"

From behind the bar Billy poked out his head. A huge wave of relief washed over Jake. He grabbed his brother. "Come on."

Dragging Billy by the sleeve, Jake hurried across the saloon to the double doors of the kitchen. They slammed through them and escaped into the kitchen. Inside was a quiet oasis. None of the workers were there, and Jake guessed they had gone to help stop the fight. He took Billy into their room, closed the door behind him and locked it.

Billy sat on the bed as Jake lit the lantern. When the wick was glowing, Jake brought the light to his brother's face. "You alright?" he asked.

"Yeah," said Billy. "Thanks. Jake?"

"Yeah?"

"I could've handled it with that man."

"I know," said Jake. "I was just making sure."

"Jake?"

"Yeah?"

"You got real mad."

"I know't," said Jake. "I don't like nobody hittin' you."

There was a pause before Billy spoke again. "Do you think that man will be alright?"

Jake felt a flush of anger. Before he could stop them, the words escaped his mouth. "To tell the truth, I don't care."

Billy said nothing, and through the walls Jake could hear the noise coming from the saloon. He listened, trying to determine if everyone had left. After a while, the sounds died down. When it was nearly silent, Billy spoke again.

"Jake?"

"Yeah?"

"Mama Alice is going to be mad."

"She sure is."

As if on cue, there was a loud knock on the door so hard it rattled the hinges. "Jake? You in there? This is the sheriff."

Jake jolted back. "Just a second, Sheriff." He pulled his brother close and in a low whisper he told him what to do. Keep working. Do exactly what Mama Alice tells you. Make sure to check the money every night when you hide it and above all keep the gun close. Make sure it's oiled and loaded. As he spoke Billy nodded but said nothing.

Jake stood up and straightened his clothes. He turned to Billy. "Don't worry, little brother. It'll be alright."

The sheriff's voice boomed from the other side of the door. "Come on now, Jake. I don't want to have to come in there after you."

The click of Jake's boot heels and the creak of floorboards filled the tiny room as Jake took the two steps toward the door and opened it. In the door stood framed the sheriff's silhouette. He took up nearly the entire entryway. The light had to bend around him to reach the room. His hand was resting on the butt of his pistol, but when he saw Jake small and thin and swimming in his clothes he dropped it down at his side. Behind him stood Mama Alice, fists dug into the billowing fabric of her dress.

"Son, you gotta come with me."

Jake walked toward him. The sheriff looked over Jake's shoulder at Billy, but looked quickly away. He lowered his head and said something, but it was mumbled and Jake couldn't hear it. Then the sheriff raised his head. "Let's go," was all he said.

Mama Alice walked toward the back door and Jake followed, the sheriff behind him. The men in the kitchen lined the narrow walkway between the stations like soldiers honoring a fallen comrade. Jake did not look at any of them, but stared straight ahead and they bowed their heads as he walked by. When she got to the door Mama Alice opened it, and Jake felt the cool spring air rush in around his legs. His feet grew suddenly cold. He stopped at the door, but the sheriff didn't and nearly knocked Jake into the doorjamb. Jake looked up, and when he saw the way Mama Alice was looking at him, he knew he would never work for her again.

Once they were outside she commanded the sheriff to take Jake to the jail and watch over him, to make sure none of the friends of the man Jake hit came and tried to get at Jake.

"You sure you want me to do this?" asked the man. "I ain't gonna arrest no one else. They cleaned up their own mess."

"This is the boy who started it," said Mama Alice. Her voice was shrill, and her eyes bore holes into Jake. "He needs to be charged."

"With what?"

"Isn't that your job?"

"Come on Alice," said the sheriff. "You're being unreasonable."

"That's Mama Alice to you, sheriff. Did you forget the name of the woman who got you elected?"

The giant of a man heaved a large sigh. "No, ma'am."

"Then you figure out what you need to charge him with, and you do it."

"Yes, ma'am," was all the sheriff said.

Then she looked at Jake, fists still resting on her hips in a pose of permanent scold. "Don't worry about Billy. I'll take care of him." Her elbows almost clipped Jake as she spun around and walked to the door. She slammed the door behind her, leaving Jake and the sheriff in the silent dirt behind the restaurant.

They stood there for a time, Jake watching the sheriff and waiting. The sheriff was looking at the door almost as if he was expecting Mama Alice to come back, afraid to raise his head completely. The door remained closed and he mumbled something under his breath and looked at Jake. Without a word he started walking. Jake followed.

They walked away from Mama Alice's along the back sides of the buildings, and did not get back onto the main street until they were well away from the saloon. Dodging horses and carriages and people rushing and bumping, they crossed the street and toward the jail. Jake had never been inside it, but passed it many times on his errands to Mr. Wilkins's store.

It was a plain, squat wooden building entirely unremarkable and indistinguishable from all the others on the street save the rusted wrought iron bars bolted outside the windows. There was also a large iron lock on the door, and the sheriff pulled from his pocket a heavy black key that he stuck into the lock and turned. From inside the door the workings creaked and shuddered, and the sheriff removed the key from the door and put it in his pocket.

Inside there was a small desk with two chairs and a dilapidated cabinet with peeling, faded varnish. Above the cabinet teetered a single shelf secured by nails toed in yet not hammered flush. On top lay two law volumes, one flat on its side and the other tilted on top the first. A small ceramic vase held a browned, bent flower that wilted toward the floor. The dim light creeping through the bars on the windows cast eerie striped shadows that warped to cover the floor and furniture.

To the right of the shelf was a large nail with a ring of keys, and the sheriff took the key from his pocket and removed the ring of keys before placing the lone key on the nail. A wheezing, rattling cough from the next room startled Jake. His eyes adjusted and he could see through a doorless frame vertical iron bars that formed part of a cell. When he followed the sheriff he saw the cell was empty, but the cell next to it held an old man who sat in shadow in the corner. The man said nothing.

Sheepishly the sheriff opened the door to the first cell and beckoned Jake inside. Jake took one step and hesitated. There were no windows in this room and when Jake saw the dark recesses of the cell he could not move forward nor look away, as if the sheriff had put on him manacles and nailed those manacles to floor. The sheriff cleared his throat and made a sweeping motion with his arm ushering Jake like a doorman at a fancy hotel. Jake looked at the man standing there, paunch pushing his shirt untucked and pudgy cheeks red and flushed. Jake tried to look him in the eyes but the man could not or would not raise his eyes to meet Jake's. For a while Jake stood there and even contemplated turning and leaving but the sheriff looked up finally. "Come on, Jake," he pleaded.

Jake looked at the man then into the cell and sighed and walked inside and sat down on the long wooden bench tilted against the wall. He did not look at the sheriff but only heard the metal clang as the man closed the door and locked it. Then the shuffle of the sheriff's feet and the groan of the chair as he sat at his desk. Another croaking cough from the man in the cell next to him and Jake sat in the darkness and fixed his eyes on the sparse sunlight that illuminated a small patch on the floor in front of him.

That patch had long since carved its path across the floor and disappeared before Jake received his first visitor. It was not who he expected. Billy maybe, although he'd doubt Mama Alice would let him go. Maybe Mama Alice would come, or Henry in her place. But instead it was Mr. Wilkins who

179

walked through the door. Before he said a word to Jake, he turned back to the sheriff who was still seated at his desk.

"What you got him locked behind these bars for, John? You think he's going to run away?"

Jake could hear the sheriff bumble to his feet. "Well, Mama Alice said—"

"Is Alice sheriff or are you?"

"Well, I just—"

"Let the boy out a minute so I can feed him this dinner the missus made for him."

"I don't know, Bill. You know the law as well as I do."

"Come on, John. You can even lock the front door if you like."

There was a pause before the sheriff spoke. For a while Jake thought he wouldn't let him out. "Aw, hell. Who the hell am I? Just the sheriff, that's who." The man pushed past Mr. Wilkins and opened the cell door. Its hinges creaked as it swung open. The sheriff moved out of the way, and only then did Jake notice the smell coming from the basket in Mr. Wilkins's hand. Corn bread. Chicken. Something sweet like pie. His stomach growled.

Jake looked at Mr. Wilkins and Mr. Wilkins smiled. "Come on, boy. Let's get you a proper supper."

Despite the sheriff's protestations Mr. Wilkins commandeered his desk and placed the dinner on it, and he and Jake pulled up the two chairs and ate. At first Jake said nothing but tore away at his food. All day his stomach had been in knots over his fate and more importantly his brother's fate that he had no appetite. But Mr. Wilkins's arrival meant Jake would get news of Billy, and since the man hadn't said anything yet Jake figured his brother was okay. As Jake ate

Mr. Wilkins sat there hands folded, smiling at Jake. The sheriff stewed in the corner, pretending to rearrange something in the cabinet.

The first words Jake spoke to Mr. Wilkins were after he stopped eating. "Thanks for supper, Mr. Wilkins. I sure appreciate it."

"My pleasure, boy."

"And thanks to Mrs. Wilkins, too. She sure is a good cook."

"She'll be glad you liked it, Jake."

Jake stared at his plate and picked up cornbread crumbs with his fork as he tried to figure out how to ask about Billy.

"I suppose you're wanting to know about Billy," said Mr. Wilkins.

Jake's head came up quickly. "Yes, sir."

"I went and checked on him this afternoon before coming over here. He's fine, Jake. Just fine." Mr. Wilkins looked at Jake as the boy kept his eyes lowered on the clean plate in front of him. "How are you doing, son?"

Jake felt a tightness in his throat and the beginning of a tear well up in his eye. He pretended he had to cough and wiped it away with his sleeve. "Alright," he said barely above a whisper. He cleared his throat. "I'm alright."

Mr. Wilkins nodded. "They told you anything about what they're thinking of doing with you?"

"No, sir."

"Well I wouldn't worry about it, Jake. There's been plenty of men got off easy for doing a lot more than you did. Looks like a clear case of defending your brother." This last sentence he said loudly enough for the sheriff to here, and when Mr. Wilkins paused for breath he even looked up at him. When he turned back to Jake he lowered his voice. "Besides, the man ain't got nothing but a couple cuts on his head."

Mr. Wilkins moved close and spoke in a whisper. The sheriff did not look at them, but he stopped what he was doing to listen. "Jake, Mama Alice is hopping mad. She says you drove away her customers. Talking about how her saloon was the only saloon in town that never had a fight, and now she's just like the rest of them."

Jake nodded. "I know't. I shouldn't have done that."

Mr. Wilkins reached across the table and grabbed Jake's wrist. "Hey, look at me." Jake's eyes made it only to the man's shoulder before they couldn't go any farther. "You did the right thing, Jake. Don't let anybody tell you different."

Jake looked like he would speak but then didn't, pulling away from Mr. Wilkins and leaning back in his chair, arms folded across his chest, eyes staring off into the dusty corner by the door. Mr. Wilkins stood up and walked over to Jake. He rested his hand on the boy's shoulder and patted it. The sheriff looked over at them.

"Alright, John. You can have him back." Mr. Wilkins turned to Jake. "You take care, son. I'll come back and see you tomorrow."

The man put on his hat and Jake stood to shake his hand. "Thank you, sir. And thanks to Mrs. Wilkins for the food."

Mr. Wilkins said nothing but smiled and nodded before turning toward the door. The open door let in light unfiltered by iron bars and for a moment Jake felt the last warmth of the day, the dreary room transformed ever so briefly into something more vibrant. But then the door closed and dusty darkness fell once more. The sheriff walked him back to his cell and locked the iron enclosure.

That night was cold and dark despite the spring warming, and the snoring and coughing of the old man next to him kept Jake awake most of the night. The room was so dark it felt like the noise was surrounding him, vibrating from within the rough walls to shake the room.

Jake woke tired. That morning Mama Alice came to see him. He heard her barking orders at the sheriff as soon as the door to the street opened. Heard her heels hammering the wooden floor. Heard her exhalations of disdain as she peered at him through the bars.

"Well Jake, you got us in a fine mess now."

"Ma'am?" He was not sure what she meant by 'us.'

She ignored Jake's question and began pacing the room. The man in the next cell was still asleep, muttering to himself. Motes of dust floated in the lone, stark sunbeam slicing through the room, and they scattered and swirled in eddies behind her.

"Business is already down, I can tell. My reputation is shot now that you—" she stopped right in front of Jake's cell and glared at him. "Did you know that until yesterday my saloon had never had an incident of violence? Not one?"

"No ma'am." Jake was not sure what she meant, since he had seen plenty of men almost come to blows.

"And now I've gotta deal with that idiot sheriff."

"Hey!" shouted the sheriff from the other room. Mama Alice paid no mind.

"And all the customers who'd rather look at the blood spot on the floor than order food or drinks. Do you know how hard it is to get a blood stain out of a wooden floor?" This last question she said to no one in particular. "And of course I have to find someone to take your place. That's not easy, Jake.

183

You weren't good at a lot of things, but at least you were a good worker."

"Ma'am?"

"Not now, Jake. I'm busy thinking."

"Ma'am?"

"I said not now, Jake!"

"Ma'am?"

"As usual you don't listen." She stopped in front of his cell once more, thrust her fists into her hips and snorted. "Well, what do you want?"

"How's my brother?"

The scowl on her face softened and she lifted one hand palm up. "Well, of course you'd like to know about your brother. It's only natural." She cleared her throat. "Billy's safe and sound, Jake. Don't you worry about him." As quickly as it had left her scowl returned. "I'd worry more about yourself."

Jake's head bowed low. Mama Alice stared at him, awaiting a response. "Well," she said, "I'll tell your brother you're alright." She turned to go but stopped herself. "Oh, I almost forgot. He asked me to give you this." From the pocket of her skirt emerged her fist enclosed around something Jake could not see. He stuck his arm through the bars of his cell and in that hand she placed Billy's rock. Jake drew it back through the bars and to his face. For the first time since his arrest he smiled.

Later that day Mr. Wilkins visited again. And again he brought food but this time it took much more convincing to let Jake out of the cell. After opening the cell the sheriff left in a huff mumbling something.

As Jake ate Mr. Wilkins watched in silence, allowing the boy to enjoy what little comfort his meal could bring. When Jake finished Mr. Wilkins eyed him a while longer, clearing his throat before he spoke.

"You know, Jake. That old boy you cut up ain't doing too good."

"No?" Jake swallowed though he had no food in his mouth.

The man shook his head. "Went and got himself a fever. And his head is all swollen and sore. Doctor said he's seen something like this before, and it ain't usually good."

"How'd you find out?" Jake stuttered.

Mr. Wilkins smiled. "Everybody in this town's gotta buy food, and my store's the place to do it." He cleared his throat again. "Jake, you know what that means for you if he dies."

Jake nodded. "Yes, sir. I suppose so."

The man lowered his voice even though the sheriff was gone. "Normally this town don't mind a killing or two, especially if you're defending someone, but Mama Alice, she's got...a certain influence around here."

"Yes, sir." Jake carved into the wooden desk with the handle of his fork.

"I don't suppose I need to tell you her intentions."

Jake carved a long semicircle before answering. "No, sir."

"Long time ago she lost a child, Jake. A boy, a bit younger than Billy."

Jake nodded. "I understand."

Mr. Wilkins leaned even closer. "We need to get you out of here, son. Tonight."

Jake nodded again. "And Billy?"

"Of course."

"You gotta talk to him."

"I don't know if he'll remember me."

"He'll remember you."

"All the same I'd like to have something only you and him know about so he can trust me."

Jake fingered Billy's magic rock in his pocket but thought better. He eyed Mr. Wilkins, wondering if he could trust this man with his life and Billy's. He realized he had no choice. "Just tell him to trust you like he trusted Mr. McCready."

"McCready is it?"

"Yes, sir."

"Alright, son." He pushed himself away from the table and stood up. "I promised the sheriff I'd put you back in there." Jake got up and walked back to his cell and Mr. Wilkins closed the door behind him and locked it. "Don't worry. This won't be for too long." He smiled but Jake did not. The lump in his throat prevented it.

Mr. Wilkins put his hat back. "Don't sleep too heavy tonight."

Jake shook his head. "No, sir. I won't."

The shadows in the jailhouse grew longer as Jake waited, and the pall of night encompassed the whole of the town and the Kansas plain and the moon and stars shone their pale gray glow so that the buildings seemed illuminated by some internal lantern and then clouds covered the sky and the shadow spread darkness over the world and still Jake waited. The jailhouse quiet save the stuttered snoring of the night watchman. The wick in the lamp long extinguished. The drunken cacophonies of the saloons rising and falling with the wind from the west.

Jake's nerves and anticipation kept him awake but after hours of dark inactivity his energy waned. His head nodded as he sat on the bench that doubled as his bed and he kept jerking his head up against the yoke of sleep. Yet still no sound or movement or sign and soon sleep overcame him and he rested his elbows on his knees and head in his hands and slept.

The sound of grating metal and then a loud click woke him. Then the slow whine of rusty hinges and the groan of a floorboard. Another whine and click. More groans. The wakening snore of the night watchman. The man cleared his throat. "Who's that?"

"Go back to sleep, Jimmy. It's just me, Bill."

Again the floor groaned but it stopped when the night watchman spoke. "Hold up, Bill. Where you goin'?"

"You know where I'm going and what I'm doing."

Jake expected more groans but this time there was only silence as the two men waited for the other to speak.

"I can't let you do that, Bill."

"Yes you can."

"But John will kill me."

"John couldn't kill anybody if he tried."

"But he'll throw me in jail."

"Just say someone came while you were out back taking a leak and by the time you got back the boy was gone." Mr. Wilkins began walking again toward Jake's cell, and Jake heard the watchman's chair scrape across the floor as he stood up. Then there was the loud click of a shotgun being pumped and the hollow rattling of the slug in the chamber.

"You don't want to do that, Jimmy. Take it out nice and slow. Come on, now. That's it. Now come around your desk and put it on the floor." Jake heard four slow footsteps and the rattle of something on the floor. "Now kick it over to me." There was a scrape and rattle as the pistol made its way to Mr. Wilkins.

"You gonna give it back to me?" The watchman's voice was trembling now.

"Don't think that's a good idea," said Mr. Wilkins.

"But what am I going to tell John when he asks where my pistol went?"

"You should've thought of that before you put your hand on it. Now grab them keys and open the boy's door. We ain't got all night."

Jake heard the man sigh before the rattle of the keys pierced the quiet. Footsteps approached in the dark, then the amorphous black forms of their bodies emerging through the doorway.

Mr. Wilkins spoke first. "Evening, Jake."

"Sir," responded the boy.

"Open the door, Jimmy."

The watchman stepped forward and inserted the key, then turned it and opened the door while Mr. Wilkins stood back and watched with the shotgun held across his waist. When the door opened Jake stood and walked through. He kept going through the doorway to the entry room and Mr. Wilkins followed backing in, and without a word the two walked out the jailhouse.

The clouds still covered the night sky and Jake stayed close to Mr. Wilkins so they appeared one being as they walked. They stuck to the shadows before finding an opening to duck off the main street and sneak around the backs of the buildings. Neither spoke as they made their way back to

Mama Alice's, where Jake hid behind the outhouse with Mr. Wilkins. Jake moved toward the door and Mr. Wilkins grabbed his arm. "He'll come," said the man.

Before long the light on the ground outside the kitchen changed. From his vantage point Jake saw a triangle of light spread wide across the dirt and heard the door slam. Footsteps scraped along the gravel and loose dirt and Jake poked his head around the outhouse. Mr. Wilkins yanked him back and Jake tumbled into the man. He held Jake still as someone opened the outhouse door and slammed open the lid and sat down and grunted and groaned as the sounds of his efforts reached the waste below. Jake shoved his face into Mr. Wilkins's coat to keep from gagging at the smell.

The man finished and opened the door before walking back to the kitchen. He had closed the lid so the foul emanations abated to tolerable levels, and Jake and Mr. Wilkins continued their wait. There was no sound or movement or change in light from the kitchen other than the normal clanks and clangs and flitting of shadows as men moved in the lantern light. The triangle appeared and disappeared several times and each time man and boy suffered silently behind the outhouse as men used it. Still no sign of Billy.

For a while there were no visitors to the outhouse and Jake began to think his brother would not show. But then the triangle appeared once more, this time with no sound. The triangle grew and shrank and disappeared. Jake strained his ears to hear footsteps but still there was nothing but the fading sounds of the night.

Then a form rounded the corner of the outhouse, the face of the person backlit and in shadow. Jake startled. The form kept moving toward them and Jake saw it was only a boy. In two steps he recognized the gait of his brother.

Billy's face emerged from the shadow of the outhouse and the moon glow gave features to his face. He looked at Mr. Wilkins and his brother and nodded. They nodded back.

In the pale starlight of the clear evening their breaths hung cold around their heads like vaporous auras. The soft, rhythmic crunch of their boots on the dirt underfoot faded into the wooden walls of the buildings they walked behind. Jake did not know where they were going and Billy gave no indication he knew but they both followed Mr. Wilkins as he headed west.

They passed silent black buildings and saloons with light and sound still spilling out as the moon continued its descent toward the horizon, boys and man and celestial object all pulled west as if by some force great and inexplicable and implacable. When they reached the edge of town Mr. Wilkins signaled them to stop and hide in the corner shadow of the last building and they did. Jake squinted his eyes against the glare of the moon and tried to see where Mr. Wilkins walked. In the distance he could make out vague shapes in the prairie grass like small hills or burial mounds that broke up an otherwise endless flatness. But then one of the shapes moved and Jake saw they were wagons.

Mr. Wilkins came back toward town, his pin-thin shadow slicing through the wide swath of silver moonlight sprawling over the grass. For the first time since they left the jail Mr. Wilkins spoke, yet only in the lowest of whispers.

"You boys got all you need?"

Jake turned to Billy and his little brother nodded.

"Well, alright then. Follow me. Single file and close behind. We don't want to take any chances."

Billy grabbed Mr. Wilkins's coat and held his belongings slung over his shoulder with his other hand. Jake looked like Billy's larger twin as they walked toward the wagons. Nocturnal hunchbacks inching toward black hulks set against the light-spattered sky, making no noise save the rustle of the grass against their legs. Carried on the wind were sounds from the wagons. The snort of a horse. The groan of leather and jangle of metal from harnesses.

From the long shadows extending from the wagons Jake saw a man standing behind the one closest to them. He strained his eyes and ears but no sign of life came from the other wagons. They were introduced in low voices to a man named Mr. Ferris who delivered goods to Mr. Wilkins. Jake thought he recognized the name and voice, but the man's face was still covered in shadow. When he stepped into the moonlight and Jake saw his gray whiskers and rounded silhouette, Jake knew it was the man he thought it was.

"Boys," said Mr. Wilkins. "Hide out in the back of this wagon. Hide out 'til you think you can't hide out any longer then hide some more. Mr. Ferris here is a good man and trustworthy but he ain't goin' to fight no law nor should you expect him to."

"No sir," said Jake.

That sheriff's going to be mad as hell I took you from that cell, Jake, so the longer you hide out the safer my hide's going to be."

Jake swung his bag down and reached into it. "I'd like to pay you for your troubles, Mr. Wilkins."

The old man waved his hand. "Don't even think about it, Jake. You're going to need it more than I will."

Jake removed his hand from his bag. "Yes, sir. Thank you, sir."

Mr. Wilkins stared off in the direction of town. "Alright, Jake."

Billy hid his head in Jake's jacket. Mr. Wilkins looked back at the boys and put his hand on Billy's shoulder. "You take care of each other now, you hear?"

Billy nodded.

"Good. Now let me help you up, son."

He reached a hand toward Billy but Billy just handed him his bag and climbed up before taking the bag back. Jake stood there in front of Mr. Wilkins his hand outstretched, and Mr. Wilkins took it and with his other hand held Jake's arm and they stood there in the tall grass. Jake could not see his eyes nor his face, but he knew this moment would be their last together.

"Thank you, sir."

Mr. Wilkins pulled his hands back. "Alright, Jake. Now get going."

"Yes, sir." Jake handed Billy his bag and pulled himself into the back of the wagon. Mr. Ferris handed the boys two blankets apiece. The boys lay down and Mr. Ferris covered them with the canvas tarp and tied it down. He nodded to Mr. Wilkins and the man nodded back and Mr. Ferris walked toward the horses and climbed onto the driver's seat and grabbed the reins and clicked and the horses and driver and wagon lurched forward. Jake and Billy were silent in back, and as they rolled away Jake looked through the flap at Mr. Wilkins standing sill in the moonlight and watching as the wagon swayed. He was still watching when the wagon dipped down below the dark horizon.

14

The first three days the boys could tell day from night only by the dull light that seeped through the thick canvas of the wagon cover. Other than for bathroom breaks and at night to stretch their legs Jake and Billy stayed concealed in the bed of the wagon. On the fourth day the driver poked his head through the back opening and said without ceremony, "Y'all can probably come out now," and Jake and Billy emerged with the curved backs and aching joints of old men.

Mr. Ferris stood waiting while the boys stretched their legs. He stared north at the twin threads of wagon tracks wending through infinite flatlands. Brown skeletons of prairie grasses covered the ground. No green to decorate the landscape save the occasional stand of pines. No smoke from fires. No buildings.

Jake's feet stabbed at the ground like a stumbling newborn colt and he walked to Mr. Ferris's side.

"Where we headed?"

Mr. Ferris pointed his nose north. "Mr. Wilkins said he's got a sister in Nebraska who will take you boys in. I got a letter here for her that asks her to do just that." He patted his coat pocket.

"Well thank you very much sir, but we don't want to be a bother," said Jake.

"He said you'd say that."

"Me and Billy can just find our own way from here. Thanks very much for your help."

Mr. Ferris smiled. "He said you'd say that, too. You must be crazy son, if you think you two can go off by yourselves. We're moving up toward Indian territory."

"I ain't got no problems with Indians."

"Well that may be, but they might have a problem with you."

Jake stood and stared in the same direction as the man. He spat at the ground but the wind took it away and dropped it somewhere in the waving strands of dead grass. "Just the same I don't want us to be a burden."

"Don't you worry about that. I plan to put you to work."

Jake stood for a while longer but when the man said no more Jake spat again. "I'll go check on Billy."

Jake checked Billy and Billy said he was fine so Jake came back to Mr. Ferris and asked if he could do anything. Mr. Ferris asked him if he knew horses and Jake said he did, and Mr. Ferris said he wouldn't mind napping while Jake took the reins for a little. Jake agreed and Billy sat up front with him, and Mr. Ferris lay in back where the boys once lay and slept as Jake steered the wagon north.

Another week passed without event. Mr. Ferris and Jake took turns with the horses and when Jake was up front and Mr. Ferris asleep in the back Jake let Billy hold the reins awhile despite Mr. Ferris's admonitions. On the rutted road north they saw oak and maple and pine and spruce and vast plains. A few buildings dotted the land at odd and undefined intervals and the occasional cattle moved slowly across the landscape or stood motionless save their circular chewing as they stared at the clumsy contraption reeling along the bumpy

195

road. But mostly the land was an endless sea of brown rolling in long slow smooth waves from horizon to horizon.

In Nebraska they stopped outside a small gathering of buildings not quite town and Jake and Billy unloaded the supplies for dinner and set up the tarp Mr. Ferris slept under. They built a fire and cooked dinner and afterward cleaned up. The moon rose and they stared at the fire, talking little and saying less. Eventually the conversation stopped altogether and they moved closer to the fire and lay back and looked at the blanket of stars.

"Jake?" Mr. Ferris's voice startled Jake in the silence.

"Yessir?"

"Mr. Wilkins paid me to take you to his sister and I intend to do that but you and Billy are good workers. If you'd like I can take you up to Indian Territory. I got a shipment of goods I gotta trade for up there and you're welcome to come along if you want."

For a while Jake said nothing, the stars giving no answer save their ancient light. Billy was silent beside him. "Can't get to California sitting around in Nebraska."

"What's that?" asked Mr. Ferris.

"Yeah," said Jake. "Yeah, we'll go."

"Alright." The man rolled over and repositioned his pillow and blanket. "Best get some sleep, then. We got a long day ahead of us tomorrow."

Jake nudged Billy to go to the wagon but his brother was fast asleep, so he went back to the wagon and grabbed two blankets. He placed both over Billy and lifted his brother's head and placed a rolled-up shirt under and placed his own makeshift pillow beside. The fire's light and warmth waned, flickering and distant like the stars. Next to the fire lay the last bundle of logs gathered from a nearby grove of trees and he placed half next to the blankets. The other half he rested on top the last glowing coals and he blew softly until a faint flame licked at the cold bark. When the dry wood caught fire he crawled next to his brother and pulled the blanket over himself, curling close to the pocket of warmth surrounding his brother.

The next morning frost clung to the tips of the dead strands of grass, bending them low like sun worshippers bowing to greet their god. The first rays of light reached through the icy crystals and spilled their hidden colors. Stained glass windows on the plains. The fire had died and the boys earlier in the night had covered themselves wholly with the blankets so that now they looked like two lumps of dirt dug up by some enormous prairie dog.

Jake rustled first and saw his brother was still sleeping, so he stayed in the warmth under the blanket. When he heard Mr. Ferris clunking around in the wagon, Jake nudged his brother.

"Billy?"

His brother groaned.

"Wake up, little brother. Mr. Ferris is up."

Billy groaned again, so Jake tore the blanket off both of them and Billy gasped at the cold.

"Dang, Jake. Give me some warning."

"Waking you up was warning enough." Jake glared at his brother, and Billy gave him the scowl of someone woken too soon. Jake's face broke into a wide grin. He grabbed the blanket and jumped up and ran away with it trailing behind.

Billy yelped and leapt up and ran three steps before slipping on the wet grass and falling forward. When he raised his head, stiff brown strands of grass protruded in wet clumps from his face. He yelled and pushed himself up but at first his slick boots couldn't gain purchase on the grass and his legs flew out behind him. At last he stood but by then he was too out of breath and laughing so hard he rolled onto his back and clutched his convulsing belly. Jake stared at him from a distance, hands on his knees, chest heaving and the same grin still stuck on his face.

"You boys finished horsin' around enough to help me with breakfast?" asked Mr. Ferris.

Jake stood up and stopped laughing. "Yes, sir. Sorry." He unloaded the box of provisions from the wagon and Billy scrambled to bring the large pot. The small one was already on the fire with coffee grinds swirling in the last of the liquid. The boys filled the pot with water from the canteen and watched it heat before throwing in the oats and stirring them until they were cooked and serving them in small metal cups. Mr. Ferris just nodded for Jake to add the cooked oats to the last of the coffee in his cup and the three ate in silence. When they finished they cleaned their cups with strands of grass now wet with melted frost and packed their supplies before stomping out the fire and climbing in the wagon to head north.

The coming days brought warmer winds from the north, and with that warmth came the first green shoots poking through the brown bone yard skeletons of their fathers. They passed towns neither boy had heard of and collections of buildings too small to warrant a name. As the wagon wound through the faint tracks in the tall grass, flocks of pheasant would alight in front of them and escape to the nearest shelter of trees. If no trees they would fly low over the ground, shrinking black dots vanishing into the pale prairie sky.

It had been days since Jake had seen a building of any kind when he asked Mr. Ferris when they would get to Indian Territory. They were sitting up front in the wagon, and Billy was asleep in the back.

"Already here," was his reply. "Been here for three days or so."

Jake swiveled his head to take stock of the country.

Mr. Ferris laughed. "Tough to tell unless you know what you're looking for. This here is where the Sioux live, although they don't call themselves that."

"What do they call themselves?"

"Lakota."

Jake scanned the horizon, half expecting them to appear right before him. "Where we headed?"

"What you mean?"

"Like what's the name of the town?"

"Ain't no town to speak of. Hell, almost every time I come up here they're in a different place."

"Then how you know where to go?"

Mr. Ferris smiled. "No need to go anywhere. They'll find us."

"But how you know they won't attack you?"

Mr. Ferris shrugged. "They know me 'round these parts." Just then one of the horses slowed and bent down toward a clump of new grass. Mr. Ferris clicked his tongue. "Come on, boy. It ain't lunchtime yet." The wagon lurched forward and Jake settled back in his seat, looking out over the plains for any signs of horse or man.

It was the next day when they met their hosts. Jake almost fell out of his seat when he saw them. He had been staring at the rise and fall of the land seeing nothing but grass and trees when the plains seemed to come to life. First one then two then five men in buckskin pants and shirts came walking toward them. Mr. Ferris pulled on the reins and the horses stopped. Under his breath he spoke to Jake and Billy next to him at the front of the wagon. "Don't say nothin'. Let me do the talkin'."

Jake watched as the men drew closer, staggered at uneven distances from each other. To him they had an odd way of lifting their legs high out of the grass and placing them back down on the ground, a vertical stride rather than horizontal. Yet as he looked behind them he saw why. Though he searched and searched he could find no discernible trace of a track in the tall grass.

They were up close now. Two had swung wide around the back of the wagon. That made Jake nervous but he said nothing. He thought of his pistol wrapped tightly in his bedroll and cursed to himself. Billy said nothing either but Jake could feel his brother tense as he gripped the wooden seat between them. Two more men approached the horses, eyeing them and running their hands along the head and ribs and flanks as they approached. Jake noticed one of them was no older than he. When Jake made eye contact the boy glared back at him and Jake looked away.

All of them had dark skin, some darker than others, and their long straight black hair moved slightly in the breeze as they did. In their eyes was a fierce intelligence. They moved with the land instead of stumbling over it, as if they swayed with the same motion of the grass, wholly attuned to and part of the world. They reminded Jake of the fox he had glimpsed occasionally in the woods by his aunt's house, possessing the same look of dominion over their world. He was both terrified and in awe.

One man walked right up to the driver's seat and climbed onto the wagon so he was face to face with Mr. Ferris. It startled both Jake and Billy and the boys jerked backward. The man looked at the boys, his eyes piercing them, and Jake and Billy sat frozen to their seats.

He looked at the boys for a moment longer then turned back to Mr. Ferris and flashed bright white teeth in a broad smile. "Ferris," he said. His accent was thick and guttural, and it sounded more like *Fay-lish*. He hopped down from the wagon and motioned to follow him with a sweep of his arm. Mr. Ferris nodded and the wagon jerked forward. Three of the men walked alongside the horses but Jake did not see the other two until he turned and peered through the wagon and saw them sitting on the back looking out over the land behind.

As the day grew long the wagon tracks in front of them faded until they disappeared altogether. The men walked with bundles on their backs and no horses and did not stop to eat lunch but still they did not seem to tire. The only water they drank was sips from bladders slung over their shoulders. Billy nudged Jake and asked in a whisper if they were going to stop to eat. Jake shrugged his shoulders and brought his finger to his lips and Billy hung his head and looked away.

They did not stop until the sun rested on the edge of the world. Past the distant western plains Jake could make out faint outlines of purple mountains rising out of the flat earth. Above them were layers of red and orange and yellow fading into the blue above, so pale it was almost gray. The brothers dismounted with Mr. Ferris and with the weight of habit Billy trudged toward the nearest clump of trees to search for wood.

"Billy!" Mr. Ferris called out after him. Except for Billy's quick lunch request they were the first words spoken by anyone since the two parties met along the road, and they broke the air like shattering glass. All the men stopped what they were doing and looked at Mr. Ferris.

The boy stopped in his tracks and turned only his head back to look. "Better let them take care of the fire," said Mr. Ferris. Without reaction Billy turned the rest of his body and walked back to the wagon. He stood beside Jake, who looked to Mr. Ferris for guidance. The man just signaled with a downward motion of his hands for the boys to hold back.

As the men moved to set up camp, Jake and Billy watched. The ritual was the same they had performed together countless times and yet somehow different, like they were seeing it done for the first time. The men disappeared in the forest, and though they made no sound they came back laden with small sticks for firewood. Instead of clearing a spot in the grass for the fire they searched until they found a small bare spot under the trees and put the small piles of wood next to it.

The bundles on their backs they placed on the ground and unrolled. Most were blankets made from buffalo hide and inside there were only small things. A bow drill for starting fires. Small pieces of jerky wrapped in a tanned hide pouch. One man took out his bow drill and within minutes he had a small fire going. Jake expected him to keep feeding the fire until it was large but instead he kept the flame low and the men gathered close around it.

Jake turned to Mr. Ferris. "Mr. Ferris?"

"Yeah?"

"Why are we just standin' here? Shouldn't we be setting up camp?"

The man shook his head. "I always wait until they let me know it's okay to come over. We're in their territory, I figure it's like being in someone's house. You gotta follow their rules."

"But can't you ask them?"

"I don't speak their language and they don't speak English."

"Then how do you trade with them?"

"Well, mostly we just point and count on our fingers and nod yes or shake our heads no. Seems to work."

"So we just wait here until they give us a signal or something?"

"Yup."

At that moment out of the corner of his eye Jake saw Billy moving toward the group of men huddled around the fire. Jake called to Billy in a hoarse whisper but the boy kept moving. When Billy reached them the men made space in their circle for him, and he squatted like they did and held his hands out to the fire. The sun had almost completely set now and as it did it stole its warmth back from the earth and air. There was enough of a chill to see their breaths and only now did Jake notice his hands were going numb. He thrust them in his pockets and watched his brother nervously. "Goddammit Billy," he grumbled.

One of the men took a piece of jerky from his pouch and handed it to Billy. Billy thanked him with a nod and tore off a piece with his teeth and chewed. He pointed to where his brother and Mr. Ferris were standing and the man nodded a vigorous yes. Billy stood up and cupped his hands. "Hey guys, come on over. These guys are nice."

Jake shook his head. "That's my brother." He walked toward the men and Mr. Ferris followed. At the fire they sat in the spaces made for them and accepted the offerings of food and nodded in thanks. Jake watched as Billy tried to converse with the men, much to their amusement. Billy kept pointing at things and saying the English word, then waiting for a man to say the word back in his language. Then he repeated the word the way the man had said it several times until the man nodded. Each time he learned a new word he would start from the first object he had learned and list them in order pointing at each one as he did.

"You watch," whispered Jake to Mr. Ferris. "Give him a week he'll be speaking Injun." Mr. Ferris smiled but said nothing.

The other men were speaking in low voices and when one grew tired of teaching Billy the boy would pull another from his conversation or his contemplative silence. One by one the men left the fire and retired to their spots by the woods and rolled themselves in their heavy buffalo blankets and slept. Mr. Ferris had long ago gone to the comfort of his wagon but not before bringing the boys their bedrolls.

At last the final man stood and nodded goodnight to Billy and his brother. Then he reached next to the fire and cupped dirt from a small pile into his hands. This he placed on the fire and a small smolder of smoke rose and dissipated into the night sky. He repeated the action but this time there was no smoke only a small cloud of dust visible in the starlight. Jake passed Billy his bedroll and unrolled his own and quickly the brothers got under their blankets and huddled close.

"Billy?

"Yeah?"

"You gotta be more careful around strangers, you know?"

"Oh, they're alright Jake."

"I know, but what if they weren't?"

"What do you mean?"

"I mean what if they weren't? What if for them it's bad manners or something to come up and talk without permission?"

"What are you talking about, Jake? Ain't no manners like that in all the world."

"And I suppose you been all over the world."

"Course not, Jake. But I read about it. Ain't nobody who ain't friendly enough to talk to someone if they're nice enough to talk first."

"That's another thing. What are you doin' tryin' to learn Injun? We ain't gonna be here more than a couple days before headin' back to Nebraska."

"That don't matter. What if I need it in the future?"

"In what future are you gonna need to speak Injun?"

"That's a silly question, Jake. You know I can't tell the future."

For a while Jake pondered whether his brother thought it was possible for someone to tell the future. He listened for the sounds of the night but it was too early in the season for insects. Only the occasional crackle from the forest broke the silence.

"Jake?"

"Yeah?"

"How are we gettin' to California if we're goin' back to Nebraska?"

"I ain't figured that out yet."

"California's west of here, ain't it?"

"Yeah."

"And Nebraska's south?"

"Yes, Billy." Jake's voice rose a little.

"I'm just saying."

"Sayin' what?"

There was a pause before Billy spoke again. "Nevermind." He pulled his blanket up to his chin and turned over.

Jake did the same and faced away from his brother. After a while he spoke. "Billy?"

Again there was a long pause and Jake wondered if his brother was already asleep. "Yeah?" Billy said at last.

"You did a good job talking with those Injuns."

"Thanks."

"I'm glad I got you on this trip."

"Me too."

"Good night, Billy."

"Good night, Jake."

It took a while for Jake to warm up enough to fall asleep, and he awoke in the middle of the night to the chattering of Billy's teeth.

"Billy? You okay?" He reached over and his brother's body was shaking.

"I'm cold, Jake."

"Me too."

"How come that man put out the fire?"

"I don't know. Maybe there's enemies around here or something."

Just then Jake heard a twig snap close to them. The thin starlight eking its way through the tree branch lattice was blacked out by some strange form. A small gasp escaped from his lungs and his heart pounded in his chest as a man reached for his brother. But before Jake could stop him, a heavy weight like a leaden tarp spread across both of them. The faint silhouette of a man stood over them and knelt beside Billy.

The newly risen moon cast a webbed light through the tree trunks and by it Jake saw the man reach for Billy and pull the blanket up to Billy's chin. Then he patted the boy on the shoulder. "*Siná,*" he said. He repeated it. "*Siná*" He patted Billy on the shoulder again and Billy thanked him and then the man stood and disappeared against the shadowed backdrop of the forest. Tension left Jake's body in a wave and he sank back into the ground. Already he could feel the heavy warmth of the buffalo blanket and he pulled his brother close.

In the morning they woke covered in sweat. Jake removed the blanket from his upper body and watched as the steam rose off his chest. Billy was still asleep next to him, so he left him and walked a ways into the forest. When he had done his business he walked to where the fire had been last night and the men minus Mr. Ferris were all seated talking in their strange language. It had sounds that did not exist in any language he had heard and it hurt his ears to listen. When they saw him approach they stopped talking and nodded to him and looked to the west and then continued talking.

Low in the sky cloaked in the new morning light were storm clouds, large white anvils with glowering gray bases. The air was still calm and the breeze that always announced a storm had not yet arrived but Jake could feel its impending arrival and so could the men. He strained his eyes for movement in the far trees but could see nothing. He turned back to the men and they looked at him and he nodded and they understood each other as people who both spoke the language of the land and Jake went and woke his brother and Mr. Ferris.

After a quick breakfast of cold bannock cakes eaten as they gathered and harnessed the horses, they were back on their way west. There was no road and they had to watch for prairie dog holes and dips and rocks hidden in the tall grass. The going was slow. Soon they met the storm's harbinger breeze and before long they were walking into a wind. It was a fast-moving storm but the men escorting them seemed unworried and they trundled along at the wagon's slow pace. The horses' muscles strained and rippled under sweat-glistened hides as they pulled their burden over uneven terrain.

By midday the first clouds had reached them, gauzy white precursors to their darker, more formidable brothers. The land had begun to rise and fall a little more as if trying to mimic the oncoming turbulence of the storm. In the shadows of the clouds Jake could see more distinctly the mountains in the west, undulating foothills of pine leading to taller mountains of green and gray. Even from this distance they were the biggest he had ever seen, much bigger than the muted Ozark Mountains of home.

They came over a rise and saw a large flat valley surrounded on all sides by ridges. In the southern part of the valley wound a wide shallow stream whose downstream they had crossed earlier, and dotted some distance from the stream's north bank were many teepees. They were still far away, but Jake could see everyone was busy bringing in their belongings and children and anything else lying around.

Watching over all the action were horses grazing unperturbed by the clouds gathering above.

As the wagon party got closer Jake could see the decorations on the conical walls of the teepees, animals and birds and suns and strange symbols. Smoke escaped from the small openings at the top of the teepees and was carried away quickly by the wind. By the time they reached the camp, the wind had grown strong and smelled of steel. Most of the people in the camp were already inside, and those who were out were too busy to notice or care about a wagon with a white man and two white boys wheeling through the middle of their village.

Mr. Ferris unhitched the horses and took their harnesses and bridles off and carried the trappings into an empty teepee one of the men had directed them to at the far edge of the encampment. Once free the horses scampered toward the other gatherings of horses. Some shied and others approached haughtily but the two draft horses were quickly accepted or ignored by the smaller plains horses and soon they all resumed their eating.

The boys helped Mr. Ferris pile all the contents of the wagon inside the teepee, and Jake was amazed at the amount of room there was inside. When the goods were unloaded and ringed around the walls there was room enough for the fire in the middle and all three to sleep comfortably around it. Jake walked outside with Billy and looked around. There was no one about now not even the men who had escorted them, and the first fine mist fell and coated the world with a thin layer of wet.

"Jake?" asked Billy

"Yeah?"

"We're on a real adventure now, ain't we?"

"Yes we are."

"You reckon they'd let us stay here?"

Jake looked down at his brother. "Now why would they want us to do that? Why would you want to do that?"

"I dunno. They seem nice."

"You think everyone is nice."

"Do not."

"Do too."

The boys fell silent for a time and listened to the rain pattering in the trees to the west. Fine trails of rain descended from the clouds like the thin gray hairs of an old woman. No lightning visible, but a couple distant rumbles of thunder. The soft whisper of approaching rain.

"That man that tried to get Mr. McCready's farm wasn't nice," said Billy.

"No he wasn't."

"And Mama Alice's husband wasn't nice. At least not at first."

"Nope."

"And that man you hit."

"You made your point, Billy."

"I'm just sayin' I don't think everyone's nice, that's all."

"Alright."

"Just most people."

The first larger rain drop fell on the teepee, then another. One hit Billy on the nose and he flinched and wiped it off. "I'm goin' inside, Jake."

"Alright. I'll be there in a minute."

Jake waited a little longer hiding behind the large door flap, but soon the staccato raindrops on the walls of the teepee increased their tempo and Jake went inside and closed the flap behind him.

Their hosts had left bundles of sticks of varying sizes enough to keep a small fire going all night. Mr. Ferris had already started on one. A few drops of rain found their way inside the small ceiling hole, but inside was dry and soon the fire made it warm. Mr. Ferris and Billy set to cooking dinner, and as they worked Billy asked him questions about their hosts. The man seemed to know a lot about them and had made many trips into their territory. As they talked Jake listened, trying to remember what Mr. Ferris said so Jake would know how to act around these people whose ways seemed familiar yet foreign to him. He knew Billy would remember everything, but he didn't want to have to ask his brother if he didn't need to.

After supper the talk faded with the light, and Mr. Ferris and Billy fell asleep under the buffalo blankets their hosts had left in the teepee. There was one more for Jake but he stayed awake a little while longer. He watched the fire and listened to the lingering rain. The fresh smell of a world washed. The musty sweat smell from the leather tack of the horses. The crisp smell of the popping pine logs in the fire. Mr. Ferris's gentle, rumbling snore and his brother's breathy one.

Jake's eyelids began to droop and he placed a few more sticks in the fire before wrapping himself in his blanket. The word *sipá* kept repeating in his head and the image of the sky turning black and the man placing the blanket over them and kneeling close to Jake and the saying of the word. *Sipá. Sipá.* He drifted to sleep with a lullaby from the dying rain and wind and thought, *what the hell are we doing here?*

By morning the storm had moved on and left spring behind. From the nearby trees birds trumpeted its arrival. A warmth hung in the air that had not been there the night before. Last year's grasses heavy bent with remnant rain revealed their green progeny rising from the shelter of their strands. One last act before their brown skeletons dissolved into dirt.

Billy was helping Mr. Ferris arrange his wares for trading when Jake awoke. Jake grabbed a bannock cake from the pack and joined them. When they had finished, Mr. Ferris spoke.

"Y'all can go check out the camp if you want."

Billy tugged at his older brother's shirt. "Can we, Jake? Can we?"

Jake looked down at his brother and then at Mr. Ferris. "You think it's alright?"

"Yeah. Just don't be offended if no one talks to you. Ain't nobody here who can speak English."

"Please, Jake? Please?" Billy's tug on Jake's shirt had become more of a yank.

Jake sighed. "Alright. But you stay close." Billy darted out the door flap and Jake nodded to Mr. Ferris. The man nodded back. "You sure you don't need any help here?"

"I'm fine, Jake. You go watch your brother. He looks like he's going to be a handful."

Jake smiled painfully. "You got no idea." He adjusted his hat and went outside to catch up with Billy.

The two boys walked the perimeter of the camp watching people emerge from their teepees and perform their morning rituals. Smoke rose through the interlaced poles at the tops, and the smell of wood smoke was thick in the air. Some people stared at the boys but most either nodded politely or ignored them as they passed.

At first the boys said nothing and no one addressed them, but before long Billy got the courage to speak. A woman with her toddler was walking toward the boys and Billy said, "*Hau*." She smiled but said nothing and kept walking. Next came an old man dressed in buckskin pants and long-sleeved plaid shirt and cowboy hat and Billy repeated his greeting. "*Hau*," he said but the man said nothing and gave no more than a stare in reply and kept walking.

When they were out of earshot of the man Jake asked Billy, "You sure you're saying the right thing?"

"Of course Jake," said Billy with a dismissive wave of his hand. "Everybody knows that's how Injuns say hi, Besides, those men taught me it last night."

"How do you know they weren't just messin' with you?"

Billy's eyes widened and he stopped to look at Jake. "You don't think they'd do that, do you?" Jake cocked his head and raised his eyebrow. "Aw, Jake. You're the one who messes with me. Maybe I should watch out for you."

"Maybe. I just don't want you goin' around thinkin' you're sayin' hi when you're insultin' their mothers or something."

"Hush, Jake."

Jake tousled Billy's hair and Billy swiped at his brother's hand, but Jake pulled it away before he could hit it. A younger man came walking up this time, and Jake thought he recognized him as one of the men who met them on the road but couldn't be sure since to him they all looked so much alike.

"*Hau*," said Billy. The man stopped and so did the boys and they stood there staring at him waiting for a change in his stony face. The man looked at Billy and then at Jake and back at Billy without acknowledging their greeting. Then Jake saw a smile develop in the man's eyes, moving down toward his mouth before he laughed. *"Hau,* Billy. *Tanyan yahi."*

From his face and from the trick he had played the day before Jake recognized the man as the one who first greeted Mr. Ferris on the wagon. Billy proceeded to point at and name all the things he knew words for—tree, bird, fire, pants, hair—and the man smiled and nodded and repeated what Billy said. Through gestures he communicated he was going to see Mr. Ferris, but the boys should continue walking and so they did.

Every time Billy saw an object he knew he pointed it out to Jake and named it, and Jake pretended to listen and repeat what Billy said but as soon as the word left his tongue it left his brain and the next time he saw the same thing Billy would have to repeat the word until eventually Billy gave up and just said the words to himself.

The boys spent the morning wandering around the camp. Jake counted around forty teepees and tried counting the people but lost track. By mid-morning most people were outside taking care of daily chores, talking, repairing leaks in the teepee walls. The sun stretched its rays over the lazy rises and falls of the terrain and warmed the water left by the rain. The land grew dry and the air grew humid, and by the time the boys had walked all the way around the camp and back to their teepee large beads of sweat ran down their faces.

Mr. Ferris had spread out several large blankets in front of their teepee. On top of these he had placed all manner of goods that before had been stored in the large wooden boxes stacked inside the wagon. Pots and pans and knives and hammers. Several saws. Woolen blankets and blue jeans and flannel pants. A paint-flecked frame that held a mirror bearing the long scar of a crack sustained during the journey.

People came and looked and picked up the items and tested them out or tried them on. Some bought items with money and some traded with Mr. Ferris. No one spoke the same language, but they managed with gestures and nods or shakes of the head. Billy sat down next to Mr. Ferris and quickly people saw he was trying to learn the names for things. They told him and helped him when his pronunciation was bad and smiled and nodded when he got it right. Soon most of the items on Mr. Ferris's blankets were either gone or replaced with something from the people of the encampment.

Sorted in piles was the array of items Mr. Ferris had collected. Buckskin shirts and pants and moccasins with intricate patterns of colored beads. Beaver pelts and buffalo hides and deer antlers. Leather pouches and satchels. Jake picked them up and turned them over in his hands, inspecting the craftsmanship and construction. He ran his fingers over the beading and through the tassels of the fringe and marveled at the quality.

Billy was deep in conversation with another boy about his age or maybe a little younger. It was slow and halting but Jake could hear his brother learning the language, those foreign words with their strange sounds coming out of his brother's mouth so well he almost sounded like one of them. Jake was both proud of his brother and ashamed of himself. He knew he could never do that.

Mr. Ferris had started to pack the traded items in the empty boxes, so Jake went into the teepee and grabbed more of the containers. He brought them out and set them next to Mr.

Ferris, collecting things out of the man's reach and bringing them close.

"Good haul today," said Jake.

"Sure was. Best I've ever had."

"Why do you think that is?"

Mr. Ferris shrugged. "Guess it's 'cause nobody comes out here anymore, what with the fightin' and all."

Jake looked east, half expecting to see blue-shirted cavalry riding over the crests of the far hills. "We heard somethin' about the fightin', but we didn't get much news of it where we're from."

"Where's that?"

"Missouri."

Mr. Ferris nodded. "Yeah, lots of folks don't know about it. But I can tell you these folks do."

Jake picked up a pile of blankets and handed them to Mr. Ferris. "You seen a lot of fightin' up here?"

The man shook his head. "Nope. Don't want to. Didn't want none of the Civil War, neither. I'm a business man, not a fighter. I just stayed out here and made my runs and waited it out." His face darkened like a shadow on the ground when a cloud passes over the sun. "I come across a battle once. After it were done. Bodies everywhere. Just...red."

Jake waited for Mr. Ferris to continue but he did not. An awkward silence followed and Jake thought he saw a tear in Mr. Ferris's eye. "You want me to get some more boxes from the wagon?"

Mr. Ferris cleared his throat. "We out of boxes in the teepee?"

"Yes, sir."

The man looked at the items before him remaining to be packed. "Naw, I think we're good with what we got. Looks like we'll be headin' out tomorrow."

Jake looked at Billy but his brother was too engrossed in his conversation to hear. "Then off to Nebraska?"

"Yup. To the sister of Mr. Wilkins. You boys will like her. She's a real nice lady. I met her a couple times taking goods back and forth for Mr. Ferris."

Jake nodded, but his thoughts were west, where the last remnants of his father lay waiting. He still did not know how they would get there, or what they would do once they did. He also did not know how he would tell Billy that he had been lying all this time, that the quest for their father was nothing more than a quest for ashes.

"You need me anymore here, Mr. Ferris?"

"Why? You wanna walk around and check out the camp one more time before we leave?"

Jake looked toward the camp. A group of boys younger than Billy was running toward the stream screaming with joy. "I was thinking I might."

Mr. Ferris smiled. "It's nice here, ain't it?"

"Yes, sir."

"I mean real nice. Like you can't put a finger on it but there's somethin' here that's just different."

"Yes, sir."

Jake said no more but continued to stare at the camp. A group of young women were busy tanning hides, an easy rhythm to their work and talk.

"Go on boy," said Mr. Ferris. "I can take care of this stuff."

Jake spent the rest of the afternoon among his hosts. By now news of his arrival had spread throughout the camp, and most people smiled or paid him no mind. A few tried to start conversations in their language, but Jake's reticence and red face made them quickly give up their efforts. Instead he walked among the teepees and watched the people work. The joy and care they took in their daily tasks reminded him of Mr. McCready, and he knew why his brother liked it here so much, why he himself did, though they had been here a short while.

As the sun sank lower Jake headed back to their teepee. Mr. Ferris was sitting in front of the blanket with a few remaining items spread out before him. A middle-aged woman was casually examining them, but Jake guessed both she and Mr. Ferris knew she was not going to be buying anything. When Jake got close, Mr. Ferris looked up.

"Any more business?" asked Jake.

The man shook his head. "Not much. I do enough business here most people know what they're gettin' 'fore I even come."

The boy nodded. "Seen Billy?"

"He's over yonder talkin' to that same kid."

Jake searched the near bank of the river and saw his brother pointing at things and repeating words. Jake smiled and shook his head. "Guess I better round him up so we can cook supper."

"Don't bother," said Mr. Ferris. "Them men who took us here already invited us to eat with them. They usually do that when I come."

"Alright." For a while Jake watched his brother. "What they normally eat around here?"

"Don't know the name. I think it's buffalo."

"Buffalo? What's that like?"

"You ever had beef?"

"Yeah."

"Well, it's like that but better. They put it in a stew with some crazy grasses and stuff that I don't eat, but that meat sure tastes good."

"Mr. Ferris?"

"Yeah?"

"I been eatin' jerky long enough they could take dirt and throw it in a stew and I think I'd like it."

Mr. Ferris laughed. "I don't blame you, son. I feel the same way."

"All the same I better get Billy. He'll be wantin' to prepare his questions about the meal, I suppose."

Mr. Ferris laughed again but the crunch of Jake's boots in the river gravel drowned out the sound. Jake fetched Billy and brought him back to the teepee and after a short while they followed Mr. Ferris to dinner.

They arrived at a small circular clearing where people clustered around small cooking fires. The rich smell of cooked meat and wood smoke hung thick in the air and it made Jake's stomach growl. By now the sun had all but set. In the diminished light the shadows lengthened and the light from the fires distorted and bent and played with them so that the hide walls of the teepees looked alive, like the animals that once wore them had come to reclaim them and their surfaces rippled with the muscles underneath. Jake moved closer to Billy.

A man squatting by one of the fires beckoned Mr. Ferris. He came and the boys followed. As Jake got closer he recognized some of the men from the party that first welcomed them into the territory. Most of them were eating from small bowls or biting meat off large bones.

Mr. Ferris sat and so did the boys, and Mr. Ferris took their food and so did the boys. The men knew Billy now and started telling him the names for things before he even asked. Jake asked Mr. Ferris a few questions and the man answered, but soon they fell into a comfortable silence as they ate and watched the people eat and talk and laugh. They listened to the men instruct Billy in their strange and ancient tongue, and Jake found himself melding into the shadows as if he had become a part of the night and the earth, letting their rhythm overcome him. He could not understand the words coming from the mouths of the people he saw, but he understood their meaning and he saw their smiles as the firelight danced on their faces and he was happy.

He snapped out of his trance and looked around for Billy. His brother was where he last saw him speaking with the men. Jake scooted closer to his brother, and Billy looked up and smiled and Jake smiled back and Billy turned back to the men and began talking and asking questions again. Mr. Ferris had lay back and was now snoring lightly next to Jake. The rest of the evening Jake watched his brother out of the corner of his eye, and when he noticed his brother start to nod off then jerk his head back up Jake stood up and walked over to his brother. He tapped Billy on his shoulder. Billy looked up at Jake and looked back at the men and said something. Without argument Billy got up, and the two brothers navigated their way in the darkness through the teepees until they found their own on the edge of the village and crawled inside.

The morning sun filtered through the small cracks in the walls of the teepee, its rays casting a mottled light inside. By the heat Jake could tell the sun had been up for some time. Mr. Ferris and Billy were still asleep, and Jake lay quiet under his blanket listening to the muffled sounds of the morning coming from outside. Today they would be leaving, and he did not know what lay ahead. Some part of him had felt an odd and tentative peace here and he wished they could stay.

Mr. Ferris stirred and Jake woke his brother. Soon they were making breakfast and packing their things to go. Jake watched Billy, and his little brother sang as he worked.

"Billy?"

"Yeah?"

"You doin' okay?"

"What you mean?"

"I mean are you doin' okay?"

Billy stopped folding his clothes. "Course, Jake. Why do you ask?"

Jake lifted his hat with one hand and scratched his matted hair with the other. "Cause normally you don't like leaving a place, especially one you like."

"We only been here a day, Jake."

"I know't"

"And it ain't like we're never comin' back."

"It ain't?"

Billy shook his head. "We're going east now, right?"

"Yeah."

"And we gotta head back west to get to California, right?"

"Yeah."

"Well, we can just head back through here when we come."

Jake looked at his brother with a mixture of curiosity and bemusement. "What makes you think they'll let us?"

"I asked Two Bears last night and he said it was okay."

"Two Bears? What the hel—what the heck is Two Bears?"

"Not what, Jake. Who. Two Bears is one of the men I was talking to."

"Well how do you know you asked the right question? You ain't started learning their language before two days ago."

"I just know, Jake."

"Well I'm not sure I'm willing to trust that just yet. Come on, let's stop talkin' and finish packin'."

Billy grabbed a shirt and threw it into his pack. "You're the one who started talkin'."

Once the wagon was loaded they climbed on and rolled east out the village. All three rode up front and waved as the people took a break from their morning chores to bid goodbye. Though many people waved and spoke smiling words as they left, no one accompanied them on their journey east. When Jake asked Mr. Ferris about this the man said this was customary. Coming out he never knew where the people would be camped, but he knew the way back. The men from the village only headed east with him if they had some other errand. Then he turned to Billy.

"Billy, you done real good here. You learned more of their words in one trip than I have in twenty."

"Thank you, sir. I like them."

"Yeah, they're alright. I don't know much about all the Indians but these guys are fine by me. I been doin' business with them a long time and I ain't never had no trouble."

Billy nodded and looked out over the wide plains and spat over the side of the wagon. "They're real nice."

Past noon they came to the shallow spot in the river they had crossed coming out. Only this time it wasn't as shallow, since the rains had filled in the spaces between the river rocks. The melted snows from higher elevations added still more water so that now what had been ankle high looked like it came up at least to the waist.

Mr. Ferris stopped the wagon and sat for a long time looking at the water. He gave the reins to Jake and climbed down from the driver's seat, walking to the river's edge and staring at the water some more. Hands on his hips. Stone still.

His head jerked down and even at this distance and even over the roaring rush of the river Jake still heard the curse word that came with the movement. He looked at Billy for a reaction but there was none, and Jake figured they had both spent too much time in Mama Alice's saloon to worry about those words anymore.

As Mr. Ferris stomped back to the wagon he mumbled under his breath and climbed back into his seat. He took the reins from Jake and looked at the river in silence a little while longer before speaking. "We're gonna have to chance it, boys."

Mr. Ferris clicked his tongue, and the wagon lurched forward and down toward the river. At the edge of the grass the horses stepped down onto the loose gravel and rocks of the riverbank. It sloped slightly steeper, and they picked their way carefully down. When the wagon wheels reached the edge Mr. Ferris leaned back and so did the boys. The wagon tilted forward and then dropped. Its momentum started to roll the wagon into the horses, but the harnesses pushed against them and the animals kept it from running them over. On the uneven terrain the wagon swayed and bucked like a drunkard, and the three of them gripped the seat to stay on.

When they reached the water's edge Mr. Ferris stopped and let the horses drink while he studied the river. Small standing waves rippled and crested where before there had been only exposed rocks. Jake asked Mr. Ferris if there was anything they could do to help prepare for the crossing but the man shook his head.

"Nope, he said. "Ain't no two ways about it. This here is the shallowest spot for thirty miles. It'll be close, but we'll be alright."

Jake turned to Billy. "You do exactly what I say when I say it, okay?"

Billy was staring straight ahead at the river. He nodded.

"Just hold on to the wagon and stay on top of it and you'll be alright," said Jake.

Billy nodded again.

Mr. Ferris looked at the boys and then the river. "Well, here goes nothin'." He clicked his tongue again but the horses did not move. "Come on, boys, we ain't got all day. Water ain't gonna get any warmer." This time he let out a yell and slapped the reins against the horses' rumps, and the horses strained against the harnesses.

The current was coming from the right, and as they entered the water it formed little peaks at the horses' legs and troughs on the downriver side. River rocks clicked and thudded as the horses disturbed them. Plodding deeper into the river the sound grew louder and soon all noise was drowned out save the roar of the water forcing its way downstream.

They were only a third of the way across the river but already the water reached halfway up the horses' legs. Jake looked at Mr. Ferris, but the man's gaze was fixed ahead and Jake knew better than to break his concentration. The horses balked and protested more and Mr. Ferris kept urging them on with tongue and leather. The water rushed through the horses' legs and tugged at the wheels and each step now required great effort. Their muscles strained under their harnesses.

For several steps the water level remained the same, and they came to the middle of the river. Jake looked down and saw the water whirling and eddying around the wheels. Mr. Ferris turned to the boys and said, "Halfway, boys. We should be good now." One of the horses stopped and Mr. Ferris admonished him forward and the horse took one more step before his head disappeared into the river.

Horse, wagon and human lurched forward, left and down. The current lifted the wagon's right wheel, and the whole tilted conveyance balanced on the left wheel clinging tenuously to the riverbed. All three riders stood and gripped whatever wood they could and leaned into the wagon. The tethered beasts' hooves churned violently in the water but could gain no purchase on the gravel below.

A huge groan came from the wagon as if in protest, and for a moment, time and movement and nature's relentless campaign against man seemed frozen and within man's power to control. But then the boxes in the wagon fell one then two then five and the shifting weight pushed the wagon completely over.

Billy fell onto Jake and Jake braced himself against the side rail and Mr. Ferris fell backward into the water. The man let out a terrible scream an unearthly scream that reminded Jake of a rabbit's wailing in the death throes. There was a look of terror in Mr. Ferris's eyes and the last words the man said were, "I can't swim," before he disappeared under the water. Then the side rail snapped in two where Jake held it and he and Billy crashed headfirst into the river.

The wagon above them clipped Jake's legs and sent him somersaulting into his brother and the two of them tumbled under the wagon. Eventually Jake was able to grab Billy and cover him until he was sure the wagon overhead had passed. His heart was racing and his lungs were burning and he felt like they were trying to explode through his chest and when he surfaced he pushed up and out of the water as high as he could. His arm was hooked under his brother's and he pulled Billy with him. The two boys took huge grasping gulps of air.

For a few seconds they floated downriver trying to catch their breath. In the current they bobbed like hapless logs and when Jake had regained his wits he sidestroked to shore, his brother in tow. Jake's feet reached a shallow bar and he dragged his brother until Billy could stand. They sloshed through the water to the sloping bank and collapsed on the coarse gravel. Chests heaving. Staring at the blue above. Dripping wet.

When he had the energy Jake sat up and looked downriver. In the distance he saw the horses and wagon beached in some shallows on the same side of the river as Billy and Jake. All three were on their sides, and the horses were flailing and struggling to stand. He turned and saw his brother was crying softly and he looked back at the horses and thought of getting up to help them. But just then they stood and kicked and strained until they broke free of the wagon. Up the bank they scrambled and, still attached to each other and trailing their harnesses, they galloped off onto the wide plain until Jake could see them no more.

When Jake looked back Billy had stopped crying and sat up but he stared at the ground between his legs.

"You alright?" asked Jake.

Billy said nothing so Jake asked again.

"Hey, bud. You alright?"

Billy gave an almost imperceptible nod and Jake knew his brother was not ready to talk, so he sat and looked at the site of their accident. They had floated several hundred feet downriver. Upriver where they had fallen in the water looked deceivingly gentle, and if Jake did not know better he would choose again that place to cross. He thought of Mr. Ferris's calm assurances before they fell and the sounds of his terror after and he tried to shake both from his mind. Billy was still in silent mourning so Jake got up and walked down toward the wagon.

It was on its side and one wheel spun back and forth as small waves lapped it into motion. Most of the contents were still inside and Jake pulled the boxes out one by one and poured the water out before lugging them to shore. A wave of relief washed over him when he spotted both their bags bobbing in the shallow water. After hauling everything to the grass above the high water mark of the river, Jake painstakingly removed all the contents and laid them on the grass. The sun was starting to descend but still high and only a slight breeze blew down from the mountains in the west.

Billy walked over but did not help. He sat silently looking at the river and Jake did not protest or ask for his aid. In the array on the grass he found a woolen blanket. He shook out all the water he could and wrapped it around his brother's shoulders. Billy gave no response other than to pull it closer to his shivering body, and Jake went back to work.

When everything was out and drying in the afternoon sun Jake sat next to Billy. For some time they sat in silence and stared at the river. The sun was warm and Billy had stopped shivering and the blanket now hung loosely around his shoulders. The water in the river and the breeze through the trees sang the same song and the birds' voices were carried on the wind. A bee landed on a flower and gathered pollen and flew off to another cluster of flowers. Jake watched it fly off again downriver and he thought of Mr. Ferris and wondered if they should try to find his body to bury it.

"He's dead, ain't he Jake?"

"Yeah."

Billy stared at the ground in front of him. "I ain't never seen a man die before."

"Me neither."

"How come he never learned how to swim?"

"Dunno," Jake was squinting against the sun. "I guess some folks just never get around to it."

Silence once again fell over them. The sun was now at the angle just before its warmth would wane and Jake knew they would have to pack the things up soon. A crow cawed in the distance. Jake got up and walked over to the scattered clothes and blankets and beads and housewares. From Billy's backpack he pulled something and he walked back over to his brother and gave it to him.

"Look what I found in your stuff."

Billy looked up and took his rock and twirled it as if to check it was the same one.

"Guess it still works," said Jake. "We're still alright."

Billy nodded. "What are we goin' to do now?"

"Well, we gotta pack this stuff up and set up camp. I figured we'd camp in those trees over there."

"I meant what are we goin' to do now that Mr. Ferris can't take us to Nebraska?"

"Oh," said Jake. "Well, I guess we'll just head back there ourselves. See if we can find a town and find work and save money before headin' west again."

Billy looked west toward where they had just come from. He watched for some time as if he were waiting for something to appear before turning back and looking at the river. "What about goin' back to the village?"

"What would we do that for?"

"I liked it there, Jake. The people were nice and they treated us real good and I liked learning their words. Maybe I could learn enough and ask one of them to take us to California."

"I don't doubt you can, little brother. But we don't belong there. That's their village and I don't want to bother them."

"It won't be a bother, Jake. They liked us."

"They liked you, Billy. I don't know if they have an opinion about me one way or another."

"They'll like you, Jake. Please, can we go?"

Jake bent down and picked up a rock and straightened and threw it into the river. It disappeared into a wave with barely a sound or splash. He did it again with a larger rock but to the same effect. "We can talk about it in the morning, Billy. Right now we got to get to work packin' and settin' up camp."

"Jake?"

"Yeah, Billy."

Billy's gaze dropped back down to the ground in front of him. "I don't want to try to cross that river again."

Jake's heart sank and so did his head and when he spoke it was barely audible. "Okay. We can go to the village."

Without looking at Jake or saying anything Billy pushed himself up and walked over to the contents of the lost wagon. He began picking up the stuff and Jake helped him and when they finished they took all the stuff over to the stand of trees. It took many trips and when they finished they did not rest but set up camp. They made a small fire but were too tired to cook so they used their teeth to tear off soggy bites of jerky. They chewed in silence and though it was still light their heads were nodding and they wrapped themselves in as many blankets of buffalo and wool as they could and fell asleep just as the sun did.

In the morning they ate breakfast and as they ate the horses from the wagon chomped on the grass in the field north of the river. Sometime in the night they had returned, and although they were alive and apparently unscathed they were still fastened together by the harness. From a distance they appeared as one beast with two heads. They had spent so much time shackled together they still moved as one.

After breakfast Jake tried to catch them but each time he approached they ran off so he would have to walk some more. After several tries he said to hell with them and turned and walked back to where Billy was breaking camp.

"What happened?" asked Billy.

"Them two don't want to be caught."

"What are we goin' to do with all this stuff?"

Jake peered into the trees. "Guess we can just stash it here and tell someone at the village to come get it if they want. Can you say that in their language?"

"Not yet."

"Well you better learn quick if we're goin' to stay there. I can't understand a word they say."

Billy smiled. "I can teach you as we walk, Jake. It'll be fun."

"Whatever you say, little brother. Let's pack up and get movin'."

Carrying their bags the boys followed the river back and by late afternoon they crested a hill and spotted the village. Not long after, a man rode out to meet them. He uttered crude approximations of their names and the boys nodded but no one said anything more. He dismounted and led his horse and walked with the boys back to the teepees. Preparations were under way for dinner and Jake smelled the food. His stomach growled and he brought his hand to it as if touching it would cease the noise. While they stood, more people came to greet them. The men who first brought them to the village. The boy who played with Billy down by the river. Others passed by or stood looking at them and talking from a distance.

A woman with long silver hair tied in a braid that ran the length of her back walked up and stood in front of the boys. She wore a plain buckskin dress cinched with a knotted leather belt. At the cuffs of the sleeves and the neckline there were small simple patterns of beads. Her brown eyes were set deep in her dark canyoned face and she eyed the boys silently for some time as if inspecting them. With her hand she motioned for the boys to come with her and they followed her. Jake kept an eye on her swinging braid as she wove through the maze of teepees.

When they reached a teepee indistinguishable to Jake from the other teepees the woman opened the flap and the boys followed her in. There was only one blanket for sleeping and the rest of the floor was bare dirt and trampled grass. She pointed them to the empty space across from her bedding and they sat. In the center of the teepee was a small cooking fire and over the fire a U.S. Army issue pot blackened with use. It hung from a small whittled log hooked into forked sticks on either side of the flames. Wisps of steam rose from the pot and the smell made Jake's stomach growl again.

With a metal ladle she poured the stew into a chipped ceramic bowl and handed it to Billy and then did the same for Jake. The boys waited politely for spoons but she gave none so they brought the bowls to their lips and tested the heat before drinking. The warmth of the day had faded and the bowls felt good in Jake's hands and the stew good in his stomach and the warmth held the cool of the night at bay. The stew was plain but good and the boys did not linger in finishing it.

When they had finished the woman took the bowls and nodded and turned back to her side of the teepee. She put the bowls down and without turning back toward the boys she opened the flap and left. The sun was now low in the sky and its orange light spilled through the opening and cast a warm glow inside. Dust motes danced in the beam.

The woman returned with a large bundle under each arm. Jake jumped to help her and Billy was not far behind, but she clicked her tongue and shooed them away with a look. They stood out of her way as she laid the buffalo blankets on the ground, and when she gestured they sat down. She shook her head and said something as she pointed at the ground again. Jake looked to Billy for translation but Billy shrugged. The woman said something again and pointed again so the boys lay down. When they did she nodded and turned and left. Behind her she closed the flap.

The last of the sunlight lit the walls of the tent and gave them a reddish tint that faded into night. Outside, the murmur of activity sounded at once distant and close, unfamiliar and familiar. Normal nocturnal noises and yet disembodied voices speaking strange tongues.

The next day the man Billy called Two Bears visited their teepee. In a series of gestures and broken sentences Jake and Billy tried to communicate what happened the day before. In the end Two Bears was still shaking his head, so Jake and Billy got up and started walking toward the site of the accident. When Two Bears saw this he stopped them and headed toward where the horses were kept. He came back leading two gray horses without bridles or reins or saddles and left one standing next to the boys.

Jake turned to Billy. "You ever rode bareback?"

"Nope."

"Well now's your chance."

Two Bears boosted Jake up and then Billy, who wrapped his arms around his brother. The man then grabbed the mane of his horse and rested his hand on its back and in one smooth motion vaulted onto it. The boys sat in slack-jawed awe but Two Bears did not seem to notice. He nodded to them, and when he clicked his tongue his horse began moving forward.

"Hold on," said Jake. "And make sure you squeeze your legs." Billy squeezed so tight Jake let out a grunt. "You don't have to go that tight."

"Sorry," said Billy.

"It's okay. Just give me some room to breathe, alright?"

Billy jerked his arms tight around his brother. Jake grunted even louder and started laughing. Billy giggled, and they only stopped when Two Bears looked back at them.

What had taken them all day to walk took only a couple hours by horse. The river had receded and the site of the failed crossing had returned to shallows. Two Bears dismounted and helped the boys down before walking to the river's edge. He stared at the water gently wending its way through the rocks on the riverbed.

"What happened to the water, Jake?" asked Billy.

"Looks like it finished running downhill."

"Too bad we didn't wait until today."

There was a tinge of sadness in Billy's voice and Jake looked at his brother to see if he would start crying again but he did not. Jake put his hand on his brother's shoulder. "Yep. It's too bad."

Two Bears descended the gravelly bank to the water and squatted. With cupped hands he reached into the water and scooped the clear liquid to his mouth and drank. He repeated this motion as if in ritual and when he was done he stood and walked downstream.

The wagon was where the boys had left it, but now instead of rocking back and forth in the current it lay beached on the bank with half the wagon completely out of the water. Two Bears peeked inside and then turned to the boys. "Fay-lish?" he asked Billy.

Jake pointed downriver. He hoped the man would understand the gesture since the thought of mimicking Ferris's drowning made him shudder. Two Bears looked downstream for a long time. He stood completely still, the only motion the slight swaying of the fringe on his buckskin shirt. Jake could not see his face but he wondered if this man and Ferris had been friends and if his stoic face would show some sign of sadness at the man's passing.

Without speaking or even looking at the boys, Two Bears walked back up the bank to the wide plain above. He scanned the tufts of grass bowing gently in the breeze. It looked to Jake like waves rippling across a pond. Two Bears turned to Billy and said something Jake did not understand. Billy said a word back and with his fingers mimed two people running and pointed in the direction where the horses had gone. Two Bears nodded and headed back to the horses.

He waited by the boys' horse and held his interlaced hands for Jake to step in. Jake waved him off and grabbed onto the horse's mane. As hard as he could, he jumped and at the same time yanked on the horse's mane. He landed on his chest and tried to stifle the sounds of his struggle as he wormed his way on top of the horse. The horse waited patiently as Jake got into position, and when Jake finally sat the horse he looked at Two Bears. He could have sworn he saw the hint of a smile on the man's face before Two Bears turned to help Billy up.

The three rode their horses east until they came across the two escaped draft horses. They were still attached to their harnesses, and their heads hung heavy and low as they munched the grass. As Two Bears approached they did not even move, and he made quick work in detaching them from their equipment now laden with dirt and grass. Once free they skittered away but stayed close as Two Bears jumped back on his horse and headed west. Jake kept turning back to see if they would move and for a while the horses stood still watching as they got smaller and smaller. But finally he turned and saw them trotting to catch up, and the horses followed them all the way back to the village.

It was late afternoon when they made it back. The boys and Two Bears dismounted and the man led all four horses to where the others grazed. Jake and Billy got back to the teepee and the woman was there cooking dinner. She motioned for the boys to sit and they did, taking the bowls she handed them. It was the first food they had eaten since breakfast, and soon they were handing the empty bowls back to the woman.

Billy told Jake he was going to find his friend from the other day. Jake nodded and sat by himself outside the teepee. The woman busied herself inside, so Jake got up and walked through the teepees now yellow and orange and pink in the waning evening light. People were eating their suppers and talking and laughing and as Jake passed they nodded or smiled and said words he did not understand and Jake smiled and nodded in return. When it was dark he wound his way back to their teepee where the woman was already asleep and he lay down on his bedroll and waited for Billy.

He thought he heard his brother's voice outside the tent but it was not speaking English, and only when Billy's head popped through the flap did he know it was his brother. Billy spread his bedroll next to Jake and in whispers told him about his adventures with his friend and Jake told Billy how good it was he was making friends and learning a new language but inside Jake wondered how he could ever fit in here like his brother already did. Worse yet he wondered what he would do when his brother learned the truth about the dead father they journeyed toward in California.

15

The late spring sun painted the sky the palest blue and high wisps of clouds dotted the canvas white. Grasshoppers sprang from tall stems and butterflies alighted on flowers. The slow pulse that had beaten under the snow was quickening. Once devoid of sound save the wind the prairie was now filled with the cacophonous chorus of life.

Jake sat eating lunch with a group of men while he watched Billy play some variation of tag with several of the boys of the village. The words spoken by the men still fell on Jake's deaf ears. Only occasionally did he recognize an odd phrase, and that was because Billy had drilled them into his head. Still, Jake liked the sounds of the words and the men did not mind his company so he ate in silence while they talked.

By now Billy was fluent or at least seemed so to Jake. At this distance he could not hear what the boys were saying but the ease of their conversation could have been in English for all Jake could tell. Billy went whole days speaking with the people of the village, and Jake teased him he would forget how to speak English if he kept it up.

When the men finished they nodded goodbye to Jake and Jake walked to the small hill overlooking the village and sat. He tore the tufted top off a stalk of prairie grass and watched the life of the village at a distance. People weaving in and out of teepees. The joyous cry of the children at play. Smoke rising from cooking fires and the smell of them lofted by the wind. The barks of dogs. The crushing silence brought by a shift in the breeze.

Jake stayed up there for hours. The boys stopped their game and adults finished their daily chores and the women prepared dinner and the people ate in small congregations around their homes and still Jake sat in the ache of solitude on the slope of the hill. When the lights from the small fires waned and the people began to retire to their teepees, Jake descended into the village. A thick black blanket of clouds covered the sky and almost no light shone on him as he walked through the teepees back to the one he and his brother shared.

Billy was lying down and Jake tried to be silent until he heard his brother's voice.

"Jake?" asked Billy.

"Who else?"

"Where you been?"

"Just up on the hill. Looking out over the village."

"You do that a lot."

"I like it up there." For a while neither boy said anything and Jake took off his boots and lay on his bedroll. The nights were warmer now, and there was no need for the buffalo blanket.

"Jake?"

"I'm still here." Jake's voice had an edge to it he hoped his brother didn't hear.

"You don't like it here, do you?"

"I like it fine."

Billy turned over on his side and propped his head up with his hand. "No you don't, Jake."

Jake's head dropped and for a moment he didn't say anything. "Well, what do you want me to say?"

"I don't know. Just say you don't like it. It's okay."

"But these people ain't been nothin' but nice to us."

"I know't."

"It just feels like we don't fit in here. Like we don't belong."

"I know, Jake. It's okay."

"But you like it here."

"Yeah, but like you said I like it anywhere we go."

A small smile escaped the clutches of Jake's mood and raised the corners of his mouth. Even in the darkness it lightened the air. Billy lay flat on his back and put his hands behind his head.

"Tell me about Pa," he said.

"What do you want to know?"

"I don't know. I just like it when you tell stories about him. You know him better than me."

"Well, did I ever tell you about the time we tried to catch the chickens that got out from Mr. Cooper's yard?"

Billy laughed. "Yeah, but tell it again. That's a good one."

Jake cleared his throat and sat up. "It was springtime. Early spring. When it's warm during the day but there's still sometimes frost on the window in the morning? You remember what that's like back home?"

"Yeah."

"Anyway, me and Pa was out early in the morning huntin' bobwhite quail. We had our huntin' rifles with us and we was walkin' down the road a ways before cuttin' through the woods behind Mr. Cooper's house. Remember that field behind those woods?"

"You mean the one we used to play in with Edward and Sue?"

"Yeah, that one. Well, it used to be flush with bobwhite quail in the spring. Anyway, we'd just come up on Mr.

Cooper's farm when we heard a whole bunch of noise coming from the yard. Like a fox had got in the henhouse only it hadn't."

"What did happen?"

"They heard a gunshot comin' from the direction of the woods. Probably someone else shootin' bobwhite. Anyway, they all get spooked and start runnin' all over the yard, over our feet, scramblin' to get away from the sound. So me and Pa figured we'd help out our neighbor, even if he wasn't too kind to us, just because we thought it might smooth things out between us.

"We started chasing the chickens around tryin' to get them back into the chicken yard, but the grass was still wet with dew and we didn't want to put our rifles down. So we're chasin' all these chickens all around the yard and we're tryin' to shoo them with our rifles. Only I tripped while I was chasin' one and accidentally pulled the trigger."

Billy gasped. "Did you kill it?"

"Naw, didn't even hit it. But I scared the shit out of it. Scared the shit out of myself and Pa, too. Then old Mr. Cooper comes out in his undershirt and he's yellin' at us. He's got his shotgun pointed at us and he's tellin' us to get out of his yard and stop tryin' to kill his chickens or he was gonna get the sheriff. And Pa stops chasin' the bird and says, 'Don't be a damn fool, Emmet. I was trying to catch 'em, not kill 'em.'"

Billy started laughing, and so did Jake.

"It was the first time I ever heard our dad cuss," said Jake.

"So what'd Mr. Cooper say?"

"He looked at Pa and looked at me and he didn't say nothin' or put down his gun. Then Pa says, 'We can help you put 'em in the yard, Emmet, but not if you shoot us full of holes.' Then he walks over to Mr. Cooper's porch and walks right past where the man's standing and props his rifle up against the house. I couldn't move until Pa looked back at me and held out his hand for me to give him my rifle, too. Then we spent the next hour puttin' them chickens back. Mr. Cooper just stood there the whole time with his shotgun. I think he got tired so he lowered it but he still held onto it like we was gonna take some of his hens.

"When we finished he didn't say thank you or nothin' and me and Pa walked into the woods. I thought Pa was gonna whup me for sure for firin' my rifle but when we got past the woods he started laughin'. He couldn't stop and neither could I. Every time we tried to get quiet we'd just start laughin' so after a while we just gave up and came home. When we got back Ma asked us what happened to the bobwhite and Pa said we didn't get none but we almost got us some chickens and we started bustin' up all over again."

Jake could hear his brother chuckling softly and he felt good. He had not spoken that much in more than a month. He waited a while longer but Billy did not speak so Jake lay down and pulled his thin blanket over him. Billy's next words took him by surprise.

"You miss him?" asked Billy.

"Who, Mr. Cooper?"

Billy laughed. "No, Pa."

"Yeah. You?"

"Yeah."

Silence fell once more and Jake's ears rang with the song of the crickets and the distant rush of the water over the rocks in the river. His breathing slowed and he could hear his brother's light breathing next to him. The circle of ground under the teepee was wide but the brothers still slept close. Jake thought Billy had fallen asleep and was letting the weight of drowsiness pull his own eyelids when his brother spoke again.

"Jake?"

"Yeah?"

"We can go to California if you want."

"Get some sleep, Billy."

The day broke cloudy and cool and the air smelled like the metal of impending rain. The sky was a blotchy gray that darkened in the west. Jake woke early, slipped on his jacket and boots and left the teepee without breakfast. The village was just beginning to murmur the sounds of morning and Jake wanted to be away from it before they became a din. He climbed up his normal hill but instead of stopping in his normal spot he ascended to the crest to look out over the plains they traveled weeks before.

The grasses were now full, and their green stalks stood in brilliant contrast against the gray light of the sky. The gentle breezes portending a storm stirred the stalks and they moved in winding rivers. Jake took a deep breath and breathed the pure air coming down from the mountains. He looked farther east and saw more movement. More gray. At first he thought it was just stronger winds and darker clouds but he squinted and when the distant image sharpened he saw an harbinger of change not of this world but of the one they had left and Jake turned and ran down the hill.

He sprinted all the way to their teepee and tore open the flap. Billy was laying kindling for a fire.

"Billy we gotta get Two Bears."

"What for?"

"Just hurry up and put on your boots."

"Okay, Jake. Alright." Billy fumbled for his boots as he spoke. "What's the big rush?"

"I saw somethin' over the hill."

"What'd you see?"

"I ain't sure but I think it's the army."

"The army? What army?"

"The U.S. Army."

Billy's eyes grew wide and he put on his other boot in hurried silence before springing to his feet. "Follow me." He bolted out of the teepee with Jake behind and together they ran toward Two Bears's teepee. The man was sitting outside the door with his wife and baby eating his breakfast, and when the boys ran up and he saw their faces he turned to his wife and said something. She scooped up their son and headed back into the teepee.

Billy started saying something Jake didn't understand but he was only a couple words into it when Jake grabbed his shoulder hard. "Not here," he said. Billy looked back at his brother and saw his face and nodded. He turned back to Two Bears and said something. Two Bears nodded and followed the boys toward the eastern edge of the village.

When out of earshot of the closest teepee Billy began to relay Jake's message. They crept slowly up the side of the hill, Two Bears asking questions and Jake answering with Billy translating. Two Bears showed no outward concern or hurry but as they neared the crest of the hill his gait slowed and he crouched down until he was on all fours, peering just through the grass at the top. He said nothing and moved not an inch but stayed there for a long time quiet and still as a deer. Billy tried to peek and Jake held him back, but Billy gave his brother a stern look and went anyway.

After looking out over the hill, Billy pulled back from the edge. For a while longer Two Bears remained but then slowly almost imperceptibly he lowered himself out of view. He spoke a handful of words to Billy, but before his brother even translated he knew the meaning.

"He said we gotta go," whispered Billy.

Jake nodded and without another word the three hurried down the hill and ran to the teepees. Several people noticed them coming, and when Two Bears spoke those people turned and set to work. The first thing they did was snuff out the fires, and as other villagers saw them they did the same. Next, people began removing the large leather wrappings that made the teepee walls.

By the time Jake and Billy got to their own teepee two women were already pulling down its coverings. The two boys dove into the wooden skeleton and packed their bags. Jake pulled out his father's revolver and swung the straps of his bag over his shoulders. Billy did the same with his bag before he noticed the revolver and froze.

"What you going to do with that, Jake?"

"What do you think?"

"You ain't plannin' to kill the whole army, are you?"

"No, but I ain't fixin' to let any of these people get hurt, neither."

"But Jake--"

"Ain't no buts, Billy. Just keep movin' and I won't even have to use it."

Billy shook his head and ran out past the women taking down the teepee. He and Jake raced through groups of people preparing to leave, past bundles lashed on travois made from teepee poles, past scolding adults and crying children. When they arrived at the site for Two Bears's teepee, his wife, child and all their belongings were already packed and gone. Only Two Bears remained.

Jake still held the revolver in his hands, and when the morning sun glinted off it and into Two Bears's eyes he winced and turned away. Instinctively Jake pulled the pistol out of sight, but when Two Bears turned back he looked down at Jake and pointed at the hand behind Jake's back. He said only a few words but in those words Jake heard a sternness he had not heard before from Two Bears.

"What'd he say?" Jake asked Billy.

"He said you won't need it. We ain't gonna fight anybody."

Two Bears kept pointing at Jake's hand and Jake stared back at him but did not put the pistol away. "Tell him I have it out just in case."

Billy translated, but Two Bears shook his head and pointed more vehemently. He spoke again, this time louder and faster.

"He says no, Jake. He don't want any fighting."

For a moment Jake did not move and kept looking at Two Bears. Two Bears's finger frozen in a point. Then Jake held up his hand and stuffed the pistol in the back of his waistband. "What does he want us to do?"

After talking with Two Bears Billy said, "He wants us to be up toward the front of the caravan. He says he don't want the army to see us with them."

Jake looked at Two Bears and nodded. "Tell him we can go our own way if he needs us to. They done enough for us already and we don't want to be a burden no more."

Two Bears listened to Billy and nodded before speaking. "He said that's nice but he ain't gonna let us go by ourselves. Says we're a part of the tribe and we can stay as long as we like but right now we all gotta go."

Jake nodded again. "Alright, then. Tell him thank you. Tell him we'll start walking now."

Two Bears listened to Billy and nodded and walked off, so the boys walked toward the group of people already leaving. It took a while for them to make it to the front even walking quickly, and when they did they settled in with the rest of the people and headed toward the dark mountains looming in the west. A teenage boy turned to Billy and said something.

"Billy?" asked Jake.

"Yeah?"

"What is it these people keep callin' you? That boy just said it."

"*Numpa I.*"

"What's it mean?"

"It means 'Two Mouths.'"

"Why they call you that?"

"I guess 'cause I speak English and speak their language."

"What's their language called?"

"I don't know. I don't know if they got a name for it. They just speak it." Just then a woman broke off from the main group to chase her young son who had run after a butterfly.

"They got a name for me?"

"Yeah."

"Well, what is it?"

"I don't want to say."

"Why not?"

"I just don't."

Jake looked around and as if on cue a man walked passed them and as he smiled at them he said, "*Wana Gi.*"

When the man was out of earshot Jake shot a question at his brother. "What was that? What did he call me?" Billy's head lowered into his shoulders and he did not speak. "Billy?"

He said, "*Wana Gi.*"

"What's that mean? Don't lie to me now."

Billy squirmed but under Jake's unrelenting gaze he finally spoke. "It means 'Ghost.'"

"Ghost?" said Jake. He walked a few steps before repeating it. "Ghost? Why they call me that?"

"I think it's 'cause you're always disappearing. Going on your long walks and stuff."

"Oh," said Jake. "I guess that makes sense."

"Yeah," said Billy. "That and you're really pale. White like a ghost."

A smile cracked Jake's face. "Shut up," he said. "You'd be just as pale if you washed yourself every once in a while."

Billy smiled but said nothing. The brothers followed the sad and hurried procession of people as they escaped deeper into the wilderness. Looming far in the west were pine-covered mountains and closer the forested foothills sloping toward them. To the left the river that had claimed Mr. Ferris's life diminished as they headed up toward the springs and mountain runoff that fed it. The tall grasses of the prairie were giving way to scattered stands of trees, and the people and horses walked along the edge of the river.

Two Bears came up and nodded to Jake and Billy. Billy said something to him, and he and Billy spoke for some time before Two Bears fell back to return to his family.

"What'd he say?" asked Jake.

"He said we're gonna follow the river for a while until we get to a shallow part. Then we'll cross it and head into the woods so the soldiers can't see us."

Jake looked upstream and shook his head. "How they gonna hide all these people in the woods?"

"I'm sure it'll be alright."

"What makes you say that?"

"He said they've done it before. Lots of times."

Jake looked up at the people in front of them and then behind, dragging all their worldly possessions. "That ain't no kind of life," he said.

Jake was concerned about the crossing but in the end they went far enough upstream the river barely flowed over the tops of their boots. He and Billy waited on the far side of the river for Two Bears, who was bringing up the rear with five other men. Where the grass had been trampled the men were carefully lifting the stalks as much as they could. It did not cover the tracks completely, but it looked to Jake like the caravan had passed days earlier.

The men crossed together but stayed in the water to cover the tracks etched into the muddy banks of the river. When they finished they walked up the far banks in different places and continued their work until most of the traces of the hundreds of travelers were gone or faded.

On the far side of the river grasses gave way quickly to pine forest, and when Jake looked he could not see anyone in the trees. He peered again, but still could not see anyone and shook his head. The men with Two Bears walked into the forest, and Two Bears walked up to them and looked at their boots. He said something in his language and Billy laughed and Jake turned red.

"What'd he say?"

"He said our boots make bigger tracks than a buffalo."

"Well tell him I'm sorry for the inconvenience but I ain't about to start wearin' no moccasins."

"He knows, Jake."

"I tried 'em once and my feet were sore for three days after."

"He knows, Jake. He was just kidding."

Jake looked at Two Bears but Two Bears did not change expressions. "He don't look like he's kiddin'."

Two Bears looked at Billy and Billy started giggling and Two Bears cracked a smile. Jake smiled too but a red smile of shame and that made Two Bears laugh. "*Tatonka*," he said. "Jake *Tatonka*."

"He called you Jake Buffalo," said Billy.

"Very funny," said Jake. He tried to keep a straight face but a smile won out and the three of them laughed their way into the woods.

The forest was full of ancient trees. After the initial bushwhack through shrub brush the walking was easy, and they put good distance between them and the river. On the forest floor Jake saw the odd disturbed patch of needles or broken low-lying branch, but for the most part he could not tell anyone had just walked through the trees, let alone hundreds of people. They walked in the forest the rest of the day, and when the slanting sun slipped sideways through the large trunks they came across the rest of the village setting up camp under the canopy of pines.

No one had built a fire, and people ate jerky or cold stew carried in dented pots. Some people were lashing their long teepee poles low to the trees and draping the leather coverings over them. Others were simply piling pine needles into beds and setting blankets on top. There must have been a stream running down from the mountains to the west of the forest because Jake saw several people carrying water back from that direction.

Everyone talked in hushed tones if at all, and as the light between the trees faded into darkness a silence crept over the people and their makeshift camp. The soft pine needles dampened any sound, and that night as the brothers slept with Two Bears's family Jake felt the awful silence crushing him and took solace in the sounds of snoring coming from Billy and Two Bears. Yet he could not sleep, and the blackness and silence and loneliness ached until he felt suffocated and he had to whisper to himself just to hear something to calm himself. Only when the first stirrings of light from the late-rising moon eked through the treetops could Jake fall asleep.

It was a fitful sleep and when Billy woke him the next morning he felt like he had not slept at all. There were still no fires so Billy ate dried meat and Jake nothing. "Two Bears and some of the men are going back there to see what's happening," said Billy.

"Back where?"

"Back to the river."

"Why would they do that?"

"I guess this happens every once in a while. Two Bears says the soldiers usually come for a day, look around, then head back east. The people in the village just wait it out here."

Jake looked to see if there were any fires, and there were still none so he asked his question. "Ain't no fires for cookin' and it don't look like there's much in the way of plants to eat. How long can these people last?"

"You mean we?" asked Billy. "I don't know. Two Bears didn't seem worried."

"He looked worried yesterday."

"I guess so."

"So he's goin' to check it out. What are you goin' to do while he's gone?"

"I'm goin' with 'em."

"No you ain't."

"Aw come on, Jake. I can do it."

"I know you can. You just ain't."

"You know I'm not a little kid anymore."

"No? Well what are you?"

"I'm a big kid."

"Well what's that make me? A grown man? I ain't even started shavin' yet."

Billy looked off at some of the men preparing to leave. His lower lip stuck out. When Jake spoke Billy did not look at him.

"What you wanna go there for anyway?"

"I don't know. Beats sittin' 'round here."

"Well that's as good a reason as any to get shot at."

"We ain't gonna get shot at, Jake. We're just goin' to take a look. We're gonna be sneakin' up on 'em."

"Sneakin' up? What, you walk like them now, too?"

Billy lifted his feet and only then did Jake see his brother was wearing moccasins. "What are you wearing those for?" Jake's voice had risen and several of the families close by turned to look at him.

"I told you," said Billy. "They're for sneakin' up on people."

Under his breath Jake spoke. "If I didn't know any better I'd say you've become half Injun."

"Have not."

251

"Have too. Look at you. Talkin' like them, now you're startin' to walk like them."

"So what if I am?" asked Billy. "There ain't nothin' wrong with that, Jake."

"I didn't say there was. It's just--"

Billy jumped up. "Forget it, Jake. If you don't want to come you don't have to. But that don't mean I'm not goin'. I'm tired of you tellin' me what to do all the time. I'm gettin' older."

"Well don't let me stop you from gettin' your crazy fool head shot off."

"Fine," said Billy. "And if you just want to sit there and do nothin' and say nothin' just like you been doin', well don't let me stop you."

Billy walked off and Jake watched him leave but said nothing. He watched Billy approach the group of men with Two Bears and Two Bears look back at Jake. The men said something to Billy and Billy said something back. They walked off and were swallowed by the forest. Only then did Jake look away, and he grabbed a handful of pine needles and threw them as hard as he could. A woman was passing by their camp and he almost hit her. She stopped and glared at him. He said what he thought was sorry in their language and waved a pathetic hand before wrapping his arms around his legs.

Sunbeams filtered through the latticed pine canopy and bathed the forest in a hazed glow. The air was thick with insects and they rose and fell and floated along the slanting shafts of light in an ethereal dance. Ornery crows squawked from upper branches and sparrows flitted on the ground in search of food.

People busied themselves, repairing their teepees and weaving baskets and carving tools and washing clothes in the stream. Children played in a small clearing amongst the horses chewing on the sparse grass underfoot. The whole village seemed transplanted to a different setting and nothing had changed except now they moved in silence, a pantomimed performance of the normal lives.

Jake sat and watched and waited but before long he could not take the tension and got up to walk around the camp. His boots cracked twigs and thudded against rocks and people gave him disapproving looks so he removed them and in his stocking feet boots in hand he walked with painful steps to an outcropping of rock jutting through the pines covering the hill overlooking the camp. There he sat and waited the interminable hours for his brother to come back with the men of the village.

The sun had traced its long arc across the sky and been pierced by the spires of the tallest trees before the scouting party came back. In his obstinacy Jake remained where he was and watched as the men trickled through the camp to find their families. Through the spider web of pine branches and needles he watched Billy look around Two Bears's camp and talk to people who had remained behind. Only when someone pointed up to the hill where he sat did Jake push himself up and pick his way down the hill.

On his tender feet it took time to descend, and before he reached the hill's base Billy had climbed to meet him.

"Hey," said Billy.

"Hey," said Jake. Though they were out of earshot of the camp they still spoke in low voices. Jake spit to the side. The brothers stared at the ground at opposite angles and for some time they did not speak.

"I'm sorry for yellin' at you, Jake."

"Me too."

"It's just--"

"I know. You're gettin' older. You're right."

For a long moment another silence hung between them, broken only by a chittering squirrel in a nearby tree. Both looked in the direction of the sound to give themselves something to do before returning their gazes to the ground.

"So what did you all see over there?" asked Jake.

"There's a lot of 'em, Jake. Over a hundred. They're still campin' out. Two Bears says that's normal, but that he hasn't seen this many men before"

"What does he think it means?"

Billy shrugged. "He didn't say."

"So we wait?"

"Yeah. We wait."

"How long?"

"Long as it takes, I guess. Two Bears says they normally leave after a day or two."

"Well, alright then. Guess we better get back down the hill before they start wonderin' what we're doin' up here." Jake started down the hill and was past Billy before his brother spoke.

"Jake?"

Jake stopped and turned his head enough to see Billy in the periphery. "Yeah?"

"Sorry again for gettin' mad. I know you were just lookin' out for me."

"Well, looks like you didn't need it."

"You oughta come with us next time. It was fun."

Now Jake looked at Billy and his eyes bore into his brother and Billy did not move, did not breathe. "Ain't nothin' fun about almost gettin' killed." He continued his descent, and only when he was almost at the bottom of the hill did he hear Billy start to follow him into the twilight forest.

16

The seventh day began as the first. Same and yet different. As if the people engaging in the same routines had forgotten the meaning and purpose of them but continued with the stubborn persistence of habit. The silence had grown so thick and heavy, people walked with stooped shoulders and looked sideways at any snapping twig.

Jake lay on the ground outside their teepee, breathing slowly with the sway of the treetops in the wind. From his right he heard the soft crunch of footsteps and he knew without looking it was his brother.

"Jake," whispered Billy as he shook his brother. "You sure you don't wanna come today?"

Jake looked at the sky, the same sky he had stared at for hours and days and he closed his eyes and let out a long, deep sigh. "I'll go."

"Really?"

"Really."

"You sure?"

"Don't ask me again or I might change my mind."

"You'll have to wear moccasins."

"I know."

"Just a second." Billy jumped up and quickly returned with a pair of leather moccasins. "Try these on."

Jake sat up and took off his boots. He tried to put the moccasins on over his socks but Billy stopped him. "You gotta take those off too, Jake."

"Pa always told us to only take our boots off in bed and our socks off in the bath."

"I know. But..."

"But what?"

"But Pa never wore moccasins before."

"Alright. You win." Jake pulled off his socks and shoved his pale, wrinkled feet into the moccasins, wiggling his toes. "Looks like they fit."

"Try and walk on 'em."

"I know how to walk, Billy."

"I know, but try 'em anyway. They feel weird at first." Jake stood and shifted his weight side to side. He took a couple tentative steps forward.

"You walk like your feet hurt," said Billy.

"I'm alright," said Jake. "We gonna do this or not?"

Billy smiled. "Follow me."

With Billy's back turned, Jake reached under his bed roll and slid out his pistol and slipped it into his pants so the handle fit in the small of his back. He lifted his shirt over it and hurried to catch up with his brother.

Pine trunk shadows striped the brown needles on the forest floor the boys padded across. In a clearing, a group of ten men stood in a circle, but when they heard the boys arriving only some of them turned and looked. The others were watching an animated discussion conducted in harsh whispers between Two Bears and another man. The boys stood back from the rest of the group.

"Who's that talkin' to Two Bears?" Jake asked Billy.

"That's Eagle Claw," said Billy.

"What's he sayin'?"

Billy listened a while before speaking. "He's sayin' somethin' about how he's tired of waiting. That he's tired of running from the soldiers. That we should attack them now when they don't expect it."

"Well, that's a damn fool thing to do," said Jake. "What's Two Bears think?"

Again Billy listened, but Jake could already tell by the tone of his voice that he agreed with Jake. "He says it's not a good idea."

"Good," said Jake.

As if he heard the boys at that moment, Two Bears looked up at the boys. He ended the conversation and walked to meet the boys and looked down at Jake's feet. His eyes met Jake's and smiled but said nothing before beckoning them to follow.

The journey back to the river took much longer than coming, and Jake's thighs burned at the slow, careful steps. Billy stood by him but his legs did not seem to shake like Jake's. Of the party only Billy, Two Bears and one other man were visible. The rest had fanned out and woven themselves into the fabric of the forest.

They took a break and when they did Jake sat while Billy and Two Bears stood. He rubbed his legs and shook them out, and when he rose he felt refreshed but minutes later his legs grew tired. Two Bears noticed and stopped, but Jake waved him on and so they walked and rested and walked and rested and walked again until they came upon the other men waiting in a small clearing close to the edge of the forest. The men were spaced apart and some stood while others squatted. If they were impatient waiting for Jake they showed no sign.

As Jake and Billy sat and rested the men communicated with each other in slow, silent signings. Jake watched but could not follow. When the men were finished they all nodded and slipped once more into the forest. Two Bears stood over the boys and extended his hands and the boys placed their hands in his and he pulled them up to standing. Though no one had spoken the whole trip Two Bears held his finger to his lips to signal silence. Then he used the finger to point Jake to the right and Billy to the left before turning and walking straight toward the river. As he approached the underbrush at the margin of the forest and the grassland, he began to crouch and so did the boys. Jake's thighs screamed in protest but he gritted his teeth and kept moving.

Jake kept one eye on Billy and Two Bears and the other focused ahead. He tried to mimic the man's starts and stops but soon found himself blocked by impenetrable bushes. As he attempted to weave through the maze of interlacing branches the others quickly fell out of sight. Alone in the undergrowth he inched toward the peepholes of sky poking through the tangled vegetation.

The spaces of sky between the branches grew larger and brighter and he slowed his already snail pace. He grew conscious of every noise. The small snap of a twig under his arm. The shuffle of leaves as he dragged himself along the dirt. The shrill cry of a consternated jay. His own careful exhalations.

Allowing himself to slow to the rhythms of the earth, his mind cleared and sharpened. As he drew nearer the edge of the clearing his pulse quickened and in the last shadows of the shrubs he stopped to survey the scene.

The river sliced clear and cold through the tall grass and Jake could hear the gentle rush of the water over the bed of rocks sloughed over centuries from the crumbling mountains. A soft wind descended from their eastern slopes and the trees there slowed the breeze before it roiled the rippling stems of grass in the valley. Small gatherings of clouds seemed frozen on their blue background.

On the other side of the river in a shaded cluster of trees were four soldiers. A large branch obstructed Jake's view to the right so for a brief moment he stuck his head out to scan the valley to the east. Though he strained his eyes he could not see other soldiers or people from his party, so like a turtle he pulled his head back into the cover of foliage.

The soldiers were immersed in a game of cards and seemed in no danger of noticing anything other than the suits and numbers of the cards. Jake watched as they played hand after hand. Their sounds were mostly muted by the wind but occasionally a loud curse fought its way to his ears. Much time had passed since he had heard anyone besides Billy speak English and the sound was both welcome and foreign. Against the peaceful backdrop it seemed harsh and abrasive and Jake fought the urge to retreat into the forest and return to camp.

He almost succumbed when from the pines at the base of the foothills he saw one of the men in their party emerge. The man moved slowly and deliberately, his movements barely distinguishable from the sway of the grasses as the long black strands of his hair and the fringe on his sleeves and pants moved in concert with them. Jake recognized him as Eagle Claw, the man who had been arguing earlier with Two Bears. In his hands the man carried his bow with an arrow notched but the bowstring undrawn. As he approached the game the soldiers were oblivious, and he was almost on them before one of them looked up after playing his last card.

The soldier stood, and for a moment he simply stared gape-mouthed. His legs started to shake and though Jake could not hear it looked as though the man was trying to speak. In his last moments he was able to bring his arm up to point and as he did Eagle Claw loosed an arrow that landed in the soldier's chest like another arm poking out from an unnatural place. The soldier's arm reached to where the shaft entered his body and his head dropped to see it before he keeled forward and landed with a crash onto the playing table.

Cards and coins flew into the air. The other soldiers stood and in their confusion yelled at the man felled by the arrow. Then one of them pointed at the broken shaft protruding from their friend and they looked to see from where it had come. Eagle Claw had already notched and drawn another arrow and he fired it at the soldier closest to him. It landed in the soldier's throat and the man's hands tried in vain to stanch the spurting blood before he dropped to his knees.

As Jake watched the deadly scene unfold he seemed unaware of the movements of his body. Without thinking he quickly but quietly pulled his way into the open and crouched toward the soldiers. Almost by instinct he reached behind him as he moved and closed his fingers around the curved handle of his revolver. From his belt he drew it and in a practiced motion brought it in front of him, hinged the cylinder open, inspected the ammunition and closed it before wrapping his other hand around the handle.

By now the soldiers understood what was going on, and one of them ran toward their attacker while the other fumbled for his rifle. Eagle Claw loosed one more arrow that landed in the soldier's arm as the man reached for his weapon. Then the lunging soldier tackled Eagle Claw to the ground. The two men tumbled into the tall grass and Jake could not see them. He continued forward to where the grass met the sloping banks of the river and put his moccasined foot on the rocks. A shoot of pain ran up his leg and he pulled it back. He searched for a smoother surface and tried again but his tender foot could not stand the hard protrusions through the leather soles. He muttered a curse and looked back toward the men fighting.

One soldier stood under the tree and stared at a spot in front of him in the grass, his rifle bobbing tentatively in his grasp as he tried to determine whether to shoot. The other soldier popped above the grass but was soon swept backward. Then Eagle Claw jumped up and the soldier under the tree steadied his rifle, but Eagle Claw was knocked down again before the soldier could fire.

Jake knew what he had to do and the thought made him sick. He had raised his gun to a man before, more than he ever thought he would, but this time he knew before he fired he would have to stop this man dead. So focused was the soldier he did not see Jake, and Jake would have a clear shot. But he would have to move quickly.

As his father taught him, Jake positioned his feet apart and held the pistol down between his legs. He took a deep breath, his chest and shoulders rising, then blew it out slowly to calm himself. He could feel the pounding of his heart in his chest and the blood pulsing in his neck. Eagle Claw and the soldier appeared then disappeared before the second soldier could fire a shot.

He inhaled again and as he exhaled he raised his weapon. Arms straight but relaxed. Another breath. Pulse slowing. The soldier with the rifle still unaware. Still pointing his weapon into the grass. As his breathing tempered his nerves, Jake's focus sharpened on the soldier, the metal nub of the sight aimed slightly higher than the soldier's head to account for distance. The surrounding sights and sounds of the periphery fused into a haze of dull colors and muffled noises.

Doubt slithered into Jake's mind. He imagined the soldier's family. A crying mother. An army bent on revenge. The man's bloody corpse. Jake's grip tightened and the pistol trembled and his eyes focused back on his weapon and the gleam of the metal. He tried to regain focus and slow his breath but the pistol seemed to vibrate on its own and at last he lowered it to take a deep breath and gather his nerves.

Eagle Claw emerged from the grass panting and covered with the crimson sheen of blood and sweat. He stared at the man with the rifle and Jake could see the whites of both men's eyes. In an instant Jake raised his pistol and shot wildly at the soldier. The sound shattered the silence and in the trees far behind the soldier Jake saw a branch wince and knew he had missed high and right.

Both the soldier and Eagle Claw dropped into a crouch and the soldier whipped his rifle around searching the source of the shot. He peered across the river and saw a boy standing with a pistol aimed at him and to Jake's surprise the man stood up.

Jake tried to exhale but his lungs did not work, and there was a fierce pounding of his pulse reverberating in his ears and a fierce burning in his chest and gall in his throat and he tried to corral his recalcitrant weapon and he aimed and closed his eyes and pulled the trigger.

A loud bang filled the valley. Jake stood paralyzed, bracing for the return shot. In that moment he felt certain he would die and he thought of Billy and what would become of him. He thought of his mother and his father both gone from this world and he saw their faces warm and welcoming and sad. No shot had come and he dared to open his eyes. Where the soldier had stood was now a background of trees and to the left stood Eagle Claw staring at Jake.

At long last Jake's lungs began to work and the cool air burned his throat and his chest. His pistol dropped to the ground and his hands to his knees and he struggled to keep his head up. Eagle Claw looked down and walked under the tree to the soldier hidden by the grass and he bent down and tossed the rifle away. He drew his knife and raised it and as he glared at the ground he uttered a piercing and undulating cry. His hand came down hard and fast and again it rose and again it fell and in the blur of his arm Jake could see the blood and hear the shrieks of the soldier dying.

A hand rested on Jake's shoulder and the boy startled and tumbled forward onto his hands and knees. He looked up and saw the kind face of Two Bears looking down. Jake attempted a smile but he felt the bile in his throat rising and turned to face the ground and vomited.

He retched until his stomach was empty and he retched some more and his chest heaved and his eyes stung. His whole body shook. When he was done he sat and wrapped his arms around his knees and put his head between. His breath rattled and his throat and mouth burned. A circle of men stood around him and Billy too and when Jake looked up he felt them all staring at him. No one spoke. Jake was vaguely aware of the sound of splashing water and he saw a few men look in the direction of the river. Soon after they made a space in the circle that Eagle Claw filled.

The man saw Jake and nodded. He spoke but Jake did not know what he said. Jake looked at Billy but Billy said nothing, his face slack with shock. Two Bears stepped toward Jake and held out his hand and Jake took it. With ease the man pulled the boy up. He patted Jake on the shoulder and nodded. Jake nodded back. Then Two Bears turned and walked toward the woods with the men following.

Eagle Claw and Billy waited with Jake and when Jake had picked up his revolver and was ready they walked on either side of him. Jake looked at his little brother and then at the man and he saw the water dripping off him. He realized Eagle Claw had rinsed the blood, and Jake looked closer and saw red swirls in the clear drops clinging to the man's body and glistening in the sun. Jake's stomach turned and his vision blurred and his legs seemed to lose all function and his body tilted toward Billy.

Eagle Claw reached out. So did Billy. They held him there suspended between. Jake's head cleared and he felt his legs again and stood on his own.

"You okay?" asked Billy.

Jake tried to speak but only a gurgle came out before the bile burned. He nodded.

"Let's get home then, okay? We'll help you."

Jake nodded again. He felt Eagle Claw's hands clasping his arm but did not look. He knew if he did he would faint or vomit so he looked straight ahead and staggered toward the shelter of the forest.

The whole way back no one spoke. When Jake regained his strength his brother and Eagle Claw still stayed by his side. The other men had gone ahead and Jake could not see or hear them. Jake made no attempt to lead but let Billy guide him back. In the afternoon light the trees looked buttressed by the slanting sunrays and Jake and Billy and the men like weary pilgrims come to beg forgiveness from their wooded gods.

The trip out had lasted excruciating hours of anticipation, but the flight back passed before Jake realized it was over. His mind clouded with thoughts. He and Billy said goodbye to Eagle Claw and returned to their teepee.

Two Bears was already back and when he saw the boys he walked over. For a while he stood in front of Jake and Billy, saying nothing. He looked directly at Jake and the boy was unsettled, but neither spoke and in the silence Jake could hear the quiet frenzy of the forest, chirps and buzzes and the rush of the wind through the trees. With surprising tenderness Two Bears placed his hand on Jake's shoulder.

"*Pilamaya yelo*," said Two Bears.

Billy translated. "He said--"

"I know what he said," Jake spoke without taking his eyes off Two Bears. Then he nodded and Two Bears nodded back and without another word turned and left.

Jake could feel the oppression of eyes on him and he looked up to see several people openly staring at him. He tried to ignore them and sit and look away but each time he checked people were looking. He told Billy he was going for a walk and Billy protested but Jake pretended not to hear. Up he climbed into the forested foothills and soon found a place secluded from the encampment yet still visible.

Until the green of the forest turned yellow then orange then red in the waning light Jake stayed and watched the movements of the people below. The wind descending from the hills carried the sounds of the people away from him and Jake felt as if he were observing strange and silent creatures foreign and unknown to him go about their lives. In the quiet desperation of his solitude the knot in his stomach began to grow and if he had food in his stomach he might have gotten sick again. Tears welled just below the surface but like a capped geyser could not escape. His eyes burned.

From the left he heard a twig snap. His body tensed. Quickly he scanned the black spires of trees now barely distinguishable in the twilight. Another twig snapped and Jake moved to stand when he saw his brother's head poke out from behind the darkness of the trees. Billy ambled up the hill toward him. Jake tried to relax but could not and his whole body trembled and when his brother reached him and sat next to him Jake began to cry. The tears came slowly at first and Jake tried to hide them by turning away.

"I killed a man, Billy."

"I know."

"I ain't never killed a man before." His voice started to break.

"I know, Jake. It's okay. You done the right thing."

Jake sniffled and his breathing became labored and tears starting flowing and soon his whole body was sobbing. Billy let his brother cry and told him it was okay over and over until at last his body quieted into soft tremors. Jake took two deep, purposeful breaths and his body stilled.

"I suppose we all gotta pack up and move somewhere else now," said Jake.

"That's what Two Bears says."

"Billy?"

"Yeah?"

"You know we can't stay with them now, right?"

"I know't."

"I'm sorry, little brother. I know you like it here."

267

"It's okay, Jake. I know you didn't like it much here anyway."

"It's not that," said Jake. "It's just...I don't feel like I belong here."

"I know."

"I'm not like you. I can't learn their language like you. I can't--"

"I know, Jake. It's okay. We gotta get to California anyway. We gotta go see Pa."

Jake felt a sharp stab of guilt in his chest. He took a deep breath.

"Billy?"

"Yeah?"

"I got somethin' to tell you."

"What's that?"

"Pa. He ain't with us no more."

"I know," said Billy. "He's in California."

"No, Billy. I mean he ain't with us no more."

"What are you sayin', Jake?"

Jake drew a long breath, as if that breath might unburden him. But only saying the truth would. "Pa's dead, Billy."

Billy said nothing and for a moment Jake wondered if he had heard him. He was about to speak again when his brother responded.

"You lied to me."

Jake swallowed hard. "Yes, but I did it to protect you."

"From what?"

"From gettin' hurt."

"So this is better?"

"Don't get smart with me, Billy."

"How come you didn't tell me before?"

"I don't know. I just couldn't."

There was a thick and weighted silence as Jake waited for his brother to speak.

"Goddamn you, Jake."

"You take that back."

"Goddamn you, Jake."

"You don't mean that."

"I mean it and I want you to leave."

"Leave and go where?"

"I don't care. Just away."

"You don't mean that."

"You don't know what I mean."

Jake paused and thought and gulped at the air, hoping words would come to him.

"All this time you been lying to me," said Billy. "You said we'd always have each other and that we should always be honest with each other and you lied to me."

"I know't. I'm sorry, l'il brother."

"Don't you little brother me," said Billy.

"Well you're still my little brother, ain't you?"

"Brothers don't lie to each other."

"Brothers protect each other," said Jake. "I've been protectin' you."

"And I've been protecting you!" Billy stood as he shouted. Finally he looked at Jake, but his eyes were red and angry and Jake had to look away, ashamed. "You know what it's like here, having to defend you? Having to tell all my friends that you're alright when you're not alright? Having to explain that you don't think you're better than them when it sure as hell looks like it?"

The sounds of his brother angry and cursing grated on Jake's ears. "You know I can't talk like they do. Like you can."

"You don't even try! And so now I've got to do all the work. So don't talk to me like you do. Those days are long over."

Jake tried to summon the anger to match his brother's, to put him in the place Jake thought he should be. But the words stung and the truth hit him hard and the shame he felt could not be lifted. "How come you ain't never told me about this before?"

"How come you never told me about Pa?"

Jake tried again to say it was to protect his brother but the excuse took the air out of his lungs and it came out as no more than a mumble.

"I can't believe you've been lying to me all this time," said Billy.

"I want to make it up to you."

"Why'd we leave Missouri?"

"That man our aunt was with. He was no good. He was comin' after her and would've come after us."

"I don't believe you."

"You got to believe me," said Jake.

"No, I don't. Not anymore."

"Billy, I'm your brother."

"I don't know what that means. You lied to me."

"Well, what do you want me to do?"

"I want you to go."

"You know you don't belong here," said Jake. "Just 'cause you talk like them don't mean you are them."

"I know't," said Billy. "But at least they don't lie to me."

Now the anger welled within Jake, and it gave him the energy to stand. "You really mean it?" he asked.

270

"Mean what?"

"That you want me to go?"

"Yeah!" Both were shouting now.

"If I go, I might not come back!"

"Who said I'd want you to?"

Jake wanted to say more but his tongue failed him and instead a mixture of growl and bark came from his throat and he turned and ran down the hill. Branches tore at him but he did not care and when he reached the bottom he did not stop or say hello to anyone in the camp who eyed him with curiosity. Only when he reached his belongings did he pause to pick up his pack and shove his bedroll and knife in with his father's gun and envelope containing the letters. Not even bothering to tie the strap closed, Jake stomped away from the camp.

He pounded through the forest, not caring the noise he made or the danger to himself if there were more soldiers coming to avenge their fallen friends. His anger at his brother and disgust with himself carried him far, but with each step they lessened. The slow march of reason took over and soon he stopped. He looped his thumbs through the straps of his pack and caught his breath as he stared in the direction of the camp, waiting to see if Billy would emerge from the trees. For a long time he stood like that, waiting as the darkened forest grew so quiet his ears rang with the silence.

When at last he gave up hope, Jake sought out a flat, dry spot that was raised and sheltered by a tree. There he rolled out his blankets and pulled them over his lean frame and shook slightly until he fell asleep.

The night's sleep was fitful. Every snap of a twig or rustle of a leaf woke Jake, and each time he looked up hoping his brother would be there. Yet each time he would stare into the unmoving blackness until his eyelids grew heavy and he fell half asleep once more.

The first of the dawn light seemed to emanate from the tall spires of pines blanketing the sky, pouring slowly downward until it reached Jake on the forest floor. His body ached from the nocturnal contortions of a restless slumber and only now as the day approached did Jake long for a few more hours of night. When he could no longer fight the inevitability of the morning, he sat up and rubbed his eyes.

The forest was unusually quiet. Though he did not know how far he had walked the night before, he did not think it was far. He could not hear any of the usual sounds of morning coming from the camp, though that did not surprise him. They were a quiet people, and after the incident with the soldiers, he knew they would be silent. But there was something else, as if the birds and the insects and the wind through the trees had all lost their voices. Each movement of Jake's seemed to echo through the forest, and he had to pause and listen for signs of anyone approaching.

When he had packed his bag he took a deep breath, staring first at the way ahead, then back into the part of the forest from which he had come. Again he looked away from the camp, sighing once more. "Aw, hell," he said before turning and walking toward his brother.

In the daylight it did not take him long to return to the site of the camp. But when he arrived there was virtually no trace of Billy or the others, no sign that anyone had even been there. Jake shouted his brother's name a few times, but his own echoed voice was the only reply. Then Jake scrambled up the side of the hill, hoping to see some sign of their trail. There was nothing but the trees and the birds and the fat humming of insects.

Jake cursed and kicked the ground and sat down, kicking at the loose loam a couple times before wrapping his arms about his knees and sulking. Anger coursed through him and made his limbs shake. Anger at his brother and at himself. Always they had fought but always they had come back together. This would be no different, Jake thought. He just had to wait.

After climbing back down the hill Jake scoured the forest floor for anything he could use to see which direction they went. But every broken twig or dent in the dirt led him on a false or inconclusive trail. Several hours of searching left him kicking the trees and cursing the sky, but no closer to finding Billy.

His stomach growled and he looked up. The sun was now well into its descent to end the day. He had neither eaten nor drunk so he walked to the stream and brought his mouth to a pool of water, taking long pulls. It was too late to set traps, and he did not want to use his father's pistol. There had been no sign of soldiers, but Jake did not want to take the chance. He did not even want to build a fire, so he found a place to unroll his blanket beneath a tree.

Soon the weight of fatigue pulled on him, and as the late afternoon sun trickled through the trees he fell into a deep sleep without dreams and when he woke the stars were starting to poke through the fading light of the sun. Jake took one look at the sky, wrapped the blanket tight around him and fell back asleep.

This time in the darkness of the night his sleep was filled with dreams, troubled and troubling dreams not remembered upon waking save for the feeling of dread that remained when he awoke in the middle of the night. After that he tried to get back to sleep, but the feeling stayed with him and he could not shake it to slumber.

Jake was rested but worried when the forest began to lighten. Except for his brief stint in jail, Jake had not spent this much time apart from Billy since before he could remember. Since a long-ago hunting trip with his father, perhaps. He felt the absence of his brother like the absence of an arm. The surrounding silence made him ache.

His stomach growled again. The creatures of the forest began to stir, and the sharp whistles of the birds' calls pierced the quiet of the woods, echoing in the emptiness. He rummaged through his bag for anything to eat, but there was nothing. For so long he had depended on the kindness of his hosts, he had no food of his own.

Jake had seen the women of the tribe picking berries and foraging, and he had watched them enough to recognize some of the edible plants in the area. He stood and emptied his bag before heading into the woods to find something to eat. The soft loam gave way underfoot, and his boots slipped on the pine needles. The branches and stems close to the now deserted camp were mostly picked bare, and Jake ate as he trekked farther into the forest.

The forest grew thicker and darker and the only way to tell time was by the occasional glimpse of the sun through the canopy of trees. The underbrush thinned, and Jake had a harder time finding anything to eat. At last he gave up his search and followed his footprints back to his belongings.

By now the sun was high in the sky. There was still no sign of Billy or the others, nor had any soldiers come looking for whoever had killed their fellow fighters. But Jake couldn't risk waiting too much longer for fear of being found by them.

With weary legs Jake walked over to the stream and stooped to drink from the cool pool of water swirling over the smooth stones. He looked up into the gray and green pine hills and wondered if he should spend the night up there. His belly ached from hunger but he had suffered worse on the journey and could last another night without eating more than he had that day. Being up in the hills would allow him to see down below to where he was in case Billy came back, and it would keep him out of sight of any soldiers coming.

He looked up at the sky. A cloud passing slowly in front of the sun cast a large splotch of shadow that reached halfway up the hill. A hoarse whisper of wind descended through the trees and Jake's slender frame shivered. He made his way to his bag, stuffed his belongings inside and walked back to cross the stream.

The hillside was mostly loose gravel, and Jake had to dig his toes into the earth for enough purchase to climb. Where he could he planted the sides of his boots above the roots of trees that reached into the soft dirt. The going was slow, and he had to stop several times to catch his breath. At last he reached a relatively flat spot sheltered by trees and a large boulder that obstructed the view from the valley.

As Jake leaned on the boulder he could see the stream snake along the valley floor. The sun slanting behind him shone gold on the trees and rocks below. The sky blue and pale and painted with wisps of clouds covered the earth and kept it close, and Jake felt as if he were the only person in the world.

Night came quickly. Though it was summer there was a chill in the air, and Jake huddled against the boulder, pine needles piled against his blanket for insulation. The wind had died down but an occasional gust would stir him awake and he would wrap the blanket tighter around his shoulders and try to fall asleep again.

Morning brought a weary warmth, and as the sun heated the earth Jake closed his eyes against the light and hoped to capture the sleep that had eluded in the night. At last he fell into a deep slumber.

When he awoke his body was damp with sweat and he shook the blanket off in a cloud of dust and needles. A fly buzzed around his face. He shooed it. Picking himself slowly up the rock, Jake took in the morning, scanning and scanning and scanning once more but still seeing no sign of anyone. He sighed.

"Well, shit." He beat his blanket against the rock to shake out what dirt and needles he could, then rolled it neatly and slid it into his pack. Then he slid his hand to the bottom of the bag and worked his fingers around the butt of his pistol. This he pulled out and slid into the back of his waistband.

The trip downhill was much shorter than the previous day's ascent, and Jake took long, sliding strides as his heels carved scars into the gravel and dirt. At the bottom he took another drink from the stream and stood, thumbs hooked into his pack straps.

To the right he looked toward where his brother had most likely gone, into the forest and into the hills. He could follow the stream as far as possible, hoping to run into Billy and the others. But he had seen how fast they moved, how little trace they left as they traveled. Tracking them would be little more than hopeful guesses, and on the barren pine forest floor the food was sparse.

To the left was where the soldiers had been. It was a terrain Jake understood, but Billy was in the opposite direction. If he saw soldiers he might run into trouble, but there was also probably a town close by. He could find food, but not his brother. As if in response his stomach grumbled.

Once more Jake looked into the dark reaches of the forest. His heart ached and pulled him toward his brother, but then a sheen of anger covered that emotion.

"Damn fool," he said. As he turned left, he didn't know if he meant his brother or himself.

It took him most of the morning to wind his way back along the stream to the site of the battle. It was oddly quiet when Jake got there, as if the trees were holding silent vigil over the fallen. Jake kept to the edge of the field as he circled around the bodies. At first he could not see them, but then a carrion crow flew down and disappeared into the tall prairie grass. For a while it remained out of sight, but then a breeze blew and the grass bent down and he saw the bird picking at a corpse. It cawed twice. Jake shuddered.

He continued walking until he got to the clumps of trees on the other side of the field. The old camp lay to the east, but Jake feared the rest of the army would still be there. There must be a town nearby, he thought, since a large army could not have traveled far without restocking somewhere. On their journey from the east he had not seen one, and with mountains to the west and south there was only one way it could be: north.

Jake stood at the fringe of the field and forest and took one last longing look toward the forest in whose fold his brother now lay hidden. A tear began to form in his eye, but he coughed it away. "Damn fool," he repeated before heading north.

Jake spent the rest of the day ducking in and out of the forest. A small creek ran along its edge, and he was able to drink when he needed. The food was more abundant here, too. Though he was still scared of using his pistol for hunting, he was able to fill his belly with berries. At nightfall he tucked himself into a soft pine bed and slept.

In the morning the forest was filled with fog. It swirled in slow eddies around the clumps of trees dotting the prairie. When Jake saw it he breathed a sigh of relief. Now, under cover of fog, he could hunt.

Leaving his belongings, he walked a few hundred paces from where he slept until he spotted a pool of water at the edge of his vision. There he pulled his pistol and sat with his back against the tree, slowing his breathing. The forest that had gone quiet as he walked through it slowly became alive again, birds chirping and squirrels skittering along the branches.

It took awhile but at last from the fog emerged a small rabbit. Ears perked, it sniffed the air back and forth until it emerged from the tall grass and hopped gently toward the water. As it took its first hesitant sips, glancing about furtively for any sign of danger, Jake raised his pistol so slowly his arm ached. But he knew not to move it faster.

He was worried the rabbit would finish before he had aimed, but the animal was so skittish it hardly drank before taking another look around. Just as he thought his trembling arm could bear no more without starting to shake violently, Jake set his sights on the rabbit and fired.

In a harsh spasm the rabbit jerked back and landed with its feet sticking straight up. For a moment the report from the pistol hung in the air, but then like a sponge the fog absorbed it and the morning was quiet again.

He cleaned and cooked the rabbit and the still scalding meat tasted good. Jake ate hidden in the trees and as he chewed his eyes moved across the horizon looking for anyone who might approach. No one came. When he finished he buried the carcass and ashes under clumps of wet dirt and rocks from the streambed and then continued north.

17

It was night. Jake lay on the bank of a lake so flat and calm he thought he could walk across it. No one was around. The great moon shone its large and round reflection on the surface of the water so it glowed white. Crickets hiding in the shore grasses emanated a low hum.

It had been two hard weeks of travel since he left his brother, and only now was he able to enjoy the peace this pleasant scene offered. But the joy was fleeting. He slept well, but in the morning he woke with the same pangs of loneliness he had felt since Billy left.

Jake broke camp and continued his journey north. After cresting several grassy hills, he spied in the distance a cluster of buildings along the river. As he approached he saw around the bend in the river there were more buildings and scars in the earth that resembled wagon ruts. Jake straightened the straps of his pack and loped down the hill.

An odd feeling rose inside him, a mixture of joy and dread as he re-entered a world now strange to him. In the months he had spent with Two Bears and his people, Jake had grown accustomed to the wilderness and its ebb and flow. Even the simple shacks along a rough road seemed out of place, unearthly elements in the natural world.

The gravel of the road crunched beneath his worn boot heels, and he was acutely aware of the sound he was making. No one was around that he could see, but after so many months of quiet the sound grated his ears.

Only when he was past the first set of buildings did he see someone on the road. It was a man sitting atop a wagon and for a moment Jake thought of Mr. Ferris and was sad. The man looked nothing like Mr. Ferris, though. Tall and lean, freshly shaved and washed. As he approached, the man stared down at Jake. Jake tried to nod but the man didn't respond. He was almost on top of him when Jake decided to cut the tension.

"Morning," he said.

The man seemed startled, and gave no more than a nod before looking straight ahead and clicking his tongue to get the horses moving.

Jake watched as the man and cart wound around the bend in the road and disappeared behind the hill. He turned and kept walking, and as he continued toward the town he was able to see more of the town tucked into the narrow valley. Larger, more tightly grouped buildings lined a main street, and from this distance he could see people scurrying back and forth on their daily errands. In the hills above the town several small structures and fans of rock and gravel running down the mountainsides. Mining, he thought.

Closer to the town another wagon carrying passengers lurched toward him. It was black and decorated with gilded flourishes, and Jake had never seen anything like it in his life. The driver looked at him scornfully. The people inside were hidden by a lace curtain but Jake could still hear a woman's voice and see her faint silhouette.

"Oh, that poor orphan," the voice said.

Jake looked around to see who she was talking about, but no one was on the road besides him. Before he could respond to the woman, the cart had moved on.

The closer he got to the town, the more people he encountered. Some ignored him, some stared with a mixture of pity and curiosity, and others hurried on their way as if the boy carried some deadly communicable disease.

Though the terrain was much different, the town reminded him in some ways of Dodge City. The clumsy, hurried construction of the buildings, the hardened looks of hard laborers returning from work covered in dirt. Saloons lining the street.

Yet other details differed. Instead of selling tack and riding gear, the stores sold mining equipment. The noise and hustle of this town in summer stood in stark contrast to the desolate depression of the Kansas cattle town in the dead of winter. Jake could only guess what this place was like in winter, or what Dodge City looked like now.

As he passed by a glass storefront he caught his reflection in the window. What he saw startled him, and he had to look several times to make sure it was really his face staring back. Framed in the glass was a gaunt-faced waif in tattered clothes, bearing only a passing resemblance to the boy he recognized as himself. The face was thinner and dirtier, the eyes weary. The clothes hung loosely from a wiry frame.

More passersby were eyeing him suspiciously, so he pulled away from his reflection and continued down the street. He had no money, and though he knew he could survive off the land away from the town, he also knew that would not work in the winter. And Jake had no idea how long he would be here.

After ducking down a side street and washing his face and arms with water from a catch basin, Jake tucked in his shirt and straightened it out as best he could. Then he slicked back his hair, tried to smooth out the dents in his hat, placed it back on his head and re-entered the main drag.

The way he looked he knew he wouldn't get work at a store, so he first went to the stables he had passed at the edge of town. They were run by a stoop-backed man with thin tendrils of gray hair poking out under his hat. Even above the smell of manure, Jake could smell his foul odor when he walked into the man's stable. He was talking to a horse when Jake wished him a good morning. The man did not respond, and Jake almost had to shout to be heard.

"Sir?" said Jake.

"What? What's that?" The man whirled around. His eyes raked over Jake. "What do you want, boy?"

"I was wondering if you could use a hand around here." Jake took off his hat and and spun it nervously in his hands before putting it back on.

"What do you mean? I can still do the work by myself, thank you very much."

"No sir," said Jake. "I meant do you want an extra hand to take care of more horses."

"No, I don't want to buy more horses. I got enough."

"No, sir. I mean—"

"Say what you mean, boy!"

Jake sighed. "Sorry to trouble you, sir."

"Next time don't waste my time!" the man shouted at Jake as he walked out the door.

Continuing down the street, Jake kept looking for places he might work. From his time in Dodge City he had developed a strong aversion to saloons, and though he thought he could work in one if he had to, he preferred almost anything else.

Yet the street soon ended with nothing promising. A preacher had tried to bless him before Jake shooed him away, but other than that no one seemed to want to talk, much less offer him work.

At the far edge of town Jake tilted his hat to shield his eyes from the sun and looked up into the hills. Sounds trickled down from the slopes. The rushing of water. The clang of metal on stone. The occasional shout. Jake turned back and looked at the town, then back up at the hills. If he found work it would be there among the trees and rocks and streams, not among the buildings behind him.

After looking around until he found a path that led to the mines tucked into the trees, Jake scrambled down scree to the river. There he hopped the slippery river stones to the other side and walked up the trail, a small plume of dust following.

The path was rough and Jake's boots loosed several rocks as he walked, sending them crashing through the trees. Large branches arched overhead and shaded the way as the trail switched back and forth up the mountain.

Along the way Jake passed the remnants of claims that had been exhausted or never panned out. Broken tools and parts of sluice boxes littered the terrain, rusting and decaying back into the earth. From above he could hear the din of workers pounding on stones, and he walked toward the sound.

There along a small tributary to the creek below was a group of men huddled around a small section of the stream. Each one held a small pan, and was sifting through the stones on the screen. Behind them was a man wailing away at the side of a small cliff with a pickax. The noise was deafening to Jake, but the other men seemed to pay no mind as their eyes fixated on their work with the glint of greed.

When at last one of them saw Jake, the man let out a sharp cry. "Christ almighty! Where the hell did you come from?"

"Sorry, sir. I was—a"

"Get the hell away from my claim, kid," said another. "We don't want you here."

Jake braced himself for his temper to flame up, but it did not and instead he nodded coolly and touched the brim of his hat. Without speaking, he turned and continued to walk up the hill.

He passed several more claims, receiving mostly the same unkind welcome or feigned ignorance of his presence. A few were warmer in their greetings, but politely declined his offer to work.

For a while there was no one and the trail became faint and overgrown, the forest trying to reclaim what was once its own. Jake had almost decided to turn around when he heard a rise of laughter come from the other side of a large boulder ahead. He skirted around the rock to investigate.

A small rivulet trickled down the hill on the other side, and Jake followed it upstream until he came across a group of men in a small clearing where the stream bent slightly. All but one had their backs to Jake, but the man facing him quickly caught sight of him.

"Well, hello there," said the man. The others whirled to face the boy.

"Howdy," said Jake.

"What brings you all the way up the hill? You lost?"

"No sir. Just lookin' for work."

"Sir?" The man looked at the others. Hell, I ain't been called sir since...well, since ever in my life. Why don't you all call me sir?" He looked at the other men.

"'Cause sir is for royalty. Fine folk and the like," said one of the others. "You're the complete opposite."

In response the first man let out a loud, long fart followed by a cackle. "You got that right!" He laughed some more and took off his hat to fan the fetid air away from himself. It took a while for the man to stop laughing.

"What kind of work you looking for?" the man asked Jake.

"The kind that pays," said Jake.

The man bent his head and talked low with one of the others. Jake waited patiently at a comfortable distance. He wasn't sure about these men. Not yet, at least.

"Can I trust you, boy?" The man had stopped conferring and looked back up at Jake. The others looked at him, too, and he began to get a little uncomfortable with the attention.

"Yes, sir." Jake did not hesitate.

"You see," said the man, "it's a pain in the ass for us to go up and down this goddamn hill every day. We need someone to fetch us stuff if we need it."

"I can do that," said Jake.

"Alright," said the man. "We need some food. We've been up here a couple days, and we done run out this morning. Can you fetch us some oats, some beans and some cured pork?"

"Yes, sir."

The man laughed again. "I'm going to get used to this 'sir' stuff, kid."

"Anything else?" asked Jake.

"Nope," he said. "Go on and head down. I reckon we'll be hungry here in a little bit." He picked up his pan and scooped it into the stream.

Jake stood for a moment, rocking back and forth on his heels before speaking. "Sir?"

"What is it, kid?"

Jake cleared his throat. "I ain't got no money to buy the food."

"Hell, kid. That's okay. I'm good for it. I'll just pay you back when you get up here."

There was another pregnant pause as Jake rocked back and forth again. "Sir, I mean ain't got no money at all."

"Oh," said the man. "Well no wonder you don't mind hauling up and down the hill. Come on over here, then."

Picking his way through the bushes and hopping the stream at a narrow spot, Jake walked toward him. When he got there, the man took some bills out of his pocket and put them in Jake's hand. Jake tried to pull the money away, but the man held his hand firmly. When Jake looked up, the man was staring into his eyes.

"Don't think of stealing from me, boy." The jocular tone was gone, and his voice had a rough edge.

"No, sir," said Jake. "I ain't never stole from nobody, and I don't plan on starting."

The man let go. "I don't imagine you would."

Jake stuffed the money into his pocket and stuck out his hand. "My name's Jake, sir."

The man's stern face faded back into a smile. "Well, where are my manners? My name's Marvin."

"Pleased to meet you," said Jake.

"Likewise." Marvin turned to his companions. "That there's Tom." Tom touched his brim. "Then William." William nodded, and at the mention of his brother's given name Jake felt a strong wince of shame and longing. "And that one's named Tim but we all call him Bope."

The man Marvin had pointed at was massive, even bigger than he remembered Mr. McCready being. Another stab of sorrow poked at Jake. "Bope?" he asked.

"Don't ask," said Marvin.

Jake touched his brim and nodded to all three of the men. "I better be going," he said.

"Don't get lost," said Tom.

"No, sir." With that Jake turned and hopped back across the stream toward the boulder.

As Jake headed around the rock, one of the men shouted to him. "Bring us back some pussy, too!" All the men laughed. Jake felt a hot flush burn in his cheeks.

Back in town Jake quickly found the general store and walked to the entrance. At the door he hesitated, knowing his appearance might raise suspicion. He removed his hat, and in the warped reflection of the storefront Jake flattened his matted hair as best as he could. Then he took a deep breath and pushed open the door.

Inside was vast and dark, and it took his eyes some time to adjust to the low light. When they did, he saw several people staring at him, including the man behind the counter.

"Morning," said Jake. He reached to touch his brim but his hat was in his other hand so he tried to play off the motion by pretending there was something in his eye he needed to rub out. When he finished the people were still looking at him, but turned away once he caught their eyes. Jake swallowed and walked toward the man working there.

"Morning, sir," said Jake. The man nodded and looked him up and down, so Jake took the money and set it on the counter. The man's eyes drifted down to the wad of bills in Jake's hand.

"I've been sent here to buy some supplies for some miners working the hills," said Jake.

The man's rigid body and face loosened considerably at the mention of a possible sale. "Okay, son. You know what they want?"

"Yes, sir. They want some oats, some beans and some cured pork."

The man used the nub of a pencil to write the items on a pad. "How many men?"

"Four," said Jake.

"Including you?"

"No, sir. I reckon that's five, then. Although I ain't fully worked out the arrangements with them yet. I don't want to buy myself food with their money."

The man behind the counter looked strangely at Jake. "Where you from, son?"

"Missouri, sir."

The man nodded as if this had somehow confirmed his suspicion. "You can always trust a man from Missouri. What's the name of the man you working for?"

"His name's Marvin. And there are three other men with him."

"Marvin?" The man laughed. "Marvin would hire you. He'd let anybody work for him."

"Sir?"

"Hell, I don't mean anything by it. I just mean he's friendly enough to get along with everyone. You'll be alright. I'll throw in some extra and if he don't want to pay for your food, you can pay me back. Deal?"

"Yes, sir. Thank you."

"What's your name?"

"Jake." Jake stuck out his hand.

The man grasped the boy's hand. "Farnham," he said. "Now let me get that stuff for you, Jake."

Working swiftly the man brought each item to the counter after weighing and bagging it. When he was finished he used the pencil to tally all the amounts and prices. "$2.50."

Jake slid the bills across the counter and the man counted them and handed back Jake's change. "Thank you, Mr. Farnham."

"You heading up the hill with all this?"

"Yes, sir."

"You got anything to carry it in?"

"I'll be fine, thank you."

"You sure you don't want a larger bag or something? I trust Marvin to bring it back."

"I can manage."

"Suit yourself."

One by one Jake put the bags on the floor, arranging them by weight. With his left hand he lifted the oats, holding the other two bags in his right. They were heavier than he thought they would be, and he tried not to show strain as he carried them toward the door.

Several times on the street he stopped to renew his grip on the slipping bags, and he even thought about returning to the store to get a bag. But instead he doggedly continued toward the edge of town, shifting and readjusting the bags as he crossed the creek and hiked up the hill.

By the time he reached the boulder Jake's hands were shaking and burning and his grip had weakened so that he couldn't carry the bags more than fifty feet without stopping.

He rested his hands, took one big grip and carried the bags around the rock.

When Marvin saw him, his eyes grew big and he stood up. "Finally! What took you so long?" Marvin took the bags from Jake and immediately they fell to the ground. "Jesus, boy." He lifted them again. "You carried these all the way from town?"

"Yes, sir."

"Did Farnham sell you these?"

"Yes, sir."

Marvin laughed. "That no good sumbitch sold you enough for ten men for a week."

"I'm sorry, sir. I—"

Marvin waved his hand and laughed again. "Shit, son. That's my fault. I should've warned you." He turned toward the others and hefted the bags of food. "Hope you boys are hungry."

With a series of grunts and exclamations the men assembled around the cold gray fire pit and devoted themselves to different tasks. Tom dug through the pack to find the cooking and eating utensils. William set off into the woods and began collecting firewood. Bope used the remnants of wood from the last fire and began to construct a small teepee of twigs. In his enormous hands the wood looked like fine pieces of hair.

When Jake turned to Marvin and tried to hand him the change, Marvin waved him off. "Keep it," he said. "You earned it."

"Thank you, sir."

"Hell, Jake. I know I said I liked being called sir, but I was just messin'. It makes me feel old. Just call me Marvin."

"Okay," said Jake. "Can I help?"

Marvin walked over to where Tom had laid out the utensils, grabbed a large pot and brought it to Jake. "Fill this boy up about halfway."

Jake nodded and with his still cramping hand he gripped the blackened pot. The stream was close but he had to walk a bit downstream before finding a pool deep and clear enough to fill the pot. When he brought it back to the camp Marvin inspected the water.

"Shit, I'm going to like having you around, Jake. Them boys usually just get the water from the closest spot an bring it back all muddy and swimming with rocks. Bope even brought back a pot with a fish in it once. Too small to eat, though."

Jake said nothing, and when he looked at the other men he was surprised to see they had no reaction. Bope was blowing with surprising gentleness on a small fire now licking the insides of the twigs he had propped against each other.

Marvin told Jake to set the pot next to fire, then took the bag with beans and poured some into the water. "You know how to cook, Jake?"

"A little."

"Well, that's more than I do. I reckon you know how to make salt pork and beans?"

Jake nodded.

"Alright, then. Make sure you cook them beans good so we don't spend all night fartin'. We smell bad enough as is."

Jake smiled and walked toward the pot. He saw the fire ring actually contained a smaller ring, and inside that loose cobbling of rocks the fire was beginning to burn bright and hot.

"Here," said Marvin. He handed Jake an iron grate, heavy and sooted. "Give it to Bope, but you gotta wait for his signal."

292

The fire grew hotter and hotter under Bope's care and several times Jake tried to give him the grate. Each time Bope either ignored him or waved him away angrily. When at last the coals glowed orange and red and white hot, Bope reached back and took the grate out of Jake's hands without even looking at him.

With great ceremony, Bope lowered the grate onto the rocks and adjusted it, the flames curling around the cuffs of his jacket. Twice he had to pat the flames out, and only then did Jake notice the scorch marks pocking both forearms of the fabric. Though to Jake the grate seemed level, Bope raised and lowered the corners until he sat back, satisfied. As if asking permission, Jake looked at Bope as he brought the pot to the fire. The giant eyed the pot askew and nodded, and Jake gently placed the pot on the grate. When the waves of water inside stilled, Jake saw the level of the water now dotted with beans swirling in the slow currents was exactly level with the lip of the pot.

"Damn," said Jake. He felt a hand grip inside his arm and Marvin pulled him away from the fire.

Marvin spoke in a low voice. "We call him Bope because he's a big-ass dope. I never met anyone dumber or stronger. He can lift an ox but he can't hardly talk and other than lifting things the only thing he's good at is building that fire. It's like it's a religion for him or something. But once William—who's also dumber than shit—tried to start the fire and Bope broke his arm without even trying. Just grabbed it and snapped it clean."

Jake stared at the thing at the end of Bope's arm more paw than hand and shuddered. "How'd he come to work for you?"

"Me and my brother Tom came up here from Kansas looking for gold and found this unclaimed piece of land to work," said Marvin. "It ain't much but so far we've got enough out of it to feed ourselves and get some whiskey and maybe even buy some time with the ladies in town."

"Anyway, me and Tom was in town one day and seen Bope fighting about half a dozen men. He was pounding them all good but he looked scared doing it. Tom and me had a guy who worked on our farm when we were kids, and he was a lot like Bope. Like a big, sweet kid scared of the world.

"Well these boys was picking on him and Tom and me didn't like that too much so we joined in and yelled at the men to leave him alone. Bope never said nothing but when we tried to leave he followed us. We kept telling him to git, but he wouldn't leave so we just took him up here with us. We don't let him go to town, though, unless we're with him."

"What about William?" asked Jake. He looked at the pot and saw whirls of steam rising above the lip.

"Now William's a curious individual," said Marvin. "Tom and I debate about him all the time. Tom thinks William's a shade smarter than Bope, but sometimes I see William looking at us like he knows exactly what's going on. He's like Bope 'cause he don't say shit, but there's something in the way his eyes look at the world that makes me think there's something going on behind them.

"Anyway, his story's like Bope's. He found us and we took him in. Tom gets mad at me and calls me Sister Marvin 'cause he says I always take in the charity cases, but they're good men and they don't steal nothing and they work hard and do what we ask them to do. Better than all these stories I hear of men killing each other over nuggets. And they seem happy with what we give them as pay. Bope eats as much as three horses but we don't pay him in gold because he eats that, too. He just eats a lot."

Marvin fell silent as if all the air had been let out of his lungs and he were slowly filling them back up. After a while Jake said he would check on the beans and Marvin simply nodded.

Periodically Jake checked the beans and when they were halfway cooked he threw in several hunks of salt pork and looked at Bope and threw in a couple more and stirred them in with a wooden spoon. At regular intervals he stirred the pork and beans until the mixture turned a grayish brown and the bubbles of fat from the pork pooled on the surface.

Jake said it was ready and the men came and Jake spooned the meal into their tin cups. Marvin came last with two cups and when Jake had filled them both Marvin handed one to Jake.

"Thanks," said Jake.

"You were the one who hauled it and cooked it, so you deserve your share," said Marvin.

"I can pay you for it."

"Jesus, Jake. You're too polite. Don't worry about it. Just eat."

The men dispersed to their own spots. Bope and William walked far apart from everyone and Tom, who had not spoken much since Jake arrived, sat beside his brother near the fire. Jake sat by himself too, but after a long time of eating lean he was quickly full. Soon Marvin yelled at him to come over.

"Here," said Marvin as Jake sat down. "Have a swig of this."

Jake peered at the bottle in Marvin's hand. "No thanks."

"What's a matter, you don't drink?"

"Ain't never tried."

"Well Jake, you don't know what you're missing. Here, take a swig. The trick is to start slow. Don't drink it like water or nothing."

Whether out of fear of offense or merely a sense of obligation to the man who now seemed to be taking him in, Jake grabbed the bottle and took a small sip. His lips burned and so did part of his mouth but it didn't reach past that. He could barely taste the liquid through the sensation so he brought the bottle to his lips again and took a longer swig. In a rush the burn went all the way down his throat and he forced himself to swallow everything before bringing his free hand to mouth and coughing.

Marvin slapped his thigh and laughed and even Tom smiled. "Now you're doing it right, Jake. Whaddaya think?"

Jake handed the bottle to Tom and shook his head, coughing some more.

"Oh, don't worry," said Marvin. "You'll want some more soon enough."

Tom took a swig and then Marvin again but when Marvin tried to hand it over, Jake refused and coughed once more.

"Suit yourself," said Marvin.

A warm happy feeling started to creep over Jake, as if someone had lit a comforting fire from within him. He liked the feeling, but was scared it would morph into something far more sinister, the drunken stupors and rages he had so often seen working in a saloon. To fight it off he asked a question.

"What kind of farm did y'all have in Kansas?"

"Mostly wheat," said Tom. His voice was lower and scratchier than Marvin's. "But we grew and raised everything we ate."

"That's a good life," said Jake. "Why'd you leave it?" Jake surprised himself with asking so frank a question. It was as if the words came out before he could stop them.

Tom seemed a little taken aback, but Marvin didn't flinch. "Our pa had to sell our farm. So we took the money we had and headed out here."

Jake nodded. "Sorry," he said, not sure if he meant for the tough turn of events or for his asking about them.

"What about you?" asked Tom. "Where you from, Jake?"

"Missouri."

"Uh oh," said Marvin. "Looks like we got ourselves an enemy in the midst." He laughed.

"You have a farm?" asked Tom.

Jake nodded. "Used to. Not much land, though. We grew what we could and hunted the rest."

Tom and Marvin looked at each other. "You say you can hunt?" Marvin and asked.

"Yup."

"That might come in handy," said Marvin.

Jake did not respond, but when Marvin handed him the bottle he took it. The warm feeling had started to disappear, and he wanted it to come back. This time he took two swigs, and they went down much more easily than before.

Marvin laughed. "Slow down there, Jake. You don't want to end up puking it all back up."

Jake's face burned and he wiped his mouth before handing the bottle back. His limbs felt loose and warm now, and he listened as Tom and Marvin reminisced about their farm. He liked to hear them talk, and he didn't know if it was because they were nice or because they talked about a farm or because finally he could understand what they were talking about after months living in a foreign language. Occasionally he drank from the bottle but mostly he didn't. Yet still the world seemed a warmer, happier place each time he did.

He heard Marvin's voice, but he didn't understand what he said.

"Sorry?" asked Jake.

"I said, how the hell did you get all the way out here?"

Jake cleared his throat and in his mind he started to construct a lie. Though he tried to keep it as simple as possible soon it started spinning out of control and when he opened his mouth the truth spilled out.

He told the whole story about Billy and his aunt and her husband and the McCreadys and working in a saloon and Mr. Ferris and the tribe who took them in. The words tumbled out and no matter how hard Jake tried to stop them from escaping they kept coming. Only once did he look up at the brothers and they were staring back at him with open and silent mouths so he lowered his eyes back to the ground.

When he was nearing the part about the soldiers Jake suddenly found his filter and merely told Tom and Marvin that he and Billy had gotten into a big argument so Billy stayed with the tribe and Jake came here.

At last Jake stopped speaking and he felt as if a great weight had been lifted. He felt like laughing and crying but did neither and felt the weight return as the brothers stared at him quietly. The darkness and silence seemed to press back down on Jake, and he almost spoke again to break the tension. But he didn't know what to say.

"Damn, Jake." It was Marvin. "Either you're one hell of a story teller, or you've had the most interesting life any thirteen-year-old ever had."

"My brother's the story teller," was all Jake could say. At the thought of Billy and his stories Jake felt a tear well up in his eye. He stifled it and stood. "Thanks, Marvin, for taking me in. I best get to sleep now."

"You go ahead," said Marvin.

"Good night Jake," said Tom.

"Night," said Jake. He picked his way around some trees to a flat spot and spread out his bed roll and lay down. Through the thin lattice of pine boughs he could see faint stars twinkling far above. Alone now, he let the tears come and he cried softly for a while.

He could hear Tom and Marvin walking close by and they stopped not far from where he was. Their voices carried in the still night air, and Jake heard Tom say his name. "Well, Sister Marvin. It looks like you're taking on another charity case."

"Jake ain't no charity, Tom. And neither are Bope or William. They do their share. The boy can cook and fetch us food and hell, he can even hunt."

"He says he can hunt," said Tom.

"If he says it, I believe it."

There was a pause before Tom responded. "I do, too. Just as long as he doesn't start asking for shares of our gold."

"I don't think he will," said Marvin. "Besides, I need someone else to talk to around here. I'm tired of just talking to you."

Tom laughed. "Good night, Marvin."

"Night, Tom."

By now the weight of sleep was heavy on Jake, and he was having trouble keeping his eyes open. Soon he gave up the fight and fell into a deep slumber.

Early summer bled into high summer, and Jake found his place with the brothers and Bope and William. They gave him more work like removing rocks and working the sluice box, but more often than not they let him go hunting. It saved them money, they said, and the eating was better than anything they could get at the store.

In the river they found flakes and the occasional small nugget of gold, and sometimes when the brothers went to town to sell it they brought along Jake. With their money they bought supplies and paid small amounts to Jake and William. With his money Jake bought new pants and shirts and drawers but he kept his hat and boots.

Jake worked hard and ate well and before long he felt his muscles starting to move against the inside of his shirt. His voice seemed to grow deeper and deeper and every night Tom and Marvin drank he drank too. He found he could drink more and more, and Marvin teased him that Jake would soon be able to drink more than he could.

One morning Jake woke before the sun and decided to go hunting. The animals had now become aware of his presence, and he had to hike farther away from camp to find ones who weren't skittish at the slightest sound. Jake and the men had subsisted well enough on smaller game, but Jake was itching for something bigger. He knew it would be difficult to fell a deer with only a pistol, but he had seen it done before and wanted to try. He imagined the looks on the faces of the others if he brought a deer back to camp.

The silver rays of the morning moon sliced through the trees at a steep angle, and a milky band of stars blurred the light from the other stars overhead. Not even the earliest risers of the birds had begun their calls, so each sound Jake made seemed to rise all the way to the sky arching above. It was hard for Jake to slip his boots between the twigs on the ground, and for a moment he found himself wishing for a pair of moccasins. He shook off the thought with a smile.

After a while he reached the top of the hill and began descending the slope to the valley between it and a much taller peak to the north. On his wanderings he had once spied a white sliver running down the lowest crease between the hills. It was there he hoped to find his deer.

By the time he reached the water the eastern sky glowed the palest of yellows, and the early morning shadows played tricks on Jake's eyes. Though he was tempted to drink, he walked down the stream at a distance until he found a quiet pool where on the opposite bank lay a slim trail trampled in the underbrush. On the cool side of a pine Jake sat and watched and waited. He became as still as the tree, and the forest around him began to stir with the sounds of a new day.

At first the slow passing of minutes calmed Jake, slowing his pulse and his thoughts. But as the sun climbed and the world warmed there was still no sign of deer. His mind began playing tricks, and soon Jake was imagining a deer head every few minutes. He wondered if the whiskey he had drunk the night before caused his imaginings, and he vowed not to drink any tonight. Still, he couldn't return his focus to the reality of the woods, so he stood and turned to walk back up the hill.

By the time he reached the top it was past midday, and the sun had heated the landscape. Jake was perspiring and his sweat smelled of alcohol and again he vowed not to drink tonight but already he was learning that those promises are sometimes broken. Descending the hill Jake felt the breeze rising from the valley. It cooled him and he stopped and took off his hat to let the air wick away the moisture and heat. And as he stood there he heard shouts coming from farther down the hill.

Fearing something had gone wrong, Jake drew his pistol and ran as quickly and as quietly as he could toward the camp. His mind raced with possibilities. A fight between the brothers and William and Bope, or maybe another group of men who came to take the claim. But the noises sounded happy, and when Jake entered the clearing, pistol in hand, he saw the brothers hugging and jumping in a circle. Before they could see him, Jake put the pistol back in his belt.

Marvin whirled around. "Jake! Jake! We're rich! Goddammit we're rich!" He held up a nugget the size of his palm. "We're rich!"

His eyes never leaving the gold, Jake rushed toward it and, with a nod of permission from Marvin, took and held it in his hand. The weight of it was more than he anticipated, and his arm sunk a little.

"See how heavy it is?" said Tom. "That's how you know it's pure."

Letting the nugget settle in his palm, Jake hefted it up and down, eyes wide. "Dang," said Jake.

"Dang is right!" said Marvin. "We're heading to town now to sell it. Come and join us!" From his pocket he pulled a flask of whiskey and handed it to Jake. And Jake, forgetting the promises he had made moments before, grabbed it and took a long drink.

By the time they reached the bottom of the hill the bottle was empty. William and Bope had stayed behind to watch the camp, and Tom at least had the good sense not to take more than a few sips of whiskey until they sold the nugget. That left the majority of the drinking to Marvin and Jake. And as they climbed the small hill to get into town, Jake felt the familiar loose and wobbly feeling in his legs.

In town they headed straight for the gold merchant. As they walked Marvin shouted over Tom's shushing that they had pulled a large nugget from the earth so that by the time they reached the merchant, a small group of people trailed in their wake. The man behind the counter was with another customer, but Marvin grabbed the gold from Tom, brushed past the customer and slammed the nugget onto the counter.

The man's eyebrows raised and eyes widened and he stared at the hunk of metal in front of him. Then he looked up and saw the mass of people wriggling over each other like puppies trying to get a better view. He took a deep breath and pointed at all of them before shouting, "I talk to one man. Everyone else, out!"

In unison, like a flock of birds changing direction in an instant, the crowd hung their heads and shuffled out the door. Besides the other customer only Jake, Tom and Marvin remained. The merchant looked at the three of them.

"One man," he said, holding his index finger aloft for emphasis.

Jake backed away, and after a quick, whispered conversation Marvin nodded to Tom and walked toward Jake. "Come on," he said. "Let's wait with the rabble."

They pushed through the door to see an even larger group than had accompanied them waiting outside. An audible gasp rose from the mass of people when Jake and Marvin emerged.

"How much?" shouted one of the men.

"We'll find out soon enough," said Marvin. He scanned the crowd, smiling as he hooked his thumbs into his belt loops. "Anybody got any whiskey?"

A few snickers came from the group.

"I'm good for it."

Another, louder round of laughter. From within the crowd a bottle flew toward Marvin, and he ducked. Fortunately, Jake was able to catch it and when he did the men cheered. Jake felt a small flush of pride burn in his cheeks. Marvin grabbed the bottle from his hand and held it aloft, and the crowd cheered again.

He unscrewed the cap and took a drink. When he finished, he lifted the bottle again. "As soon as I get my pay, I'm buying the first round of drinks for everyone!"

The crowd erupted.

Marvin handed the bottle to Jake, and with a big smile he took a long drink. He was starting to get past the point he had ever been before, past the comfortable, loose and happy feeling drinking had given him before to a place where his body seemed to move of its own accord, refusing or at least delaying the commands his brain was sending it. A voice in his head was warning him to stop, but he drowned it out with another drink.

At last Tom emerged from the merchant, pulling Marvin and Jake close to him. Into Marvin's hand he shoved a large wad of folded bills. "Count it later," he said. Then he turned to Jake and handed him a smaller, though still sizable amount of bills. "Don't spend it all in one place, kid."

Jake looked down and saw more money than he had ever seen in his life lying in his palm. Afraid and almost ashamed he would lose it, Jake thrust it all into his pocket. He felt Marvin's hand grip him on the shoulder.

"Come on, kid. Let's go celebrate."

With the mass of onlookers following close behind, Jake and the brothers walked directly to the saloon. It had been a long time since Jake had even set foot in one, and never as a customer. The men inside all turned and looked as the large group of people entered. At first the barman eyed them suspiciously, but when Marvin threw down several bills the man's expression changed completely.

"Buy a round for everyone in here!" he said.

Out of the corner of his eye, Jake saw Tom shake his head. But he ignored it and sidled next to Marvin. When the whiskey came he took his, and though Marvin encouraged him to drink it quickly Jake decided to wait a while. That voice in his head had come back, and something told him he should listen.

The brothers and Jake moved to a table some men had cleared for them, and when they sat down the entire population of the saloon seemed to huddle around them, peppering them with questions about how they came across their find. Jake tried to listen intently as Marvin and Tom, who had now had several drinks, regaled them with the details. Yet each time something caused Jake to lose focus. The jostling of people behind him, a random thought popping from his increasingly cloudy mind, the passing breasts of a woman.

Throughout the storytelling Jake held firm to his full glass, at times staring solely at the amber liquid in front of him. Though he had not drunk since outside the merchant, he felt his body losing more and more control. Even as he sat there he felt his head loll, his free arm slip off the table. He feared if he had one more drink he would pass out. But then Marvin turned to him and said, "You gonna drink that or what?" Jake brought the glass to his lips and tilted it back, drinking it as if it were water.

After that Jake didn't remember much, just a scattered collage of faces and sounds. At one point someone placed a loaf of bread on the table, and Jake tore off a piece and shoved it in his mouth. As he chewed some drool escaped his lips and he wiped it with his sleeve. After several bites the rumbling in Jake's stomach subsided and his head seemed to clear a bit, so he tore off another piece and kept eating.

Religiously he made his way through half the large loaf, and despite the ringing in his ears he began to hear what Tom and Marvin were saying. At this point both were slurring their words with hoarse voices, and the crowd had thinned considerably. Most of the men had gone, and next to each brother sat a woman. The woman next to Marvin had the largest breasts Jake had ever seen, and even though he knew it was rude he couldn't stop staring at the long line of cleavage exposed by the low, loosened neck of her dress.

The woman noticed and laughed and Jake felt ashamed and pretended to become very interested in the empty barstool over her shoulder. She whispered something to Marvin and Marvin laughed and nodded and looked at Jake.

"You need a girl," he said.

Jake shook his head, too embarrassed to speak.

"Come on, Jake. This is a celebration. You need someone to celebrate with. Pick anyone you want, and I'll introduce you." Marvin waved his arm and knocked over his glass. The woman laughed. Tom was too busy kissing the neck of the woman next to him to notice.

Again Jake felt his cheeks flush but he could not bring himself to say anything. Almost involuntarily, though, his eyes moved around the room. Talking to a man at the bar was a woman with long, blonde hair. Unlike most of the women in the saloon her figure was slight and Jake watched with fascination as the strap on her dress kept slipping off her shoulder, and she would reach with her hand and flip back her hair and pull the strap up in one coquettish motion.

The next thing he noticed was Marvin walking up next to her. He said something to her and she looked directly at Jake and Jake turned away. But he couldn't help looking back and when he did he saw her sashaying toward him, the man at the bar raising his arms and shouting in protest.

She was too quick for his drunken eyes to follow her as she circled behind him. But he heard the squeak of a chair to his right and when he turned she was sitting next to him, her head resting in her hand as she stared at Jake.

"What's your name?" she asked.

Jake tried to say his name, but no more than a cough came out.

"Aw, he's shy," she said, turning to Marvin. Her hand touched Jake on his shoulder and slid down his arm, and it thrilled him.

"Jake," said Marvin. "His name's Jake."

"Hi, Jake," she said, looking back into Jake's eyes. "I'm Annie."

Again the heat of shame warmed his neck, but he could not muster a word.

"Where you from, honey?" asked Annie.

Why the state of his birth was the only word he was able to pronounce, Jake did not know. All he knew was that "Missouri" came out of his mouth before he could stop it.

Annie gasped. "You don't say. Me too! Whereabouts?"

Suddenly Jake found his voice. "South of Sainte Genevieve. On a farm."

"Well, I'll be. A farm boy from Sainte Gen. I'm from just down river. Cape Girardeau."

Jake smiled but said nothing.

"You don't talk much, do you?" she asked. "Well, that's okay. Most men I'm with want me to listen to all their boring stories about mining or their stupid relationships with their mothers or which women they fucked in which towns coming out here."

Jake was shocked to hear such a dirty word come out of the mouth of a woman who looked so innocent, but he quickly forgot that as Annie rubbed both his thighs with her hands. He felt a warm prodding between his legs.

"You just sit there and I'll do the talking," said Annie.

Jake swallowed hard and nodded. As Annie talked he listened, staring at her blue eyes and soft, white skin, catching glances of her breasts before looking away. She spoke of an angry father and protective brothers lost to disease or drink, of an absent mother and a journey west with a man she thought loved her but left her as soon as they reached Kansas. And all the while she touched Jake, holding his hand or

308

rubbing his arm or running her fingers through his hair. He thought Annie was the most wonderful thing he had ever seen.

When she got to the part of her story where she had arrived in town, her voice took a darker, angrier tone. But she cut through that quickly and a smile returned to her face. Then she stood up, pushed out Jake's chair and sat on his lap.

"You were so sweet to listen to me," she said, arms wrapped around his shoulders, fingers caressing the back of his head. "Why don't I take you upstairs and show you how grateful I am?"

Jake was afraid she could feel him poking her from underneath. He tried to reposition himself, but she just rubbed herself up against him and he felt a rush of joy run through him.

She stood up and only then did Jake notice Marvin and Tom and their women were gone. Annie held out her hand and not thinking Jake took it and stood. When Annie looked down he became acutely aware of a protrusion just below his belt and he bent over to hide it.

"Looks like some of my work is already done," she said.

Before Jake could stop her she pulled him by the hand and led him through the tables to the stairs at the back of the saloon. As they passed, men looking into their glasses cheered and shouted encouragement to Jake but all he could do was focus on the touch of Annie's hand and the warm feeling filling every part of his body.

The stairs creaked as they walked up them, and for a moment Jake wondered if they would hold. Never letting go of his hand, Annie led him past closed doors until they found one that was open slightly. The room smelled of alcohol and smoke and sweat and something else Jake had never smelled before.

Annie walked him to the bed and told him to sit down so he did. Without warning she started unbuttoning his shirt, and in reflex Jake's hands shot up to brush hers away.

"It's okay, sweetie," she said, holding his chin in her hand. "I'm going to take good care of you." She took his hands and put them on her butt and as much as he tried Jake could not get them to move.

When she was finished unbuttoning she opened his shirt and slid it down his arms. His hands slipped from behind her and now he could not keep his eyes off her breasts. She laughed and he looked up and she said, "Go ahead and touch them, honey." Afraid she would change her mind he hurried his hands up to her breasts as soon as they were free of his shirt.

Annie laughed. "Whoa, easy boy. They're not going anywhere."

Jake massaged them and wondered at their softness and firmness like nothing he had felt before and when she pushed him back into the bed he tried in vain to hold onto them. Annie made quick work of his pants and soon Jake was lying stark naked on a bed in front of a woman for the first time in his life. That realization so utterly froze him, Annie had to lift his stiff body to the center of the bed before straddling him.

Slipping her shoulders and arms through the straps of her dress, Annie let her dress fall around her waist and Jake's eyes widened and hands rushed back up to her breasts. "Okay now," was all Annie said before reaching between Jake's legs.

He felt the warmth and wetness and burning shame and all he could do was hold onto Annie's breasts as she moved on top of him. The alcohol still had its hold on him and he did not know what was going on but soon he felt a rush and his whole body seize up and Annie moved closer and he wrapped his arms around her and hugged her tight as she lay on top of him.

His whole body was shaking but he wasn't cold and soon he felt very sleepy. Annie whispered in his ear, "You can let go now," and he did. He turned so she couldn't see him and he felt her lift the sheet over him. "Take as long as you like," he heard her say.

Only then did he look and he saw her pulling some money out of his pants pocket. Before he could say anything she padded to the door and left. Jake fell asleep.

When he woke the room was dark. A pulsing pain pounded on the inside of his head and his tongue was dry and swollen and he wanted nothing more than water to drink. His senses slowly returned and he saw a sliver of light under the door and muffled sounds on the other side.

Quickly he swung out of bed and put on his pants and shirt and boots and hat and walked toward the door. There he paused for a moment, half expecting Annie would be on the other side waiting for him. Then he realized he did not want to see her or anyone but wanted to find some place to be by himself so he opened the door and entered the hallway.

Sporadic candles on the walls gave off a faint glow, and as Jake walked toward the stairs more light lifted up from the saloon below. Without even looking at who was there, Jake hurried down the stairs and through the tables mostly empty now and out the door. The street was dark and empty and almost noiseless and Jake kept his eyes to the ground as he stumbled through the shadows and out of town.

When he reached the slope to the river he picked his way through the rocks to the water. After finding a pool deep enough to drink from, Jake took off his hat and bent his face to the surface but went too far and dunked his whole head. The cold shocked him and he recoiled, more awake and alert now, before slowly lowering his head again.

His lips touched the water and he took several long pulls. It tasted cool and fresh and filled his body with energy and he drank more and more until his belly was full. When he could drink no more he rocked back on his haunches. Immediately he felt queasy and lightheaded and he turned to his right and vomited.

His throat burned with bile and in the moonlight he saw his spew swirl in the eddies of the river before being carried downstream. After he had spit it all out he brought his lips back to the river and took only a mouthful. With the water he rinsed out his mouth and when he spit that out he took another mouthful. When the taste was mostly gone Jake dared to drink again, taking cautious sips and pausing in between. Then he crossed the river and walked into the trees, searching until he found a flat spot to fall asleep again.

Jake woke drenched in sweat and completely without his bearings. It took him several minutes to figure out where he was and piece together the previous night's events, and when he did he felt ashamed. The thought of returning to town terrified him, but then he thought of Annie and her golden hair and blue eyes and the feel of her skin in his hands and he knew he had to see her again.

Before heading back to camp he had to descend to find the trail by the river. It did not take him long, and then he began the painful march back up the hill. His legs and lungs burned and his heart and head pounded but by the time he reached the top he felt better.

Marvin and Tom were there asleep under trees and Bope was eating from his cup in the shade of another one. The pot was sitting next to the ashy remnants of a fire, and Jake looked inside. There was still some pork and beans left so Jake ladled it into a cup and ate and it tasted salty and good. He was so absorbed with the eating he almost didn't see William skirting the fringe of the clearing.

Over his shoulder William had slung all his belongings and when Jake looked at him he flinched but didn't stop walking. Jake stood chewing his food like a cow with its cud and watching as William moved closer to the boulder bounding the edge of camp.

"See you, kid," said William. It was the first words Jake had heard him speak, and the shock of it was so much Jake could not respond before William slipped out of sight behind the boulder.

When Jake finished his meal he went to where he stashed his bag, checked that all his clothes and his father's pistol and the letters were in there, and headed down the trail toward town. He had fresh clothes in his bag, but he didn't want to wear them until he had cleaned himself up.

In town he went to the wash house and took a bath and afterward he went looking for flowers. Some part of him knew it was silly but he wanted to make a better impression on Annie than he had the last time. Very cautiously so he wouldn't sweat too much, Jake went down the hill outside of town and picked some.

By now the sun was sitting low on the horizon, and Jake hoped Annie would be in the saloon. At the door he dusted off his pant legs as best he could, and clutching the thin cluster of wildflowers Jake walked inside. The large room was bustling now, and several people recognized him as he wandered through the tables looking for Annie. More than once someone asked if Jake would buy a drink, but Jake ignored them.

After several fruitless laps around the room Jake walked up to the bar and asked if Annie was there. The man pointed toward a table close to the stairs, and Jake saw Annie talking with another man. His heart leaped and he began walking toward her, practicing what he was going to say. But as he did Annie stood and grabbed the man by the hand. She led him to the stairs and began to climb and when the man grabbed her ass she laughed and shook it and he grabbed it again. Then he came up from behind her and fondled her breasts and began humping her before she laughed again and pushed him away. As she did she looked out and saw Jake standing there flowers wilting in his hand and smiled and winked and took the man upstairs and disappeared down the hallway with him.

For a while Jake just stood there as sorrow and shame and anger washed over him in waves. He felt like everyone in the room was staring and laughing at him, but he could not bring his feet to move. A thousand possibilities entered his mind, going up there and stopping her, waiting for her to come out and pretending he hadn't seen, waiting and seeing her and pretending it was no big deal. But soon the swirl of emotions became too much, and all Jake could think to do was walk to the bar and order a drink.

When the bartender brought a shot of whiskey Jake slammed it back and asked for another. The bartender obliged and Jake drank that too and asked for another. Almost apologizing the bartender explained he knew Jake had just earned a lot of money but he needed payment to pour another. Jake searched in his pocket and took out a bill and put it on the table. He explained to the man that he wanted to drink and the man said no problem and left the bottle on the bar before walking away with the money.

Jake poured another drink and then another. He wanted the feeling back and he wanted it now, but it would not come. This was not a warm, happy feeling. More a dulling of pain. His throat burned and he stopped drinking for a while, but the alcohol still worked its way through his body. His arms tingled and the sights and sounds around him blurred and finally he began to feel it. Warm. Happy. Invincible.

He would wait until Annie came and would tell her how nice it was to see her and would she like to sit and talk a while. He took another drink because now he could handle it. It would give him the extra confidence and coolness he would need to talk to her. Jake turned to see if she had come back down yet, but before he could look for her he saw Marvin sitting at the table closest to the bar.

He was talking with a woman but Jake could not tell if it was the same one or different from the night before. They too stood up and as they walked by Marvin turned and saw Jake. With a slow smile he said, "Hey Jake," before walking upstairs. It warmed Jake to see him, and a few minutes later when he saw Annie coming down the stairs by herself, he was sure his plan would work.

His eyes followed her, and as she descended she smiled and looked about the room. As Jake hoped her eyes caught his, and she smiled more broadly and gave a little wave. He waited patiently until she made the walk over to him, and when she was close enough he stood to greet her. Immediately his legs gave out from underneath and he tumbled headlong onto the floor.

Jake thought he felt Annie's arms try to catch him, but the next thing he knew he was rolling around on the wet wooden floor. After the initial jolt he started laughing. Annie grabbed his hands and tried to pull him up, but he was laughing too hard. Soon he felt someone hook underneath his arms and throw him up against the bar. There he was able to fumble around until he was on his seat again.

Then Annie appeared at his side. "Hey stranger," she said.

Jake felt her hand rub up his arm, and he smiled. "Hey."

"I had fun last night."

"Me too." To Jake, something didn't sound quite right with his words, as if there were a delay from his tongue to the air.

"How you feeling there? You look like you've been tipping back a couple."

"Good," said Jake, but the word was much more elongated than he intended. "You wanna go upstairs?" Jake was horrified the request came out so soon, but there was no catching it now.

"Well," said Annie. To Jake's relief, she laughed. "That's a little forward, even for me. You don't want to talk to me for a little?"

"Yesh. Yesh. I like...talk." Jake leaned in closer to her but lost his balance as his elbow slipped off the bar. His head landed squarely in Annie's chest.

"Okay there," she said as she lifted him back up. "Earl, can we get some water for this young gentleman here?"

"Good idea," said Jake. The words sounded normal to him and he gained courage to speak some more. "I like you Annie."

"I like you, too."

"I mean I like you a whole lot."

"I know, Jake. Let's get you some water."

"I don't need it, Annie. I'm fine, honest. Look." Jake stood triumphantly, hands on hips, and Annie laughed. Encouraged, Jake attempted to dance a jig, something he had never done in his life, and tumbled backward into a table of men playing poker. They yelled and one of them shoved him hard so that he slammed back into the bar. Again Jake laughed.

"Jesus, Jake," said Annie with surprising scorn. "Come back and talk to me when you are sober."

Before Jake could stop her she marched away. He turned to the bar and saw a glass of water in front of him. Remembering his experience from earlier in the day he tried to sip it, but ended up spilling half of it on the bar. When he asked for another drink the bartender scolded him and told him to get out. After a small, unsuccessful argument Jake managed to stand himself upright, leaning against the protesting patrons at the bar as he made his way for the door.

A shout and a kick to the ribs woke Jake next. He rolled over and saw the storeowner Farnham standing above him.

"Get off my porch, you filthy drunk."

Jake mumbled sorry and rolled over to his hands, pushing himself up to all fours. He felt nauseous and dizzy, and for a moment he swayed there despite Farnham yelling at him to

317

move. Finally he was able to stand and, not wanting Farnham to recognize him, Jake turned away and stumbled down the stairs into the street.

Jake knew he shouldn't drink but now the drink had gotten hold of him and he wanted nothing more than to taste the burning and feel the warmth. The sun was brighter than he could stand and he shielded his eyes as he staggered toward the pub. He was almost at the door when he remembered Annie and how embarrassed he was about the previous night and he vowed never to drink again.

Then he felt in his pockets and pulled out his money. There were a few coins and a lot fewer bills than he remembered, but still enough to get something to eat. But then he thought of his bag and panic took hold of him. Where had he left it? Was it up at the camp? In his mind he tried to retrace his steps. No, he thought. I took it from the camp. So where did I leave it? After picturing the wash house and the field where he picked the flowers Jake finally remembered that he entered the saloon still holding his bag.

He rushed to the doors and slammed them open. Earl the bartender from the night before was there, and he yelled at Jake to be more careful with the doors.

"Sorry," said Jake as he hurried to the bar. "Did you see my bag from last night?"

Jake got closer and Earl squinted at his face. "Oh," he said. "It's you. Yeah, Annie gave it to me and told me to hold onto it. You're lucky she was looking out for you, kid. It would've been gone otherwise."

After opening it up, a huge sigh of relief whooshed out of Jake when he saw his father's pistol and the letters buried under his clothes at the bottom of the bag.

"Thanks," said Jake. He took out a coin and placed it on the bar. "Really, thanks."

"Don't sweat it, kid. Here." Earl poured a drink and slid it across the bar.

Jake held up his hand. "Thanks, but I really shouldn't."

"Don't worry, it's on the house."

Though Jake tried not to his hand was already reaching for the glass. "Thanks." He brought the drink to his lips and attempted to sip slowly, but soon he was pouring the whole shot down his throat.

Jake was shaken awake by Earl, a puddle of drool pooling under his mouth on the bar. He had no idea what time it was, but it was dark and the bar was empty save the bartender and a man mopping the floors and wiping the tables.

"Time to go, boss," he said.

"What time is it?" Jake slurred.

Earl pointed outside and even through the leaded glass Jake could see a lightening sky. "Daytime," said Earl.

As Jake lifted his head off the bar he could feel the dull pain that was just beginning its residence in his head. Soon he knew his whole body would be racked with an unbearable ache. His head was still foggy as he mumbled an apology on his way toward the door. The sky was turning from black to slate, but there was light enough for Jake to see the street as he plodded toward the edge of town.

He knew he had to get away. From town, from the brothers, from alcohol. He wanted to see Annie again, to feel her soft skin and blonde hair and gentle touch. But he knew he had to clear his head first.

319

Across the street from the store, Jake waited for it to open. The streets were mostly empty, with only the occasional passerby, industrious miners heading for the hills, the stumbling drunk wandering home. At last Jake saw Farnham enter the store. He watched as the man lit the lanterns and removed the dust covers from the shelves and counters, putting on his apron when he was finished.

For a moment Jake hesitated, not wanting another confrontation like the last he had with Farnham. Jake could smell the whiskey seeping out of his pores, so he was sure everyone else could. Still, Jake needed to leave town fast, and he needed supplies to do it. As best he could Jake flattened his hair and straightened his clothes before walking across the street and into the store.

Farnham looked startled when the door opened, and when he saw Jake his face lowered into a scowl. "I'm not selling you any alcohol!"

"And I ain't buyin' it, sir. I just need a few days' supplies."

"For you and the brothers?"

"No sir. Just myself."

Farnham's face relaxed a little. "Good. That's good. Those brothers have been different people ever since they struck it."

"Yes sir. That's why I need to get away for a bit."

"Alright then. What do you need?"

"Just some beans, some salt pork and some oats. And I suppose I need a pot for cooking. You got one?"

"Sure do. I've got everything you need if you've got the money."

"I do," said Jake. His heart jumped as he realized he had not checked his pocket to see if he had any money left.

"Give me a minute," said Farnham. He disappeared in the back and when he did Jake shoved his hand into his pants pocket and breathed a sigh of relief as he felt coins and a few bills still there. Looking up to see if Farnham was still gone, Jake pulled it out. He didn't have nearly as much as he started with, but it was enough to buy what he needed.

Finally Farnham emerged from the back room with a shiny new pot and set it on the counter. He measured out the oats and beans and salt pork and put them in burlap bags.

"Do you have any used pots?" asked Jake.

Farnham scowled again and heaved a dramatic sigh. "Let me check." He went back into storage room again and emerged a short time later with a blackened, dented pot. "It doesn't have a handle."

"That's alright," said Jake. "How much do I owe you?"

Farnham took out his pad and pencil and scratched a few numbers on there. "$1.65," he said.

Jake counted the money and handed him coins and Farnham took them and rang up the register and dropped the change into Jake's hand.

"Be careful out there, son."

"Thank you, sir. I will. Although I reckon it's a lot less dangerous out there than it is here in town."

Farnham looked at Jake and for a while said nothing but then let out a small laugh. "Amen to that."

He smiled and Jake smiled back and took his bags and pot out the door and out of town.

Jake knew exactly where he wanted to go. He walked up the trail as far as it went, skirting the brothers' camp and over the top of the hill. Then he descended toward the river he had been to before and when he reached it he looked for a place flat enough to make camp.

When he found a spot, he placed all his earthly possessions on the ground and set about to find rocks for a fire ring. The exercise had invigorated him and the sweat and alcohol poured out of his body as he dug in the dusty earth for suitable stones. Avoiding rocks too close to the river in case there was water inside that would explode them open in the fire, Jake eventually found enough to make a small ring. There were no signs of other humans besides himself, so Jake had an easy time finding enough firewood. After starting a fire he filled the pot halfway with water and began to cook his meal.

The coming of dusk brought familiar yearnings, and several times Jake was tempted to make the hike up the mountain and down to the town. He told himself it was because of Annie but he knew she was not the only reason. His hands shook a little as he ate, and no matter how much water he drank he could not seem to get enough. A rare craving for something sweet occupied his mind. Jake watched the sun drop down below the trees on the ridge and watched as the sky grew dimmer and dimmer. The last of the gray light was still in the sky when Jake curled up under a tree and went to sleep.

18

For five days Jake stayed in the mountains, away from any sign of civilization. The shaking and craving abated, and he began to fall into the familiar rhythm of the forest. Images of Billy kept filling his head, and he knew it was time to try and find his brother. Only he had no idea where. And there was one other thing. He could not stop thinking about Annie.

On the sixth day he couldn't hold out anymore. His supplies were running low, and though he knew he could hunt and forage he convinced himself of the lie that he needed to go into town for more food. In the river he washed his best set of clothes and scrubbed himself until his skin was red and raw. He waited naked save for his boots as his clothes hung on a sunny branch, the breeze coming down from the hilltops drying them quickly. When they were only a little damp, he put them back on.

Up the hill he went and down, again avoiding the brothers' camp. By the time he reached town it was nearing night, so he ducked behind a building and changed into his good clothes. Several deep breaths later, he gathered the courage to walk to the saloon.

The first thing he did when he entered was walk straight to the bar and summon Earl. When the bartender came, Jake spoke.

"Earl, I don't care what I say, I don't want you to let me drink anything. Not a drop."

"Alright," he said. "But you can't just loiter. You gotta buy something."

"I'm here to talk to Annie, and that's it."

"Well, she's busy at the moment." Earl looked upstairs.

"I'll wait over there." Jake pointed to the door.

"Suit yourself."

From where Jake leaned against the wall he could see the entire place, the men with their drink and the women trying to tease their money away. Jake felt he was no longer one of them, and was glad.

After a small eternity Annie appeared at the top of the stairs. Something about her seemed different to Jake. Gone was her smile and light, easy way and in their place was a rougher edge. He was afraid to talk to her. She ignored men as they whistled at her and grabbed for her and walked straight to the bar. Jake heard her order a drink and watched as she slammed it back and heard her ask for another and slam that one too.

Without realizing it Jake crept closer and closer until he was standing next to her as she downed her third.

"Hey," was all he managed to say, and he winced at how stupid it sounded.

Annie whirled around in her chair and looked at him. "Shit, it's you. You come to fall all over yourself again?"

"No, I ain't had nothin' to drink. You can ask Earl."

Annie looked at the bartender.

"Like a preacher on Sunday morning," said Earl.

Annie scoffed and looked back at Jake. "So what do you want?" Jake fumbled for words. "I want to talk. I mean, I want to listen, Annie. Listen to you." He felt like an idiot.

"I'm all talked out," she said. "If you want to go fuck, I'll fuck. But I ain't got nothin' to say." She signaled to Earl for another drink.

Her words grated on Jake's ears. "But...did I do something, Annie?"

She scoffed again. "How much you got?"

"How much what?"

"How much money, Jake."

"A couple dollars."

"A couple dollars? You know I cost more than that. Get lost, kid. I don't do charity work."

With that Annie got up, ran her fingers over her hair and dress and cleared her throat. She forced a painful smile and turned toward the men sitting at the closest table. "Hey, boys," she said, wrapping her arm around one of them and sitting on his lap. "How are you all doing tonight?"

Jake kept looking at Annie, hoping she would glance back at him, but she did not. So he turned and without another word walked out the door. Numb, his mind tumbling with a thousand thoughts he could not grab onto, Jake wandered the street. It was full now, of people returning from work or heading out to drink, to gamble, to spend the money they had worked all day, all their lives for.

It was then he saw Marvin, so drunk he could hardly stand, bouncing back and forth between people. Marvin grabbed a man by the arm, but was pushed to the ground. Then he got back up, yelled in another man's face and was elbowed away.

"Marvin! Hey, what's going on?"

Marvin wheeled and saw Jake and stalked toward him. "You!"

"Hey, it's Jake."

When he was close enough, Marvin landed his fist on Jake's jaw. The blow took Jake by surprise, and he spun around from the impact and landed on his face. Before he could push himself back up, Marvin was on top of him.

"Where's my money, you little shit? You thief! You stole the money we stashed at the camp."

Jake squirmed to his back while Marvin flailed his fists into him. Some hit on the ground, and others Jake was able to block. But some landed and sent shocks of pain through Jake.

"Hey, Marvin! Hey! Wait a second!" yelled Jake. "I didn't take it!"

Marvin's pounding ceased, but his foul whiskey breath made Jake cough. "What do you mean?"

"I don't know what you're talking about," pleaded Jake. "I only took the money you gave me. I swear."

Marvin seemed to contemplate this information before speaking again. "I don't believe you," he said. "I've been asking around. You've been drinking at the saloon every night, and then you just disappeared. You went to hide the money, didn't you? Didn't you?" The punching resumed.

"I swear I didn't!" yelled Jake. He could feel blood trickle down his face, and he tried to piece together the events after they struck gold. Then he remembered William and the words he spoke as he left. Jake recounted that story to Marvin.

Marvin stopped the beating long enough to listen, then hit Jake a few more times. "You're a lying sack of shit, Jake. William ain't never said a goddamn word to us. Why the hell would he say anything to you?" A few more punches. "I took you in and shared our money with you and this is the thanks I get? Where's your money?"

Rooting through Jake's pockets, Marvin found the last of Jake's meager bills and coins and stuffed them into his own pocket. Then he pinned Jake to the dusty street. "Don't ever show your face around here again or I'll knock it off." With one more shove into the ground, Marvin stood and walked in the direction of the saloon.

For a while Jake lay there, breathing hard and wiping the blood running from his nose. But after a crowd began to gather he mustered the strength to stand, grabbed his bag and staggered toward the edge of town. Sitting propped against one of the buildings was a man drinking in the shadows. His head nodded toward the half-empty bottle in his hand, and it seemed every ounce of his energy was dedicated to holding up his head and maintaining the grip on the bottle.

Jake snuck over to him, snatched the bottle from his hand and ran off, ignoring the man's shouts from behind. When he was a safe distance away Jake stopped and took a swig. The whiskey burned and he no longer liked the taste but he took another swig and then a longer drink. A few more steps and another drink and then bottle in hand he wiped away the blood and the tears as he wound his way into the darkness of the trees.

The ground was cold and wet. Jake's whole body hurt, his face was swollen. Eyes swollen almost shut. Then he felt something warm and dry placed over him, and he fell back asleep.

Again he woke, the pain still there. The wetness gone. A vague image formed in front of him. He was dreaming, he thought. That couldn't be who he thought it was.

Sleep again, and then awake once more. It was light out. His head was clearer, the pain still there but bearable. His eyes could open more and when they did he saw a fire. Beyond it moved two figures, two pairs of legs. Jake groaned. The legs disappeared then reappeared much closer. They bent so the faces above came into view.

One face was dark, at once young and ancient. The other was lighter and vaguely familiar, like something out of a dream of childhood, but a childhood that never was. Jake opened his eyes even more.

"Hey, Jake."

Jake pushed himself up on his elbow, but the world started spinning so he lay back down and closed his eyes. When he dared open them again the faces were still staring at him.

"Billy?"

"Yeah."

"Is that really you?"

"Yeah."

Jake began to cry and through the tears he struggled to speak. "I'm sorry, Billy."

"It's okay, Jake."

"I'm sorry, little brother."

For a while Jake continued to cry and Billy disappeared but when he came back he placed a steaming bowl of stew in front of his brother. "You hungry?"

Jake nodded and slowly propped himself up on his elbow. He wiped his tears and sat up and grabbed the bowl. It was hot, so he set it back on the ground. Billy handed him a spoon and Jake lifted a spoonful to his mouth and blew on it.

The first few bites he took cautiously, not wanting to throw up. But soon his body was craving the salt and the meat. The soup had cooled and Jake was now shoveling it into his mouth, pausing only to breathe. When he finished he set the bowl down. "Thanks."

Only then did Jake look up. Billy was seated across the fire from him. He was tan and lean and though his face looked the same it was also different. Older. More the lean lines of the teenager, as if the intervening months had been years. He seemed taller, too, although Jake thought he might be imagining that. His hair was longer and the moccasins on his feet were now worn. He wore buckskin pants, too. Only his shirt was the same as Jake remembered.

To the left of Billy sat Two Bears, calm, expressionless. The shame he felt in front of his brother was even more when he looked at Two Bears, so Jake chose to stare at the fire. "How'd you find me?" he asked.

Billy shrugged. "After you and me argued, I figured you'd just follow us. But you didn't."

"I tried," said Jake. "But y'all disappeared."

As if he hadn't heard, Billy continued. "We set up a new camp and I waited for you to show up. When you didn't, I told Two Bears I was going to look for you. I figured you tried to find a town or something. Two Bears said he'd come with."

"How long did it take for you to find me?"

"It took a while. Two Bears knows the towns out here, but he doesn't like comin' into them."

Jake scoffed. "I don't blame him."

"We looked for you in two other towns before we came here. This one's the biggest. I had to ask around and look a lot."

"I'm glad you did." Jake exhaled and continued to direct his gaze at the small fire in front of him. He still didn't have the courage to look at his brother. "I'm sorry I left, Billy."

"Me, too."

"I was mad."

"So was I."

"And I'm sorry I lied about Pa. I was just--"

"It's okay, Jake. I know why you lied. I know you were trying to protect me."

"That don't make it right."

"Yes it does."

Jake smiled ruefully as a small feeling of relief started to cleanse his conscience. He looked up at Two Bears, who still sat there observing him silently. "*Pilamaya yelo*." Jake thanked Two Bears.

The man's eyes brightened and face wrinkled into a slight smile. He nodded.

"You remembered, Jake," said Billy.

"Yeah, that's about the only thing I remembered how to say."

"Well, that's the most important one."

"I reckon so," said Jake. His head was clearing and energy returning to his limbs. "So, what's the plan?"

Billy turned to Two Bears and said something Jake didn't understand, and Two Bears responded.

"You got anything back in town you need to get?"

"There ain't nothin' there I ever want to see again."

"Alright. Two Bears says when you feel up to it we can start heading back to camp."

"That's a long walk," said Jake.

"Not on horses it ain't."

Jake looked around until he saw three brown and white horses grazing in a clearing nearby.

"Where you all camped out now?"

"Not far from where we were last," said Billy. "A couple days' walk on the other side of the forest there was another open plain where we set up camp. Two Bears says it's farther away from the soldiers, and they probably won't come through the forest."

Jake paused and thought before speaking, wondering if Two Bears would understand. "You know that probably ain't true, right?"

"I know't," said Billy. "I didn't tell him, though. Not yet."

"Well," said Jake. He stood up and his legs wobbled but soon they felt steady. "What time you reckon it is?"

Billy shrugged. "The sun rose a couple hours ago."

"You all ready to move?"

"Whenever you are."

"Let's get the hell out of here, then. The sooner I'm away from that town, the better."

Billy turned to Two Bears and spoke again and without a word Two Bears scattered the fire and covered it with dirt. Occasionally using trees for support Jake walked toward the horses who stood eating and watching as he approached. Billy moved ahead and so did Two Bears and as Jake watched Billy he noticed his brother moved more like Two Bears than like himself. Smooth and fluid and graceful, not the bouncing steps of the boy who started out with him from Missouri.

Then Billy walked up to a horse and without hesitating grabbed the mane and leaped on top. Jake shook his head. "Guess you've been practicing," he said.

A wide smile stretched across Billy's face. "Yeah," he said.

"That's good. Maybe you can teach me a couple things." Jake stood next to his horse and rubbed its neck and flank and haunches and let the horse smell his hand. When the horse stopped shaking Jake gently grabbed its mane. Just then a burp formed in his throat and though he tried to hold it back it leapt forth in a great burst and sounded out across the clearing.

The horse flinched. Billy giggled. Even Two Bears smiled. Jake tasted the stew and the whiskey before it and a bit of bile and he grimaced as he swallowed the taste down.

"Billy?"

"Yeah?"

"Don't ever let me drink whiskey again. Ever."

"Okay."

After tightening his grip on the mane Jake bent his knees and jumped up, swinging his leg over the horse's back. The horse did not move. Jake situated himself on its bare back and nodded to Two Bears and Billy who sat watching him. "Ready," he said.

19

They traveled for five days, each day rising with the sun and stopping only when its western rays were long. As they rode Billy talked of his life during their time apart, and Jake was happy to listen to the sound of his brother's voice. To Jake's relief, Billy asked little about Jake's adventures. Jake said even less.

Toward evening of the fifth day they crested a hill and looked down on a wide plain. The grasses rippled and bowed and bent in the wind. Jake thought it was peaceful, but when he looked at the faces of Two Bears and Billy, he knew something was wrong.

Billy said something and Two Bears replied. His voice was tense.

"Hey Billy," said Jake. "Look over yonder." He pointed at a thin spire of smoke rising out of the plains to the east.

Billy looked, then pointed and said something to Two Bears. The man nodded.

"What's going on?" asked Jake.

"This is where we were camped," said Billy. "But now everybody's gone."

Two Bears spoke, and before Billy or Jake could say anything he galloped toward the smoke on his horse.

"He says it's probably just a small grassfire," said Billy. "He says they happen out here from time to time."

"And what if it's not? What if it's another tribe? Or more soldiers?"

Billy shrugged. "Two Bears will know what to do. Let's go over to the forest there and camp. He'll find us when he comes back."

Jake smiled at his brother taking charge, but said nothing. He followed as Billy rode into the pines.

Later that day as the boys cooked their dinner under the darkening sky, Two Bears returned. As soon as Jake saw his face he knew what happened, but he waited for Billy's translation.

"The soldiers are back," said Billy.

"How many?"

"Lots. He's a little worried because they've never come this way before."

"I'm worried for him."

Billy said something to Two Bears, and Two Bears nodded and got up, walking some distance away.

"What'd you tell him?" asked Jake.

"I said you and I needed to talk in private."

"I thought he didn't speak English."

"He doesn't."

"Well?" asked Jake. "What do you want to do?"

Billy plucked a stalk of grass from the ground. On one end was a small tuft, and Billy took the other end and folded it over the top part just below the tuft. Aiming like with a bow and arrow Billy snapped the tuft off the grass and it flew in a short arc into the fire. It was a trick Jake and Billy used to do back home, one Jake had not seen for a long time.

"I think we should go," said Billy.

"But you like it with these people," said Jake.

"But you don't."

"I like it fine."

"Well, that doesn't matter. It's too dangerous for them if we stay. Might be too dangerous for us."

"Where would we go?" asked Jake.

For a while Billy didn't say anything, and Jake listened to the fire as it popped and hissed.

"I was thinking maybe we could go to California," said Billy. "Maybe find where Pa went."

"I got the address where his last letter came from, and one from his old boss. Says he's still got some stuff of Pa's."

"You do?"

"Yeah."

"Well, maybe we can go there for a start."

"And do what?"

"I don't know," said Billy. "Look for work, maybe."

"Work? What kind of work."

"I think we can do lots of things."

"I think you're right," said Jake.

An owl hooted nearby. Then a bullfrog in response. Lightning bugs like stars come to earth danced to the rushing rhythm of the creek. The sounds of the night grew louder. The boys sat and listened a long time before Billy spoke again.

"So what do you think?" asked Billy.

"I think you're right."

"When should we leave?"

"Soon as we can, I guess."

"Jake?"

"Yeah?"

"Can we wait until tomorrow to tell Two Bears?"

"I think that's a good idea."

Billy got up and walked to Two Bears, and when they returned the three of them walked the horses deeper into the forest. That night they went to bed without food or fire, sleeping on pine needles in the darkened woods.

When they woke Two Bears stood over them in the morning and shook them from their slumber. The boys stood up and the man said something and then Billy turned to Jake.

"He says we gotta pack up and get moving."

"I guess we should tell him we ain't going with him. Tell him we thank him for all he's done but we can't go with him," he said. Billy hesitated. "Go on, tell him."

Billy told him and for the first time Jake saw anger flash across the face of Two Bears. When the man spoke his voice was louder and more forceful.

"He says we are now like family and we can't be separated."

"Tell him I appreciate that but we are too dangerous to them. They might feel like we're family but if the army finds us with them they're gonna think we were kidnapped and then it'll be even worse."

"I don't know how to say 'kidnapped' in their language," said Billy.

"Well figure somethin' out, 'cause I sure don't know."

Billy spoke and Jake could tell where he stumbled in the translation. Two Bears nodded as he listened but when Billy translated he said it did not matter to him because Jake had saved the life of Eagle Claw and now they had shared the field of battle and were united and they could not break that bond. A blood debt was owed and Eagle Claw could not repay it if Jake and Billy left.

Jake listened and understood and turned to Two Bears and in English spoke directly to him. He looked into the man's eyes and spoke of family and loyalty. He spoke of his brother and their bond and the bond of a promise given long ago to a father who was no more. A promise to protect his brother no matter what. A promise which Billy had not known.

Billy tried to translate but quit when Jake did not stop talking. Jake spoke of their journey to chase the ghost of their father and his voice broke as he spoke of the power of the bond of family and his admiration for Two Bears and his people and how they all belonged to this world and yet were not a part of the same world. Two Bears listened in silence and when Jake was finished and Billy spoke to translate Two Bears held up his hand to stop him and in his own language spoke directly to Jake.

"I don't know how much English he knows but he says he understands," said Billy. "He says he knows where his people are. They are safe in the hills, and he will take us to the train."

"*Pilamaya yelo*," said Jake. Two Bears nodded.

As the brothers packed their bags Two Bears retrieved the horses and brought them to the boys. Billy took that one and gave the other to Jake. They slung their bags over their shoulders and Two Bears boosted Billy on his horse before doing the same for Jake. He jumped up on his own horse and clicked his tongue and the horse started forward.

They rode along the edge of forest and plain, always with an eye to the east. At first the sky was clear, but before long the smoke appeared again. Two Bears shook his head. Just then a figure emerged from the woods, and their horses startled. Jake was behind the other two, and could not see who or what it was until Two Bears dismounted.

A man approached and greeted Two Bears. When Jake got close enough he saw it was Eagle Claw. Jake halted the horse,

337

and he and Billy sat while the men talked. They were within earshot, and Billy translated. The soldiers showed up several days ago, said Eagle Claw. The tribe had left but Eagle Claw stayed behind to wait for Two Bears. His people needed him. The old hiding places were running out, and they needed to find new ones away from the soldiers. Two Bears said he would come, but first he had to take the boys to the train.

At this Eagle Claw walked past Two Bears and stopped in front of Jake's horse. He gestured for Jake to dismount and he did.

Jake had not seen him since the last incident with the soldiers. In his hand the man held a knife. It was the same knife he had used in his attack on the soldiers and Jake's stomach turned at the memory. He held it out for Jake to take and when the boy did the man spoke.

All Jake could understand was *Pilamaya yelo*, the word for thank you. He turned the knife over in his hands and admired the bone handle and the honed steel blade, the sheath of beaded buffalo hide. Still looking at the knife Jake thanked the man and fumbled for something to give in return. He had nothing of value but his father's pistol and that he could not give so he looked up to explain but Eagle Claw had already gone back to Two Bears. They talked for a little while, and Eagle Claw disappeared into the trees. The knife Jake placed in his bag and he jumped back onto his horse.

"Where's he going?" asked Jake.

"Back to his people," said Billy. "Two Bears will meet up with him later."

Without a word, Two Bears jumped onto his horse and started forward again.

They moved along the margin of plain and forest. In front of Jake the dust kicked up by the other horses clouded the grass and the trunks of the nearby pines and the morning haze illuminated the forest. Beams of light bent and swirled in the air like milk in water. The dust got in Jake's eyes and his mouth so he covered his face with his sleeve and kept one eye squinted open. He looked into the forest to see if he could spot Eagle Claw, but the man was already gone.

20

They traveled four days through the forest and at the edge of the other side was a large, sloping hill down to an immense plain. They waited two more days for a large storm to pass. From the distance they saw formidable anvil clouds marching slowly across the plains and they took shelter in the trees at the base of the foothills. They watched as the sky crackled and lit up with electricity and they felt the boom of the thunder in the ground. Fierce winds brought rain horizontal and bent the long stalks of grass down penitent and prostrate at the mercy of their god.

The morning after the storm passed Two Bears announced he would not be joining them the rest of the way. There was no sign of people but he knew there might be. If they ran into white people Two Bears would be seen with two white children and be taken for a kidnapper. If they ran into people like him yet not of his tribe he would also be unwelcome. Billy told Jake all this and Jake searched his brother's face for signs of sadness but saw none.

Jake shook Two Bears's hand and thanked him then walked to Billy's horse. His own horse grazed close by and he stood watching his brother and Two Bears. Billy rummaged through his bag and pulled out his magic rock. Jake could not remember the last time he saw it. For a while Billy held the rock, running his fingers along its grooves and ridges. Two Bears watching intently. At last Billy looked up and held the rock out to his friend. With great care Two Bears let the rock come to rest in his hand.

He said something to Billy and Jake did not know what he said but he understood as Two Bears did that the rock held a great and powerful medicine and it was not given lightly. Two Bears stood there frozen as if he himself had been turned into the stone. The rock held between man and boy like a bond. The man's lips barely moving speaking as if in chant.

He stood in silence for a while longer before putting the rock into his satchel. Then from around his neck he took the loop of rawhide and lifted it over his head. Pendent from the string were a feather and some talisman Jake could not discern from this distance. Two Bears reached out and put it over Billy's head and Billy nodded in thanks. Then they clasped hands and Two Bears turned and without looking back mounted his horse and headed back into the forest.

Billy walked over to the horses and Jake thought he could see the glimmer of a tear in his brother's eye, but he was not sure. His brother jumped up on his horse and so did Jake and the two of them rode into the wide sea of grass.

In its wake the storm left a warm dry summer air. A gentle breeze came from the west and by the end of the day their clothes had dried. They did not speak. That night they made camp under a family of trees and rocks that seemed to have risen straight from the ground for the purpose of giving them fuel for their fire and refuge from the elements. Nothing in this land gave them reason to believe otherwise.

Two weeks after they left the encampment Jake and Billy arrived at the train tracks. They followed them another half a day before finding a cluster of buildings where they met the man who ran the trading post. He told them the train would stop there the next day and agreed to give them food and lodging and a small amount of money in exchange for the horses. The boys took the horses to the stable out back and fed and brushed them and without any emotion said goodbye to their mounts.

The boys washed their clothes and themselves out back and changed clothes, leaving their wet ones to dry on the line. For dinner they ate with the man. Before each he placed a simple plate of pork and beans, and when they ate that he filled their bowls and then another and still one more. He seemed glad for the company and talked of his trade and of his wife now gone and of his new life at this train stop on the plain. Of their own adventure the boys spoke little.

After dinner he led them to the spare room where he had placed two straw mattresses. In the drowsy last moments before they fell on the beds the man assured them he would wake them before the train came in the afternoon.

At midday the man woke them and told them to get ready. He fed them and walked them out to the train now waiting on the tracks. After a mild protest the engineer agreed to let them ride all the way to San Francisco as long as they stayed in the empty cargo car and kept their space clean. The boys agreed and thanked both men and climbed into their temporary home. There was a loud whistle and a lurch forward, and as the train and the rhythm of the wheels increased the air rushing in through the cracked door cooled the car and stirred the stalks of hay on the floor. The car rocked back and forth like a cradle and for a fleeting moment the boys were children again lulled to sleep by the chug of the engine and the rush of the world going by.

For days the boys watched the scenery from the train. They saw great herds of buffalo and plains extending horizon to horizon. New settlements and old mountains carved by ancient glaciers whose remnant snows still clung to the peaks. They felt the heat of the desert on the other side of the Rockies and the cool breezes descending from the eastern slopes of the Sierra. They talked as they traveled and built the image of their destination on rumor and innuendo and the descriptions in the few letters their father had sent.

"Jake?"

"Yeah?"

"What are we going to do when we get to San Francisco?"

"We're gonna strike it rich."

"No, I mean for real. What are we going to do?"

Jake shrugged. "I figured we'd go to the man Pa worked for and ask him for Pa's things. Maybe ask him where we can find a job and a place to stay."

"Where did Pa work?" asked Billy

"A general store, I think."

"We could do that."

"Don't count your chickens, brother."

21

It was early morning when the train pulled into the city and the jolt of the stop woke the boys. They rubbed their eyes and cracked the door and hopped down. The engineer was still up front and the boys climbed the engine and thanked the man.

"You boys know where you're going?"

"You know where Wilson's General Store is?" asked Jake.

The engineer shook his head. "Sorry. I only know the two blocks between here and my hotel. I always wanted to see more but the company doesn't let me stay very long. Maybe they're afraid I'll never come back." He laughed and wished the boys luck and Jake and Billy climbed down and walked through the clouds of steam emanating from the engine and onto the streets of San Francisco.

The streetlights still hummed as they wandered and the boys asked passersby if they knew the store. In the air was the salt-sea smell and the odors of fresh bread and other less pleasant ones. Gulls cried in the distance. More people emerged from the doors of buildings that towered over the boys and soon they found someone who pointed them toward the store.

They found it and when they entered the man at the counter was busy with other customers so they walked the aisles pretending to be looking for something to buy. The man watched them out the corner of his eye and when the customers left he called them over and asked if he could help them in a tone that meant buy something or get out. Jake introduced them both and recounted the story of their journey. The man listened and his eyebrows rose at certain parts and when Jake was finished there was a long silence before the man spoke.

"You boys have come a long way."

"Yes sir," said Jake.

"What did you say you're names were again?"

"Jake and Billy, sir."

"And you're Jim Crowley's boys?"

"Yes, sir. We were wondering if you had any of his personal effects."

"Hold on a minute." The man disappeared through a door behind the counter and the boys could hear rustling and clanging before the man emerged with a box in his arms. He set it on the counter in front of the boys and all three peered inside. There were some old clothes and photos and a knife along with a few toiletries. The last remnants of a man besides the two boys looking at them. The room had fallen silent. No customers entered.

The man coughed awkwardly and disappeared into the back room again. When he returned he held in front of him a small, plain urn. He coughed again, his head bent, and placed it in front of the boys.

For a while Jake and Billy stared at it, saying nothing. The air was still and uncomfortable.

Softly, almost inaudibly, Billy spoke. "Is that--"

"Yes," said Jake. He wrapped his hands around the vessel containing the remains of their father and looked up at the man who stood before them, head still bowed. "Thank you for taking care of this." He turned to Billy. "Let's go."

Without a word Billy nodded, and the two of them headed for the door. From behind the man called to them, but Jake did not hear what he said.

The boys walked west toward the water. The city was alive now and bustled with men in suits and women in their finery and other men in working wear. From the street and storefronts people sold wares and exotic clothing and food Jake and Billy had never seen. They walked through sections where no one noticed them and others with no white people where everyone watched as they passed.

The hills made their legs burn but after a while they reached the gentle slope down to the ocean. The city gave way to sand dunes and scrub brush and the boys slogged through the sand until they stopped on a ridge of sand overlooking the beach. A lone fisherman stood down the beach a long way, barely visible in the haze.

"I ain't never seen anything like this," said Billy. "Look how big it is, Jake."

"I know."

"You wanna go in?"

"Race you," said Jake.

They set down their belongings and stripped their clothes as they ran and dove into the water and screamed at the cold and ran back up the beach collecting their clothes and putting them on as they went. They got back to their bags and stood shivering and covered in sand.

"It's salty," said Billy through chattering teeth.

"Yeah."

"I don't need to do that again anytime soon."

"Me neither."

They grabbed their bags and their father's remains and brought them down close to the water. The sun was burning through the thin gray layer of moisture in the air, and it warmed the boys as they sat.

From where they sat the sand sloped down into a swirling froth of white and beyond that great white walls of water crumbled their way to shore. Beyond that still were the rippled and dappled dark waters of the Pacific.

Jake turned to look at his brother, then back at the ocean. He stared for a long while in silence as his little brother grabbed handfuls of sand and let them sift through his fingers.

"Billy?"

"Yeah?"

"We're gonna be okay, you know that?"

"Yeah." Billy slid next to Jake and rested his hand on his brother's shoulder. They sat like that a long time, watching and listening to the waves roll onto the sand.

About the Author

Axel Schwarz is a writer and teacher. He lives in San Diego with his wife Melanie. Find him at axelschwarz.com and on Facebook.

Acknowledgements

Mel, Lee, Lynn, Patrick, John and Leyla, my faithful first readers. For all the feedback and encouragement. This book is better because of you.

John and Wright, my high school English teachers. For introducing me to the beauty of a well-told story and the magic of words.

Kathy and Fritz, my parents. For everything.

Kurt, my big brother. For being both protector and teacher. You have no idea how much I've appreciated it.

Melanie, my First Reader, editor, muse, best friend and wife. You hold a lot of job titles, and you do them all better than anyone. Thanks for hitching your wagon to mine.

Made in the USA
San Bernardino, CA
24 November 2015